JANE

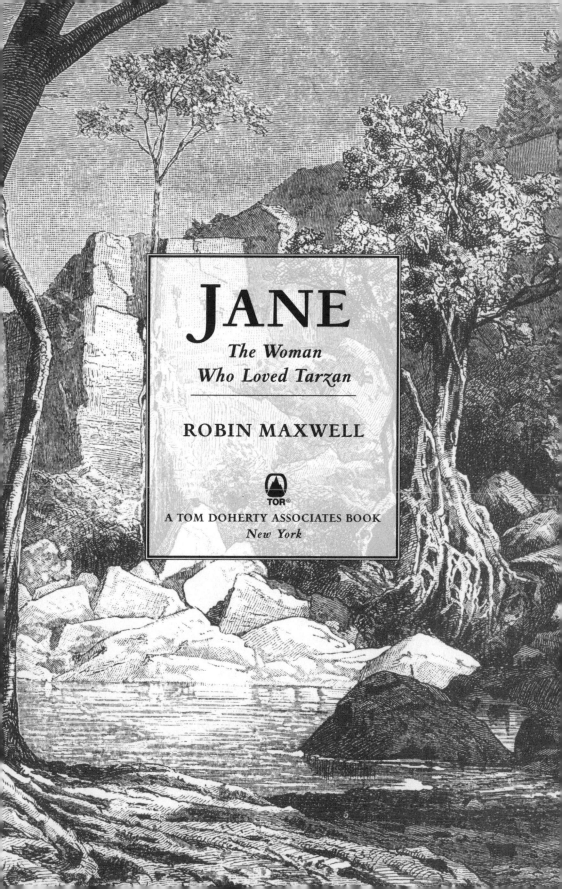

JANE

The Woman
Who Loved Tarzan

ROBIN MAXWELL

TOR®

A TOM DOHERTY ASSOCIATES BOOK
New York

JANE: THE WOMAN WHO LOVED TARZAN

A Tor Book
Published by Tom Doherty Associates, LLC
175 Fifth Avenue
New York, NY 10010

www.tor-forge.com

Tor® is a registered trademark of Tom Doherty Associates, LLC.

Library of Congress Cataloging-in-Publication Data

Maxwell, Robin, 1948–
    Jane : the woman who loved Tarzan / Robin Maxwell. — 1st ed.
        p. cm.
    "A Tom Doherty Associates book."
    ISBN 978-0-7653-3358-2 (hardcover)
    ISBN 978-0-7653-3359-9 (trade paperback)
    ISBN 978-1-4668-0321-3 (e-book)
    1. Young women—England—Fiction. 2. British—Africa—Fiction. I. Title.
PS3563.A9254J36 2012
813'.54—dc23

                                                                    2012019452

First Edition: September 2012

Printed in the United States of America

0 9 8 7 6 5 4 3 2 1

For Edgar Rice Burroughs

There is no Tarzan without Jane.

—John R. Burroughs

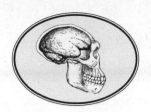

Chicago Public Library, April 1912

ood Lord, she was magnificent! Edgar thought. Infuriatingly bold. He had many times fantasized about women such as this Jane Porter, but he honestly believed they existed only in his imagination. The vicious heckling she had endured for the past hour in the darkened room would have broken the strongest of men, yet there she stood at the podium casting a shadow on the startling image projected by the whirring episcope on the screen behind her, back straight as a rod, head high, trying to bring order back into the hall.

Her age was indeterminate—somewhere approaching thirty, but her presence was one of striking vitality and self-assurance. She was tall and slender beneath the knee-length suit coat of fine brown wool. Her honey-colored hair was tucked up beneath a simple toque of black felt, not one of those large frivolous feathered creations that these days hung perilously cantilevered over a woman's face. Emma wished desperately for one of those freakish hats, and Edgar was secretly glad they were still too poor to afford it.

"These claims are preposterous!" cried a man seated halfway back in the crowded room. He had the look of an academic, Edgar thought.

"These are not claims, sir. They are the facts as I know them, and physical evidence, here, right before your eyes." There were hoots of derision at that, and catcalls, and Jane Porter's chin jutted an inch higher.

"This is clearly a hoax," announced a portly bearded man who brazenly walked to the table in front of the podium and swept his hand above the massive skeleton displayed on it. "And a bad hoax at that. Why, you haven't even tried to make the bones look old."

The audience erupted in laughter, but the woman spoke over the commotion in a cultured British accent with more equanimity than Edgar thought humanly possible.

"That is because they are *not* old. I thought I made it clear that the bones came from a recently dead specimen."

"From a *living* missing link species," called out another skeptic. The words as they were spoken were meant to sound ridiculous.

"All you've made clear to us today, Miss Porter, is that you should be locked up!"

"Can we have the next image, please?" the woman called to the episcope operator.

"I've had enough of this claptrap," muttered the man sitting just in front of Edgar. He took the arm of his female companion, who herself was shaking her head indignantly, and they rose from their seats, pushing down the row to the side aisle.

This first defection was all it took for others to follow suit. Within moments a mass exodus was under way, a loud and boisterous one with rude epithets shouted out as hundreds of backs were turned on the stoic presenter.

Edgar remained seated. When someone threw on the electric lights, he could see that the episcope operator up front in the center aisle was wordlessly packing up the mechanism of prisms, mirrors, and lenses that threw opaque images onto the screen as the speaker began her own packing up.

Finally Edgar stood and moved down the side aisle to the front of the meeting hall. He rolled the brim of his hat around in his hands as he approached Jane Porter. Now he could see how pretty she was. Not flamboyantly so, but lovely, with an arrangement of features— some perfect, like her green almond eyes and plump upward-bowed lips, and some less so, like her nose, just a tad too long and with a small bump in it—that made her unique.

She was handling the bones as if they were made of Venetian glass, taking up the skull, shoulders, arms, and spine and laying them carefully into a perfectly molded satin receptacle in a long leather case.

She looked up once and gave him a friendly, close-lipped smile, but when he did not speak she went back wordlessly to her task. Now it was the lower extremities that she tucked lovingly away, using special care to push the strange big-toe digits into narrow depressions perpendicular to the feet.

Edgar felt unaccountably shy. "Can I give you a hand?"

"No, thank you. They all fit just so, and I've had quite a lot of practice. London, Paris, Moscow, Berlin."

"I have to tell you that I was completely enthralled by your presentation."

She looked at Edgar with surprised amusement. "You don't think I should be locked up?"

"No, quite the contrary."

"Then you cannot possibly be a scientist."

"No, no, I'm a writer." He found himself sticking out his hand to her as though she were a man. "The name's Ed Burroughs."

She took it and gave him a firm shake. He noticed that her fingernails were pink and clean but altogether unmanicured, bearing no colorful Cutex "nail polish," the newest rage that Emma and all her friends had taken to wearing. These were not the hands of a lady, but there was something unmistakably ladylike about her.

"What do you write, Mr. Burroughs?"

He felt himself blushing a bit as he pulled the rolled-up magazine from his jacket pocket. He spread it out on the table for her to see. "My literary debut of two months ago," he said, unsure if he was proud or mortified.

"*All-Story* magazine?"

"Pulp fiction." He flipped through the pages. "This is the first installment in the series I wrote. There was a second in March. My pen name's Norman Bean. It's called 'Under the Moons of Mars.' About a Confederate gentleman, John Carter, who falls asleep in an Arizona cave and wakes up on Mars. There he finds four-armed green warriors who've kidnapped 'the Princess of Helium,' Dejah Thoris. He rescues her, of course."

She studied the simple illustration the publisher had had drawn for the story, something that'd pleased Edgar very much.

"It really *is* fiction," she observed.

"Fiction, fantasy . . ." He sensed that the woman took him seriously, and he felt suddenly at ease. It was as if he had always known her, or *should* have known her. She exuded something raw and yet something exceedingly elegant.

"When I was ten I came home from school one day and told my father I'd seen a cow up a tree," Edgar said, startling himself with his candor with a complete stranger. "I think I said it was a purple cow. I was punished quite severely for lying, but nothing stops a compulsion, does it?" When she shook her head knowingly, he felt encouraged. "A few years later I moved to my brother's ranch in Idaho and stayed for the summer. By the time I was enrolled at Phillips Academy I could spin a pretty good yarn about all the range wars I'd fought in, the horse thieves, murderers, and bad men that I'd had run-ins with. It was a good thing my father never heard about them."

A slow smile spread across Jane Porter's features. "Well, you've shown him now, haven't you. A published author."

"I'm afraid my old man has yet to be convinced of my myriad talents."

She snapped both cases closed and took one in each hand.

"Here, let me help you with those."

"No, thank you. Having the two of them balances me out."

"I was hoping you'd let me take you out to dinner. Uh, I'd like very much to hear more about your ape-man."

She stopped and looked at him. "Honestly?"

"Yes."

"You must pardon my suspiciousness. I have been booed and hissed out of almost every hallowed hall of learning in the world. This is the last. I tried to have my paper heard at the Northwestern and Chicago universities, but I'm afraid my reputation preceded me and they said absolutely not. That's why you had to listen to my presentation at a meeting room at the Chicago Public Library."

"So will you come out with me?"

The woman thought about it for a very long moment. She set down her cases and walked to the man at the episcope, quietly conferred with him, and returned. "It's really not a good idea for us to talk in public, but my hotel is nearby. You and I can go up to my room."

"I wouldn't do that if I were you," Edgar said. "Chicago police keep an eye on even the nicest hotels. They might arrest you for soliciting. But my apartment's not too far. The wife and kids have gone to her mother's for the weekend. I mean . . . sorry, that sounds . . ."

"Mr. Burroughs, your apartment's a fine idea. I'm not afraid of you. But don't you care about the neighbors?"

He eyed the woman's bulky luggage. "I'll tell them you're selling vacuum cleaners."

She smiled broadly. "That will do."

They were largely silent on the taxi ride across town to his Harris Street walk-up, except for the exchange of pleasantries about the lovely spring weather they were having and how April was almost always horrible in England.

It was just Edgar's rotten luck that the only neighbor who saw them come in was the landlord, a petty, peevish little man who was looking for the rent, now more than a week late. Edgar was relieved to get Jane Porter up the three flights and inside, shutting the door behind them, but he cringed to see the empty cereal bowl and box of Grape-Nuts that he'd left on his writing desk. There was a pile of type-written pages on letterhead lifted from the supply closet of the pencil sharpener company he worked for, a mass of cross-outs and arrows from here to there, scribbled notes to himself in both margins.

"It's a novel I'm writing, or should say rewriting . . . for the third time. I call it *The Outlaw of Torn*." Edgar grabbed the bowl and cereal box and started for the kitchen. "I turn into a bit of a bachelor when my wife is away. By that I don't mean . . ."

"It's all right," she called after him. "You have children?"

"A boy and girl, two and three. Why don't you sit down? Can I get you something to drink? Tea? A glass of sherry?"

"Yes, thank you. I'll have a cup of water. Cool, please."

When Edgar returned from the kitchen, his guest was sitting at the end of the divan in an easy pose, her back against the rounded arm, her head leaning lazily on her hand. She had taken off her suit coat, and now he could see she wore no stiff stays under the white silk blouse, those torturous undergarments that mutilated a woman's natural curves. She wore no jewelry save a filigreed gold locket hanging between shapely breasts, and it was only when she was opening the second of the two cases holding the skeleton that he saw she wore a simple gold wedding band. He could see now where she had meticulously pieced together the shattered bones of the apelike face.

He set the water down and sat across from her. Now she sighed deeply.

"Are you sure you want to do this?" Edgar asked, praying silently that she did.

"Well, I've never told this in its entirety. The academics don't wish to hear it. But perhaps your 'pulp fiction' readers will. I can tell you it's a story of our world—a true story, one that will rival your John Carter of Mars."

"Is it about you?"

"A good part of it is."

"Does what happened to you in the story explain your fearlessness?"

"I told you, I'm not frightened of you. I . . ."

"I don't mean me. You took an awful lot of punishment this afternoon . . . and in public, too. You're a better man than I."

She found Edgar's remark humorous but grew serious as she contemplated his question. "I suppose they did toughen me up, my experiences." She stared down at her controversial find, and he saw her eyes soften as though images were coming into focus there.

"Where does it begin?" he asked.

"Well, that depends upon *when* I begin. As I've said, I've never told it before, all of it." She did some figuring in her head. "Let me start in West Central Africa, seven years ago."

"Africa!" Edgar liked this story already. Nowhere on earth was a darker, more violent or mysterious place. There were to be found cannibals, swarthy Arab slave traders, and a mad European king who had slaughtered millions of natives.

"It just as well could start in England, at Cambridge, half a year before that." She smiled at Edgar. "But I can see you like the sound of Africa. So, if you don't mind me jumping around a bit . . ."

"Any way you like it," Edgar said. "But I know what you mean. It's not easy figuring out how to begin a story. For me it's the hardest part."

"Well then . . . picture if you will a forest of colossal trees. High in the fork of a fig, a great nest has been built. In it lies a young woman moaning and delirious. Her body is badly bruised and torn."

"Is it you?" Edgar asked.

Jane Porter nodded.

"I have it in my mind. I can see it very well." Edgar could feel his heart thumping with anticipation. He allowed his eyes to close. "Please, Miss Porter . . ." There was a hint of begging in his voice. "Will you go on?"

July 1905

It was the hurt that woke me—white-hot needles at shoulder and calf, and deep spasms the width and length of my back. My head throbbed. Fever seared. Limbs like lead. Bright patterns dancing behind closed lids. Too much effort to move a finger, a toe. Frightening. Did I have the strength to open my eyes? And what was the cause of my agony? What had happened? Where was I? Then I remembered. Recalled the last sensation that was pure terror made corporeal.

I was a leopard's next meal.

Why was I not dead? Was I even now in the cat's lair? Would I open my eyes to a pile of bones and rotting corpses of its earlier prey? Was the cat waiting an arm's length away to finish me?

No. Beneath me was softness. My arms and legs were gently positioned and cushioned. But this was not a bed. The air was fresh, fragrant. I was outdoors. I could make no sense of it. I strained to remember. Called out for help.

I dared to hope.

"Father?" My voice was so weak. How would he ever hear me? I drew a long breath to give me strength, but that small act was a knife to my ribs. I fought to raise my lids, but the minuscule muscles defied me.

"Fah-thah." It was a male voice, deep and resonant, even in its youth. Fevered as I was, a chill ran through me.

Who was this stranger? Dare I speak again?

A wave of pain assailed me and crushed the words into meaningless cries and moans. I was so weak, buffeted, helpless in a sea of suffering. Then two strong, comfortable arms cradled me, lifted me tenderly, held me to a broad male breast as a father would a small, ailing child.

Relief flooded me and I sank gratefully into my protector's chest. The skin was smooth and hairless, the scent richly masculine. The throbbing heartbeat against my ear was strong and I heard the mindless humming, a familiar lullaby. I was rocked so gently that I fell into a swoon of safe repose.

How long it was before I awoke again I did not know. But with the pain having substantially subsided, when I opened my eyes this time I could see very clearly indeed, and my mind had regained sense and order.

I was in the crook of a tree where four stout limbs came together, lying on a thick bed of moss. I saw the naked, heavily muscled back of the man I remembered only for his fatherly embrace. He squatted beside me in what could rightly be called a "nest." His skin was mildly tanned, marred only by several fresh scratches and puncture wounds, the hair a matted black mass hanging down below his shoulders.

When he turned, he was spitting a just-chewed blue-green substance from his mouth into his hand, and was as startled at my waking state as I was at the entirety of him.

We were equally speechless. He never took his eyes from me as he finished chewing, then spat the rest of the paste into his palm. I lifted onto my elbows but winced at the pain this caused my left shoulder. I turned my head and saw the appalling injury—four deep gouges in the flesh.

He gently pushed me down and began to pack the green substance into the wounds. His ministrations were straightforward, and in the silence as he tended the shoulder scratches and another set on the back of my right calf, I gazed steadily at his face, overcome with a sense of wonder and unutterable confusion.

He was the most beautiful man I had ever seen. Perhaps twenty, he was oddly hairless on his cheeks, chin, and under his nose, with only a soft patch at the center of his chest. The face was rectangular with a sharp-angled jaw, the eyes grey and widely set, and alive with intensity and inquisitiveness. Jet-black brows matched the unruly mane.

Though a stranger and clearly a savage, he touched me intimately, but he did so unreservedly, like a workman at his job, and I felt no compulsion to recoil from that touch.

Then he did the strangest thing. He raised his hand to my face and, turning the palm up, laid the back of it on my forehead, as a mother would to her child to check for fever. I thought I detected satisfaction in what he'd found, and indeed, I felt the fever had gone from my body.

Now he met my gaze and held it with terrible intensity. His lips twitched for several moments before any sound emerged. Then finally he spoke.

"Fah-thah," he said.

"Fah-thah?" I repeated. Then understood. "Father."

The sound of the word and the thoughts it evoked suddenly tore through my being and, lacking all restraint, I began to wail. *Where was my father? Was he alive or dead? Did he have any knowledge of my whereabouts?*

Everything in me hurt, but most of all my heart.

The young man moved to take me into his arms as he'd done before, but now I began to struggle, pushing him away, crying out with pain of my torn shoulder and thoughts of my father. With a stern countenance, the man opened his palms and, spreading them across my chest, pushed me back down in the moss.

My face and body went slack in surprise, and I ceased struggling. He withdrew his hands and in time I calmed. I never took my eyes from him. Now I placed my own hand on my chest and spoke again.

"Jane," I said.

He was silent, eyeing me closely.

"Jane," I repeated, this time tapping my chest.

Understanding glittered in his eyes.

"Jane," he said.

I refused to give in to false or premature hope, but I rewarded his victory with a small smile.

He grew excited. He tapped his own chest and said, "Tarzan." *So this was his name? Odd. Tarzan.* He placed his hand over my hand, then said his name once more.

But I shook my head and finally said "no."

He nodded his head yes. "Tarzan. Tarzan," he repeated.

I laid my head back, closing my eyes and sighing deeply. I wanted to shout, "No, I am not Tarzan. You are Tarzan!" But I must be patient.

And then very suddenly, as though he, too, was spent from the frustrating conversation, he left me and climbed from the nest, disappearing from my sight.

I lay there alone, trying to order my mind. There had been a brief moment when I thought the savage might possess intellect, and my heart had soared. He was able to mimic words. I must have uttered "Father" in my delirium, and he'd remembered it. And he had repeated "Jane" instantly and clearly, and even appeared to understand that this was who I was. And then . . . oh, I grew heavy with disappointment—he had called us both by the same strange name: Tarzan. He was clearly an imbecile, a feral child, grown up. A freak of nature. And while he was at least gentle and had nursed me so carefully, I despaired that this creature was the one and only key to my salvation, if that was in fact a possibility.

Now that he was absent from the nest, I gazed around. It was a rough home to be sure, but a home all the same. I saw a depression in the moss beside where I lay—long and deep. It was clearly where the tameless man had been sleeping—so close to me. There were few artifacts. A stone-tipped spear. Near my head a pair of half coconut shells, and next to them a pith helmet—my own?—all of them filled with clear water.

But where was I?

I looked up and around me. I recognized the tree as a fig, and a large one at that.

It seemed that this nest was quite high off the ground. *How on earth had I gotten here?* Certainly it was by virtue of the gentle savage, but I had been injured. As a deadweight, I'd been carried up a tree!

Although every movement was still an agony, my mind was clearing moment by moment. But still I found myself tumbling fearfully in an avalanche of questions.

How serious were my injuries? Will I live or die? Where was my father? We had come together into this forest. Was he even alive? Deathly ill? What has he been told about my whereabouts? Was he searching for me even now? And who or what, in heaven's name, was this man . . . my savior?

Then suddenly, unaccountably, the pain subsided like an outgoing tide. I found myself soothed, lulled into comfort by the sounds and the scents around me. It was an incessant thrum—trilling, piping, and whistling of birdsong. Calls and answers. Clicking and chip-chipping of insects. The rumbling roar of a distant waterfall.

I should think! Plan! But I could not. The sudden absence of pain, the delicious stillness of my body, the comfort of the bed, the sweet and pungent fragrances and the sounds. Oh, the sounds made me lazy, indolent. I allowed my mind to drift. *Not like me. Not like me at all.* Always too busy. So much to accomplish. So much to prove. Here there was no accomplishing. Here there was only being, and gratitude that I was alive and safe and not a leopard's dinner . . .

Only then did I think to look down at my body. My left shoulder was bare—the sleeve from my bush jacket gone. The terrible wound packed with green-blue paste no longer throbbed. *Was it this strange medicine that relieved the pain?* The rest of my jacket, I could see, covered me, but the front—still buttoned—was lying atop my chest like a small blanket. I felt with my right hand. The jacket's back was beneath me, the two parts unattached, the seams apparently ripped apart.

I needed to lift my head to observe my lower body, but the spasm that racked my neck and back with even the smallest movement forced a speedy look. It revealed a similar configuration. The lower right trouser leg was gone. A dull ache in my right calf reminded me of the claw wounds there and the blue-green poultice that packed it. The front of my trousers loosely covered my bottom half, and I assumed the backs were underneath my buttocks and legs.

The thought struck me that such an arrangement of my clothing had to have been accomplished by my new friend, and I wondered at his inventiveness. *Would an imbecile have achieved so ingenious a sick-bed?* He had applied medicine that appeared to have prevented infection of my wounds, ones that while severe showed neither redness nor swelling nor suppuration, and provided substantial analgesia.

How long had I been unconscious? I realized with horror that my modesty must certainly have been compromised. *What of my bodily functions?* I felt clean and dry below, and detected no unsavory odors from my nether regions. *Stop!* I ordered myself. The accomplishment of urination and defecation in the presence and with the help of a strange male was certainly an embarrassment, but it was far from my greatest concern.

Suddenly a tight packet of leaves plopped down on the opposite side of the nest and a moment later came the man, leaping with utter grace and agility up over its side. Thankfully, his private parts were covered with a loincloth of sorts, really just a short animal skin tied at the waist covering the front of him, with what appeared as the wooden hilt of a large weapon protruding across his taut, rippling belly. His long legs were exquisitely muscled, as were his buttocks, and even his feet, bare of coverings of any kind, possessed great definition and obvious strength. As he came close and squatted unselfconsciously beside me, I thought that the sinuous toes, flexible and as powerful as fingers, were much like an ape's—good for climbing.

He held my gaze, seeming pleased at the clarity he saw in my eyes, and spoke.

"Tarzan," he uttered with great certainty.

All right, I thought, *he is not an imbecile. We have simply not learned proper communication with each other.* I touched the center of my chest lightly with my right hand.

"Jane," I said and nodded my head, smiling. I touched my breastbone again. "Tarzan . . ." I shook my head with definitive negativity and frowned.

His expression was at first quizzical. Then he smiled. He tapped my chest lightly. "Jane," he said. Then he tapped his own. "Tarzan."

He understood!

I returned the smile to encourage him, though to be honest, my smile was entirely sincere. There was hope to communicate with this creature. *No*, I corrected myself. *Not a creature. A man.*

And a beautiful one at that.

I lay still and quiet as he opened the banana leaf he had tied up with thin vine and revealed inside it wood mold and nuts, and the fruit of the pawpaw tree.

He first applied the delicate fuzz to my wound, and the moist paste caused it to disappear. Then he grabbed the flat rock from the nest's rim and, pulling out his blade, broke the nuts' shells with the hard handle. He offered the nut meat to me in the palm of his hand. Yet I did not take or eat them. I was staring hard at the blade.

He held it out flat in front of me to see.

"*Boi-ee*," he said proudly.

"Bowie?" I said, astonished. *What was this man, this "Tarzan," do-*

ing with a Bowie knife, and how on earth did he know its proper name? My father had such a blade in his collection of weapons. I had heard the story of Jim Bowie, the frontiersman who had died at the American Battle of the Alamo and had given the famous knife its name. There was nothing else about the man squatting beside me, or his home, that remotely bespoke of the civilized world.

And suddenly a Bowie knife.

This was a mystery, but perhaps more confounding was my trust in the man—Tarzan. I'd not questioned the grey mold he had rubbed into the poultices on my shoulder and calf, but I somehow assumed that it would improve my condition. *How had I come to trust this wild man, a being whose life and mind were becoming more bewildering to me with every passing moment?*

He again extended his hand holding the nuts, and though I felt no hunger I was moved to accept them. It was a token of faith and friendship. Indeed, he seemed pleased when I put them in my mouth and chewed. He smiled and went to work peeling the pawpaw, gutting it of its black seeds.

When he held out a portion to me—the simple sharing of food between members of a family—I wondered how it had come to this so very quickly.

I brought the yellow fruit to my lips and took a bite. Nothing I had tasted in my life, I thought, had ever been so sweet.

Together we quickly devoured the meal, and when he rose again, I knew that he was off to gather more. As he stood on the lip of the nest preparing to slide the Bowie knife into its sheath, a rare ray of sunlight pierced the thick canopy above to glint blindingly off the blade. I closed my eyes and saw . . .

. . . reflected January sunlight glittering off the razor-edged scalpel in its small wooden chest. The sight of the serrated bone saw, knives and drills and probes with their ebonized handles filled me with satisfaction. My very own dissection kit.

Yet standing there alone in the bright high-ceilinged chamber with two rows of sheet-draped cadavers—alone if one did not count the bodies of the deceased—I could feel a nervous flutter in my chest. The sickly sweet and acrid smell of formaldehyde, and the flesh it prevented from putrefying, stung my nose. *Get your bearings, girl. You're in the gross-anatomy laboratory at Cambridge. No time for floundering!*

The medical students would be arriving any moment. Would it be the jocular, shoulder-bumping playfulness that I saw in the lecture hall, courts, and arches, I wondered, or would they quiet and grow still in this strange sepulcher?

There was a clattering at the door as a laboratory servant, his arms piled with tin pails, hurried in and began placing one at the foot of every table, for discarded parts I guessed.

I recognized the young man, Mr. Shaw, a graduate of the medical college who had yet to find a position in the world. The professor of human anatomy had happily taken him on to this posting that was both lowly in its tasks and most necessary to the smooth functioning of the laboratory. Servants, though they were called, were valued very highly, and the best of them, like Mr. Shaw, fetched and carried and mounted specimens that were produced by the students' work. Some servants were paid as much for their services as college lecturers.

"Your first day, Miss Porter?" Shaw inquired.

I nodded.

"Make sure you keep the face covered," he said of the corpses. "That's the bit that can give you a nasty shock. My first day the towel fell off and I found myself staring at a granny with half of her skin flayed down to the muscle and an eyeball hanging down by the optic nerve. I retched into one of these buckets every few minutes till the end of the session." He set down one of the pails near my feet. "Apparently it was a record-breaking spew . . . my classmates never let me forget it."

"I'll take your advice, Mr. Shaw. I'll wait a bit to uncover the face."

"Good luck to you, miss."

The laboratory was filling with young men, two to a table. Presently one of them took his place across from me. He was a fresh-faced boy with skin so pale and translucent that blue veins formed a delicate map across his cheeks and forehead.

"I'm Woodley," he said. "You're Jane Porter."

I could hear snickering from the tables on either side of us and the row across the aisle. I'd prepared myself for all manner of derision. The first woman to gain entry into this hallowed laboratory was sure to stir controversy and even indignation. *I have every right to be here*, I repeated to myself for the hundredth time that day and almost unconsciously pulled back my shoulders and thrust out my chin.

The movements, subtle as they were, did not go unnoticed by a too-handsome young man I knew from the anatomy lecture hall. Arthur Cartwright's family was old, and they had managed to preserve their wealth and prestige in the previous century that had seen so many of them collapse into genteel poverty. Cartwright wore his arrogance like a badge of honor. All he did was smirk at me.

"Shall we?" Woodley asked.

Leaving the face covered with a small towel, Woodley pulled the sheet away, revealing what looked to be a middle-aged man. It was already a partly dissected cadaver, as I had joined the class in the middle of its term. I could see that the skin of one forearm had been peeled away, revealing musculature that looked decidedly like the stringy meat on a dried-out turkey carcass. A large opening in the abdomen exposed the intestines and multitudinous folds of the mesentery tissue. A repulsive odor wafted up from the belly and hit me with a force that knocked me back on my feet.

"I know," said Woodley. "The gut stinks far worse than the rest. You'll get used to it. Or you won't."

I was aware that even though work had begun on all the tables around mine and Woodley's, everything that was being said here, and probably my reel backward from the odor of the abdominal cavity, was being closely observed by Cartwright and the others. They were all most certainly waiting for an opportunity to chime in with a barb, a pun, or their idea of a witty rejoinder . . . at my expense, of course.

"Mr. Woodley," said Cartwright in a most unctuous tone, "perhaps you should help Miss Porter with the dissection of the rectum."

I thought how apropos was my fellow student's choice of body parts, as that was the precise orifice I'd just silently affirmed I would associate with Arthur Cartwright for the rest of my days.

But what I said aloud was, "Thank you, but I can take care of myself very well."

"I'm quite sure you can." The five words were spoken by Cartwright with such lewd innuendo that his corner of the laboratory erupted with laughter.

I gathered my wits and fixed my eyes on the flayed corpse. In the most demure tone I could summon, I said, "Mr. Woodley, might you show me this man's testicles?"

There were roars of laughter, hoots and howls. Not a full minute had passed before the professor of anatomy, the most revered of lecturers, was in our midst. He was a clean-shaven man, and his barrel chest lent power to his otherwise tall, rangy appearance.

"Gentlemen!" The single word was close to a shout, and he spoke it with blatant irony. These were ruffians he was addressing, his tone revealed—anything but well-bred university men. The professor's usual good nature and easy manner had vanished. His Midwest American twang seethed with gravitas as he continued. "You are working on human cadavers that were once living, breathing men and women. Somebody's father, mother, child. It is the reason that we in the dissection room wear black coats, not the white of scientists and physicians—out of respect for the dead. There will be no laughter in the anatomy laboratory. No horseplay. Ever. Now get on with it."

In that moment, the silence of the dead filled the room, and the students returned, chastened, to their grisly business.

I felt the professor looming above me, He whispered into my ear, "You should have known better."

I turned and spoke so softly I doubted Woodley, across the table, could hear. "Sorry, Father. You may come to regret the mountains you moved to get me into this classroom."

"I'll be the judge of that," he said and, moving away, called over his shoulder, "Button up that coat, Mr. Cartwright. You look like a trash collector."

I returned my eyes to the cadaver.

Woodley addressed me with mock dignity. "Was it the testicles you wished to be shown, Miss Porter? Or the scrotal sac?"

"Neither, Mr. Woodley. I think I'll investigate the larynx."

I felt his eyes on me as I removed the smallest of the scalpels from the instrument kit and attempted to make my first incision, this to remove the skin in the center anterior of the neck. Nothing happened under the knife.

"The human hide is tougher than you think," Woodley told me. "Pressure should be firm, but not so firm as to slice through any more than the derma. Think of cutting into an overcooked heel of roast beef."

I tried again. To my delight, the bloodless flesh parted. Having exposed what lay beneath, I closed my eyes and recalled what I had studied so carefully in my anatomy text.

"I had the larynx last term," Woodley said. "Remove the mucous membrane posteriorly to expose the laryngeal muscles and the inferior laryngeal nerve. Then you can remove the lamina of the thyroid cartilage on one side to view the remaining laryngeal muscles."

I thanked him and set to work carefully and assiduously in the soft tissue. I found myself handling the new knives and probes with unexpected dexterity. It was as though I had used the tools all my life. Nothing was so sublime or miraculous as the human body. So many secrets buried in flesh and bone.

Ah, there they were, the vocal cords!

I paused, awestruck, as a treasure hunter would before opening a long-lost cask of golden coins. I was startled when Woodley spoke again.

"You seem to know what you're looking for in there."

"Are you familiar with Dubois's paper on the development and evolution of the larynx? That the mammalian larynx issues from the fourth and fifth branchial arches of the embryo, implying," I continued, perhaps too zealously, "that the human voice box evolved from the gill cartilage of fish? Those structures that once filtered oxygen from water now filter air . . . and make sound!" I remembered then that I ought to keep my voice down.

"Ah, this is what all the excitement is about," Woodley said. "Dubois's 'missing link.' His 'Java man' fragments."

"I'd say they're rather more than *fragments*. A tooth. A thighbone . . . and a complete skullcap."

"It hasn't been proved that they've come from the same individual."

"Rubbish! They were found at the same depth, and only fifteen yards away from each other. Their color and texture are identical."

Woodley never took his eyes from the long, ropy intestines he had extracted from the cadaver and placed for examination on its still-intact chest.

"Well," I demanded, "do you have an opinion on it?"

"Not really. I'm studying to be a physician, not a fossil hunter."

"Certainly you have an opinion on so important a scientific question."

"It's important to some people."

"*Some people?*" I was incensed. "So you don't care whether your forebearers were ape-men, or creatures that came magically out of Adam's rib?"

Woodley was clearly unused to such a highly opinionated lady.

"The apes, I suppose," he finally muttered.

Truly, I would have been shocked had he chosen the rib. Few educated men and women denied Darwin, but fewer still were courageous—or some said idiotic—enough to make paleoanthropology their career. In other than the scholarly crowd, such a calling was laughable. This was a contradiction that drove me mad.

"Are you coming to hear Dubois at the congress?" I asked.

"The congress?"

"The International Congress of Zoology. He's presenting his Java man finds here, later this month. Are you coming?"

"Are you?"

"Oh, Mr. Woodley. I really hope you're not the type who's always answering a question with a question."

He gave me a sharp look. "I'm trying to like you, Miss Porter. You make it very difficult."

Aware that my impatience was getting the better of me, I resumed my dissection. "Yes, I'm going. My father and Eugène Dubois are friends. But you knew that."

"Everyone knows that." There was a strained silence. "Miss Porter . . ."

"What?"

"Be careful with the vocal folds. They're very delicate."

"Thank you," I said, contrite. Perhaps Woodley was a decent sort of man after all. There were so many I would just as soon send to the bottom of the ocean. I looked up and managed a smile. "Can you tell me which tool you suggest?"

U nladylike though it was, I dashed across the Newnham College green clutching my valise in one hand, hat to my head with the other. The scarf ties flew out behind like wind-whipped banners, and the young women walking two by two with great decorum skewered me with the evil eye. But my father was waiting just beyond the hedge in the Packard, eager to make an end to his week's work at the university. And I hated to keep him waiting.

As many weekends as I was able, I went home with the professor. I lived for these times, working with him in the manor laboratory and keeping company with my animals. The courses at Newnham—one of the two women's colleges at Cambridge—were adequate, and I appreciated the extreme privilege of participating in higher education, but the restrictions imposed upon my sex irked me beyond measure. Women could attend classes at Cambridge and write examinations. But Newnham had its own library and separate laboratories, as girls were prohibited from sullying those hallowed halls in the men's colleges. Worst of all, females could not graduate or qualify for a degree of any kind. It was maddening!

That was why my admission into the anatomy laboratory—the only one at Cambridge—had been such an unimaginable coup. Certainly it had stirred numerous debates and ruffled whole hatsful of feathers, even prompting several of the fellows to suggest my father's termination as a lecturer.

But to hell with them! None of the other girls at Newnham had a fraction of the ambition that I did. I was going to make something of myself. Leave a mark on the world. And that was that.

It had been my great good fortune to have a champion for a father—one who so openly applauded my audacity and who, in every way within his power, was clearing the path for my success.

As I came around the high hedge, I heard the Packard running before I saw Father—Professor Archimedes Phinneaus Porter—behind the wheel of his pride and joy—the bright blue two-seater Mother had recently given him for his fiftieth birthday. I smiled whenever I thought of my father thusly. "Archie" was what he called himself, undistinguished as that might sound. He'd never forgiven his parents for saddling him with such a ridiculously antiquated name, which was why, he explained, he had given his daughter such a plain one.

I strapped my bag to the back platform and slipped in beside him. The door was barely shut before the car lurched into forward motion and we were off. I grabbed the two side scarves and tied them under my chin for the drive into the countryside south of Cambridge town.

"Will I ever get the smell of formaldehyde out of my hair?" I needed to shout to overcome the wind blown directly into our faces and the "infernal combustion engine," as my father called the Packard. I put my wrist to my nose. "I think the stuff's in my skin as well!"

"It is!" Father called out cheerily. "Formaldehyde is organic and seeps into the skin. You'll smell like a cadaver for the rest of the term! Perhaps longer. Every year before the summer break all the anatomy students get together on King's Court, set a huge bonfire, and burn their odious black coats!"

I liked the sound of that tradition and imagined the heat of the fire, the raucous shouts, and the glow of the flames on the faces of the Messrs. Woodley, Shaw, and even Cartwright. There was something wonderfully pagan about the ritual.

Everyone knew Professor Porter's blue Packard and waved merrily to him as we tooled along Gwydir Street and the Brewery, then passed the Mill Road Cemetery and on out of the city limits. Cambridge was a smallish town. It wasn't long before we were driving southwest on Whimpole Road through green farm- and pasturelands.

"Well," Father said, "what did you find in your specimen's throat?"

"All the organs and structures necessary for the muscles of speech! The hyoid bone, the larynx, the tongue and pharynx. I took a good hard look at the supralaryngeal air passage. I've studied the voice box in theory and lecture, but it was amazing to finally see the very organ that makes our species human!"

"Don't let's forget upright posture in all the excitement. You'd have quite a fight on your hands with our fellow evolutionists if you showed them a knuckle-dragging ape, even if he could sing 'The Star-Spangled Banner'!"

I carefully considered my father's words. He was right. Sometimes my enthusiasm got the better of me. I tended to forget the obvious.

"Remind me tomorrow," he continued, "but I think I've got the larynx of a mountain gorilla in the pantry!"

Much to Mother's dismay, Archie Porter called the specimen closet in his home laboratory the pantry. It truly was a grotesque chamber, worse in ways than the human dissection laboratory at the university. Before Father had become a lecturer of human anatomy, he had been a morphologist—a comparative anatomist—studying and dissecting a variety of animal species. He therefore kept, in row upon row in his pantry, body parts, embryos, specimens, and skeletons of every sort of wild and domesticated animal.

In this one instance, and possibly this one instance alone, I found myself in agreement with Mother. Even as a young girl I'd hated the sight of half a dog's head in a jar, the rather large phallus of a stallion, a pig embryo, a skinned cat. And not because they were hideous or frightening. In fact, they'd fascinated me. But I adored animals (in their *living* condition) and felt nothing but pity for the poor creatures who had been so unceremoniously cut into pieces, ending up pickled in Father's closet. It suddenly occurred to me that I'd had no such qualms that morning in the human anatomy laboratory. But then, I had more love for animals than I did most people I knew.

"While the human is fresh in your mind," Father said, "you should have a look-see at the ape!"

"That would be brilliant!" I called out, grateful enough for the extraordinary opportunity just offered to overcome the revulsion I felt for the unfortunate simian.

Father was proud of his collection. Every summer for the past six years he had gone on expedition to Kenya, timed between that country's two rainy seasons, in furtherance of his lifelong quest. He, like his friend and associate Eugène Dubois, had been searching for Charles Darwin's missing link. Dubois, in 1891, had had the good fortune to find in the wilds of Indonesia the fossil remains of Java man, what my father believed was "stunning proof" of an interim species, part ape, part man. But this had, ironically, proved to be only the beginning of the poor man's travails. The scientific establishment had, by and large, repudiated Dubois's finding. Ever since his return to Europe with his precious bones, having nearly lost the case holding them in a shipwreck, the Limburgian paleoanthropologist had been compelled to defend his fossils against those "too dense or jealous," as Father would say, to admit his accomplishment. And all this after years of intensive work and massive personal sacrifice— the appalling loss of an infant daughter to a tropical fever and a wife who had lost her love for the man with the death of their child.

Father's only dispute with his friend was one of location. Eugène Dubois, on the urgings of his professor at Jena University—the esteemed Ernst Haeckel—had gone looking for the ape-human link in the jungles of Asia. Professor Porter, a more literal Darwinist, was certain the fossils would be found in equatorial Africa.

Dubois had returned home from Java carrying tangible evidence of an upright anthropoid with a large brain—far larger than any ape's, though not quite as fulsome as the Neanderthal skulls discovered in Europe. Alas, it had no neck vertebrae or any evidence of the power of speech. But Father had so far found less than that. Nothing at all but fossils of extinct flora and fauna of the Pleistocene epoch. He had also harvested quite a collection of unwanted body parts as specimens from the carcasses of apes taken down by the numerous great white hunters now making a fine living in Kenya with their wealthy clientele, out for adventure and trophies for their library floors and walls.

Certainly he was frustrated, but each year without fail he mounted a new, insanely expensive expedition, financed by my mother's vast fortune. The money was grudgingly given, as Samantha Edlington-Porter loathed the months her husband disappeared into the "Dark Continent." She was mortified by his theories and endeavors, which were similarly disavowed by his fellow scientists. While they might agree with Darwin's theories in *Descent of Man*, few had any interest in finding physical proof of them. Well respected though Archie Porter might be in his professorship at Cambridge, he was merely an "enthusiastic amateur" in his paleoanthropological adventures. I always thought it to my mother's credit that despite her dreaded misgivings and the whiff of scientific heresy that surrounded the hated safaris, she repeatedly funded them.

Father did, however, pay a price. There were the acid comments at Mother's dinner parties and the incessant harping about the dangers of these expeditions. In one respect, at least, she did have firm ground upon which to level her assaults.

For beating in Archie Porter's broad, manly chest was a questionable heart. It was a family thing, he liked to say, much like the Hapsburg lip. His father, two uncles, and a brother had died young from what Father referred to as "a bum ticker." But he insisted—quite rightly, I thought—that his kin had been wholly unfit individuals, carrying before them massive bellies and jowls hanging heavily from their chins that shook like beef aspic on a platter. Father was an altogether different sort—a bona fide outdoorsman. He fished, he rode, he bicycled. He took miles-long striding constitutionals every single day that weather permitted. And I, the only one of his and Mother's children who had survived infancy, had taken very much after my father.

Samantha cringed when anyone called her daughter a tomboy, but that was a perfectly reasonable description of me. Much as I loved reading and the study of science, I honestly preferred the out-of-doors. Never was I happier than on the back of a galloping horse, my yapping hounds running alongside. Not to brag, but I was a crack shot, too. I could outshoot Father at skeet, and my begrudging nickname on the college archery range was "Robin Hood." Long ago, Mother had given up seeing me descend the staircase slowly and decorously, my hand pressed lightly on the rail. I had proved myself to be little more than a female ruffian.

"So were they horrible to you today, the young men in the class?" Father shouted over the wind.

"Only one true dolt!" I shouted back in answer to his question, thinking of Mr. Cartwright.

I noticed that Father's wavy brown hair, blown backward, was growing rather longer than Mother liked, and it was always an unruly mess by the time we returned from the college. He had refused to grow the full beard that was all the rage now, especially among English academic men, choosing instead the clean-shaven American style. His wife approved of the beardless look but strenuously objected to the too-long hair. "You look like the Wild Man of Borneo," she would complain every time he came in from a drive. And when it attained a dangerous length—as it had now—Samantha would have the barber make a special house call.

"But it makes me so angry, Cambridge segregating the men and the women!" I said. "Why haven't they come into the new century? Look at Marie Stopes at University College London. Not only are females training side by side with male physicians, but Marie, a girl *my age*, is already a lecturer there!"

"You could have gone to University College!"

"I know I could. But then I would have had to leave you!" I

looked over at my father, affection threatening to spill over as tears. "And your laboratory!"

"*Our* laboratory!" He smiled, never taking his eyes off the road. Archie Porter was nothing if not a careful man.

I was warmed to be reminded that he trusted me as his assistant in his private work at home. Depended on me more and more all the time. It was why I relished every weekend I could steal away from the university. To work at his side.

"If you test well in human dissection—you're already top of the class in lecture—you just might open some doors for young ladies in the future!"

The Packard turned into the long manor drive and pulled up to our stately home—the Edlington-Porter manor house with its fine stonework and high arched windows. Now Father spoke in normal tones, filled with the warmth and familiar affection I so loved.

"Meanwhile, you'd best sneak upstairs and stick your head in a bucket of lemon juice before coming down to dinner. I'm afraid I'll never hear the end of 'our reeking daughter smelling of the dead.'"

The doorman came to my side and opened the Packard's door. "Welcome back, Miss Jane."

Then the hounds were there to greet me, setting up a fine racket, sniffing wildly at my new and enticing fragrance.

"Come on, boys," I said, eager to get to the stables, "let's go see if Leicester wants to have a ride"

Home

I woke to find my tabby cat licking my neck and the sound of crinkling paper at my feet. *Not good*, I thought. *Not at all good.* I opened my eyes and winced to see my Pekingese, Harry, sprawled on the silken coverlet gnawing wetly on the pages of the book I'd fallen asleep reading. No wonder I had dreamed of Africa again. It was Mary Kingsley's magnificent account of her journey up the Ogowe River to collect fishes and fetishes, an expedition she—a woman!—had planned, led, and executed by her very own devices. I snatched the volume from Harry's teeth and found the pages crumpled and soggy but largely intact.

I'd been forbidden by Mother to utter the name of Mary Kingsley aloud in the house, as any thought of her daughter traipsing off into the filthy, parasite-ridden jungle was entirely out of the question. At twenty I was already considered by most as a spinster, and my outrageous ideas, atheism, and radical education were every year diminishing my prospects for a good marriage, any marriage.

I sat up and gazed at the feather-decorated spear and elaborate Maasai tribal necklace that hung on either side of my overcrammed bookshelf. They were my proudest treasures, gifts from Father's Kenyan expeditions. I rose and padded quietly across the floor, trying hard to avoid the squeaks in the old planks that would, inevitably, bring Constance, Mother's lady's maid, knocking on the door to inquire, as she did every morning, if Miss Jane wished assistance dressing. Every morning I firmly but politely declined assistance. It was mad that a grown woman with all her body parts intact would need help putting on her clothes.

I knew that the refusal was founded on my abhorrence to the idea of servants in the first place. But that was an argument, like the subject of Mary Kingsley (or myself) traveling to Africa, that was simply unwinnable. Even Father, who was similarly uneasy with servants at his beck and call, had long ago given up trying to change Mother's mind. The maids, butlers, cooks, gardeners, and stable hands were as integral to country life as the stove and mortar and wood beams of the manor house.

A floorboard squeaked under my toe, and barely a breath later came the inevitable tapping at my door.

"No thank you, Constance, I'm already dressed," I lied before the question could be asked. I pulled my riding habit from the clothes cupboard and put the cinch-waist jacket on over a clean starched blouse and the hated corset. I glared at the ankle-length skirt as I did every morning I dressed for riding, furious that Mother was yet unmovable on the subject of the split skirt for the sport. How senseless it was to ride horse sidesaddle with petticoats and flounces hindering natural movement.

It brought to mind the ongoing bouts with Mother on the subject of swimming, an activity she thought most unbecoming for a lady. Father, bless his heart, had insisted on teaching his daughter "that manly art," as my mother called it. What I remembered best was the feel of his strong warm arms enfolding me, bracing me against the slap of cold breakers. His laughter and mine mingled with the sounds of the seashore. "Are you ready, sweetheart? I'm going to let you go." I'd splash doggy-style as he backed away, his long sopping hair clinging to his neck. "Swim to me, Jane!" And I would. Anything to please him. Facedown I'd slap arm over little arm, turning my head to gulp air the way he'd taught me. But something was dragging me down. Water filled my nose. I flailed, panicking.

He'd caught me up in his arms again. "Blasted weight!" Propping me on one arm, he raised the long skirt of my wool bathing dress and with the other hand ripped at its hem. The lead weights were thrown into the sea along with the flat-sole shoes. "Let's try again." Now when I swam I felt light as a bubble. I could hear his encouraging shouts above my slapping arms and the roar of the surf. He was proud of me, proud of his little girl. He'd carried me up and onto the beach past the demure ladies wading in the shallows. Past a horse-drawn bathing wagon filled with giggling girls in their princess dresses and bloomers being drawn into the waist-deep sea. Mother had been waiting for us in her three-sided tent, scowling at the sight of her wild-haired husband and shoeless daughter, the ragged, weightless hem of my dress. "Oh, the pair of you!" she'd cry. She was always exasperated with us.

As I'd grown older, I'd insisted on continuing "real swimming," but she wouldn't hear of my wearing a form-fitting French maillot—a sleeveless, body-hugging garment that covered only the upper thighs. This was another skirmish in which my father refused to engage.

"We need to choose our battles with your mother," he reminded me frequently. He was right, of course. My refusal to "come out" at age sixteen to be presented at court in a fluffy white ball gown—its cost would have paid the wages of six servants for an entire year—had nearly brought the Edlington-Porter house down around our ears. My decision to attend college had sent Mother to bed for two weeks. But in both of those instances, Father, still very much the head of this household—even if not the holder of the family fortune—had prevailed.

Father's insistence that I be allowed into his human dissection laboratory had been met with Mother's unqualified horror. His spirited rebuttals had been at least in part selfishly motivated, as he depended on my help more and more in his home laboratory. None of the assistants he'd hired over the years had exhibited a fraction of my aptitude or enthusiasm. I suspected there was a sense of pride passing on his vast knowledge of morphology, anatomy, and evolutionary science.

Once fully outfitted in my riding habit, I drew out of a wooden trunk at the foot of my bed a pair of men's trousers and pulled them on under my skirt. I'd sat up by candlelight for a week wielding a needle and thread—tools with which I was not on the friendliest terms—and hemmed the pant legs so that they wouldn't show beneath my skirt. Satisfied that I looked sufficiently dignified and ladylike, I left my room, taking the stairs quickly.

My parents were already at the table, Father at the head, though his eggcup was still covered in its quilted cap, his buttered toast uneaten. He had his head stuck into his *New York Times*—one of a week's worth that had arrived that morning, another luxury his wife's money afforded him. "My guilty pleasure," he called the weekly delivery of newspapers from America. Father prided himself on keeping up with current events "from the colonies," as he called them—a playful dig to the Edlingtons, several of whose staunch ancestors had died in America's revolution against Mad King George III.

Mother had not touched her kippers and tomatoes, and only a tiny nibble had been taken from her apricot scone, as she was busy jotting down notes for Cook for the evening's dinner party.

At the sideboard, I filled my plate with kippers and toast, ignoring the sausage floating in grease, and pondered an egg, which I did take. I sat at Father's left hand across from my mother. Neither looked up from their occupations, which was just fine with me. I could eat in peace or, rather, quickly so as to get on my horse as soon as humanly possible.

But it was not to be.

Mother put down the pen and regarded me with that beady eye of hers. I could see her nostrils fluttering in an attempt to discern any residual odors from the laboratory. She had strangely refrained from any arguments about the dissection class at the dinner table the night before. Now seemingly satisfied on the olfactory front, Mother examined my face with the discernment that Leonardo would his model for the *Mona Lisa*.

"Your nose is covered in freckles, my dear. I suggest you wear a broader-brimmed hat when you ride. And Constance will bring you some of my bleaching salve. If you use it regularly, the freckles will fade."

"And the skin on my nose will be burned by the caustic chemicals that the salve contains."

"The burn is superficial and will heal. It's a small price to pay for beauty."

Choose your battles, I repeated sternly and silently to myself and made a sandwich of my kippers and toast.

"Well, Roosevelt's been inaugurated for a second term," Father said without taking his head from the *Times*. "And it looks as though the Industrial Workers of the World are calling themselves 'Wobblies.'"

Clearly Father had chosen to steer clear of this particular mother-daughter spat, so I cracked the top off my soft-boiled egg, spooned the contents onto my kipper sandwich, and began to devour it.

"Louisa Pomphrey-Bell tells me that all of Melanie's right-hand blouse and dress sleeves have had to be let out." Mother was speaking now of our neighbors' pretty, very popular, and equally vapid sixteen-year-old daughter, the one for whom suitors were falling all over themselves, seeking her attention. "It seems that every one of those sleeves has become too tight from the constant tennis she plays."

The statement was so utterly inane that neither Father nor I replied in any way. Melanie was one of the simpering, always-cheerful, and agreeable girls of Cambridge society whose lives were filled with trifles and, I was sure, had never drawn a single rebellious breath.

The silence from her husband and daughter must have come as an insult to Mother, for a moment later she erupted. "That is a disgusting habit, Jane!" She was glaring at the sandwich in my hand.

"What? Egg on my kippers? Mother, I don't mean to be rude, but I think you've gone off your bean."

"That *is* rude! Archie, will you put down your paper and speak to your daughter? She seems to have lost the last vestiges of good manners she was ever taught under this roof."

Father folded his paper carefully and set it down next to his plate. He looked at me and then at Mother.

"Well, Jane, you do seem to have a few freckles on your nose. And Sammie"—this was a pet name he used only in the privacy of our small family gatherings—"you seem to have a problem that I suspect has to do less with Jane's egg on kipper than bone saw on femur." Mother's face was set in stone. "So why don't you just come out with it?" he finished.

"What good would it do? The two of you have already made up your minds. I have nothing to say about it. Besides, the damage is done. What decent man is going to want a woman—*a twenty-year-old woman*—who cuts up human bodies and smells like the basement of a charnel house?" She glared at Father. "I ask you!"

I thought I detected a glimmer of guilt on my father's face. We all knew that no decent English gentleman would want a woman such as myself to become his wife and the mother of his children.

The thing was, I didn't care.

"I'm going out for my ride," I said, standing from my chair. "I apologize for my rudeness, Mother. I love you, and I wish I could make you happier. But boat races and domestic bliss make me want to scream. Do you have any respect for me at all, or know one *single* important thing about me?"

I looked at Father, then. There was nothing more to say. He wore an expression that bespoke both pride and remorse, the very sentiments warring in my own head. I took leave of the dining room. I heard a single, choked sob but, steeling myself from all further emotion, headed down the hall to the back door and out to the stables.

Peter, the stable boy whom I liked the most for his gentle way with the horses and whom I trusted with my little secret, came out to meet me, averting his eyes from my scowling face.

"It's all right, Peter," I said, trying to lighten my voice. "I'll ride Leicester this morning."

"Which saddle, miss?" Peter whispered, knowing that some days his outrageous mistress wore breeches beneath her skirts.

"Give me a man's saddle today," I told him. "And every day hereafter."

"Yes, miss," he said and turned back to the stable. "Very good, miss."

I could see the boy was smiling.

Bones of Contention

The scientific lecture hall at Cambridge was magnificent. Oak paneling rose to the high, elaborately carved ceiling, and its black horsehair chairs set within the steeply curved gallery afforded the large, murmuring crowd a perfect view of the still-empty podium and exhibits below.

Father had secured the best seats for us near the bottom center, but he was, at the moment, deeply engaged in heated conversation with several of Oxford's morphology lecturers.

The Fourth International Congress of Zoology was an enormous affair. Peppered around the chamber I recognized some of the preeminent scientific minds of the day—from not only Britain and America but the Continent as well. There were fellows of the Royal Geographical Society, nobles, professors, military men, and a smattering of clergy. There was Sir Francis Galton who believed in the existence of a natural elite in mankind; a physiologist of note, Professor Sayle; and Mr. MacColl, the editor of the *Athenæum*. It was a distinguished crowd indeed.

I peered around, curious to see who from Cambridge had come. The whole of the biology, zoology, geology, and chemistry departments were there, lecturers and students from the college of comparative anatomy. Most of my cohorts from the human dissection laboratory had come, and I had to smile noticing that Woodley (who was "studying to be a physician, not a fossil hunter") and a rather smug-looking Mr. Cartwright had made an appearance.

A small crowd was gathered around the table set to one side of the podium upon which the precious Java man bones were displayed. "Bones of contention," some called them, and the black-frock-coated men surrounding the specimens were, I could see by their posture and gesticulations, already in heated debate as to their worth.

Mr. Shaw, the laboratory servant who apparently possessed skills beyond those of the anatomy laboratory, was at the base of the center aisle fussing with the episcope, a recent innovation that allowed opaque materials, such as book pages, drawings, mineral specimens, and leaves, to be projected onto a screen behind the lecturer. Cambridge was very proud of its episcope, and hardly a serious discourse was held anymore without it being employed.

A fellow of Trinity College with a loud ringing voice called the meeting to order, and we all took our seats. Father sat down beside me looking a bit red in the face with his jaw set hard as it always was when he was angry. "Eugène is not going to have an easy time of it," he whispered.

"Did you ever think otherwise?"

Father sighed. "Scientists are among the most pigheaded people alive. Wouldn't you think it should be just the opposite?"

Now Harold Gardiner, dean of Trinity College, a man whose heavily veined florid face betrayed his love of drink, came to the fore. "Good afternoon. I'll not waste any precious time with a long introduction. We all know our esteemed speaker. He was recently awarded the Prix Broca for outstanding achievement in anthropology, Professor Eugène Dubois."

Tall and fair-haired, with a handsome face and open, rather hopeful expression, Father's old friend strode into the room, taking his place at the podium to what could generously be called polite applause. He squared his broad shoulders, looking for all the world like a man hard-pressed to allow anyone to undermine his most dearly held convictions. I'd heard my father say that Eugène's assertions about *Pithecanthropus erectus*, which he called *P.e.* for short, were something akin to a holy crusade, and from the fire in his eyes I knew this to be the whole truth.

"I am here to present my riverside findings at the Trinel site in Java, the Dutch East Indies."

The lights in the lecture hall dimmed, and with the episcope whirring, a schematic section of the geologic formations at Trinel was projected on the screen behind and above the podium, highlighting the all-important layers in which the *P.e.* fossils had been found. Almost immediately there were loud, skeptical mutterings from the audience.

Someone just behind Father and me wasted no time in calling out loudly, "Our esteemed colleague, Rudolph Virchow, is no longer with us . . ."

"I'm glad that old fossil is dead," Father whispered a bit too loudly, referring to the recently deceased pasha of German science.

". . . but if he were here, I'm sure he would strenuously object, as he had many times before, to your contention that the three bone fragments in question were part of the same individual. The skull is most certainly that of a giant gibbon of some kind, and the femur is clearly human. You yourself have pointed out the grievous injury to the thighbone. That injured man—"

"Pardon," Dubois interrupted, "*P.e.* was a female."

"The injured female," the skeptic continued, sounding quite annoyed, "lived long enough for the bone to ossify. Apes do not perform those kinds of caretaking of their own species, as humans do."

Dubois moved to the table and, picking up the skull in one hand, the femur in the other, demonstrated that they were extremely weighty. "These are thoroughly fossilized—stone—and the color of the two specimens is identical. Numerous geologists have confirmed the level at which they were found—and they *were* found at the same level, Dr. Ellenbogen."

Near the front at the side aisle of the hall, a strapping fellow in a tan linen shooting jacket with padded shoulders that looked to be quite unnecessary stood up and called out, "Correct me if I'm wrong, Professor Dubois, but wasn't a great deal of flora and fauna extracted from this same level at Trinel, fossils that confirm that their geologic histories are identical with *P.e.*'s?"

I noted that the outspoken man was clean-shaven except for a small pale mustache and looked altogether out of place in the room full of black-clad academics.

Indeed, every eye in the room fell on the man—clearly an American—defending the beleaguered speaker. He seemed to my eye "rakish," if I'd had to describe him, and he'd made his declarations in bold, deliberate tones, evincing admiration from a few, irritation from the greatest majority of others.

"To whom do I have the pleasure of speaking?" Dubois inquired.

"The name is Conrath. Ral Conrath. I'm an expedition leader and engineer by trade, and I've worked on every continent in the world. I had the great fortune to visit the Trinel site, though sadly after you'd left. Your team's efforts there were unimpeachable."

"Thank you." Dubois, while certainly pleased at the kind words, was eager to get on with it and turned back to the subject at hand. "So I stand on my assertion that the skull, the femur, and the tooth, as well as the *entire collection* met their end in either the late Pliocene or early Pleistocene epoch."

"Here the fantasy passes beyond all experience!" called out another heckler in the first row.

Father could no longer contain himself. He stood and faced the rotund and bespectacled clergyman who, from the fine cut of his robes and scarlet sash, could be identified as a cardinal. "Can't you even devise your own ignorant insult? That was Rudolph Virchow's boneheaded rejection of Charles Darwin's evolutionary theory, for crying out loud! How can you take seriously anything that idiot said?"

Arguments broke out all over the chamber now, and Dubois allowed them to swirl around him with admirable equanimity. But out the corner of my eye I caught a small, swift movement. Father's hand had darted quickly to his chest. I glanced at his face and saw pain there, brief though it was, before he let the hand drop to his side and took his seat again. This alarmed me, but there was little to be done at the moment, and with order restored, another image was projected onto the screen, this a drawing of the inside of *P.e.*'s skullcap.

"With a foot-driven, diamond-tipped dentist's drill, I was able to remove every bit of matrix from the inner skull," Dubois went on, unable to conceal his pride. "I discovered the *Pithecanthropus erectus*'s cranial capacity to be one thousand ccs."

There was a general murmuring of approval from the assembled. This was an undeniable fact, even to the disbelievers. Every paleoanthropologist and zoologist in the chamber knew very well that the largest anthropoid ape skull held no more than eight hundred ccs.

"A damn dental drill," Father muttered. "Why didn't I think of that?"

"While Neanderthal skulls hold two hundred ccs more than *P.e.*'s, they share the same elongated cranial shape and strong brow ridges," Dubois added. He moved behind the podium and signaled to Mr. Shaw for the next image. It showed a photographic cast of what I assumed was *P.e.*'s brain. Eugène must have poured plaster into the meticulously cleaned brain cavity. The foramen magnum, the bony hole through which the spinal cord exited the skull, was clearly visible.

Dubois pointed at the projected photograph. "Can you see how far forward the foramen magnum is on my specimen? This position is typical of animals with upright postures. This affords me, or should I say my beautiful *P.e.*, anatomical consistency between the skullcap and the femur—one more piece of evidence proving they came from the same animal.

"I'd say you've proved that beyond a reasonable doubt," called out Ral Conrath.

"Hear, hear!" Archie cried.

"I have therefore come to the inescapable conclusion that *Pithecanthropus erectus* is neither ape nor human. She is a transitional creature between two species—Charles Darwin's missing link in human evolution!"

Now there was general outrage in the hall, a roar that drowned out Dubois, who was attempting to continue.

"Isn't there anything you can do, Father? I know he was expecting resistance, but this is appalling behavior."

Archie had begun to rise from his chair when he noticed that a dapper older gentleman was already halfway to the podium, and that Eugène Dubois's face had lit into a broad smile. Silver haired and silver bearded, the stranger was quite handsome and strode with the strength and vigor of a much younger man. Eugène Dubois put out his arms to welcome the distinguished interloper, and they shook all four hands before Dubois stepped aside and let him take the stage.

"Who is that?" I whispered to Father.

"That, my dear, is Professor Ernst Haeckel."

I was speechless. I knew the zoologist and professor of comparative anatomy at Germany's University of Jena to be one of the world's foremost authorities on evolution and the author of one of my most prized volumes, *The History of Creation*. His early drawings of embryos had been singled out for praise by Darwin himself in his *Descent of Man*.

More to the point on this day was Haeckel's very presence, as he had been the greatest personal influence on Eugène Dubois's career. Haeckel's theories on "ape-like men" and "man-like apes" had been the cornerstone of Dubois's quest. His suggestion that evidence of human evolution—"the missing link"—was to be found in the Dutch East Indies directly led Dubois to explore Java.

So nonplussed was I that my brain cleared only when Haeckel was partway through his summary of the evidence for human evolution of all life on earth. I was stunned. It was not simply that Ernst Haeckel's arguments were clear and brilliant. But the man—bless his great heart—was publicly defending Dubois and denigrating Rudolph Virchow!

"I believe that fossil remains of a form intermediate between ape and man do exist, and that the *Pithecanthropus erectus* of her able discoverer, Eugène Dubois, is in fact a relic of the extinct group—intermediate between man and ape, to which as long ago as 1886 I gave the name *Pithecanthropus*. This is the long-lost 'missing link' in the chain of the highest primates, an intermediate form connecting the lower races of mankind to anthropoid apes!"

Now the murmuring in the room was more polite, for no one dared to disrespect Ernst Haeckel.

"The Neanderthal skulls of Spy and Moulin Quignon were declared by the sagacious Rudolph Virchow to be nothing more than 'pathological specimens,' produced only through disease and not, in fact, an early race of mankind. Virchow denies even Neanderthal man!"

Father reached over and gave my hand a happy squeeze. Things were going much better than he'd ever expected.

"It must be remembered, gentlemen and ladies," Haeckel went on, "that for more than thirty years, Virchow regarded it as his special duty as a scientist to *oppose* the Darwinian theory and the doctrine of evolution. The 'descent of man from the ape,'" he continued with real disgust creeping into his voice, "Virchow attacked with unmitigated zeal and unnatural energy. According to him, the ape-man is a mere 'figment of a dream.' I say here today that the petrified remains of *Pithecanthropus erectus* are the palpable contradiction of such an unfounded theoretical assumption!"

Unable to control myself, I began to applaud loudly. Father joined me, and though there was heard only a smattering of it in the gallery, from one corner it rang out unabashedly. Ral Conrath was on his feet, clapping enthusiastically. Finally the grudging scientists relented and gave Ernst Haeckel the ovation he deserved. Certainly it must have rankled many that by their applause they were, by association, applauding Eugène Dubois as well.

My eyes strayed to the strange Mr. Conrath, and I found to my embarrassment that he had been regarding *me* quite openly. Just then feeling happy and rather bold, I smiled back at him. He touched his fingers to his hatless head in a return salutation.

Something quivered inside me, somewhere below my belly, and I quickly turned away, glad for an excuse to avert my eyes.

Ernst Haeckel had begun speaking again.

It occurred to me that the food on my plate and that of my dinner companions lay almost altogether untouched. No one was the slightest bit interested in eating.

Talk was the thing.

Father and I, Dubois, and Ernst Haeckel, the latter a guest at the De Vere University Arms Hotel, were dining in its elegant restaurant. The Zoological Congress behind us, the ideas and debate it had engendered had set the air all around afire with controversy, raised voices, and laughter.

"How frustrating it has been," Dubois opined, "to have my femur to prove the upright stance but no cervical vertebrae to relate the hyoid bone with the mandible."

"So you've got no proof of speech," I sympathetically concluded.

"And what do you suppose your Java man would say if he *could* speak?" Father asked with a wry grin.

"I will tell you what he would say," Ernst Haeckel replied. "He would call Rudy Virchow a nincompoop!"

We all roared with laughter and raised our glasses in a toast.

"All that's water under the bridge," Archie insisted. "Let's get to the real point here."

Dubois groaned theatrically. Everyone knew that the two paleo-anthropologists' favorite argument of all—where in the world other missing links might be found—had hardly been touched upon this evening.

"Well, you know what I think," Ernst Haeckel said, eyeing his untouched dinner, "so I will spare you, Archie."

"Thank you for that, Ernst. You should eat. They know how to cook a mean pork chop here."

Truly, Father did not need reminding that though a staunch evolutionist, Haeckel was not a dyed-in-the-wool Darwinian. And with Eugène having found such stunning success in following his teacher's urgings to search for his fossils in the Dutch East Indies, the two of them needed no further convincing that they were right.

"You sure you can't be moved about a major find in equatorial Africa?" Father persisted. "My distinguished colleague, Mr. Darwin, were he here with us at this table, would agree that an ape-man will be found in Africa."

"But you have been trying and trying, Archie," said Eugène Dubois, finishing with a bit of gentle teasing, "and with all of your work, you've got less than a leg bone to stand on."

My father laughed ruefully.

"There is only one way this dispute can authoritatively be decided," Ernst Haeckel said. "You will arm wrestle."

We collapsed into such a fit of laughter that the four of us were shocked to find Ral Conrath standing beside our table. He was smiling broadly, having overheard the challenge made in jest.

I was unable to take my eyes from him, thinking how handsome he looked when he smiled, how large and virile was his presence.

"Mr. Conrath," Eugène said with much congeniality. "I never had a chance to thank you for your generous support this afternoon."

"Well, it didn't hold a candle to Dr. Haeckel's brilliant discourse, but it certainly was heartfelt."

Eugène looked behind him. "Are you alone?"

"I am, as a matter of fact. I'm staying at the De Vere tonight and thought I'd have some dinner before I turned in."

"You must join us."

Father and Haeckel immediately made room, and the waiter was called to bring another chair.

Within moments the conversation picked up where it had left off, as easy and convivial with the newcomer as it had been before. This Conrath fellow fit right in, I could not help but observe. I saw that

Father liked the man, or at least felt some kinship with a fellow American. Ral was a Midwesterner, too, he from a small town in South Dakota. Ral was particularly attentive to Father, listening to his arguments, brow furrowed with intense interest.

"I'm a tad reluctant to state my humble opinion in such illustrious company," Conrath began, then paused for a long enough moment that the others all chimed in with encouragement to go on.

"From what I've seen at Trinel and other East Indies digs, the European Neanderthal cave sites, and my work with Petrie . . ."

"Petrie!" Archie exclaimed. "You worked with Flinders?" William Flinders Petrie was the most celebrated Egyptian archaeologist of the time.

"I worked on the excavations at Luxor."

"That was an impressive find," Dubois said, "and quite a feat of engineering, too."

"Bill's a bit of a madman about those things. He insists on acting as his own engineer."

"One must have men one can trust with such delicate matters," Dubois offered.

"I've been on both coasts of Africa now," Ral went on.

"Kenya?" Father asked.

"On safari there. Hunting big game. In fact, I took our president's best friend into Amboseli, and he tells me Roosevelt can't wait to leave office to 'go shoot him some elephants.' "

I winced at the mention of big-game hunting, the thought of which upset me deeply.

"But that's neither here nor there," Ral continued. "I'm no expert, mind you, but I follow with great interest the adventures of pioneers like yourselves, and I've decided that I'm going to have to throw my hat in the ring with Professor Porter and the late, great Mr. Darwin. Africa's the next place the missing link is going to be found."

"You sound very sure of yourself, Mr. Conrath," I said, finally finding my voice.

He looked me dead in the eye. "And you are . . . ?"

"Jane Porter," I said and put my hand on Father's arm.

"This is my daughter, Mr. Conrath."

"I'm very glad to make your acquaintance, Miss Porter, and the truth is, yes, I'm close to one hundred percent sure West Central Africa is going to give up some extraordinary ape-man fossils in the next few years."

"West Central Africa? Do you mean Gabon?" I felt myself grow suddenly warm beneath my high-necked blouse and serge jacket. Gabon was the location of the Ogowe River. "Then you must be familiar with Mary Kingsley and her several expeditions."

Ral Conrath looked momentarily blank, but Ernst Haeckel, certainly progressive in some quarters but not, as it appeared, with a woman's right to be heard as well as seen, interrupted, dismissing Miss Kingsley's adventures as mere trifles—"fishes and fetishes"— and clearly unworthy of serious discussion.

"A woman alone has no business trekking around Africa," Haeckel said. "It is unseemly. Very unseemly."

The professor's words left me chastised and uncomfortable, and I began tucking into my untouched roast beef with less gusto than violence. Father noticed, of course, but it was neither the time nor the place to defend independent womanhood.

In fact, the talk had turned to the plight of the Belgian Congo in the past fifty years—King Leopold's horrible slaughter of ten million black Africans in that country he claimed to own. The men argued about whether the Englishman Sir Henry Morton Stanley had been tricked or had gone willingly at Leopold's behest, leading one of the great exploratory expeditions into the Congo. One that led to further exploitation.

"Well," Father observed wryly, "it wasn't much worse than what President Andrew Jackson did to the American Indians with his Indian Removal Act."

And with that, I found my voice once more. *Who was any man— even the great Ernst Haeckel—to shut me up?* "I believe the urge to colonize and subjugate is universal in the human species."

All the men quieted and turned to look at me. I put down my knife and fork and straightened my back. "My once-favorite monarch, Elizabeth Tudor, ran riot over Ireland. She killed damn near half the Irish population in her lust for power."

Ernst Haeckel looked scandalized and Dubois amused, but the only reproach I perceived from Father for my vulgar language was a single raised eyebrow.

That said, I felt my appetite return, a real appetite, and I finished my dinner, every carrot and pea and roasted potato, sopping up the gravy with a bread roll.

I was well aware that Ral Conrath was appraising me with great interest, but I refused to meet his eye.

Later, as we stood in the grand lobby of the De Vere, Eugène, who was coming home with us, was saying his good nights and giving final thanks to Professor Haeckel. Mr. Conrath took the opportunity to approach Father and me.

"Like I said, Professor, you're right on the mark with Africa, but take my word for it, Gabon's got the limestone formations you fossil hunters have the most luck with, and I know where to find 'em." He handed Father his card and spoke to us in low tones. "I've got something of great interest to show you. Why don't you let me tell you more about it?" Then he looked straight into my eyes and said quite suddenly and entirely out of context, "It's rare to see a woman with a steel backbone."

"That's my Jane," Father said, not in the least offended by the man's familiarity.

"It's refreshing in the extreme," Ral added.

Far from blushing with embarrassment, I felt a rush of excitement that shuddered through my frame, and I said, "I hope you do come and talk to us, Mr. Conrath. We would be very happy to hear what you have to say about West Africa."

"It would be my pleasure," he said, pumping Father's hand. When he gave me his little finger-to-forehead salute, I hoped nothing in my expression gave away my strange discomfiture.

The Snake Charmer

Ral Conrath had been expected at noon and by five had neither come nor called on the telephone. I was sorely disappointed at missing the larger-than-life expedition leader. I'd spent an afternoon of unspeakable boredom with Mother's idea of a fine suitor at a riverside picnic and had rounded on her at the front door of the manor. Could she have chosen anyone more perfect to annoy me? I'd demanded. Mother's lips quivered in outrage at having been spoken to so rudely by her ungrateful spawn, and for a moment I thought I might receive the first slap of my life. But at that very moment the sound of an automobile puttering up the drive froze us both in our places.

And there came Father, striding out past us to meet the black Ford Model A and the solitary figure at the wheel—Ral Conrath, his hair tousled by the wind, his face weathered and tawny, and his presence a very breath of fresh air to sweep away the poison swirling around Mother and me.

Ral did not use the door. With a hand on the frame, he vaulted athletically over the side and came down gracefully on the gravel drive.

I could hear my mother's sharp intake of breath and her chuckle to see Father greet this hale fellow with an ardent handshake.

"Is *that* Mr. Conrath?" Mother asked me, as though all the recent unpleasantness between us had never occurred.

"It is. A very late Mr. Conrath."

He and Father were walking toward us, already sharing a laugh.

"Mrs. Porter," Father said, "may I present . . ."

"Mr. Conrath," my mother finished for Father, putting out her hand, which, to my utter astonishment, the man kissed with all the gallantry of a high nobleman.

More surprising was the girlish giggle that escaped from Mother's lips. She had never, in all of my memory, come out with more than a cultured chortle.

"Madam," Conrath said, gazing into her eyes, "I do believe the beauty of the mother surpasses that of the daughter." Then he turned and winked at me as if to say there was no slight to me at all. It was only praise for an older lady so much more in need of compliments than a beautiful young women like myself.

"You have my sincerest apologies for the tardiness. A milk truck— what do you call them here, 'lorries'? Well, one of them crashed smack into a telephone pole, knocking down the lines to Cambridge, so I couldn't call to say I'd been tied up with some outfitters in London." He turned to Father. "What they showed me today will hold great interest for you, Professor Porter."

"'Archie,'" my father ordered. "None of this Professor Porter business. What is it these outfitters are selling?"

"Metal canoes. Fantastic, I tell you. Perfect for the tropical climes. No mildew. No rot. Nothing gets to the hulls. Barnacle won't stick. Three or four of these boats and we're home free up the Ogowe. But look here, I'm getting ahead of myself. I don't even have the job yet."

I watched astonished as Mother slipped her hand through Ral Conrath's arm and led him inside. I had just seen her being charmed, as an Indian fakir with a flute does a hooded cobra.

I took my father's arm, and without a word we followed Ral and Mother into the manor.

It was going to be a very interesting evening indeed.

My amazement extended through dinner, during which Ral regaled us with stories that he promised would "curl Mrs. Porter's hair." He spoke of living for months at a time with a tribe of cannibals; of a pride of lions and pack of hyenas who were at war with each other and into whose path Ral had unintentionally stepped; of ruthless Arab slave traders on the Barbary Coast who did not stop at stealing Negro tribesmen but had a going concern in kidnapping and delivering beautiful white women to the harems of Persian sheikhs. His adventures were something out of H. Rider Haggard's *Allan Quartermain* or *King Solomon's Mines,* and when he took the great liberty of teasingly calling his hostess "She Who Must Be Obeyed," I had a brief but sinking sensation that if I were to re-read the fictions of that famous author, I might discover among the chapters the very tales being told at our dinner table.

But surely Ral Conrath was who he claimed to be. He knew far too much about exploration and site engineering and fossil hunting to be a charlatan. I quieted my racing heart and suspicious mind and allowed myself to be swept away, as were my parents, into the wonders of our guest's world.

"Won't you tell us about yourself, Mr. Conrath?"

I regarded my mother with astonishment. Under normal circumstances, Samantha Edlington-Porter would consider rude such a personal question of a stranger. Even our guest seemed for a brief moment to be caught off guard. Then Ral's lips set themselves into a wry grin.

"Bit of a rough start. Drunk for a father. Put-upon mother. Four older brothers who enjoyed beating me to a pulp."

"And how was it that you became so accomplished a man?" Mother persisted.

I saw out the corner of my eye that Father, too, was most curious about Ral Conrath. This man who seemed never to be lost for words went very still for a long moment. Clearly, he had never been asked this question before.

"To tell you the truth, it was a book that changed my life."

"A book?" I said. "Which one?"

"The first of Donnelly's studies."

"Was it his treatise on Francis Bacon as the author of Shakespeare's plays?" Mother asked. "I remember when he came to Cambridge to argue it. I found it quite fascinating."

Ral shook his head.

"Let me guess," said Archie. "*The Antediluvian World.*"

"That's the one, Professor."

"Well, you certainly weren't alone in your interest. There was a time when everyone was talking about that book."

"I don't know what you're referring to," I interjected.

"These books were published before you were born," Father told me. "An American senator . . ."

"Did he not run for the vice presidency of the United States?" my mother piped in.

"He did indeed . . . and lost," said Father. "His name was Ignatius Donnelly and the book in question was *Atlantis: The Antediluvian World*. It caused quite a sensation in its day. Some people loved it, some thought the man was a crackpot."

"I was one who believed a lost continent existed in the middle of the Atlantic Ocean . . ." Mother said. She went inward then, remembering, ". . . just beyond the Pillars of Hercules. There were colonies in Egypt and South America, too. I was very impressed with the man's scholarship."

"He did a hell of a lot of research," my father said, "but Donnelly never had me convinced."

"You were in the minority, dear," Mother said, smiling prettily and turning back to our guest. "Please go on."

"For me it wasn't so much about whether the man was right or wrong. It just got a poor young boy thinking about the world outside the South Dakota dirt farm he'd grown up on. All his brothers who were taking up the plow and would probably never leave."

Ral lifted his wineglass and took a sip before continuing. I noticed that his fingers, though clean, were rough and unmanicured.

"I decided to become an adventuring man because of that book. See the world. Meet interesting people." He lowered his eyes and his tone grew suddenly humble. "Like all of you."

"Well, you're a very interesting man yourself," Mother insisted.

Ral flashed his hostess a brilliant smile, encouraged to go on with his story.

"Of course all the action was in Egypt," he said.

"That's where you met Petrie?" Father said.

"Nope. Met him for the first time in Jerusalem. In 1891."

I caught myself leaning forward in my chair, then forced myself to ease back. I would remain reserved, unlike my mother, who was acting uncharacteristically dazzled.

"Petrie was excavating at Tel-el-Amarna, and I went to work for him as a common digger. That's where I first got my hands dirty with ancient sand. But within the year he left for London to take up the chair Mrs. Edwards created for him at the university . . ."

"The first ever professorship in Egyptian archaeology," Father told me. "It was a big moment, that. Took what had been a mere pastime for enthusiastic amateurs and turned it into a respectable science."

"What we expect will happen soon with paleoanthropology," my mother added.

"'Course with Petrie in England," Ral went on, "I was out of work. I tried hiring up with some of the other digs but, frankly, they were haphazard. Some of them were still using dynamite in their excavations."

"It was Professor Petrie, wasn't it," I asked, "who taught that dirt should be pared away inch by inch to see all that was in it, and how an artifact lay in the surrounding earth?"

Ral nodded. "I was spoiled by the best. But I couldn't sit around waiting, could I? So I took myself off to whatever part of the world interested me. India, Tibet, Java. Not much digging going on, but there were a few natural history museums that paid well for specimens for their collections, and lots of wealthy men who wanted trophies hanging on their library walls. I was a damn good shot—pardon my French—and I wasn't afraid of exotic locations. So I took up biggame hunting for a bit. While I was in the Javanese jungle I heard that a pal of mine—an engineer who'd worked at Tel-el-Amarna—was digging at Trinel."

"That's how you came to Eugène's site," Father said.

"Exactly. But Dubois was in India trying to get someone to believe he'd found the missing link. So I missed the great man." Ral paused and, quite daringly, I thought, caught and held my eye before continuing his story. "It was my good fortune that the next year Petrie was back in Egypt, digging at Luxor. I signed on, and to my delight, he remembered me."

Ral's expression softened, an attitude, I thought, that was most uncommon in the man.

"We had some good times, Bill and me. He didn't mind a few whiskeys at night after Hilda went off to bed."

My father said to me, "Hilda was Petrie's wife. The love of his life. She went on all his digs with him. Assisted him."

"And never grumbled about living without the comforts she was used to," Ral added with obvious admiration. "Quite a gal, Hilda." He paused for a breath, then added, "You know, everybody always called Bill Petrie difficult. Arrogant. Even insensible. But to me, he was just eccentric. Do you know what he told me?" Ral leaned forward as though to tell a secret. All of us Porters, entirely enthralled, leaned forward, three eager conspirators.

"Now I grant you we'd had a few, maybe one too many, but he said that when he died, he was going to have his head cut off and donated to science so they could study his brain."

I watched as my mother's jaw fell open, and even Father sat back hard in his chair.

"That was a *touch* arrogant, wouldn't you agree, Mr. Conrath?" I said.

"Yeah, but he was a genius," Ral countered. "I can only hope to have a career half as fine as his."

"I don't doubt you're looking at a great future ahead," Father said, thoroughly pleased with our unusual dinner guest.

Ral glowed with the praise. "From your lips to God's ear," he said.

"You'd best find someone else for Archie to talk to," said Mother. "My husband and daughter are avowed atheists."

"As so many thinking men and women are today," he observed, then turned. "And you, Mrs. Porter?"

"I'm an Episcopalian. Nonpracticing."

"Good Lord, I've landed in a hotbed of heretics!"

"I say we drink to that!" Father cried, and the four of us clinked congenial glasses.

"Eleanor," Mother called out in the direction of the kitchen door, "bring us more wine." She smiled prettily. "We seem to be having a celebration."

The talk went on uninterrupted for hours, and while the many courses were consumed, no one at the table, if asked, would have had the faintest idea of what we had been fed. Finally, before Ral and Father retired to his laboratory for cigars and an after-dinner drinks, my mother, in her most authoritative voice, put her hand on Mr. Conrath's arm.

"You must spend the night with us," she said.

He began to object.

"I won't hear of you riding back to Cambridge in the dark. Besides, you and Archie haven't even begun to discuss your business. I'll have Maggie make up the Blue Room for you. I insist."

"Well, how can I resist a direct order from She Who Must Be Obeyed?" Ral said with a winning smile.

The men disappeared and I was left with Mother, who seemed—if I'd had to describe the expression—a bit dreamy eyed.

"What a nice young man he is," she said.

"Yes he is," I agreed, but in my heart I knew that "nice" was not precisely the word I would have chosen to describe Ral Conrath.

That night my dreams were startlingly real. They involved, as they did so many times, the jungle, but there amid the greenery was a hotel all of giant bamboo, and lounging in its soaring, thatch-roofed lobby was Mr. Conrath in a damp white linen shirt and trousers that clung to the strong lines of his body. He reclined on my mother's rose silk chaise longue, and without invitation, I went to him and sat down next to him. I saw that the thin lips were unsmiling, yet his hands came up and cupped both my breasts. I moaned with pleasure and awoke in a sweat.

The rest of the night sleep evaded me, and I was glad to see first light. I dressed and went down to our laboratory, hoping to finish my sketches of two specimens side by side—the craniums of a mountain gorilla and a human.

"Your father's determined to find his bones in Africa."

I startled at Mr. Conrath's voice, just behind me.

"Most people call him obsessed." I turned and eyed Ral directly. "Don't you?"

"Maybe he is. But who's to say obsession's a bad thing? Bill Petrie had one of his own."

"And what was that?"

"Well, he was quite the Greek scholar and had taken something written by Herodotus to heart."

"Herodotus. The Father of History."

"That's him. The thing was a passage written five hundred years before the time of Christ. Herodotus said that on one of his travels to Egypt, he'd had a walk through an 'ancient labyrinth'—*three thou-sand* rooms, half above-, half belowground. The officials only let him see the ones above because the kings who built the place, and some crocodile gods, were buried on the lower level. The old man said this ancient Egyptian labyrinth was bigger than the Great Pyramid. It was the most amazing thing he'd ever seen in his life, and he'd seen a lot. One of the 'Wonders of the World,' he called it. It was apparently a maze of interlocking courts and chambers and crypts and pillared corridors made out of white stone, 'exactly fitted,' engraved with spectacular figures and painted with frescoes that told the whole history of the world. Herodotus said that a person who didn't know his way through the ancient maze could get lost in it and never see the light of day again.

"So Petrie decided that come hell or high water he was going to find the damn thing. He'd already done his triangulation survey at the Giza pyramid and his explorations at Tanis, but all that time he had his eyes peeled to find this place. He drove everybody crazy with it—'his obsession.' Then after that big find at the Fayum Oasis—a good-sized pyramid and sixty well-preserved coffin portraits from Roman times; you were probably still a little girl when that happened—he stumbled onto a huge heap of rubble, stone chips six feet deep. The location was right, the dimensions—bigger than Karnak and Luxor combined—were grand enough. He'd also found parts of columns and statues, and a giant plaster foundation he reckoned was the floor of the complex. Putting it all together, he concluded that this was all that was left of his great Egyptian labyrinth."

"Not even proper ruins?"

"A pile of gravel. It looked as if the kings from later dynasties had come in and used it as a quarry for nearby temples."

"How horrible for him."

"He's been haunted by it ever since. Now *there's* an obsession with an unhappy ending." He held my gaze. "That's not going to happen to your father. Not if I have anything to do with it."

I felt my eyes stinging with gratitude and turned away before he could see such naked emotion.

When Father arrived a few moments later, we showed Ral Conrath around the laboratory. Every bit of it was solidly appreciated by the man. The library, the maps and globes, the skeletons, the great drawers of fossil specimens. Even the "pantry" with its gruesome exhibits evoked oaths of awe and numerous well-conceived questions.

I found myself, rather bemusedly, caring very much what he thought of us.

Then Mr. Conrath unrolled his own map—that of Gabon, the coastal cities of Libreville and Port-Gentil, the spidery line of the Ogowe River, and the great uncharted areas that he said few whites had penetrated, no less explored. South of the river and less than two hundred miles inland he poked his finger.

"I took a hunting party down here. I found limestone caves. My employers came for the ivory and couldn't have cared less." Conrath fished around in his oversized pocket and removed a small wooden box. He placed it on the table between us and opened it. "Look at this." He pushed the box toward Father, who squinted in surprise at its contents. Father held the pale, rounded, and clearly fossilized bone fragment up to the light. I, too, was riveted to the piece.

"Am I seeing what I think I'm seeing?" Father asked.

"Please examine it more closely," Ral graciously suggested.

But Father stood suddenly and, moving to his wall of large specimen drawers, pulled one open. Finding what he was after, he brought a long slender bone to the table and set it down next to the fragment.

"What we have here is the femur—a thighbone—of an antelope. See how long and skinny it is? For fast running. The big bump here on the base of the femur is where the muscle, a very powerful muscle, attaches it to the lower leg." He set the fragment and the bone on the table next to each other. "The two bones are not identical but extremely similar." He looked up at Ral Conrath and me and said with almost boyish wonder, "This species became extinct in the border period between the Pliocene and the Pleistocene epochs, three to four million years ago."

"And where did you say you found this, Mr. Conrath?" I asked. Truly, I was mesmerized by the sight of the fossil.

"The Enduro Escarpment caves. Gabon." Ral turned to my father. "There are no guarantees, Archie. I'd be a liar if I said so. But I've been to the riverside Trinel site, and I saw the place your friend found his ape-man. I've been to Spy as well, where the limestone gave up Neanderthal fossils. I questioned a native near the Enduro Escarpment—needed a translator, of course—but as far as I can see, the caves there are as good as anyplace on earth to find your missing link."

Father was quiet, his eyes closed in contemplation. I saw the jaw begin to clench. I did not dare look at Ral Conrath.

"There's something else," our visitor said. "I'm loath to say it, as it'll probably get me kicked out of your house."

Father nodded for Ral to go on.

"Miss Porter here needs to go on the expedition with you. This is a dense jungle, and the dig site will be large. You'll need another set of eyes, another mind—one that thinks the way you do—if you want to make the most of the months we have between the two rainy seasons. You'll have me watching both your backs every minute of every day. It's a dangerous undertaking, all right, but there's nobody better than me to get you both home in one piece. There, I've said it." He gave Archie a crooked grin. "You going to kick me out?"

Father looked at me. "My girl, you look like a sleeping dog who's just been pecked in the ass by an angry goose. Say something."

I was so stunned and breathless it was hard to get the brief sentence out. "May I go, Father?"

"Well, if I can convince your mother you won't be sold off into white slavery or eaten by cannibals, it's all right by me."

"Let me talk to your mother," Conrath said. "I'll remind her of Hilda Petrie." He clapped Father on the shoulder. "You leave Mrs. Porter to me. In no time at all we're going to be seeing eye to eye. Trust me."

I took Father's arm. "Will you promise to do everything in your power to make this happen?"

"Scout's honor."

I loved it when my father said that. It was so American. And it reminded me of what Archimedes Porter must have been like as a young boy.

I was absolutely sure we would have been the best of friends.

The Nest

I looked up to see the scarlet-tailed grey parrot waddle in a comical pigeon-toed gait down the fig limb. He hung upside down like an acrobat from a smaller branch to take a drink from the coconut shell, then resumed his course till reaching a limb above my feet. Here he stopped and watched me silently for a long moment before ripping off a piece of bark and holding it in the grip of his claws. He began nibbling daintily, letting pieces fall on my toes. This was not the first time the hookbill had come visiting. Tarzan had said the bird's name was *Lu-lu*, but I saw the creature not as a French cancan dancer but as a distinguished professorial gentleman in a frock coat, and had taken to calling him "Mr. Grey."

I had known such a bird in Cambridge, as my neighbor, Mrs. Rys Willis, had kept one as a pet, mentioning endlessly that Henry VIII had had one like it. It had bitten my finger once, drawing blood, and as I had recently been so misused by a wild animal, I was not eager to tangle with Mr. Grey, no matter how small or how sweet and docile he appeared.

It was clear that my new protector, Tarzan, had entrusted my care to his avian friend. There were times when the young man had had to leave the nest to gather food. Every morning before first light he would climb straight up the fig and mysteriously disappear into its thick branches. Whenever Tarzan was gone, Mr. Grey would come to stand sentinel, calling out in a shrill two-part whistle if anything more threatening or untoward than a lizard came near my still largely immobile person. If the whistle sounded, Tarzan would be at my side in an instant. I could only imagine with what strength and agility he had climbed the tree to arrive at such short notice. I marveled at the bird's power of discernment. Other birds or small monkeys coming to call elicited no alarms, nor did a snorting wild pig at the base of the trunk, but an immense red-and-black spider *had*. And a small viper slithering toward me had sent Mr. Grey into a frenzy of whistling and the shouting of a word that sounded much like "hister!" Tarzan had returned posthaste with blood in his eye and hacked the head from the snake in a display both horrifying and deeply appreciated.

While I had heard the bird speak to Tarzan in words unintelligible to me as yet, Mr. Grey had not deigned to converse directly to me, as though he had found me an unworthy partner in conversation. True, I had said very little to him, finding myself more shy with the parrot even than the man.

And the man was shy with me.

Tarzan and I had continued a sort of rudimentary communication. I'd begun enunciating body parts and the objects around me that I recognized, and he had dutifully—no, enthusiastically—repeated and quickly learned them in his lovely deep voice. He was, as my father called his best anatomy students, "a quick study." Less adept was I at the strange language Tarzan employed (from what tribe could it have come?), for it was spoken with gruff, grating undertones. Speaking his words for "eye" and ear"—*yat* and *yad*—had made me feel as though I was clearing my throat of a great wad of phlegm. *Sheeta* was "leopard" and *neeta* was "bird." I had learned that *tar-zan* literally meant "white-skin," and thus our earlier miscommunication had been explained. Really, he was very clever. He had even learned that one word might have two meanings: "here" and "hear."

A sign language had developed as well. This was helpful for verbs—"come," "go," "eat," "hear"—and emotions—"sad," "happy," "angry." This was as far as we'd gotten, but it amazed me that I was understanding the wild man as well as I did, and he me. And that we should even be communicating our simplest feelings.

Most other ideas were yet beyond our capabilities. I had not known how to explain what "father" meant, though whenever I spoke the word, Tarzan flinched. I guessed that this resulted from me hearing it from Tarzan's lips when I had first awoken, and in my unstable condition, "Fah-thah" had provoked an alarming fit of tears and moaning.

Many times I wondered at the great decorum and reserve of the man. Here we were, a man and a woman, living half naked in close quarters, and never had I felt the smallest hint of fear that he might molest me.

It was the simplest of all lives and, without a doubt, the strangest.

"Hello, Mr. Grey," I said for perhaps the fiftieth time, hoping the bird would mimic me.

He said nothing, just dropped the remaining bit of bark in his claw onto my foot and reached for a fig, snapping it off the branch. He held it in one foot while standing with perfect balance on the other and began gnawing at it with gusto, depositing almost as much of the ripe fruit on his beak as in his stomach, a sack just under his throat that quickly began to bulge with the meal.

"You're a little piggy," I said.

"Piggy," the bird repeated, startling me.

Why that word, and no other? I wondered. Perhaps he liked the sound of it.

"Piggy," said Mr. Grey again and dropped the remainder of the devoured fruit on my foot.

I laughed. "Yes indeed. Now I'm a piggy, too."

Tarzan suddenly appeared at the lip of the nest. That was his way. There was never a warning of his comings or goings. It was strange, that. In my society, one was very clear about one's intentions. There were cards given and received so that one knew ahead of time of a friend's or neighbor's visit. "That will be all" would signal a servant's exit, or "I'll be going now" the departure of a guest.

Tarzan simply disappeared and materialized at will. I might be in midsentence, explaining something I desired, and suddenly he would be gone. The strange thing was, he always returned with the very object for which I had not had time to fully ask.

The plantain leaf packet was bulging. I wondered what would be contained within it this time. The past several days it had held sulfurous mud that Tarzan had packed onto my still-sore back, and the pain had lessened considerably. Other times he had returned with strange fruits, tender shoots, and tiny curled-up ferns that were sweet and delicious.

When he spread the packet now, looking very proud indeed, I saw to my horror that it was filled with chunks of bloody meat.

I looked at Tarzan and shook my head no. He cocked his head curiously, then nodded yes.

"*Dako-za*," he said.

"*Dako-za* . . . meat," I replied, learning his word for the first time and teaching him mine.

"Meat," he repeated instantly, then added with a gesture to his mouth, "*Popo* meat."

Eat meat, he was commanding me.

I shook my head again and, frowning, pointed to the blood.

Tarzan smiled. "*Galul*," he said. This must be the word for "blood." He dipped his fingers in the pile of meat and brought them to his mouth, licking the gore off with great relish.

I winced. "*Galul*," I said and started to utter the word of Tarzan's language I had learned meant "bad"—*sord*. But I stopped myself. I did not wish him to think that I believed blood was bad. Or meat. *How to say what I meant?*

"*Dako-za*," I said and smiled. "*Galul*." I smiled again and nodded my head. "Jane *popo dako-za galul*." I frowned and shook my head no. I saw a spark behind his eyes as he came to understanding.

He thought hard, then said, "Tarzan *popo dako-za galul*."

I smiled triumphantly. "Yes, Tarzan eats bloody meat. Not Jane." It was the most complex conversation we had yet had. He was pleased as well, and to prove it he took a piece of the meat and stuffed it in his mouth, chewing exuberantly.

I watched in silence, revolted and delighted all at once.

"Piggy!" cried Mr. Grey.

I barked a laugh. I wondered then if I might, in fact, still be delirious and dreaming all this, for it was almost beyond my comprehension.

In any case, it was quite an education.

It was an important day, the day that I would first leave Tarzan's nest. This had been decided between us with various words and signals. I was, of course, terrified at the prospect, for I had peered over its lip and seen the floor of the forest through the branches more than fifty feet below. While I was healed of my injuries and fevers, I was weak from inactivity and had lost a considerable amount of weight. I felt light as a hollow-boned bird.

He stood before me now, very close, a habit I found initially unnerving. Civilized people—a term I was finding mildly ridiculous these days—held greater space between themselves. Physical contact was minimal. Men shook hands or nodded their heads in greeting. An embrace between ladies was the merest brushing of lips on cheek. And proper distance was kept when two people spoke face-to-face.

Here Tarzan stood but a foot from me. He was quite tall, and so I was forced to look up to meet his eye.

And of course he had handled me. Intimately.

The thought of this had at first made me blush with shame. But the unselfconsciousness with which he had nursed me, washed me, held my head when I vomited, had been so natural that I'd forgotten many of my inhibitions. How Tarzan had dealt with my toilet functions while I had been unconscious I'd never asked, but the simple knowledge that he had, had made moot any further pretense of modesty. At my request, he had fashioned a latrine of sorts, and I took the opportunity when he disappeared up the fig before dawn to do my business. I washed with water from my pith helmet, its ventilation holes now plugged with resin by the endlessly resourceful Tarzan. It always amused me to see the hat lined up side by side with his two coconut shell halves, his usual water supply.

Now I stood there in the garments he'd cleverly fashioned for me when I'd been able to sit up and finally stand. With slender vines, Tarzan had jerry-rigged together my rent-at-the-seams clothing, tying them around my torso, arms, and legs. It was, all in all, an ensemble my mother would have been appalled to see her daughter wearing.

Unaccountably, it pleased me very much.

Take me down? I signaled to him. Sometimes the silent language we had devised was easier than juggling words in two foreign tongues. In fact, I quite liked such communication.

The English drowned in words, I thought, *so many of them unnecessary.*

Tarzan nodded a simple yes, then turned his back on me, reaching to pat it with his hands. He meant to *carry* me down!

"Oh no, I couldn't. Uh, I'm afraid. Uh . . ." We had never had cause to use any words that denoted fear. And here was something I had no way to express. While Tarzan had touched me intimately, I had never laid my hands on him. Now he was indicating that I should climb upon his back. Lay my torso, breasts, and female parts on his skin and, I reckoned, wrap my legs around his waist.

When it was clear I had not complied with his order, Tarzan turned back to me with that inquiring expression he assumed when he could make neither heads nor tails of my actions.

He gestured the question—*Did I not trust the strength of my arms to hold onto him?* I shook my head. *I was strong enough*, I signed in response. With that, he gave me his back again, this time squatting so that mounting him would be easier.

Mounting him. I thought I was through with blushing, but here I was, heat rising from chest to throat to cheeks. But I was, if nothing else, determined. I had ridden horses since the age of six, taken countless dangerous jumps. At least, I thought, smiling, I would not have to ride Tarzan sidesaddle. And here was the thing that mattered above all: I trusted him. This raw, naked savage.

I trusted him with my life.

Finally he strapped around my back an ingenious twisted-vine "harness," tying it at his front. Mr. Grey was strangely silent, but I caught him watching us intently.

"Well, I guess we'll be going, then," I said to the bird.

And then, good Christ, I was flying! First my "ride" had run along thick limbs of the massive fig till the width diminished and Tarzan sprang lightly to another tree, and another, whose branches overlapped in an intricate arboreal web of byways. Reassured as I was by the harness, I held on for dear life, unable to think coherently, my arms wrapped around his chest, my legs his waist. Crossed feet clasped at his belly, my cheek laid flat against the wild man's back. It had thrilled me, this solitary footrace, twigs and leaves lightly slapping me, a blur of green and glimpses of canopy dwellers passing quickly before my eyes.

Then all at once Tarzan had leaped out—across a void between trees—and we were airborne! My shout of terror ceased abruptly when his hand caught a thick vine, and as we swung in a wide arc, my voice rose again in a high keening wail. Another vine, another wail, and then his foot connected with hard wood. But this for only a moment, long enough for him to grasp an overhead branch. What an extraordinary aerial pas de deux, I thought.

Now to my amazement he brachiated, hand over hand through tangled liana above us, a thick crisscross of branches, creepers, air roots, and vines, this thankfully, blessedly, taking us ever groundward.

Another swift dash on foot through a roadway of lower limbs ended with an abrupt thud as finally we landed. Tarzan untied the harness and my feet hit solid ground. He turned and gazed at me with a most self-satisfied look.

The man is a show-off! He'd known I was safe on his back, but he'd taken no small pleasure in providing me with a thrill. Well, it *had* been thrilling, and if I was perfectly honest I would have to admit I was sorry it was over. He pointed at my knees and questioned if I was steady on my feet (my naked feet!). When I nodded, he turned again and began to walk away, assuming I would follow. For a moment I worried that I was barefooted, but there seemed to be clear, unimpeded single-file paths to walk along. Whether these paths had been made by animals or humans I could not say. Tarzan, however, appeared by his posture and the brief, almost birdlike movements of his head this way and that to be extraordinarily wary. He frequently swiveled to be sure that I was just behind him. Even though he moved with easy grace, I wondered if the forest floor held dangers for him that the canopy did not.

The ever-present sound of running water I'd heard from the nest became louder. We approached a long, black rock escarpment, with ancient trees growing miraculously out of the solid stone, with creepers and flowering plants interwoven on its uneven face. Tarzan disappeared through a narrow gash in the ridge and I followed after him.

Life abounded everywhere I looked. In each crack and crevice grew a delicate flower or lived a creature of such strange and intricate design I pitied Charles Darwin for having missed seeing them, for surely here were species not only startling to the eye but also yet unknown to science.

All at once the unmistakable sound of the waterfall was crashing in front of me. We rounded a rock bend and I found we were standing just behind the roaring liquid curtain. Tarzan took my hand then, for the stone here was slippery, and sharp, too. A fall here could split the skin down to bone.

On the far side of the falls, we emerged at a large pool and its narrow beach of fine black sand. Here Tarzan dropped into a squat, a pose that seemed altogether comfortable for his body. I couldn't imagine sitting. I'd been immobile with my injuries for what seemed an eternity, then confined to the nest during my recuperation for longer still. I stood gazing at the pool, the low, broad falls and next to it a high flat-lipped cliff. I noticed Tarzan gazing at the cliff with what I imagined was longing. It was odd: While he had quickly and regularly apprehended my innermost thoughts, his mind, except when he chose to converse in words or sign language, was a closed book to me.

He was staring peculiarly at me now. He nodded from myself to the pool. *Jane go in*, he was saying. I could see a narrow, shallow bar of sand at its edge, but beyond that the water looked deep. It would be perfect for a cool swim. When I looked back at Tarzan, however, he was gesturing strangely, with his fingers tugging at the skin of his chest and pinching his thigh.

Then I understood. *He wanted me to undress while he watched!*

I shook my head an indignant no! and sat down in the sand some distance from him. What an absurd circumstance this was. While I depended on this man for my very life, trusted that he had never taken advantage of me in my time of extremity, and was my protector in every way, Tarzan possessed a nature as famously prurient as an aristocratic Victorian gentleman.

But oh, how I longed to bathe!

Without a backward glance and feeling more than a bit ungovernable, I stood and walked into the water. It was oddly warm, not as warm as the mineral pools at Bath were, but more than tepid. As I stepped off the ledge into the deep and began to stroke around, I felt a strange confluence of water—cold at the surface, as if issuing from the stream and its falls, and pulsing hot plumes rising from what appeared to be bottomless depths. It was a lovely sensation, even with the vine-laced outfit covering much of my skin, but something about the intemperate mixture troubled me.

I was racking my brain for an explanation when suddenly a strong hand clamped hold of my ankle. I gasped with shock, and a moment later Tarzan exploded to the surface, water streaming off him. On his face was what could only be called an ecstatic grin.

"Tarzan, what is it?" I was unconcerned that the words themselves meant nothing to him, and he seemed to understand. He splashed at the water with his hand. He dove under and popped back up with the same silly smile and pointed at me, crying, "Jane *lul*. No *jai lul*!" I knew that *lul* was water, but what was *jai*?

He swam in mad circles around me, and caught up in his playful spirits, I swam about the pool with a forward stroke and then a backward one. At this last he roared laughing, as though it was the cleverest thing he had ever seen. It occurred to me that the noise of his laughter echoing off the water and the rock cliffs was altogether marvelous—a sound I wished to hear again and again.

Now Tarzan swam to the falls, climbed a ledge, and stood in a broad stance beneath the cascading torrent, looking no less than a majestic god of the forest. He stepped forward and beckoned. As if in a dream—my will subsumed by his, my urge to defy him nil—I simply obeyed. When he reached down his hand I took it, and he lifted me effortlessly to the ledge beside him.

I saw in his expression neither prurience nor lust, just pure joy shining on his face. His arms encircled me and he drew me protectively to him. *Or was it possessively?* I wondered. Whatever it was, was inconsequential, for the feel of my body pressed full against his was extravagantly sensual. Outrageous as it was, there was glory in the moment.

Even destiny.

But this perfect moment—light and glittering halos of sun-splashed spray, the gentle strength of Tarzan, his pulsing warmth beneath the cool smooth skin—ended suddenly. The heavy sum and substance of my past life, and the grim reality of tomorrow, came like the terrible weight of water, crashing down upon my head. My arms, poised to clasp this beautiful man to my heart, fell heavily to my sides. I must not allow myself to be enchanted by this place.

There was far too much left that I must do.

That night sleep failed to come. Lying next to me, Tarzan was restless, tossing about, muttering words in his language and mine. Once he cried out, his arms flailing above his head. At first I willed myself to sleep, annoyed at the nocturnal cacophony and the utter darkness blanketing the nest.

But the far-off whine of a great cat brought home suddenly the miracle of my circumstances, and all at once I perceived the long night ahead as a gift—a deep well of reflection sorely needed if I was ever to leave this prison in paradise and regain my life.

"Remember," I whispered aloud. "Remember . . ."

Evangeline

Firsts.

It was a game I had played from the time I was a little girl. It was simple cognizance that a thing—a place, a sight, a sound, a smell, a thought—was my very first experience of it. The playing of the game was so personal to me, so simplistic, I never believed it worthy enough to tell anyone about, even my father. How it worked was that I made mental note of such events as the first jump Leicester and I had made over a stile—I'd been seven; the first time I had worn the men's trousers under my riding habit. When I took long walks in the greenwood and went off the beaten path, climbing a particular hillock, standing on a particular rock, looking in a particular direction, I would say to myself, "I might be the first human ever to have stood in this exact spot in the whole history of the world." I thought about the man, how many tens or hundreds of thousands of years ago I didn't know, who had purposely lit a fire; the woman scouring the shoreline for food who'd been the first to discover that by prying open a bivalve there was flesh inside to eat.

And now standing on King's Dock at the Port of Liverpool amid the towers and cranes of the waterfront, I heard the chaos of bellowing, hammering, and belching engines, smelled the mixed stench of horses and sweat and urine, and watched the *Evangeline* being loaded with cargo, and I knew that the months to come would provide me the greatest profusion of firsts—a bountiful cornucopia of original and pioneering experiences—that I might ever at one time in my life behold.

The idea made me shiver with delight.

I turned from the long, low-slung cargo and passenger ship to the

"Second Port of the Empire," second only to London, to see dock after dock for seven miles, brilliantly constructed, granite-lipped piers and warehouses, looking for all the world like an immense fortress, and pondered my good fortune.

I was not unaware of the previous blessings of my life. That because of my father's progressive nature and indulgences I had been afforded freedoms that most women my age—or, for that matter, women of any age—had not. I was about to set off on a scientific expedition into the heart of Africa to search for Mr. Darwin's missing link fossils with the one man in the world I most loved and admired. It was nearly incomprehensible.

Certainly, I had dreamed about this day. Longed for it. Imagined it a thousand times over, but that the dream should become real, that I was just now standing at the brink of such a grand adventure, seemed all at once to place me in the company of the small coterie of females that I held in a place of the deepest reverence. The Mary Kingsleys of the world.

And just as suddenly, I felt foolish, falsely self-glorified. Mary Kingsley had led *her own* expedition up the Ogowe River. Annie Peck had done the same, ascending the slopes of Peru's Mt. Huascarán. Lady Hester Stanhope had dressed as a Bedouin and with twenty-two camels taken her caravan across the desert to Palmyra. I was a mere laboratory assistant to my father, and on this safari we both would be in the care of Mr. Conrath.

Ral.

That was what I called him to myself. I would not dream of speaking his given name aloud. It was only after fifteen years of marriage and much cajoling that Mother had given up calling her husband Mr. Porter and agreed to Archie.

Some parts of myself, despite my abhorrence of the values, were still wholly Victorian. Though I had no compunctions about discussing, and now dissecting, the human body, I was still modest about my own. Even with lady's maids I covered my naked breasts and my lower female parts as I was allowing myself, however infrequently, to be dressed. And I would not bare an ankle, silly as I knew it was. Mother's influence, much as I hated to admit it, pervaded my life in unexpected and irritating ways.

Perhaps it was a function of my spinsterhood. Most girls of my class, by my age of twenty, had taken part in those most primal of animal acts—copulation and childbirth. I noticed that girls who were wives and mothers—despite their prudish airs—shared an unspoken knowingness, a twinkle in the eye that denoted a sisterhood of sorts, one to which I decidedly did not belong.

Well, if I am a freak, I am quite a happy one. I'm going to Africa, and my companion—besides my dear father—is the indomitable Mr. Conrath.

He was something of an enigma, I thought. And if I was perfectly honest with myself, I would have to acknowledge more than a slight attraction to the man. It was the first real interest I'd felt in my life for anyone of the opposite sex. At the very moment these thoughts crossed my mind, I heard Ral's voice.

"No! No! Not like that, I said!" His tone was harsh and authoritarian, not the sort of thing I was used to hearing. Ral was dealing with two dozen stevedores loading the *Evangeline* with the provisions and equipment for the "Porter Expedition," as he called it. All that morning, looking very much the engineer, with a tool belt strapped around his slim waist, he had been barking orders to the dockhands with very limited patience and rising frustration.

I'd refused to miss a second of this momentous occasion and had watched, from just before dawn, the brawny "Scousers"—Liverpudlians whose own language was as salty and unrefined as their smell—begin their work under Ral's supervision. I'd caught him staring brazenly at me several times, and I found it unsettling but not unpleasant.

I was impressed with this brawny American. He was quite the administrator and had, over the previous months, procured and methodically coordinated every possible aspect of this undertaking, while at the same time miraculously assuaging Mother's doubts and fears that should, by all rights, have been *doubled* with my accompanying my father on this trek into the "green hell," as she called it.

I concluded that Ral was nothing short of remarkable. Father, too, was pleased with the expedition leader. He put his whole trust in the man. Perhaps that was why I'd fallen into fantasy about Mr. Conrath. Begun to imagine myself as "Mrs. Conrath."

Was it such an outrageous idea? He was a hardscrabble American, but so had my father been. He was big and handsome and, I had to admit, masculine in the extreme. I could for the first time in my life imagine myself as a wife—part of an adventuring team, one that would travel the world seeking exploits and enterprises, never shying from risk or hazard. It was true I did not love the man yet. His harsh outbursts grated on me. In fact, I had taken to making a jest of them to him, as I was not one to stay silent about such things. This way I could acknowledge that I saw this flaw in his character and mildly disapproved.

So far, while my tactic had not provoked anger from him, neither had it improved his disposition. But what was one fault in a man? Would not such a partnership be the perfect antidote to my mother's soul-killing idea of marriage to an effete, upper-crust Englishman?

Father had already boarded the *Evangeline*, claiming the need to make ready our cabins for the journey. "Out into the sea on a large ship" was one of my firsts. I'd rowed many times on the River Cam, sailed on Lake Como on a trip the family had taken to Italy, and even taken a ferry across the Channel to France. But this was a proper voyage. Two weeks on board. Crossing the Bay of Biscay into the wild Atlantic. Stops at several ports along the way—the Canary Isles and Sierra Leone. Away to another continent and to a clime that was as unfamiliar to me as a fish to desert dunes. The heat, my father told me, could be stifling and unrelenting, many times worse than the hottest English summer. Another first. I relished the thought.

"Idiots!"

I was blasted from my reverie by Ral Conrath's rude outburst. I turned back to the ramp where four stevedores were grappling with a long wooden crate, one corner of which was about to hit the concrete pier. The dockworker who had let the thing slip used his prodigious muscles to catch it before it crashed to the ground but overcorrected, tilting the crate to vertical.

"Damn you!" Ral shouted. "Keep the thing horizontal!"

"It's horizontal you want it?" said the Scouser who had mishandled his corner. "I'll give you horizontal, ye little turd." With a nod to his mates they all let the crate drop with a rattling crash and, saluting their taskmaster with a barrage of rude gestures, sauntered away without another word.

I could see a distinctly murderous look in Ral's eye, but the moment he caught sight of me staring at him he began to compose himself. I likewise set my features into an even expression, neither disapproving nor joking.

"The contents of the crate must be quite valuable," I said, striving for a tone of equanimity.

"I'll say they are." Ral pulled a small pry bar from his work belt and began opening the box to the tune of screeching nails. "If they've damaged it, I'll wring their filthy necks."

Now the treasure was revealed, and it came as quite a surprise to me.

"Gatling guns don't run cheap," he said. "Their mechanisms are more delicate than you'd think."

I squatted down and examined the immense gun and the folded tripod legs upon which it would stand. I knew Ral was regarding me with interest, I in the most unladylike of postures, taking keen interest in the most masculine of objects.

"The Gatling gun is a rapid-fire weapon," he said, as a lecturer would speak to a student, "the most important invention of warfare in hundreds of years, used to great effect in the American Civil War. It shoots eight hundred rounds in a minute."

"Why on earth do we need such a thing on our expedition?" I demanded to know in the moment before I realized he might take offense.

An offense was, indeed, taken. I could see it blazing in his eyes. But as he had done moments before, he reined in his emotions. Ral managed a crooked grin.

"How you do love to second-guess me, little lady," he quipped.

Then setting the top back on the crate, he pulled a hammer from his belt and nailed it shut with all the force I imagined he would have liked to hammer in the skulls of those dockworkers.

"Do me a favor and keep your eye on this," he said. "I need a word with the captain of this tub."

Ral stood and with a polite tip of his head strode up the gangway and bordered the *Evangeline*.

I stood, unsure whether I was pleased to be given the responsibility as a member of the team, or irked by this raw, churlish fellow. Perhaps, I thought, it was not worth debating.

It was simply another first.

* * *

S o, yer takin' yerself off to the wilds of Africa and you've not read
Heart of Darkness?" our Captain Kelly badgered the prim English
missionaries sitting to his right at the dinner table. The Irishman had
proved to be an intelligent and widely read person, one for whom
Father and I were every day gathering more admiration. Meals at the
captain's table were intimate affairs, as the *Evangeline* was carrying
very few passengers on this voyage. It was the only time all of us
gathered in one place during the long, otherwise uneventful days.

"The book might scare the bejesus outta ye," Kelly continued,
"but you'd have a wee taste of what ye were gettin' yerself into."

The bland-faced young man, Brother Roderick Smead, sat stiff
and straight, with a tight smile stretching the bottom of his face into
a grimace.

Father and I had several times argued amusedly about just how far
the stick must be lodged up the man of God's rectum. We had so far
controlled ourselves in impugning and provoking him, as Brother
Roderick had become the captain's favorite sparring partner (or perhaps "target" would be more precise) at the evening meals. It had become clear in the past several days that Kelly had lost patience with
the man's narrowness and naïveté. Tonight might prove the show-
down.

After the captain's last provocation, I could see Mr. Smead's wife,
Ellen, shifting uncomfortably in her chair. A plump partridge of a
woman, she had so far on this journey remained the perfect wife,
adoring and respectful of her husband and almost entirely silent on
any matters that strayed from the trivial or domestic.

"God will look after us, Captain Kelly," the missionary replied,
and his wife nodded in pious agreement. "The evangelization of the
Asian and African continents is His work, and He takes care of His
own."

I felt my blood begin to boil. I was surprised that Father had not
jumped down Smead's throat. He had nothing but contempt for all
proselytizing religions, but in the next moment the captain continued his own assault.

"I've taken a slew of German Lutherans to their missionary posts,"
said Kelly to Brother Roderick, "and they've got a sight more consid-
eration for foreign peculiarities and cultures than you lot do."

Ellen Smead looked scandalized at such an idea. Everyone at the table was startled when she spoke up with great fervor. "What is the point of a native's conversion if he is not . . . *converted*? I believe . . ."

Brother Roderick turned to his wife with such astonishment it occurred to me that he had never once heard uttered from those lips the words "I believe."

Sister Ellen went on, ". . . that the convert must live in a permanent *upright* house with a chimney in it. He must no longer be befuddled by its hot smoky atmosphere, or degraded by creeping into it." She spoke the word "creeping" as though it evoked the loathsomeness of a poisonous snake. "He must be *decently* clothed and . . ."

"That is enough, Ellen," Brother Roderick hissed at his wife.

Instantly she was silent and slunk down in her seat.

"I think you misunderstand us," Brother Roderick said to the captain. "We are all, even the lesser races, God's children. In the Bantu tribe, there is a rich folklore that demonstrates conscience in a *marvelous* way."

"Conscience?" Father barked. He had come to the end of his patience with this young man. "How kind of you to grant them the attribute. And how, may I ask, does their polygamy—even after conversion—fit into your standards of 'Christian morality'?"

"That's easy," I interjected. "Men reign supreme in every culture. They have what they want whether they are an African tribesman with several wives, or an Englishman with a mistress on the side. It is very simply a 'man's world.'"

Captain Kelly sat up a bit straighter, and his eyes shifted with the anticipation of a proper scrap. "So," he began, "do I have a 'wild woman' at my table, then?"

I presented my most demure smile. "A '*new* woman,' perhaps." The term I suggested was held by conservative thinkers to denote a woman of lax morals, overarching ambition, and other "unnatural" desires, such as rivalry with men and attendance at university.

I relished the title.

Brother Roderick fixed me with a glacial glare. "I've heard of these new women and their manly ambitions. They throw the whole social order into disarray. It's said that if given free rein they could conceivably bring down the whole of the British Empire."

I snorted derisively.

Mr. Smead grew very red in the face. His missus looked as though she had stopped breathing altogether.

"It's my understanding," Father offered, "that these young ladies simply want the same education, the same employment, and the same rights of citizenship that men have. That doesn't seem so out of line to me. What do you think, Mr. Conrath?"

Ral was taken quite off guard by the question. He'd been only half listening to the dinner conversation. Just as we'd sat down at the table he had been handed a telegram. After reading it with a scowl, he returned to it time and again. His answer to Father's question was un-thought-out and therefore perhaps a more honest one than he had wished.

"The female sex is different from the male. Women are weaker, simpler, purer creatures than men are. They need our supervision and protection."

"I don't need a man," I said in as even a tone as my rebellious heart would allow. "I may *want* one," I plunged on, "but not at the expense of my education and independence." Ellen Smead gasped and stared down at her plate, afraid to meet another pair of eyes. "Hasn't anyone else noticed that once a woman is married, she's treated under law with exactly the same rights as idiots, children, and the insane?"

"Tommyrot!" Smead cried, quite out of his missionarial character.

Captain Kelly was enjoying himself. He called for the galley mate to fill everyone's glass with wine. When the missionaries put their hands over their glasses, he muttered "stuffed shirts" loudly enough for everyone to hear.

Roderick Smead pushed back his chair and stood. His wife followed suit. "Good evening," he said with that tight-lipped grimace and, taking Ellen by the arm, frog-marched her out of the dining room.

"That pair'll have one helluva time in the bush," Kelly said.

The rest of the dinner passed in lively conversation. More than a little wine was imbibed, and of "new women" and "God's will" nothing more was said.

Sleep evaded me that night, the dinner conversation having stimulated me sufficiently that even the reading of Eugène Dubois's monograph of the whale larynx—something that always put me to sleep—failed to make me the least bit drowsy. I'd thrown a long shawl around my nightgown and gone padding out barefoot onto the *Evangeline's* rear deck.

Phrases kept repeating themselves in my head: the "lesser races," "the evangelization of the Asian and African continents," the "befuddled" African native creeping through his smoky hut's doorway. It upset me that pompous imbeciles like the Smeads were being sent in droves all over the empire to wring and bully from these ancient cultures everything that made them unique. People like them believed themselves so honorable, so righteous. Little by little the world was being dissected like a cadaver, those bits thought unnecessary sliced out and discarded—thrown in a tin pail at the feet of the chosen few believing themselves worthy of the cutting. The wealthy. The educated. The "noble."

I was part of the problem; I knew that. It always concerned me, the conundrum of my privileged position in the world. I was thankful, of course. I never wished I had been born a washerwoman's daughter.

No one was more fortunate than me, yet on nights like this I felt wretched, weighted down with guilt at the reckless colonial imperative that, like a mania, had gripped the entire world. I felt helpless to remedy suffering. I was no Florence Nightingale. On the contrary, I was selfishly ambitious. Perhaps Brother Roderick was right. Enough women like me might indeed bring the empire crashing down around our ears. But would that, in the end, be such a tragedy?

"So, you don't need a man, do you?"

It was Ral Conrath. He was very close behind me. So close I could feel his breath on my neck when he whispered, "But you might *want* a man."

"And you believe women are 'weak' and 'simple' and need protecting and supervision by men," I said without turning.

"Some women. Not all women."

I felt his hands on my shoulders, then his fingers at the nape of my neck. He'd reached under my loosed hair—I'd not tied it up before leaving my cabin, never thinking I'd be anything but alone on the deck in the middle of the night.

I tried to calm myself, but my heart was pounding. My fingers clutching the rail tightened, and my suddenly flushed face steamed against the cool sea air.

His hands on me were possessive. Entitled. I liked the feeling . . . yet somehow it repelled me. Thus entrapped by my ambivalence, I remained silent, still.

He took this for assent.

The hands slid under my arms and from behind cupped both breasts. I thought then, *This is wrong. I need to see his face. He needs to see mine.* I tried to turn, but he'd buried his face in the hair at my neck and his hands were seeking the front opening of my gown, reaching down to the tender skin. His fingers pinched my nipples.

I cried out with pain and forcefully swiveled to face him, to order him to stop. What I saw was a cruel mouth and eyes glittering dangerously in the moonlight.

"No," I said.

His reply was to kiss me hard, so hard he bruised my lips.

My self-possession returned in a rush, and I placed my palms on his shoulders and pushed him away.

"Stop. *Now.*"

There was no surprise in his expression. No hurt at the rejection. No remorse for what he must have known had caused me pain. There was, in fact, nothing in his expression at all.

This frightened me.

He moved to grab me again, and this time I lifted one arm between us.

"Touch me again and I'll geld you right here."

He smiled then with the greatest calm. "You wanted this, Janie. You asked for it."

"Maybe I did. But I don't want it now."

All at once he stepped back.

I resisted the urge to dart away from him. Instead I straightened my spine and looked Ral in the eye, willing him to withdraw farther, to give me space for a dignified exit.

An infinitely long moment passed. Then he complied, flashing his most charming smile, as if all was forgiven. But I knew very well that behind the smile was the heated desire to strike me, crush my face with his fist.

I moved slowly from Ral's presence, feeling the smooth wood of the deck beneath my feet, shaking with fury at myself for having so disastrously misjudged a man's character.

I would never let it happen again.

From the "evening of the missionaries," as Father and I had taken to calling that contentious dinner, Captain Kelly had regarded his wild woman (as he insisted on calling me) with a sight more respect than before, more than simply reminding me to take those "four grains of quinine" every day for the fortnight before the Porter Expedition reached the Ogowe River.

Kelly had extended to me a standing invitation to the bridge for company and conversation. He said he'd not had occasion to converse with "a woman of parts" in a very long time. We had crossed the Bay of Biscay and steamed past Portugal, heading for the equator. As we sailed, Kelly occasionally allowed me, under his supervision, to take the wheel, regaling me all the while with stories about West Africa and the legendary "Old Coasters" he had known. These colorful characters were the ones who always had the most outlandish tales to tell. It was they who gave the continent its reputation, much of it deserved. Like the apocalyptic epidemics of fever that ran rampant in towns and villages, carrying off nearly the whole population in a matter of days. Or the city cemetery that at all times kept two freshly dug graves open and ready for the Europeans who would most certainly occupy them by day's end. I stopped counting the number of times Captain Kelly unconsciously said, "He's dead now." And it was not lost on me that the shipping company had not bothered to sell me or my father return-trip tickets.

I'd taken to bringing to the bridge my thumbed-nearly-to-death copy of Mary Kingsley's *Travels in West Africa*, mostly to compare the author's observations of these very same sights and the turns of phrase she had used to describe them. Very early on I'd admitted to Kelly that my favorite heroine, in whose footsteps—to my amazement—I was now following, was a superior writer to myself. No praise of the beauty and mystery that I was witnessing came close to Miss Kingsley's prose.

Beneath us, Ral and Father walked into view on the foredeck. They were deep in conversation as they frequently were now, even more so since the night Ral Conrath had accosted me. I had wished very dearly to tell my father what I perceived about the character of the man who would be leading us into Africa. But I was not at all certain what it was that needed saying. The truth was, I had led him on. *You wanted this, Janie.* That had been the case, at least until the moment he had laid his hands on my body and I, with some until then unknown instinct, sensed a wrongness, a defect in him. A ragged edge to the man's soul. One that made his touch unbearable, even as my desire welcomed it.

But each time I'd found a moment to tell Father of my fears, his excitement for our venture and his ardent belief in Conrath's abilities smothered my best intentions. Only the night before, when I'd determined nothing would stop me from making my thoughts known, Father—his eyes alive—had grabbed my hand on the rail and with emotion choking his voice said, "We're going to find those bones, Jane. I can feel it in my own!"

My father was a man of the world with six African expeditions under his belt, a whole life in America, and another at the top of his chosen field in England. And what was I? A sheltered girl who had spent the whole of her existence in a small university town.

I must allow Ral Conrath the benefit of the doubt, I decided. He was certainly a cad with women, but I'd been stupid and gullible. He had so far proved his administrative talents in arranging the expedition. I must set my mind at ease and let the adventure unfold. Like my father, I should envision the very best of outcomes. For if the Porter Expedition did, in fact, uncover the fossils of Darwin's missing link in Africa, Father and I would become a very part of the history of the evolutionary theory.

And nothing could possibly make me any happier.

Libreville

After the cooling sea breezes aboard the *Evangeline*, I was altogether unprepared for the skin-searing noontime heat when we docked at Libreville. Yet I was amazed how strangely soothing I found it. Memories assailed me of England's frigid mornings and unremitting grey skies, the coal soot in the air, the dormant trees in winter, and the crunch of frozen ground beneath my feet.

The city of Libreville, I'd learned from Captain Kelly, had received its name, "Free Town," from the shipload of slaves rescued at sea by the French in 1849, set upon northern Gabon's shores, and given their freedom. It was a poor sort of port after Liverpool. Ramshackle wooden warehouses with peeling paint and corrugated metal roofs lined small rickety wooden piers. Here the "stevedores" were half-dressed natives whose black skin decorated with intricately designed scars glistened with the sweat of laboring under a merciless sun.

Clutching my black portmanteau, I stood gazing around and watched as the Porter Expedition supplies were unloaded under the vigilant eye of Ral Conrath, he resorting more to hand gestures than to verbal commands, as he seemed altogether helpless when it came to the French or Gabonese languages.

I had already said a poignant farewell to my mentor, Captain Kelly, he plying me with last-minute advice. "Keep a hat on yer head, and never turn yer back on a Frenchman."

Father was uncharacteristically beside himself. Any more animated, I thought, and he would be dithering. But everything did run smoothly, and soon our belongings and supplies had been loaded onto several rickety wagons that lacked only teams to pull them.

When I had inquired where the horses were, a native—more clothed than the rest and who appeared to be the dock foreman—replied, "*Chevaux mort par les tsé-tsé.*" Horses are killed by the tsetse flies.

Suddenly human "teams" of four raggedly dressed Negroes collected themselves along the front shafts of the vehicles and, gripping them with bare hands, began trotting away. In the next moment, Ral Conrath propelled me to a rickshaw in which sat a very pretty middle-aged lady in a proper English gown, proper except for the missing stays and corsets. Without them, her ample figure—bosom and belly and thighs—seemed to overlap one onto the other, like great folds of melted candle wax. She was smiling and holding out her hand to me as Conrath helped me into the seat with its tattered satin cover.

"Miss Porter, meet Mrs. Fournier. She's our hostess while we're in Libreville. I'm riding with your father right behind you."

As he strode away, our mode of locomotion arrived—again human and native, but this lot neatly dressed in white breeches and jackets with bright red cummerbunds wound around their waists. Two took the front, pulling, two the back, pushing.

"Welcome, my dear!" Mrs. Fournier cried. Despite her name, and her planting a kiss on either of my cheeks the way they did in France, she spoke in the King's English. In midgreeting, our faces bumped as the chariot lurched into forward motion. We laughed, and Mrs. Fournier sat back fanning herself one moment, fanning me the next, and began to talk, a pastime I would come to know was my hostess's favorite of all.

"When I learned that an esteemed professor at Cambridge was coming to Libreville, with his *daughter*, no less, I determined I must have you stay with me. There is a hotel, of course, but it is a dreadful place. You must take my word on that. Things are stolen all the time from the rooms, and the food is atrocious. I think you will be most comfortable . . ."

I was grateful for Mrs. Fournier chattering on, for it gave me leave to take in the sights from the go-cart (that was what my hostess called it) moving through the Libreville streets, most of which were dusty dirt or, the finer ones, gravel.

There was so much to see!

I could barely contain myself from gawking at the native man whose entire costume seemed to be the fabric of an umbrella with the stick and all the ribs removed from it. There was another in nothing but a loincloth, and one in a garment fashioned from a burlap rice bag. The ladies were a sight more fashionable. One ample-figured matron wore a bright printed dress yoked at the neck and falling in billows to the ground, a matching handkerchief binding her bristly hair. Her companion of a younger generation wore nothing but patterned fabric wrapped around her as a skirt, with conical breasts swinging rhythmically, one arm balancing a basket full of yams on her head.

Roaming the streets there were more animals than people and vehicles combined—goats, sheep, pigs, chickens, and numberless skinny yellow dogs. One of these canines fought with a black buzzard twice its size over an unrecognizable maggot-ridden carcass.

"I suppose the one unbreakable law is to never expose yourself to the sun's direct rays," Mrs. Fournier told me. I nodded, trying to pay attention to the well-meaning woman. But now as we passed from the bustle of dockside, there were structures to be seen, of many sizes and varieties, but hardly any of them remotely familiar to my eye. A street of native houses was terribly poor—painted wood bungalows with tin roofs and mud-and-palm-leafed huts—though each boasted its own small shop where the wares—iron pots, bolts of gaily colored textiles, tin basins, and bottles of American rum—were proudly displayed out the front.

Of course there was a cathedral—the French were such good Catholics. Except for a few European-style houses, it seemed the only solid structure in the whole ramshackle quarter of town, its large painted stones the blinding white of skeletal remains.

Strange sights were hardly my only experiences. Unexpected and breathtaking stenches assailed my nostrils, smells the sources of which I did not wish to contemplate. A moment later, the sweetest fragrance of a flowering tree would overtake and conquer the sickening miasma. Then I would be forced to slap at myself as a tea-saucer-sized beetle came nipping at my neck.

"But this is a *tame* bit of the tropics," Mrs. Fournier insisted. "If you don't count the fevers carrying away your husband and friends and servants, really a lady's biggest worry is running out of hairpins." Mrs. Fournier flicked a large mosquito that had come to rest on my cheek. "Pesky creatures. I'm sure you've been told a hundred times that your mosquito netting at night is as important as breathing. *Becomba lumbo!*" she called to the uniformed go-cart Negroes.

The coast road out of town gave way to a broad track shaded very pleasantly by tall pepper and eucalyptus trees. There were the baobabs with their massive trunks, or "monkey breadfruits" as Ernst Haeckel called them, claiming the trees lived to be five thousand years old. And now, to my utter delight and amazement, stretched before us on either side a row of "flamboyant trees," most aptly named for their spreading crowns of vermillion flowers, bright green, feathery leaves, and dark brown beans as long as a man's forearm.

I settled back into the go-cart seat thinking that if a person could die of contentment, I might end up a corpse in one of those open graves always kept ready and waiting in the European cemetery.

My African adventure had well and truly begun, and I had been on the continent a mere three-quarters of an hour.

There were still a few delicate tendrils of cool air threading themselves through downtown Libreville at eight the next morning, but I, once again a passenger in a rickshaw, could feel them being sipped quickly up by the sun. Soon the lustrous blue day would be shimmering—everywhere one looked, a mirage. I could just make out the dull thunder of the breakers against the seawall several blocks behind. The streets were alive with all manner of business going on, not simply food markets but also men in rumpled white suits making deals with one another.

"Those fellows are the ivory traders," said my go-cart companion for the morning, Ral Conrath. Father rode behind us.

Farther down the block were three roughnecks in bush jackets and straw hats identified as "rubber men," who argued with a monocled Frenchman smoking a fat cigar.

On the whole, Mr. Conrath had behaved himself on the ride into town, though he had annoyed me with his prattle about Mrs. Fournier, the kindest of hostesses. He took great delight in identifying the Englishwoman as a Parisian prostitute, "a high-class whore," as he called her, who had serviced the richest men in Europe.

It was not Mrs. Fournier's profession that disturbed me but Mr. Conrath's offhanded insults and epithets. And he had, of course, made it clear that he himself had availed himself of the charms of "fallen women" in every port in which he had ever so briefly hung his hat. I was not interested. I'd endured his nonsense as long as I was able before telling him that Mrs. Fournier's life was her own business and that if he wished to make himself useful to me he would point out the sights and explain the things I was seeing.

"Straight ahead, there's the French consulate," he said, sanguine about the rebuff.

The government offices of the Congo Français were where we were headed. I could see behind the gates a sprawling wooden house amid the most splendid garden. But as we approached, I could make out from between the shoulders of the rickshaw bearers a commotion just now erupting in front of the consulate gates.

A white-suited European was being taunted—more *besieged*—by a small gang of natives. I could see that he was standing tall, but fists were darting at him and a juju stick with feathers hanging from it was thrust in his face. He ducked from his attackers while never relinquishing his dignified posture.

"Goddamn Negroes!" Conrath shouted. "That's my man, D'Arnot!"

Suddenly I found myself alone, as Conrath had leaped from the rickshaw and run straight toward the fracas. But before he could reach "his man," a rock came flying at D'Arnot, striking him in the forehead. He went down in a heap. Conrath chased the natives, who had scattered in every direction.

I jumped down and ran to the stricken man's side. He was unconscious and bleeding profusely. A moment later, and to my great relief, Father was kneeling beside us.

"Always lots of blood in head wounds," he said. "Heavily vascularized, the skull. He'll be all right."

By the time Ral Conrath returned, breathless and furious that he'd not gotten his hands around the neck of even one of the attackers, the bleeding had stopped, and Father was helping the victim to sit up.

"He'll be all right?" Ral said, full of concern.

"Sir, will you tell me your name?" Father asked the bloodied fellow.

"Paul D'Arnot," he answered with no hesitation. He was a Frenchman.

"What day of the week is it?"

"Zee day I get my head bashed in outside zee consulate." D'Arnot's thick accent was the perfect complement to his dry sense of humor.

"There's your answer, Mr. Conrath," Father said.

"Good. We can't have a translator whose brains are scrambled. These nice folks will look after you. They're the Porters."

D'Arnot, his face pale with the loss of blood and pinched with pain, looked up at Father. "You are the professor?" Every time he said "th," my English ears heard "z."

"The very one."

"I have come here today to meet you," D'Arnot replied.

"This is my daughter, Jane."

"You are both very kind."

"Why don't you get him in?" Conrath said. "I'm off to get the ball rolling."

Inside the consulate gates, I thought it odd that none of the many officials and clerks who had surely seen the incident had come running to assist the poor fellow. In fact, the employees' expressions were blank and vapid or openly hostile. *What on earth could these people be thinking?* I wondered.

"It may be bold of me to ask, Monsieur D'Arnot . . ." I began.

Father chimed in, "You'll get used to that phrase in short order, I can promise you, my friend."

I grimaced at him, then continued more seriously, "Why did those men accost you? And why did none of your countrymen come to your aid?"

D'Arnot laughed morosely. "That is a long story. And a sad one. I will tell it to you on our safari, but suffice to say that until last year, I was an official in this consulate. The men who stood by and watched me attacked were, not so long ago, *mon amis.*"

I contained my instinct to question the man further. Certainly an interrogation would be rude, but I seethed with curiosity. My immediate impression of Monsieur D'Arnot had been overwhelmingly positive. Despite the telltale signs of a man who enjoyed his drink a bit too much, I liked him very much. Yet both natives as well as every one of his coworkers seemed to despise him. *Have my powers of judgment failed me again?*

We found a peculiar scene in the main office. Mr. Conrath sat upright on a bench meant for petitioners, listening and watching very patiently—too patiently—as the party ahead of him spoke with two French officials in their native tongue.

For all my education, I had never learned the language very well. Neither did my father speak French.

"What are they saying?" I asked D'Arnot.

"They are Belgian. Engineers."

The four men were well dressed, and their linen suits in different shades of white and cream were neat and unrumpled, even in the heat that had risen in the offices, refusing to be dispelled by the electrified overhead fans.

"Belgians? What do they want here?"

"They are in the service of His Majesty . . ." D'Arnot spoke the last words with contempt.

"Leopold?" The name was synonymous with murder on an unprecedented scale. The entire Belgian Congo was the *private property* of this monarch who plundered it for ivory, rubber, and gold.

D'Arnot continued, requiring no eavesdropping on the conversation for the intelligence he now imparted. It seemed that the Belgians were there seeking permission to enter the interior of Gabon and had been doing so for the last two years. At its far eastern edge, Congo Français shared a border with the Congo Free State. The Belgians were drowning in resources, but they were landlocked and needed a port—a trade route to the coast—and Gabon was the only way. D'Arnot said that the French government in Paris was against such a plan, even though the payment would be monumental.

D'Arnot fell silent and I was certain I saw anger simmering behind his eyes. "I will tell you that some in this office felt as I did. That such permission given would mean death, perhaps annihilation, to native tribes who came in contact with these murdering bastards. Many of these officials are gone, like me. There are others here who have no compunction about leaving the Gabonese at the mercy of Leopold's legions."

I knew then without being told that D'Arnot's post at the consulate had been forfeited over the Belgian contretemps. My heart went out to this man of principle, yet I wondered again why the natives had attacked him. I refrained from pursuing the subject, but now my curiosity gave way to another mystery.

Why was the pathologically impatient Mr. Conrath sitting like a proper schoolboy as the French and Belgian conversation dragged on and on? He should by now be demanding attention paid him. Instead he was listening. *But did he know French?* I didn't think so.

When finally the four engineers turned to go, Ral Conrath stood up and saluted them with his fingers-to-the-forehead greeting and stepped forward to the counter. Then he beckoned to Father to join him.

I could hear that one of the French officials spoke English. I thought I saw his face darken at the sight of Conrath, but I must have been mistaken. Papers were passed across the counter and the business of our passage down the Gabonese coast and up the Ogowe River was begun.

The netted, broad-brimmed hat that Mrs. Fournier had provided me this day was a lifesaver. I was protected from not only the direct rays of the African sun, which my hostess insisted "fried the brain," but also the persistent and sometimes immense bugs that constantly assailed me. Different as we were, Mrs. Fournier and I got on well, chattering like old friends from the moment we'd met. Mr. Conrath had been quite right about our hostess. She had been, in her day, a celebrated courtesan. When Cecily Willbury had seen the end of her Parisian heyday approaching, and with something of a fortune tucked away, she had accepted the proposal of the first of her customers to offer marriage. None of the stuffy Englishmen would have condescended, but the French diplomat Auguste Fournier, who had recently lost his wife of many years and whose duties of state were about to take him to a post in West Africa, conceived that he needed a genial female companion to accompany him there. He adored his still-beautiful English mistress—one of the belles of Paris—who had given him so much pleasure over the years. He was old enough, nearing sixty, to ignore all rumor and scandal that would certainly assail a diplomat with a prostitute for a wife. He also knew that they would be living at the ends of the earth. No one there would care, and if they did, *c'est la vie.*

So the Frenchman had married her, and for fifteen years he had overseen consulates from Sudan to the Ivory Coast to the Congo Français. In every one of those postings his little wife had proved the perfect hostess, was altogether uncomplaining of the most wretched of circumstances, and continued to pleasure him delightfully till the day he died.

Finally laid low by yellow fever and knowing his time was coming, he had requested that Cecily satisfy him one last time. That he was able in his advanced condition to come forth with a tumescent member was a source of some pride. That she so readily complied allowed him to die a contented man happily spent, and knowing how wisely he had chosen a wife.

Of this romance I had been spared no detail. In fact, I found it fascinating in the extreme, and there was no question I might ask—no matter how lewd or personal—that Cecily Fournier would not answer. I took this opportunity to extract many details of a sexual nature, subjects that my own mother would have found excruciating to discuss with her daughter. Subjects that even married ladies of Cambridge society would never whisper about in the privacy of their bedrooms. Descriptions of various coital positions; the preferences of males of different cultural backgrounds; interesting and sometimes alarming sexual techniques, some of which I was quite certain I would have no cause to further investigate in my life.

But much of this venereal education more than piqued my interest. It excited me physically. Hearing Mrs. Fournier speak of such subjects provoked in me feelings not unlike the ones I had experienced during my early infatuation (and dreams) of Ral Conrath.

I wondered, however, if I would ever be called upon to use this education. If my mother was correct, every passing year took me farther from the prospects of marriage, and while I did not judge Cecily for her chosen profession, I hardly saw myself in the role of a man's mistress. There was something not so much unsavory as degrading about it. I did not wish to be "kept" by a man any more than I wished to be married to a gentleman who bored me.

But what to think of the twinges and soft waves of sensuousness that more and more frequently assailed me? Was it the frank talk of

Cecily Fournier, or was it the voluptuousness of Africa that elicited such untoward phenomena, morning and night?

There was so much nakedness around me. Shirtless and fantastically muscular Negro men. Grown women who thought nothing of a similar state of undress. I wondered how it would feel to move through the world with my own breasts exposed, swinging freely before me. Were men down here not in a constant state of arousal? I had asked Cecily.

"I wondered that myself," she told me. "I asked Auguste, but he said"—Cecily smiled—"that no other woman than me excited him. He claimed to be inured to the pert bosoms of even the most beautiful native women. He may have been lying, but I chose to believe him. I was happily endowed with a very pretty bosom myself. And might I add," she said to me, "so are you."

"Do you think so?" I asked. No one had ever commented on my breasts, unless one counted the seamstresses who fitted me for my dresses and riding clothes.

"Very well shaped," Cecily assured me. "A lovely size. Enough to please any man, but not overlarge. Such appendages can be exciting for your lovers while you are young, but gravity, my dear, is a woman's greatest enemy. And the more prodigious the mammaries in youth, the more ghastly the ruin in later years." She smiled approvingly. "I am happy to see you eschew stays and corsets. Wise. Very wise."

This day Cecily had come into town for groceries. The sprawling open-air marketplace bustled with life, screaming with vibrant colors, sounds, and smells. Some of the more well-to-do vendors had simple shaded stalls, but most of the wares were spread upon the ground on blankets or rugs—piles of guava, soursop, sweet potato, and taut-skinned purple-black aubergine. I took special delight in the colorful piles of limes, oranges, alligator pears, tomatoes the size of marbles, and pawpaws—the latter reputed (and repeated ad nauseam) to be the balm for every sort of digestive malady.

Native women dominated the square, and their diversity was extraordinary. The fat were as beautiful as the slender, the old as well as the young, for their warm smiles and brilliant white teeth, sweet brown faces, sparkling black eyes with antimony-painted lids, and a vivid fresh flower tucked behind one ear made them, every one, attractive to my eye.

"The girls you may address as 'Tee-Tee,'" Cecily informed me as she carefully picked lemons from a pile and placed them in a cloth bag held open by her cook, who had accompanied us this day. "A young woman is 'Seester.' But all women of a certain age should be addressed as 'Mammy.' Do not ask their given name. They will be offended. 'Missus' is tolerated, but 'Mammy' is best."

The few men who wandered the market were much stranger to my eye, not as clean as the women and affecting costumes and adornments I found quite grotesque. Some had plucked out every hair on their heads, including their beards and whiskers and even their eyebrows. Others bore great scars on their faces from the roots of their noses, spreading out over cheeks and chins and foreheads. As I had seen at the dock, some scarifications extended over great swaths of their shoulders or backs or chests. There were raised dots, stars, and even a man with what looked like writing on his belly. They wore pieces of wood in their earlobes and even lumps of fat as earrings and hairdressings.

As I looked around me it was as though I had been transported to one of Jules Verne's other worlds—it was that contrary to all I had known. None of my father's stories, Captain Kelly's, or even Mary Kingsley's books had prepared me for the shock of Africa.

"Poor Monsieur D'Arnot," Cecily offered, apropos of nothing as she led the way on foot to her favorite seller of yams.

"Why is he so sad?" I asked my new friend. "And why does everyone hate him? I find him a most congenial fellow."

"He is that. I have great affection for Paul D'Arnot myself. There is a gentleness about him. He has an extraordinary talent for the Gabonese languages—the best of any man in Congo Français. But he broke the unbreakable rule. He married a native woman."

"Married? He did not take her for a mistress?" I was aware that virtually every married or unmarried European man in Africa (save Monsieur Fournier, of course) had a Negro lover, or a string of them.

Cecily's eyes grew soft remembering the sad story of Paul D'Arnot. His housekeeper had brought him back from the brink of death from a fever with no thought of her own well-being and no promise of reward. When D'Arnot had recovered, he was a changed man.

Shortly thereafter he'd announced his intention to marry the woman in the Catholic church. Sadly, her tribe was not fond of Europeans, believed them interlopers in their lands. So while all at the consulate repudiated D'Arnot for such a ridiculous act as marrying a native, her family, too, was incensed. They'd insisted she leave him, and when she refused they came at her with their bad juju sticks and curses. Every night they'd stood outside D'Arnot's house, chanting and praying for her death, and his. Finally she'd sickened and died."

"She *died?* Of a curse?" I was deeply stricken by the story.

"Very sad, that. But D'Arnot's troubles were far from over. By then the wicked Belgians had come with their pleadings and demands. Their trade routes and maps of the interior of Gabon with vast white tracts of 'no-man's-land' they wished to survey."

"Monsieur D'Arnot told me the government disallowed all those plans," I told Cecily. "I saw with my own eyes that, to this day, the French government *refuses* the Belgians."

"All is not what it seems, my dear. To the undiscerning eye, Leopold is spurned by the French. There are men like D'Arnot who wish to protect the native lands and peoples from scum like the king of Belgium. But there are others, officials with far fewer scruples, and *their* palms are outstretched under the table. Some of these officials were in places of great influence at the consulate and saw to it that D'Arnot, a troublemaker and a laughingstock who had married a Negress, was relieved of his posting."

I was speechless with outrage and heartbreak for the man.

"As you can see, he has not thrived. He is very close to destitution. And of course he drinks."

And there, suddenly, as though by us simply speaking of him, Paul D'Arnot was manifest in the flesh. Not thirty yards in front of Cecily and me was an odd sort of scene, of which the Frenchman was a part.

Ral Conrath had assembled around him a ragtag gaggle of native men of several tribes. All wore the most serious of faces as they listened to Monsieur D'Arnot reciting in one tongue, and then another, as Conrath demonstrated the use of a rifle.

With a terrific explosion, he fired off a round, blowing a melon stuck on a pole into a mass of yellow pulp.

Men cried out in surprise, then laughed uproariously.

Cecily and I stayed back out of sight of D'Arnot and Conrath, hidden by the angled canopy of a stall, but now we could hear a conversation in English, a dressing-down of the Frenchman by the American.

"I thought you told me you knew Waziri!"

"I told you I had spoken with one Waziri man, the same man you had met. This language is unlike any other I know. And the man went back to his tribe before I could learn it well."

"What the hell good are you to me, then?"

"I can manage," D'Arnot answered in a voice that I could hear was pleading. "From what I remember—"

"Oh, this is rich. From what you can *remember?*"

"It bears resemblance to a little-used Fang dialect. Once I am in the presence of this tribe, I can—"

"Once we're in the presence of the tribe and you can't speak the language, we're all as good as dead!"

"The Waziri man did not appear warlike," D'Arnot argued weakly.

"And you don't remember 'Sumbula'?" Conrath demanded.

"I told you, I do not remember that word."

"That's the only goddamn word you *needed* to remember, you goddamn drunken Frog!"

The insult was D'Arnot's limit. Cecily and I saw him emerge from behind the stall and stride angrily away. A moment later Conrath had caught up to him, placing a hand on his shoulder.

"Look here, Paul, I'm sorry. I'm a hothead. I admit it. Let me make it up to you. We'll go and have a drink. Just let me sign these black fellows up for the safari."

D'Arnot was simmering with rage, perhaps less for Ral's despicable manner than for his own inability to walk away from the man.

"I need you, Paul. I can't lead this expedition without you. You know that." D'Arnot was softening. "And you know the money's good. Right now, pal, I'm the only game in town. Come on, you tell these gents they'll each get ten francs for the trip, half the day we leave, half the day we get back to Libreville. It's a whole year's wages for a single trip." Now Conrath's arm clamped tight around D'Arnot's shoulder. "That's my man."

They disappeared again behind the stall. Cecily and I turned and walked back the way we'd come, silent and considering all we'd heard.

"I've never liked that man," Cecily said, both of us knowing of whom she spoke. "I've seen his kind before." She noticed something wavering in my eye. "You watch yourself, my dear. Never turn your back on him."

"All right."

Then Cecily smiled. "But what am I saying? You are the most level-headed young woman I have ever met. You would never be taken in by the likes of a Ral Conrath."

"No," I said in reply, and then silently to myself, *never again.*

Cecily had taken me to her milliner in the European section of Libreville, insisting on buying me a netted hat of my own for the safari. Hatbox in hand, we stood outside the shop, and for the first time Cecily seemed to me distracted, even nervous.

"I have a little errand to run," she told me. "One I must do on my own."

I readily acquiesced, not daring to be rude by inquiring about the nature of the errand, since it had not been offered. Cecily instructed the rickshaw bearers to take me home, promising to join me there in several hours.

But as the go-cart began its journey back, I found myself worried about my friend and confidante. *Could she be ill? Was the "private" appointment a doctor? Surely it was not one of the fevers that afflicted so many. Was it a cancer eating away at her organ?* No. That was ridiculous. The woman was the picture of cheerfulness and health.

Sunk into my musings, I was startled when the rickshaw came to an abrupt halt. We were still in the European quarter, but up ahead I could see that an overturned cart of pawpaws had stopped all traffic in the street. The farmer was restacking his fruit, arguing the whole time with what seemed to me an arrogant French gendarme. Suddenly, all four of the go-cart bearers vanished from their places in front and behind and joined the gathering crowd being entertained by the incident. I determined it interesting to listen in and hopped down from the vehicle.

But as I turned, my eyes fell on the shop before me, one in a row of proper European structures. It was a run-down bistro with its name, LE CHEVALIER, painted in thick lettering on its grubby window. A glimpse of something familiar inside caught my attention, or, more specifically, some*one*.

It was Ral Conrath. And there beside him was Paul D'Arnot.

They sat at a table of men having drinks. I began to withdraw out of sight when it occurred to me that the lettering on the window would easily hide my identity. In any event, Mr. Conrath was so deeply immersed in conversation that he'd have no cause to look in my direction. Then I received another shock.

Their drinking companions were none other than the four Belgian engineers I'd seen at the consulate. D'Arnot appeared to be translating for Ral, who leaned in, head-to-head with Leopold's men. He gestured broadly with his hands. His expression was fierce. This was no congenial gathering for afternoon sherry.

"M'amselle!"

I was startled once again to see the rickshaw bearers back at their rails. One of them had called out to me. Leaving the mysterious scene behind, I allowed myself to be helped into my conveyance, and it lurched into forward motion. A moment later Le Chevalier was behind me, out of sight. It had been a brief glimpse through a dirty glass window, but what I had seen was clear as day.

Ral Conrath was up to no good. And Paul D'Arnot was a party to it.

Heartsick, my mind whirling, I debated myself. *Something had to be done. But what? What, in fact, did I know for certain? And would this conspiracy—if it was one—spell the end of the Porter Expedition?*

Before I knew it I was under the shaded foliage on the coast road back to Cecily's. But even the spectacular canopy of crimson flamboyant flowers failed to delight me. Everything, I was certain, was falling apart . . . before it had even begun.

The tension had become unbearable on the day before the Porter Expedition was to board the steamer that would take us south along Gabon's coast and up the famed Ogowe River.

The evening before, I'd gone to Father's room and found him repacking his gear into a long waterproof sack. I'd finally found the

courage, and the words, to explain my misgivings about Ral Conrath.

It had not gone well.

Perhaps I shouldn't have begun with my qualms about the weaponry.

"The man has gone overboard," I told Father.

He looked at me long and hard, and then sighed deeply. "Jane," was
all he said.

"Well, honestly, Father, we are not marching into the Battle of
Gettysburg. He's brought a gun that fires eight hundred rounds a
minute and—"

"That's enough!"

The shock of his disciplinary tone nearly leveled me where I
stood. In all my life, Father had never spoken to me so roughly.

"We are not marching into Gettysburg. We are marching into the
deepest heart of the African jungle. Uncharted territory. There's no
telling what we will encounter there. I, for one, think our Mr. Conrath has done a bang-up job provisioning and arming this expedition." He angrily stuffed a pair of boots into his bag. "Maybe I made
a mistake bringing you along."

"No! You didn't!" With Father's cruel words I felt my world crumbling around me. "Father, I only—"

"You've been second-guessing Mr. Conrath since we boarded the
Evangeline."

So Ral Conrath *had* reported our little dispute on the dock at
Liverpool. I doubted he had mentioned his groping hands on deck at
three in the morning.

Father had turned and rounded on me.

"Why on earth do you think I allowed the man to bring all those
guns? Because of *you*. Have you any idea what would happen to our
family if any harm came to you out there? It would kill your mother.
It would kill *me*!" He turned away again and refolded for the third
time a small woolen blanket. When he tried to fit it into the bag, it
wouldn't go. He pushed and pushed to no avail, then with a frustrated cry, pulled the thing out and threw it on the floor.

I had never seen my father in such a wretched state.

"I'm sorry. Really I am. There'll be no more 'second-guessing.' I
promise." I silently vowed to be silent about my forebodings, per-

haps to calm my beloved father, perhaps—more selfishly—to allow the expedition to go on unhindered. I would never get this extraordinary opportunity again. I must be silent. I must withhold what I believed the most damning evidence against Ral Conrath.

Or was it so damning? How could I be certain? Was there a law against an American and a Frenchman having drinks at a bistro in Libreville? Could I not, for once, quiet my overanalytical mind and allow life, like a great river, to flow smoothly and naturally on?

I went to my father, still turned away, and wrapped my arms around him, laying my head on his back.

"Everything will be all right," I said with conviction. "Nothing is going to happen to me. We shall be the first Europeans to explore where none have gone before. We are going to uncover the most important scientific find in the history of the world! And we are going to do it *together*."

I'd felt Father's shoulders soften. He covered my hand over his heart with his own and gave it a reassuring squeeze.

I had willed myself not to weep with relief.

"Well, if that's the case," he said, the tone of the doting father having returned to his voice, "then you'd better find a way to fold this blasted blanket so it fits in my sack."

"Let me at it," I said.

Disaster, for the moment, had been averted.

Later that night, however, I had found it impossible to fall asleep, furious at my weakness and still harboring apprehensions about our team. I would simply have to live with it all and hope for the best. But I would never, as Cecily had advised, turn my back on Ral Conrath again.

Now, late in the afternoon, I'd taken a seat on the veranda and guests were beginning to arrive for Cecily's farewell dinner. It would end early so everyone could turn in by nine. We'd be up well before dawn. The steamer was already loaded with our supplies, but Ral Conrath was insistent on a final muster for his team—the carriers, rowers, laborers, cooks. We would leave the Gabon River estuary at sunrise.

D'Arnot was the first to come. He wore a small bandage over his injury, and about his head was a cloud of misery that broke my heart to see. But I was wary of the Frenchman since I had seen him with Mr. Conrath in the company of the Belgians. He greeted me warmly, and despite what I perceived as his questionable motives, I returned the greeting with matched cordiality.

A lanky older gentleman in a suit of pale linen so well-worn it failed to wrinkle even in the humid heat of late afternoon came striding up the flowered path. When he tipped his straw hat to me and introduced himself as Mr. Batty, I recognized his northern English accent. His face, while still handsome, was heavily lined about the mouth and forehead, with deep crinkles at the sides of his eyes. This was a man, I was sure, who had spent the better part of his seventy-odd years outdoors, and I guessed from the languid ease in his long joints that it was the tropics in which he had made his home— one of Captain Kelly's Old Coasters, I thought, the kind of man who "went to his death with a joke in his teeth."

Finally, a native man looking uncomfortable in his European bush suit, wearing on his face the telltale scarification of the Bantu, bowed formally from the waist, introducing himself as Yabi of the Ogowe Mbele tribe. He was to be our guide.

Father and Ral descended from their upstairs bedrooms, and Cecily emerged from the kitchen with a film of perspiration on her upper lip but looking lovely in a rose silk gown and hibiscus laced through her upswept hair. She had been giving the cook last-minute instructions on the lamb roast which, indeed, smelled divine.

We were seated quickly, allowing no time for chitter-chatter, but the underlying buzz of excitement for tomorrow's departure was as loud and ever-present as a thousand cicadas at sunset. I wondered as we were served a sweet yam soup whether Ral Conrath would, both this evening and in the months to come, control his obnoxiousness and antipathy toward the Negroes of our party, in particular toward Yabi. Outbursts of the kind I'd several times witnessed could be disastrous if proud native bearers, fed up with Ral's antics, walked away from the safari in the middle of nowhere.

But at least for this night, to my great relief, Mr. Conrath was as cheerful and courtly and intelligent as the day we'd met him at Cambridge. He was in very good form, entertaining us with the most shocking stories in his repertoire. His favorites revolved around the cannibal tribes whose preferred form of ritual sacrifice was, besides the hacking off of heads, burying the still-living victim in the ground up to his neck with only his "bean" sticking out. This would be gnawed upon by sundry creatures, eyes plucked out by the vultures, all, of course, while the poor man was conscious.

Yabi offered that this "head-above-ground" tradition was his tribe's usual mode of burial, but for the dead, of course. He had nothing but contempt for the cannibal tribes upriver from the Mbele. He had been chosen as our guide because his tribe lived along the tributary of the Ogowe at the point of departure into the uncharted wilds. He explained that though few of his people had ever strayed farther south from where their tributary ended in a mangrove swamp, once, as a boy, Yabi's father—a great hunter—had taken him in that direction. They had eventually found themselves at the northern edge of a small mountain range with "trees that touched the sky." They saw no other tribes, though there had always been persistent rumors of the Waziri. Before they could go any farther, the ground had begun to shake violently. This terrified his father, who quickly decided it was a message from the spirits that they were trespassing where they should not be. They returned home.

"What do you know of Sumbula?" Conrath asked Yabi.

The native shook his head.

"The Enduro Escarpment caves?" Father inquired of his guide.

"There were caves where my father and I went. I believe they are the same ones Mr. Conrath explored, coming from another direction."

Mr. Batty, as I suspected, had stories of his own, not so horrid or bloody as Ral's but steeped in the mystery and magic of the continent. As he wove his tales, I became quite convinced that Cecily's "private appointment" had been with this Old Coaster to whom she listened intently with her eyes closed and her pretty mouth bowed into a smile.

The realization made me unaccountably happy.

As the main course was served and the heat of the day began slowly to diminish, Mr. Batty's entertaining stories grew even more wild and improbable. He spoke of "lost cities of gold," which, I noticed, had Ral Conrath sitting up straighter in his chair.

Childish fantasies of antediluvian civilizations, I thought scornfully. It was unnerving that my feelings of mild dislike for the man had so quickly transmuted into revulsion. I was aware that unchecked emotions were many times the root of costly mistakes in behavior. I'd best rein myself in.

I redirected my attention to Mr. Batty, who was still holding forth about the mysteries of the Gabonese lowland jungles.

Then Yabi smiled enigmatically. "There is a tale, one that even our most wise charm doctors cannot be sure is true . . ." He paused and went inward, as if to retrieve the story hidden in the deepest folds of his mind.

"You must tell us, Yabi," I insisted.

Father poured himself another glass of wine as if preparing himself for a ripping yarn. I was glad to see him enjoying himself, all the tension of the previous evening gone from his demeanor.

"Many along the Ogowe speak of the 'Wild Ape-Man of the Forest,'" Yabi said. "He is partly a man . . . and partly an ape."

"Now that's rich," Ral Conrath said with a derisive laugh. "Which part is which?"

"It is hard to say, because most of those who have seen him have only caught a brief glimpse."

"That *is* a tall story, Yabi," Father said. "Perhaps it's a deformed lowland gorilla, or a native with a particularly hirsute body."

"No, no. He has skin, and it is *white*," Yabi said.

"What a load of horseshit!" Ral Conrath had clearly run out of this evening's supply of gracious good humor.

D'Arnot interjected, the first time he had instigated conversation the whole of the evening. "I have spoken with a man who claims to have seen this creature with his own eyes."

"He must have been as bad a boozer as you, then," Conrath said.

D'Arnot appeared unoffended. He went on. "The man was a respected chief of the Okande tribe. He had been hunting far from his lands for a tiny zebra only found many miles south of the Ogowe. He was frightened by the sight of this beast who looked like a man but swung naked through the treetops and could kill a crocodile single-handedly."

"It *is* preposterous," I said. "I'm afraid I'm going to have to agree with Mr. Conrath for once."

"Well," Conrath said, leaning back in his chair with a cynical grin, "if I were ever to lay eyes on this ape-man, I'd get out my nets and take him alive. Then I'd haul his hairy ass back to America and sell him to the Ringling Brothers Circus."

"Is everyone ready for dessert?" Cecily chirped. She fluttered her eyelids at her old admirer.

"What do we have tonight, Mrs. Fournier?" Mr. Batty asked with sweet familiarity.

"Will you dim the lights, dear?"

He did this and the dining room was bathed in the night's first shadows.

Suddenly the door to the kitchen flew open and a servant walked out looking as though her head was on fire.

"Bombe Alaska!" Cecily cried, naming the flambéed ice cream confection the cook held in front of her. "From one end of the earth to the other." She raised her wineglass high. "To the Porter Expedition. May you all find your dreams and desires!"

Everyone toasted heartily, Father muttering, "Hear, hear," and Ral crying, "I'll drink to that!"

I was silent, but Cecily's salute had, like a well-aimed arrow, found its mark. Tomorrow would begin the realization of my dreams and the culmination of my desires.

When I lifted the glass to my lips and sipped the sweet wine, the covenant was sealed.

The men had retired to the veranda for their port and cigars. Cecily and I remained alone at the table, both of us staring at the last remaining slice of the dessert. The meringue was still stiff and stood in a pretty peak at the center, but the vanilla ice cream at the base was nearly melted.

"I think we should share it," Cecily suggested. I agreed. She cut the meringue in two, placing a piece of it on either of our plates, then drizzled the liquefied ice cream on top. We ate with great pleasure, savoring every bite.

"I hope you don't mind my saying I find you a rather odd girl. You're unmarried and clearly a virgin . . ."

I felt myself beginning to blush.

". . . but unless I'm mistaken, passions run deep in you."

"I suppose so. Passions of a sort. Not the usual kind."

Cecily eyed me strangely.

"No, no, I don't tend toward the Sapphic," I said. "I'd happily chase some fossilized bones halfway around the world, but not a man, the way Isabel Burton did Sir Richard."

"She meant to have him under any circumstances, didn't she," Cecily agreed. "But Jane Digby was even more shameless."

Cecily chuckled at the thought of Lady Jane Ellenborough, our nobly born countrywoman who had in the last century famously (or rather infamously) taken into her bed three husbands and several lovers, including two kings, a count, and a brigadier general. She'd ended her life as the wife of a nomadic Bedouin sheikh twenty years her junior.

"I thought it a bit undignified the way she knelt before him in his goat-hair tent, washing his feet every night," I said.

Cecily smiled and sat back in her chair. "Yes, but she also rode out at his side into desert battles, guns blazing, on a pure white charger. And the sheikh adored her till the day she died. Really, there are far worse fates for a woman than that."

"I have to agree," I said, thinking just then of the Mr. Cartwrights of the world.

"So you haven't any interest in love?" Cecily said, taking the flower from behind her ear and slowly inhaling the fragrance.

The question took me aback. No one had ever thought to ask such a thing before.

"If I could find a man as wonderful as my father, perhaps then . . ." I felt suddenly shy. "You've known a lot of men, Cecily. Did you ever find one you couldn't live without?"

My hostess grinned wickedly. "I do wish I'd met Mr. Batty a bit earlier on."

"Cecily, what is it like to live so long in Africa?"

She fell silent, her eyes growing soft and unfocused, as though she was both remembering the past and seeing into tomorrow. Then she reached across the table and took my hand in hers.

"You do not live in Africa, my dear," Cecily replied with equal measures of tenderness and passion. "Africa lives in *you*."

I felt tears spring suddenly to my eyes and warmth spreading from the center of my chest, for this was the very core of a truth I had known from the moment of my first footfall on the continent. I had never put much stock in notions such as fate or luck or destiny.

But there was something about Africa, something calling to me now. It had always called me. *Was it too outlandish to believe it might be my future? My home?*

When I gazed again at the twinkling eyes and contented expression of Cecily Fournier enjoying the last bite of her bombe Alaska, it suddenly and forcefully occurred to me that it could.

And with that, I knew my life would never be the same again.

The Great River

It had begun to go really wrong the moment we'd disembarked from *La Belle Fille* onto the banks of the Ogowe. Prior to that moment, Ral Conrath had reverted to another period of admirable behavior. Once again he had provided excellent accommodations on the clean, perfectly maintained little stern-wheel steamer. Its two passenger cabins and saloon on the upper deck had been large and exquisitely fitted up, its lower deck used for business.

Father and D'Arnot had discovered a friendship of the heart between them and spent many long hours on the deck, deep in quiet conversation. I noticed, too, that D'Arnot drank very little, if at all, and he suffered for it with tremors and sweats of withdrawal. I thought it brave of him and the honorable thing to do before we headed into the jungle. It was, I surmised, done out of growing respect for my father. I saw clear admiration in D'Arnot's eyes as we ate dinner at the captain's table every evening.

I had once and for all given up my diary keeping, as this very river journey had been so well described by Mary Kingsley. She had captured perfectly the strangeness of the mangrove swamps with their rotting shores that comprised the first many miles of the river: "black batter-like, stinking slime" and a "fearful stench." She spoke of the water at high or low tide looking like "a pathway of polished metal . . . [being] heavily weighted with stinking mud," and the vertical aerial root of a mangrove tree keeping a "hard straight line until it gets some two feet above water-level, and then spreading out into blunt fingers with which to dip into the water and grasp the mud."

There were the "gaunt black ribs of the old hulks, once used as trading stations, which lie exposed at low water near the shore, protruding like the skeletons of great unclean beasts." Raised on piles from the mud shores were the white-painted factories and their large storehouses for oil, and just as Miss Kingsley had said, the factories flew flags at half-mast because somebody was "dead again."

I'd seen a hopping mudfish and a crocodile lying asleep with its jaws open on a sandbank in the sun. Heard the nighttime noises, "grunts from I know not what, splashes from jumping fish, the peculiar whirr of rushing crabs, and quaint creaking and groaning sounds from the trees; and . . . the strange whine and sighing cough of the crocodiles."

Finally with the mangrove swamps behind us, the morning air on the river was soft, and the song of the plantain warblers soothing to the ear. The low, dense, luxuriant shores might have been monotonous in their verdant sameness but for the climbing plants that formed thick "curtains"—sometimes forty feet wide and seventy feet high. These vegetal veils were gaily festooned with flowers, as if decorated by the hand of an artist. The trunks and branches of many trees were themselves the show-offs in hues of pink and red and yellow. Some were bone white but arrayed in patterns of thick orange lichen and vermillion fungi. Stretches of sword grass along the banks, red-dwarf clay cliffs with tiny villages atop them, or neat coffee plantations with their rows of healthy bushes made the journey along the deep, silent river a joy.

Yabi had given the captain of the steamer precise instructions as to where the Porter Expedition should be let off. His village was downstream on a minor tributary of the Ogowe, many miles before the great rapids. This was apparently to be a different route to the Enduro Escarpment than Ral Conrath had taken with his hunting party, and he was therefore dependent on Yabi—all of us were—for our very lives.

There being no dock, the ten canoes—the newfangled metal ones that Conrath had purchased—were lowered into the water. Our supplies and team, numbering fifty, were loaded into them. One by one, with the paddlers' muscular arms pumping in rhythm, the slender vessels made for the mouth of the tributary. The canoes met briefly on shore, then pushed off down the Mbele Ogowe. Its course appeared to me to run diagonally, south to be sure, but gently also to the west, back the way we'd come.

Here the real expedition began, and it was here the trouble began in earnest.

It was as if a very devil had taken up habitation in Ral Conrath's being. He did not speak orders; he barked them. He was endlessly condescending to Yabi, something that I knew to be foolhardy in the extreme. He lobbed insults at D'Arnot, who, in his newly sober state, did not take to them very kindly but bore them stoically. Ral Conrath barely conversed with me and refused to meet my eye. It was only with Father that he managed to retain the thinnest veneer of civility.

I sat with Father in a canoe behind the leading one—with Conrath, Yabi, and D'Arnot aboard. No one spoke of the change in Conrath, everyone perhaps believing that this was the demeanor he always assumed to keep control of his expeditions—his "style of operation"—though I heard my father mutter to himself after one of Conrath's outbursts at the laziness of the rowers, "Get a grip on yourself, man."

The Mbele village was nearly two days' paddling down the tributary, with Conrath refusing to allow the rowers to stop, an abominable labor for them, one that forced everyone not paddling to sleep sitting upright. But no one argued, as our leader claimed the crocodiles would have a feast of us if we put ashore on an uninhabited site.

We were welcomed ashore at Yabi's village. His mother, a skinny woman with breasts hanging below her waist and who looked far too old and worn to have a runny-nosed infant at her teat, came and put her arms around her son, giving him a great smacking kiss on the cheek.

The whites in the party were taken into the village, a place surrounded on all but the river side by large rough-hewn stakes, which Yabi explained were to protect against rampaging elephants. It was a shabby place of mud and thatch huts, their door flaps made of leathery elephant ears. All the Mbele were thin and appeared beaten down, perhaps from their lack of nourishment. But preparations were soon under way for huts to be vacated for Yabi's guests.

Then from within the largest hut, one twice the size of any other in the village, came the sound of drumming. Its front door swung open, and out strode a large native man, an amazingly attired creature—most certainly the chief. His name was Motobe.

In the main he was covered by the scarlet tunic of a militia uniform. Wound around his waist were many yards of bright yellow gingham cloth, the long ends of which hung down and trailed on the ground like a queen's train. He wore the helmet of an English life guard, carried a lady's pink parasol with gold lace edges, and around his neck was a wooden tambourine, lacking only its skin top. As the chief strode toward us, I could hear the tambourine's brass cymbals jingling. Following behind him were his six women, several carrying babies, and weighted down with row upon row of colored glass bead necklaces.

We were fed small portions of stringy goat, foul-tasting manioc paste and mashed yams, and a palm wine that reeked strangely of turpentine. But the sentiment was as gracious as dinner at a Cambridge great house, and perhaps more sincere. I was touched deeply.

Over the campfire, with Yabi and Paul D'Arnot translating, the chief was told of our plans to travel southwest in search of Waziriland. Motobe howled with laughter. This was a joke, he was sure. There was nothing down there but some mountains with "trees that touched the sky," and bad spirits that made the earth rumble and quake.

Certainly no one expected the headman to understand about million-year-old fossils or Darwin's theory of evolution, so we simply laughed along with him at our own stupidity and recklessness.

Later, as the fire burned into embers, the talk became more serious. The chief spoke of the tribe's falling on hard times. They were, in fact, facing starvation. Their crops had not failed, he told us, leaning close to the fire, but an "evil monster elephant" had decided to curse the village, and night after night it had come and trampled the Mbele gardens into the mud. Could Yabi's new friends spare some ammunition for their guns? They were all out and had nothing with which to barter for bullets. It was a useless request, for even I could see that their flintlocks were ancient. The Porter Expedition had no ammunition for such weapons.

"Yabi," Ral Conrath said, "tell Motobe that I'll kill his monster elephant for him. We'll go on a hunt. Bring him down. Say that his people's stomachs will be large with elephant meat."

Yabi's eyes lit up, but before he could begin the translation, Father objected, worried about our timetable. We could not afford to be stuck in the bush when the rains came.

But Ral Conrath was convincing. People were starving here—women and children. It was an argument a great-hearted man like Archie Porter could hardly contest.

But the next morning, Ral Conrath's mood had turned ugly almost at once. By the time we'd entered the jungle proper—Father and I armed with rifles for the first time—he was tripping over fallen trees and enormous roots, being bruised and scratched by thorny creepers, and cursing the sodden ground with such noisy vehemence it startled the birds and monkeys above. Earlier I had cornered him, demanding to know why we were carting everything we'd brought with us from Liverpool on an elephant hunt.

"You think they'd leave us a pot to piss in if we left it there?" he'd snapped at me. "I wouldn't trust a Negro as far as I could throw him."

It was late in the afternoon with everyone's nerves frayed to the snapping point. The Mbele hunters were insisting that we had come too far, that this could not be the place of the evil beast, but Ral was deaf to their pleading. Hardly a moment later, Yabi pointed to a great spreading forest of tall bamboo. Straight through its center was a path four feet wide where the stalks had been beaten into the ground—an elephant path, Yabi told us.

We were instructed to follow Ral Conrath down the path. The rustling and click-clacking on both sides of us was claustrophobic and unsettling. The giant bamboo culms were so tall and slender that they leaned inward, touching in an arch above our heads, thus no sky could be seen. The air was thick and stuffy, and D'Arnot felt faint. Father and I stayed behind to tend him, but Conrath pushed ahead, determined to bring down one of the beasts by day's end.

When Father and I caught up to him at the far end of the grove, he was opening the crate that held the Gatling gun.

"You're not using that thing on an elephant," Father said.

"Listen, old man, this is my hunt, and I'll use the weapon of my choice. I'm going to bring down an elephant today and be a hero tonight. One way or the other."

I tilted my head out the opening in the bamboo into a long, wide clearing. On its far side was a jungle, and thirty yards down to the left of us there stood a single elephant. It foraged with its trunk on the trees at the edge of the greenery.

It was not very large, certainly not the culprit from the Mbele gardens. Nevertheless, the Gatling gun was set on its tripod, and Ral Conrath, swaggering like a soldier, took his place behind it.

Then to my horror, in a thunderous hail of machine gun fire, he shot the placidly grazing elephant. Its front knees buckled and, with a confused shake of its head, fell in a mountainous heap.

Conrath wasted no time crossing the clearing to examine his kill . . . or rather to gloat. Stunned as I was, I followed him. The downed beast was a female. She lay on her side, wrinkled grey skin oozing red from a hundred cruel wounds. She was not yet dead, her trunk moving weakly in the dust, her one eye glazed with pain. I felt my blood begin to boil.

Ral Conrath was leaning over his trophy. Without thinking, I smashed him hard in the back with my rifle butt. He swiveled and glared at me with as much shock as hatred.

"You're despicable," I said. "Move aside."

He was unarmed and could see that I should not be trifled with. Bile rising in my throat, I took aim and put the poor animal out of her misery. I heard my father calling my name as he crossed the clearing, ordering the bearers to follow him out of the bamboo.

But I froze where I stood with the next sounds that came to my ear. First it was a deep rumbling vibration under my feet, followed quickly by the shrill trumpeting of many elephants.

I turned to see the most terrifying of scenes: the clearing filled with members of the Porter Expedition, my father, D'Arnot, the bearers, and Mbele tribesmen and, led by a giant bull, a herd of rampaging elephants bearing down on them.

Father had already taken aim but was knocked off his feet by a panicked bearer. I had no choice. I lifted my rifle and took aim at the bull. He was coming straight at me, so the target was, I thought with bitter irony, easier than shooting skeet.

I fired.

A single stream of blood spurted from between his eyes. The bull fell dead in his tracks. At that very moment I thought that I'd heard a lion's roar, but I had no time to look for its source, for the stampede I believed would be halted by the bull's downing was still coming toward us. The sound of gunfire had merely deflected them. Several followed the scrambling bearers and tribesmen into the elephant path and others wildly trampled down the giant bamboo stalks as if they were saplings.

Ral ripped the rifle from my hands and, using the dead female as cover, was firing into the melee. Father and D'Arnot were at my side when we heard the first human shrieks rising from the bamboo grove. Father, himself trembling, clutched me protectively to him.

"This is my fault," he whispered, his voice husky with outrage. "My fault."

There was nothing I could say to comfort him.

I felt sick.

The elephant hunt had proved a tragedy of unspeakable proportions. Five men had died, two bearers of the Porter Expedition and three Mbele, one of them Yabi's cousin. They'd been gored and trampled to death by the animals. I had felt like a rampaging beast myself as I turned on Ral Conrath when all had quieted. I'd been forced to take the life of that magnificent creature—the first elephant I'd ever seen in the wild. I shouted with almost incoherent fury at his appalling stupidity and insane pigheadedness. He was no better than a murderer. I'd never spoken like that to anyone, and I hadn't cared who was listening—the Mbele, the bearers, my father, D'Arnot . . . and no translation had been needed for their perfect understanding.

Conrath had gone stone-cold at my tirade. Even as the words flew from my mouth, I saw the venomous expression on his face and knew without question that I had made the first true enemy of my life. How dare a woman (really no better than one of the "lesser races") humiliate Ral Conrath? Cause him to lose face before his employer and members of the safari?

More stunning to me was the knowledge that the man had no remorse for those who had died because of his actions. The moment I was through shouting at him, he had turned away and, as though nothing out of the ordinary had happened, directed the bearers to butcher the carcasses, then called out orders for the Mbele hunters to fetch "reinforcements" who could carry loads of elephant meat back to the village.

Father, livid, had insisted that Conrath go with him and make apology to Motobe for the loss of his tribesmen. He had flatly refused. He would stay with the slain elephants to ensure that the survivors of the herd did not return and attack the butcherers.

"People die every day in the jungle," he'd told Father. "Think of all the lives that meat will save. The Mbele will be grateful." Further, Ral Conrath meant to dig the ivory out of the elephants' skulls. He was indignant when Father demanded that the Gatling gun not be used again and instructed the bearers to carry it back to the village. It was a grim march. Yabi controlled his agitation for as long as he was able, but when we arrived at the village I could see silent tears rolling down his cheeks. The disgrace, he believed, was all his. It was no surprise that even the meat of two elephants for a starving tribe did nothing to assuage the unnecessary loss of three of its own.

Ral Conrath finally returned wearing a false cloak of remorse and made fulsome apologies to Motobe. The chief was unmoved. Indignant, he had muttered rather loudly, "Ungrateful bastard," and turned away to set the expedition on its way again. That was Yabi's cue. Father and he came to stand before the headman. He made the deepest and most humble apologies and begged him to accept a gift, one that could never return his loved ones but something they might trade with and bring some good to his people.

To Ral Conrath's astonishment, his elephant ivories were carried right past him with great solemnity and laid at Motobe's feet. There was great satisfaction watching Conrath's face burn as his trophies were given away. Of course there was nothing he could do.

But in that moment, a second member of the Porter family became this damnable bully's avowed enemy.

Deeper, goddamn it!" Ral Conrath shouted at the bearers who were digging holes in the soggy ground.

We had paddled on past the Mbele village, and the river had ended in a mangrove swamp. A mile beyond that it had turned into this marsh, and there Ral had ordered the bearers to bury the metal canoes.

"It is very difficult digging in this soil," Yabi told him. "It is as much water as earth."

I could see by Ral Conrath's expression that he didn't care for his guide's tone. It was defiant, his anger boiling just below the surface. It made no difference to Conrath that some of Yabi's friends and family had died on the elephant hunt, but he was too dependent on the native man to simply order him to buck up and get on with it.

What he said was, "I don't want to hear any excuses. If the bearers want to get paid, they'll do as they're told. Otherwise you can tell them to turn around and go home."

Without a word, Yabi walked away.

Conrath looked up and caught sight of D'Arnot—certainly another annoyance. The Frenchman, after sobering up on the riverboat, had taken to the bottle again, and sometimes, when D'Arnot was drunk, he would rave on about seeing the "ape-man" in the trees roaring like a lion.

Following Yabi's lead, the Porter Expedition proceeded on foot. We slogged on, suffering mosquitoes, leeches, and flesh-eating fish that ripped at our calves in the shallow water. Ral stayed at the head of the column and spoke to no one but Yabi. As the two of them pored relentlessly over maps in the soggy camps they set up at night, the guide appeared less and less confident about finding the mountain range.

"That's all we need," Ral Conrath groused at Yabi, "a wild-goose chase through hell!"

The terrain had changed into a dense, steaming jungle thicket. There were no discernible paths, either human or animal. Everything was overgrown, and the bearers, with their machetes, hacked away at it, jumpy from the constant worry of poisonous snakes and a vine, they said, that grew a whole foot a day, not to mention the insects that could crawl into your ear at night and eat the eyes right out of their sockets. The diggers and cook were uneasy, too. There was much grumbling, and quarrels were breaking out between them every day. Even I was having doubts about Yabi.

Then the thicket broadened a bit, into a low, level canopy—young trees overhead, giant ferns and large-leafed bananas closer to the ground. Everyone was relieved to see narrow paths to be followed. There were larger animals, too—flying monkeys, anteaters, wild hogs, peacocks. Now in the rare clearing, we could make out—off to the east of us—a single conical peak.

"So is that the mountain range with 'trees that touch the sky'?" Conrath demanded of Yabi.

He was staring at it with unblinking eyes. "It may be, but I cannot say for certain."

"Why in the hell not? How many damn mountain ranges can there be out here?"

"We will just continue on and know very soon," Yabi said. He turned his back on Ral Conrath and continued down the jungle path.

To our surprise, the Mbele Ogowe River surfaced once more. It had been running underground and now emerged as a narrow but swiftly running river. Yabi's excitement could hardly be contained at its appearance. This was something of the early journey with his father that he had forgotten over the years and now remembered—how the river had "come and gone from sight." It meant that the Porter Expedition was on the right track.

When the river submerged again, leaving nothing but soggy ground, the party was back to slogging. Everyone took turns falling into holes in the soft earth and getting up covered in foul-smelling muck. Ral Conrath was already on edge when late in the afternoon of the seventh day a fog rose up from the swamp. Not just a normal fog. It reeked of sulfur and decay, and worse, it was so thick that we could not see the fingers of our hands stretched out at arm's length in front of us.

I was tied to my father's belt by a rope. He, in turn, was following behind Yabi, carefully finding the guide's footprints to step into. All sounds were muted, eerie. Everyone was half blind in the dangerous terrain and deathly exhausted.

Suddenly we heard the shrieking. *One of the bearers!* He should have been behind us, but he must be abreast of us. Off to our right.

There was no chance of seeing him in the mist—there was only the shrill sound of agony. Yabi untied himself from Father and quickly disappeared into the fog. My father and I were knee-deep in muck and still tethered together. But we followed Yabi's shouts and the bearer's screaming, which was getting weaker and weaker.

When we reached Yabi, he stood with an arm outstretched to keep us from going farther. Beyond was a boiling mud pot, its grey viscous soup having engulfed all but the head and one arm of the unlucky bearer. The man's eyes were bulging and he was already insensible, but god-awful sounds still emerged from his steaming lips. He slid farther down until nothing showed but his hand, as though he was reaching for rescue. But a moment later it disappeared in the bubbling muck as well.

We stood in place, disbelieving the scene we had just witnessed. But with nothing more to be done, Yabi led us back to what there was of a path. Father spoke in low, worried tones to our guide as Ral Conrath listened.

"We are moving on from here," Yabi told him. "We are soon coming to Waziriland. You will start your dig and all will be well."

"Yeah, right," Conrath said, "and I'm the king of Belgium." Then he called for camp to be made, and no more was said about the loss of the native man.

But in the morning when we woke, one-third of our bearers had disappeared.

Eden

The loss of the carriers would have been much harder to bear had the expedition not soon after passed out of the most miserable of landscapes and arrived at another that could be negotiated with comparative ease. Directly to the east was the quartet of mountains, one large peak and three smaller foothills. The range was blanketed with enormous trees as described by Yabi's father—ones that with their monstrous size indeed "touched the sky." There was a preponderance of jagged black rock that had been crushed by the millennia into the richest of all soils, which fed the vegetation. At the base of the range we observed a trail winding up and around the highest of the mountains, but there was no purpose in exploring it. More to the point, we had come to a place of almost excessive beauty.

Yabi was ecstatic, for although there was still no sign of the Waziri tribe, he recognized this location as the farthest point to which his father and he had come all those years ago.

The dense, uniform thicket with its oppressive under- and overgrowth that needed hacking through for every footstep had here broadened out into groves of huge and ancient trees—mangoes, figs, baobabs, rubber, silk-cotton, and mahogany—spread out umbrella-like above spacious clearings and well-worn tracks. In the soaring canopy, wild orchids nestled in the soft moss of heavy limbs. Giant fruit-laden trees of a species no European had ever before seen were hung with thick, ropy vines. There was an almost deafening chorus of birdsong of more varieties than one could possibly count, and though larger animals did not make themselves apparent, one could discern by the wide paths and by the great rustlings, grumblings, and not-so-distant roars that here lived big game of every possible variety. Yabi explained that what we had recently emerged from was "jungle"—new growth. This area was "forest" . . . and very, very old.

The climate was different as well. Even though it was hot and the vegetation lush, the heat was relatively dry. Certainly there were myriad insects, some astonishing and unique, but we were no longer eaten alive by swarms of voracious mosquitoes and sand flies.

As we drove deeper into the forest, we discovered rock rifts and escarpments, exquisite waterfalls, streams and ponds. Yabi guessed that the Mbele Ogowe River again ran underground here, but Father surmised that the character of the locale was, in fact, informed by its volcanism. He was no expert, but the largest of the peaks had the shape of a volcano, though long extinct.

Yabi, who was "following his nose," was finding more frequent signs—subtle, except to the most peerlessly trained eyes—of human habitation: nothing as obvious as a footprint, but a tiny hole in a tree trunk where an arrow had pierced and later been extracted; twigs on the ground broken in a certain pattern that meant a man, not an animal, had trodden; the lingering scent of a woman many days after she had gone from her seat on a rocky outcropping. If this was not Waziriland, Yabi assured us, it was very near to it.

Happily, Ral Conrath had suggested that our party make an encampment here and spend a day or two to rest. Everyone quickly agreed, as we were sore and depressed from our many tribulations and needed a peaceful respite before moving on.

All these sights were thrilling to me, and my heart began to lighten. Despite the wretched Mr. Conrath and the tragic start to our expedition, my father and I were finally on a clear path to finding our missing link. I could, for the first time since the disastrous elephant hunt, begin to forgive myself for ending the lives of the two blameless creatures. Sleep, however, was harder to come by than forgiveness. My mind, every fiber of my being, was afire.

We had finally arrived.

I walked slowly along the paths, gazing up at the wondrous canopy, stooping to sink my nose into flowers' fragrant faces. I stopped and listened to birdsong. Enjoyed the perspiration softening my skin. Following what appeared as the trail of small animals, I found myself at a pool of clear water and, wasting no time, stripped off my clothing and let down my hair. I lowered myself in, slowly, savoringly, watching my breasts float on the surface, sweeping my arms like two wings over the water, and dipped my head back to soak my hair. I heard a rustling in the bush then and found the bottom with my feet, so only my head and shoulders rose above the surface. I looked all around me but saw nothing, no one. All was benign. Still, I felt watched. A moment later Father appeared on the path I'd come from. His expression was, I imagined, all that mine had been while walking along so heavenly a road. When he saw me in the pool and my clothing in a heap, he beamed and sat down on the narrow shore.

"You look like a water nymph, sweetheart. Or Eve in the Garden of Eden."

"I am! Father, I've dreamed of this place. This *very* one. It's positively primeval. Can't you imagine that somewhere exactly like this human life could have evolved?"

"I think it could."

"Turn your back." He did, and as I rose from the water and dressed, he closed his eyes, slowly inhaling the fragrance of a thousand flowers, and we shared the sweet cacophony of life sounds around us.

"Come on, I want to show you something."

Father led me down narrow, circuitous paths to an outcropping of black basalt, a shallow cave in one side.

"Stand back." He barred me from coming too close.

"I don't see anything," I said.

"Just wait."

Suddenly a cloud of hot sulfurous steam shot from the depression and billowed all around us. After a few moments, much of it was sucked back into the vent.

"The earth is breathing!" I exclaimed. I slipped my hand into his. "Thank you, Father. Thank you for this."

"I'm afraid we have to leave tomorrow. Our dreadful Mr. Conrath assures me that our caves are not much farther." Father stood and took a more businesslike tone. "We haven't come for the beauty, you know."

I smiled up at him and finished the thought. "We've come for the beast."

He pulled me up into a warm embrace. "Or at least his bones."

I kissed my father's cheek and all our troubles of late seemed borne away on the wings of a scarlet-and-yellow bird that fluttered above us and away. Then together we walked arm in arm back to camp.

By the time I had risen, washed, dressed, and joined my father and D'Arnot around the breakfast fire, it was clear that Ral Conrath was nowhere among us. Neither was Yabi, for he had taken off the day before to discover the best route to the Enduro Escarpment.

I took up a tin cup and sipped bitter coffee. "Where did Mr. Conrath go?" I asked.

Father shrugged.

Paul D'Arnot was staring off to the east. "There," he said, lifting his arm and pointing through an opening in the canopy that allowed sight of a narrow sliver of the highest mountain in the range.

I could just make out on the slope two tiny figures climbing along a track toward the summit. It was Ral Conrath and a bearer carrying a narrow crate on his back.

No one spoke for a long while, for the implications were largely incomprehensible. What was clear was that D'Arnot knew something.

"Tell us, Paul," Archie demanded.

D'Arnot sat himself down on a log, as though his legs would no longer hold him. He cradled his face in his hands and sighed deeply. Father and I took camp chairs across from him. It set the stage for a proper interrogation.

"Last year," D'Arnot began, "Ral Conrath came to Port-Gentil, the town south of Libreville, where I had gone to live for a time. In Libreville he had drunk, whored, and gambled away most of the money he had earned on his last safari, and gotten into one too many brawls. We had met at a bistro and often drank away our sorrows together. One afternoon he sent me a message to come to the dock and meet him. There I found him with a man, a native man. I had never seen such a person in all my travels along the west coast or up the Ogowe River. This man was strong. Beautifully muscled. Fierce and intelligent. But primitive. There was no sign that he had had in all of his life contact with the world till that moment. He wore no shoes, but his feet themselves were hard as leather. His garment was a loincloth made of a textile the likes of which I had never seen. A kind of woven cotton, but not of a factory loom, hand-spun, red and yellow, with a squarish pattern that repeated over and over.

"But Ral Conrath had not brought me to meet the man to show me his clothes or the soles of his feet. Around his neck on a leather string hung an artifact *extraordinaire*. It was solid gold and very heavy. The shape was round with a round hole in the center. "

D'Arnot stopped to drink from his flask. I hoped it was water at this hour, but his lips pursed as a person's do when he has downed a great slug of whiskey.

"Were you able to speak to this man?" Father asked.

"Only a little. We made signs with our hands, but I was careful with my gestures, for as clearly as he seemed a warrior, he was fearful of the city. He had never seen a proper building. He had never seen modern clothes. He had never seen a watch, or eyeglasses, or shoes. He had come paddling out of the Ogowe in a rough-hewn canoe and had probably not spoken to a soul on his journey from who knew where, perhaps passing other native canoes and a paddle steamer or two. He called himself Ecko of the Waziri tribe. The language he spoke was not Bantu. It seemed more—what can I say?—primitive. There were no affectations of modernity. Not even the occasional French or English word."

"Why had he come to the coast?" I asked.

"I do not know. My skills as an interpreter were insufficient. But even as he had just arrived, he seemed eager to go home again—as though he had made a mistake coming. Conrath was, of course, most interested in the ornament around the Waziri man's neck. I found, by the few words we had managed to learn, and by hand signals, that the gold necklaces were very common with his people. Every grown man and woman wore one. There was, he indicated with gestures, a limitless supply of them. And if he did not seem to understand the value of the metal, it was to him a *sacred* object. Something he called 'Sumbula.' When we repeated the word, he became instantly disturbed and signaled with his arms the shape of a mountain. He squatted down and drew on the muddy dock *four* mountains. But when I tried to ask him how his necklace and the mountains were connected, he stood and started for his canoe.

"Conrath was shouting at me, 'Don't let him go! Find out where these mountains are! Sumbula! There is gold there!' But the Waziri man could not be stopped. He paddled away, and that was the last we saw of him. Well, our friend was beside himself. He hounded me, as if I should know what to do. But later that month we both returned to Libreville and I ran into Yabi and related the story. He grew very excited and told me of his and his father's adventure to a place not so far from his village, a place with four mountains and the legend of an old tribe his people had always called 'Wazir.' When he told Ral Conrath he could take him to that place, the man nearly jumped out of his skin. He wished to go at that very instant." D'Arnot laughed ruefully. "But this was not to be. His double-dealings had caught up with him. The authorities took him into custody, and before Conrath could disappear up the Ogowe, he was deported. They told him never to return to Libreville without lots of money and a passport."

Father looked grim. "So I became his passport *and* his banker. It's why he came to the Zoological Congress in Cambridge. He was looking for a 'mark.'"

"Much of your money was used for bribes," D'Arnot continued. "There were 'associates' to line up in Libreville, corrupt officials. There were guides and bearers to hire . . ." He looked ashamed. "A translator . . . desperate for money."

"He's a common treasure hunter, then," I said.

"And I am a common drunk," D'Arnot miserably confessed.

I knew the next question must be asked, but I dreaded it beyond words. "The Enduro Escarpment, the limestone caves . . . do they even exist?"

"From what I can tell, yes, they do. Conrath had questioned Yabi like a grand inquisitor. 'Are there caves? A river?' Yes, Yabi told him. He and his father had seen some caves. 'Any caves will do,' Conrath said. But the fossil he showed you, that which he told you came from the Enduro Escarpment . . ." D'Arnot hung his head and stared at the ground. "I believed it did until this morning. Today he bragged that he had brought it back from Java. A place he called Trinel."

"Jane!" Father cried, his voice breaking.

"He took the thing from Eugène Dubois's site," I said, my voice thick with contempt. "Stole it."

My heart pounded furiously, and an emotion I had never before associated with my father welled up and threatened to topple me: pity. This enraged me. I turned on D'Arnot like a mad thing.

"Stand up," I ordered him. "Stand up and look at us!"

He obeyed as a slave would his master.

"There's more that you're not telling us."

"What, Jane?" my father said. "What more can the man have done to us?"

"Why is Ral Conrath climbing that mountain?" I demanded of D'Arnot. "What's in that crate he's carrying?"

The Frenchman began to tremble—lips, shoulders, knees. But though his mouth moved, no words were forthcoming.

"I saw you and Ral Conrath in the bistro at Libreville," I accused him, "with the Belgian engineers. You were deal-making, weren't you?"

"What do you mean!" Father cried. "The *Belgians*? What kind of deal could you possibly make with those thugs?"

"In that crate," D'Arnot began, his voice pathetic with confession, "is the equipment for surveying. The Belgian engineers, try as they did, could not get past French authorities into the interior. Conrath bragged to them of his surveying skills taught to him by Petrie. So for a very large amount of money, half of which has been paid, he is doing it for them—climbing to the highest point south of the Ogowe and finding a passage through unexplored Gabonese jungle for Leopold's trade route. It is already under way."

"So I've been had not once but *twice* by that lying sack of filth!" Archie roared. "Ah, we'll see about that." He grabbed his rifle and strode out of camp in the direction of the mountains.

I ran after him and caught him up by the arm. "Father, the man is dangerous. We know that. Don't go up there. *Please*."

"And let him get away with . . . what? Murder and butchery, conspiring with a mad king? Whatever it is that you call what he's done to us? I'm going up there and I'm going to wring that low bastard's neck!"

The tensed muscles of Father's arm shuddered and suddenly became flaccid under my hand. Large and powerful as he was, he faltered, if only for the briefest moment. But I had felt it. I came around and looked him in the face. The skin was ashen. There was pain in his eyes. And the other hand was clutching the center of his chest.

"Father!"

"It's all right. It's nothing. A twinge. That's all."

"D'Arnot!" I shouted. "Come here quickly!"

The two of us helped Father back to the fire and sat him on the camp stool. His color had already begun returning. He was smiling, relieved.

"I told you, sweetheart. A tiny twinge. A hiatal hernia."

"One doesn't go grey in the face with a hiatal hernia. You need to rest."

The bearers were about to break down my father's tent. I turned to D'Arnot. "Tell them to stop. Leave the tent up." My jaw clenched in bitter fury. "It's not as if we're going anywhere." Then I said to my father, "Can you stand?"

"Of course I can stand."

"Then come. You're going to your tent to lie down. Don't argue with me. If anything happens to you, Mother will skin me alive. That was the bargain. We were going to take care of each other."

"All right."

Father allowed us to see him to the tent. D'Arnot went in after him to get him out of his clothes.

When the tent flap closed behind them, I grabbed my rifle and followed Ral Conrath up the mountain.

In all my life I had never felt such hatred for another human being. I climbed relentlessly up the steep path, barely awed by the trees in their unimaginable proportions, or the trail strangely wide and even for one so rarely trod upon. All curiosity, all delight in my surroundings had been shattered by this fiend's appalling deceit and betrayal. My father's dreams dashed, perhaps forever. He was unwell, seriously so, despite his protestations. The "bum ticker" was real, waiting only for a terrible blow such as this to irreparably wound it. He could die out here. We could all die if Ral Conrath was not stopped.

I would stop him. I must.

The Mountain

Fury propelled me. As I reached the rim of the flattened cone, the size of the trees normalized, and where before no foliage had grown in the dark clearings beneath the thick, umbrella-like canopy, now smaller trees and bushes and ferns grew in profusion. *Good*, I thought. The easier to hide my approach to Conrath, who was certainly on the eastern slope, gazing out toward the Chaillu Massif, and beyond.

Just as I had envisioned, I found a narrow machete-hacked path through the undergrowth leading out to the east. I cocked my rifle, then very carefully and very quietly moved along the track. There in a newly cut clearing with his surveyor's transit, level, and solar compass was Ral Conrath kneeling and making notations upon a large map. I could see beyond him, through the hacked limbs and twigs, the sky, the jungle spread out like a great green ocean all around the mountain, and far in the distance the peaks of Chaillu Massif.

There was no sign of the bearer.

I waited, still and barely breathing. Watched as Ral carefully folded the map and stowed it inside his bush jacket. When finally he stood, he turned and found himself staring, at close range, down the barrel of my rifle.

"I suppose the Belgians know the way as far as the eastern slopes of the Chaillu range," I said. It pleased me to see I had startled him, though he quickly regained his composure.

"There's only so much they know," he said. "Every time they send an expedition into this damn hellhole of a country, they run into a pack of cannibals and never make it out alive. My employer wants to know if there's a southern route around those mountains out there . . . and the best route from there to the coast."

Ral flashed me such a carefree and rakish grin that I wondered with a thrill of terror if even now the bearer, hidden in the bush, had his weapon aimed at my head. I must hold steady. Show no fear.

"Well, isn't it a shame Leopold won't ever receive his coordinates."

"Won't he?"

"Not if you're rotting in an English prison. Or maybe we'll just turn you over to the French in Libreville. I understand their jail is extremely unpleasant. Hot as hades."

His expression changed not a whit, but I was close enough to see a small muscle beneath his eye begin to twitch.

"I haven't broken any law," he said. "You and your father wanted to go on a dig, and I took you on one. By now Yabi's found the caves his father and he saw all those years ago. I would have delivered you there and you would have dug to your heart's content."

"The fossil you showed us in Cambridge . . ."

Ral shook his head sadly. "Ah, D'Arnot. He's such a spineless creature, isn't he? You must know the leg fragment is genuine. There's no way to prove it didn't come from here. It's my word against a drunken Frenchman's."

"And your Waziri gold?"

"Hell, I don't even know if there is any, other than one damn native's necklace. That's what got me thinking to come out here in the first place. But the deal I cut with Leopold and the Belgians . . . that's *easy* money, and a lot of it. Even if I found the so-called tribe, and even if there was a mine, I'd still have to haul the stuff out through hell." Now he leered at me. "You know my only regret? Not plucking your sweet little cherry when you were hot for me. Though I did have a nice go at your mother. Ah, Samantha . . . I sure made her squeal."

He took a step toward me, the barrel of my rifle only feet from his face. "Give me the gun, Janie." He spoke in his smoothest, most cajoling tones.

"Do you really think I'm that stupid?"

"What are you going to do? Blow my head off? I never took you for the violent type, though you've got a wild streak in you a mile wide. That's what always got me hard." Suddenly he was done talking. Done smiling. "Give me the gun. Now."

I saw the bearer emerge from the thicket into the clearing behind Ral's back, forty degrees and twenty paces from his right shoulder. He was unarmed and oblivious of the turmoil into which he was about to enter.

He was similarly ignorant of the great spotted leopard crouched on a limb above him, poised to spring.

I saw I had a clear shot. It meant losing my perfect sight on Conrath, but there was no time for indecision. I swung the barrel from him and took aim at the beast. It was all the time Conrath needed. He dove, arms and head first at my legs, knocking me off my feet. The gun discharged, firing wildly.

I went down, and the cat leaped upon its prey. As my head struck a rock, I vaguely heard the bearer's shrieks and felt the rifle being wrenched from my hands.

Quickly I stood, but I was dazed, wobbly on my feet. When my vision cleared, there was Ral, the gun pointed at my head. His look was mad, murderous. He didn't speak. He just moved forward, forcing me backward, step by step by step. I could hear faint moaning behind me and, louder, the leopard chewing, sucking, and crunching human muscle, blood, and bone. He was eating the man alive!

Suddenly Conrath's face broke into a smile. In that same moment the sound of the predator's gory feasting ceased altogether. To my surprise and dawning horror, Ral Conrath lowered the rifle, gave me his jaunty fingers-to-the-forehead salute, and sauntered away down the newly cut path.

The force of the massive furred body crashing onto my back flattened me, driving my face into the ground. But it was the searing red pain of deeply pierced flesh that was the last sensation I felt before the green jungle world went blessedly black.

The Tribe

I must find my father."

Tarzan squatted on the forest floor beneath his nest, and I knelt before him holding both his hands, staring deeply into his eyes. I knew I spoke words he did not recognize, but I must make him understand.

I said again, more loudly, "I must find my father." I rose to my feet and pounded my chest. "Jane find . . . find." He watched as I moved to the undergrowth and made the motions of searching frantically for something on the ground. Then I bent and, putting my hand in the brush, came up with a red-and-yellow frog.

"Jane 'find,'" I said.

Tarzan shook his head. "Jane *rok*," he corrected me. Of course, *rok* meant "frog." I was not being clear.

"No." Again I made the exaggerated movements of searching, of reaching down and discovering the frog.

Tarzan nodded his head. "Jane find *rok*."

"Yes, yes! Brilliant man!" I knelt before him and, taking his face in my hands, kissed him joyfully. His eyes gleamed at my sudden gesture. But there was no time to waste. I forced him to attend my words carefully.

"Jane find Father," I said.

"Fah-thah?" Tarzan repeated and made the gesture we had agreed meant "explain."

I smoothed out the dirt between us and, using a single pointed finger, made marks in it—a circle and a line coming down from that. Two lines poking out from the top and two at the bottom—a stick figure. He stared hard at it. Then I made more marks. Two circles on the line just under the head. Teats. Clearly a female. He nodded his understanding. Now I drew another figure next to the first, but this with crude male sexual organs between the two legs. A male. Seeing that he understood, I began again. The figure was much smaller this time.

"*Balu*," Tarzan said.

"*Balu*, child. Yes. Yes, Tarzan." Now I pointed to the small figure. "Jane is *balu*," I said. Then I pointed to the male figure. "Jane's father." I took Tarzan's hands again, pressing them tightly. "Jane find father."

"Jane find fah-thah," he repeated with triumphant understanding.

"Oh, my friend!"

"Tarzan see Jane fah-thah." He spoke and signed this.

"What?" I stared hard at him.

"Tarzan see Jane fah-thah." He swept his arms around him. "In *lul*." *He'd seen my father in water?* "In . . ." Tarzan had no words for what he clearly wished to describe. Instead, he took his finger and made scratches in the sand—many simple huts in a circle around jagged lines—a campfire—and more human stick figures amid the huts.

"You were watching us!" I exclaimed. *He'd seen us when Father had come to me while I bathed in that pool. And in our camp.* "Where is Jane's father?" I poked the male figure I had drawn in the sand with such ferocity that the image was broken. "Where is my father?!"

Tarzan shrugged helplessly and sadly shook his head. I slumped in defeat. Then I felt his hand on my arm. His face was lit with excitement.

"Jane, come see," he said.

Even before I noticed the square golden pendants hanging about the necks of the native tribesmen and -women, I realized they must be Waziri.

Tarzan had carried me on his back through the canopy with great certitude in a single direction that, because of the blocked sky and sun, I could not discern, but within the hour I had spotted several sites below me that I recognized—the small pool where I had bathed (and where Tarzan had secretly watched me bathing), paths I had explored, and finally the clearing under the giant trees where the Porter

Expedition had made its last encampment. Beyond that were the four volcanic peaks.

So, I reckoned, *we had been traveling from west to east.*

Then Tarzan turned sharply south. Within half an hour we had reached a long, towering black basalt ridge that looked to my untrained eye as flow upon flow of ancient lava—the Enduro Escarpment. *Damn thing!* I thought. It existed. Ral Conrath had been such a clever liar, constantly riddling truths with falsehood. How I hated him!

We did not take the escarpment head on, instead staying to the treetops and circling it. Finally Tarzan stopped and untied the vine harness, allowing me to find my footing in the crook of a tree that overlooked an astonishing scene.

At the base of the limestone cliffs we had just rounded stood a large, vibrant village. It was as different from the Mbele's as day was from night. The square mud huts within the square-within-square layout of the great compound were tall and sturdy, their roofs laid down in intricate woven patterns. Though the thatch was fresh, the enclave looked as though it had stood in this place for eons, and the dappled afternoon light filtering through the heavy branches rescued the site from the unremitting shadow of the canopy. Brilliantly plumed sunbirds flitted in the branches above the main aisle, and bright blue dragonflies beating silent wings lent the place a paradisiacal air. The sound of women's laughter and their clear, bold voices seemed to confirm it, and then I saw them, clustered in twos and threes around cook fires— handsome black-skinned women and girls, long legged, swaybacked, and supple—pot-stirring, jostling, and teasing with small pokes or the tug of an ear. Their hair was braided tightly around their heads and they wore, besides their gold pendants, thick gold bracelets on slender, muscular arms. Over their hips and legs they wore short wrapped skirts of red-and-gold-patterned fabric. Their bare bosoms were high and rounded unless the woman was very old. Many held infants on one hip while they cooked, and fed them at their milk-swollen breasts most unselfconsciously.

That was it, I realized. *They are altogether unselfconscious, immersed in natural movement and female conversation, unencumbered with the suffocating rules and manners and protocol of civilization.* But was it presumptuous of me to think so? They would have their own manners and protocols. They were different. That was all.

Men squatted together in small groups talking or milling about a hut several times larger than the rest. They were beautifully proportioned, with sharp-cut musculature and proud posture. But if they were as handsome as their women, it was not easily discernible, for their expressions were so fierce as to be frightening. They looked to be fearsome warriors. *Were they cannibals as well?* I wondered with a sudden chill.

At my side, Tarzan had, too, been observing the village in silence. Then, as was his way, he departed without a word to me, untying a thick vine wrapped twice around a tree limb, and with a loud undulating cry I had never before heard—one I suspected was his announcement of arrival—he swooped in an arc over the village and dropped down, landing with almost balletic grace in the central clearing.

The Waziri responded with moderate surprise. There was a somewhat more admiring welcome from the women, but that so sudden an appearance had provoked no alarm from the bellicose-looking men demonstrated that Tarzan could not be a stranger to them, or a threat.

In that moment I realized that my protector must of course be the legendary "Wild Ape-Man of the Forest." *How could I have not recognized such a thing before now?* But Paul D'Arnot had claimed to have seen the creature at the scene of the elephant kill. Heard him "roaring like a lion." No one had taken Paul seriously. But if it was true, that would mean that Tarzan had been following the expedition from Mbele territory onward. What an extraordinary and unnerving thought!

I watched as Tarzan strode past the women's cook fires, exchanging smiles with them. A small boy came up and hung on his leg as he walked. After a few steps, Tarzan lifted him and, to the child's squealing delight, threw him up in the air and caught him. He put the boy down, and as he continued along the main aisle of the village, all the small groups of males stood and gathered around him as he approached the clutch of villagers standing at the front of the large central hut.

And now two men emerged from it. I could see by the tribesmen's deferential gestures as the pair came forth that they were important men—perhaps the chief and the tribe's charm doctor.

I was too distant to hear the voices, but aside from talking, there were many gesticulations, signaling that Tarzan's grasp of the Waziri tongue might be no greater than it was of English. Clearly he was not unknown to the tribe, and was respected, but he appeared to be an infrequent visitor. The women, who had not left the fires, were straining to see and hear the congress between their men and the ape-man.

Finally the mass of tribesmen parted and out strode Tarzan. He made his way back through the village at the edge of the clearing, and with a running start he leaped with stunning strength and dexterity up into the trees. A few moments later he was by my side.

"Come, Jane," he said, gesturing down to the village.

It was a strange collection of emotions that assailed me. Excitement. Fear. Curiosity. I thought perhaps my recent injuries and invalidism might have sapped a bit of the natural fearlessness I had always possessed, and then I remembered my reticence at climbing on Tarzan's back the first time he had offered it. *Pull yourself together, woman!* I scolded myself. I must be done with all fear and reluctance. This was an adventure that exceeded my dreams and rivaled—no, *outstripped*— Mary Kingsley's expedition up the Ogowe. And besides, if Tarzan had brought me here, then the tribe must know something of my father's whereabouts.

I inhaled and straightened my back, then nodded my agreement to go down and meet the Waziri.

Tarzan and I walked through the village side by side. I had not been scrutinized with such bald-faced stares by so many men since my first day in the Cambridge dissection hall. Up close I could see the raised scarification on their bare shoulders—that same square-within-a-square pattern of the village itself.

Midway to the large hut, Tarzan stopped by one of the cook fires and with the women now coming to gather around said to me, "Jane here." But of course. As much as I wished to be party to any conversation pertinent to myself, I was merely a female in this place. I wondered if this was a tribe that held women as inferior, the way Ral Conrath had spoken of all native peoples. In any case, custom must certainly forbid mixing of the sexes in important palavers. I must simply be patient.

The moment Tarzan went on, I found myself closely surrounded by the Waziri women. They commenced speaking to me in their language in rather more melodic tones than Tarzan used, and they touched me quite uninhibitedly. My hair was of the greatest interest, as it was so different from their own crisp wool that had been braided and wound tightly in concentric circles, its center at the top and back of their heads. What appeared to be a small golden pyramid ornament sat in the center of the "bull's-eye." Multitudes of curious fingers lightly brushed the bare skin of my face and the arm and calf where my injuries had necessitated the jacket sleeve and trouser leg of my safari suit be removed. Some women sniffed at me to detect my scent. Suddenly they were all laughing raucously, but I sensed no maliciousness in it, so that when the whole group, with me in the center, moved like a rugby scrum toward a hut and I was hustled inside, I did not protest.

All but a dozen of the women remained outside the door, leaving me in the care of the matrons. A rough wooden bench was placed behind me and gently I was pushed down to the seat. Suddenly, with fingers working at my limbs and torso, the vine laces were untied and the remnants of my clothing fell away. In a state of total undress before this determined quorum of female strangers I felt unreasonably comfortable and altogether safe. They began, with wet squares of undyed cotton, to scrub every inch of my person. No one had taken a sponge to me since my nana at age eight. I was in sore need of a good bath, and if I was perfectly honest, it was rather pleasant. Something like the queen of Sheba's daily ablutions, I imagined with an inward smile.

Once I was clean and patted dry, gourds filled with palm oil were produced, and the oldest, most wrinkled woman, with long flattened breasts reaching almost to her waist—a "crone," I thought—brought forth a small but finely wrought golden vessel, itself covered with symbols I could not discern. Wafting from it came an intense but gorgeous floral aroma. A few precious drops of this concentrated perfume were mixed into the palm oil, and the women began anointing my skin with it.

Suddenly all ministrations ceased and what I perceived as an argument among the women commenced. I felt my hair being lifted and twirled from several sides. A decision made, they began to braid it. It was a long process and I squirmed at my rigid confinement on the bench. Just as I felt myself growing faint, I was made to stand, like Aphrodite in all her nakedness. A woman came forward holding a length of their textile—the ubiquitous motifs of both concentric circles and concentric squares woven intricately and beautifully into the cloth—and wound it around my hips. By their satisfied expressions they indicated that their guest was fully clothed. I looked down and saw my two breasts in all their unbound glory.

"I'm sorry, ladies," I announced as if to my Cambridge seamstresses, "this will never do." Smiling the whole while, so not to offend, I unwound the length of fabric and held it up before me. The textile was simple but very fine, and it pleased me greatly that this would become my new forest habiliment. I tried tying it around me like a shroud, making sure my bosom and genitalia were fully covered, but the sheath left very little room for the movement of my legs, something that was most essential in my present circumstance. There must be a better way. This time I hung the cloth loosely by a knot at the left shoulder, covering the ugly scar left by the leopard.

All at once there were cries of dismay from the Waziri women. One of them untied it, I thought rather indignantly. But then it was rehung in exactly the same fashion with the knot over my *right* shoulder. By a flurry of gestures, facial expressions, and words that were altogether foreign to me but whose meaning I clearly comprehended, I understood that the scars left by the leopard were anything but ugly. They were to be worn proudly, even venerated.

Part of the slender vine of Tarzan's original creation was used to belt the little dress that covered only the top of my thighs, but I was satisfied that all my female parts were covered and I could move my limbs freely.

Finally a thick gold bracelet was slid above the elbow to my upper arm, and one of the square gold pendants on a leather thong was hung about my neck. Now properly attired, I was led outdoors, where the larger crowd of women had dissipated not in the least. They all nodded their approval at my appearance and many reached out and touched my coiffure. With so much more hair than the Waziri women, I could hardly imagine what the braided creation must look like. *My kingdom for a mirror*, I mused.

Thus I was escorted around the village. I was handed wiggling babies to hold. I wondered if I was meant to give my blessings, so I kissed them all on the top of their foreheads to a chorus of "ahhs" from my companions.

What I saw in the village both delighted and confounded me. There were structures and tools and artifacts that were primitive in the extreme—huts and pottery of mud and stone and thatch, tools and weapons of crude iron—but the patterns on jewelry and textiles, woven into basketry and carved into the sides of the thick-walled houses, were unusually complex and clearly meaningful to the tribe. What could these symbols possibly mean to the Waziri, I wondered, for them to repeat the designs so frequently and in such a variety of ways?

Well, I decided, it would all be revealed in time. I did wish very much to be reunited with Tarzan, but there were yet sights the women wanted me to see.

The tribal garden was indeed a wonder, vast and crowded with every sort of crop, from yams, eggfruit, and sugarcane to plantain, pawpaws, and oil palms. And here were rows of cotton, something that I had been astonished to see growing in a dense forest. But the size of the garden and the industry with which it was being tended was not what startled me most. In the clearing, the massive trees had been cut down, and giant limbs that had hung over the edges had been hacked away, some of them quite recently, so there would be no impediment to full sunlight blanketing the garden rows, allowing for the growth of sun-dependent plants such as cotton. At the edge of the plot was a square-walled hut, quite large, where inside many women sat at looms weaving the raw fiber into cloth.

At the far back of the village, serious industry was under way. All up and down the wall of the Enduro Escarpment men hung from woven rope hammocks chipping away at the basalt, areas where thick veins of gold ran through it. Chunks of the mineral were thrown to the ground and collected by other tribesmen, who carried them to iron cauldrons heated by blazing fires—a primitive smelting operation. This, then, was the source of the Waziri gold.

Back in the village proper with my "ladies-in-waiting," I was drawn forward toward a smaller hut. The women parted for me to enter, and I found myself suddenly in a dim space, faintly lit at the far end with wicks floating in cups of oil. It reeked of old smoke and something vaguely sweet and hoary. The crone took my hand and led me forward to the lighted altar. There through the haze I made out the figure of a seated woman and around her feet other tribeswomen in poses of prostration.

This must be an important wife of the chief, I thought, and following the crone's lead, I knelt before the queenly figure. I made to kiss the right hand resting upon her knee, but when my eyes, having accustomed themselves to the darkness, fell upon the fingers I was about to kiss, I recoiled in mute horror.

The seated woman was a corpse, an unwrapped mummy! I lifted my eyes to see the brown, leathery face and found not a wizened old hag but what had clearly been a beautiful and stately young woman. She was bedecked in beads and gold and feathers and, from the look and smell of her, appeared to have been embalmed by a process of smoking.

I longed to know why this female was so venerated to be so carefully preserved and set out for worship. Would Tarzan know? Or would I ever learn the Waziri tongue well enough to find the answer? I steeled myself, kissed the hand, and withdrew, allowing those who had followed me in to pay homage to the cadaver.

By the time my escort and I had come out, the sun had begun setting, and the dappled light gave way to darkness illuminated by a single massive bonfire in the middle of the central clearing.

On the ground, large banana leaves had been laid out in a huge circle around the fire, and upon this table food had been set out, from the look of it a veritable feast. Tribesmen, -women, and children were all taking their places around this tribal groaning board, and to my relief I saw that Tarzan was already seated. He looked as odd and uncomfortable here as he might have at my mother's polished mahogany dining room table. Next to him on his left was the man I guessed was the charm doctor, now bedecked with an awe-inspiring headdress of scarlet feathers, ones I suspected had been plucked from the tails of hapless parrots like my guardian, Mr. Grey. Next to the wizard was an empty space, and beside that sat the chief—himself a sight in a leopard skin hat topped by a gold circlet that could be nothing less than an antiquated crown.

I was deposited at what I supposed was a place of honor, and I took my seat of pounded and beautifully painted bark cloth, mimicking a cross-legged pose that everyone else naturally assumed. Because of the charm doctor's placement beside me, I was unable to speak to or even see Tarzan. But the dinner partner between us now turned his eyes on me.

"Ulu," he said, thumping his breastbone above his gold amulet. He opened his palm toward me, and without the slightest change in his menacing expression intoned, "Jane." Tarzan, I realized, had begun communication with the Waziri headmen on my behalf. Oh, how desperately I wished for intelligence of my father!

I thought it somewhat unwise to smile, so I simply repeated his name. "Ulu." *Doctor Ulu*, I thought and wished the physicians at Cambridge Medical College could see their Gabonese counterpart.

"Jane," I heard from the other side and turned. "*Shango* Waziri," my other dinner partner said. Shango *must mean* "chief," I thought.

"*Shango* Waziri," I repeated, with what I hoped was appropriate gravitas.

Suddenly he pointed to the leopard skin under his crown and then placed his hand over the quartet of healed gashes on my shoulder. He held my eyes and nodded somberly, acknowledging, as the women had, my most honorable scars.

Neither man had smiled, but I suddenly felt that their fierceness was benign, and knew I was not sitting amid a tribe of cannibals.

Now Chief Waziri and Ulu the charm doctor lifted metal bowls of liquid, urging Tarzan and me to do the same. Ulu raised his voice in a speech unintelligible to me, but the sentiment was altogether clear. With a nod to either side of him, he acknowledged his honored guests and after a great cry of "*Napesi bolinga nzambe mokola!*" the assembled drank.

I sipped from my bowl. Palm wine. I had tasted a more refined version on *La Belle Fille*. It was a strong intoxicant, so I had better measure my consumption of it. The congregated began to pass the heaping plates of food. While alien in its spicing, it was delicious. I noticed that around the table, many pairs of Waziri—a man and a woman—were sharing food off a single leaf dish. I leaned forward as if to reach for a dish of yam and turned in order to see what Tarzan was eating. His cup of palm wine did not appear to have been touched.

I caught but a brief glimpse of his face as he stared down at his banana leaf plate piled with steamed fish, monkey stew, and grilled lizards on sticks, and saw that he was perhaps more flummoxed than I was. Could this be the first time he had sat down to a meal with the Wiziri? The first time he had been confronted by cooked food?

He caught my eye, and I quickly took up a piece of meat and popped it in my mouth, chewing ardently. I wished to say, "*Tarzan, popo koho dako-za*," Tarzan, eat this hot meat, but felt that good manners prevented me from speaking over the charm doctor's plate.

It seemed the feasting went on for an eternity, but I, to my surprise, found that I was famished and partook of bits of everything I was offered. Tarzan's seeds and nuts and flowers and ferns had been most appreciated, but there was something comforting even in so outrageous a dining room as this, with such exotic dinner companions, to be eating food that tasted like *food*.

And then all at once the drumming began.

In all my life I had never heard such a sound or, more rightly, *felt* one. The booming was loud and deep and sonorous, and it throbbed disturbingly in the pit of my gut. Across the clearing, my eyes found the drummer and the drum itself. It was monstrously large, the entire base of a hollowed-out tree stump, the skin-covered ends of the drumsticks the size of an infant's head. I had barely accustomed myself to the hedonic thumping when a great cacophony of smaller drums rent the night with frenzied clattering and pounding.

All at once the Waziri men stood in their places and, leaping across the banana leaf table, began to dance around the fire. Incomprehensible was the sight! A hundred native men, naked but for their feathers and skins, with jumps and gyrations and stamping feet thrust their shoulders to one beat, their chests to another, and their hips to a third, never losing the beat. Their dark bodies—now taut, now rippling—glistened in the flickering flames, and the faces I had once thought fierce now contorted with frightening sensuality. On a silent cue, Chief Waziri leaped into the fray and commenced a dance more rousing and convulsive than the others. Ulu, the charm doctor, joined him, but before beginning his own dance, he threw a gourd full of dried tobacco leaves into the fire, sending up a cloud of pungent smoke that, from the expressions of approval on the Waziri faces, was a most welcome addition to the festivities.

I must remain calm, I thought, though my pulse was beginning to race—if I was not imagining it—to the rhythm of the drumming. Impossibly, the thunderous pounding quickened. The leaping and whirling grew wildly ribald. My head swam. My body was afire and suddenly I felt the urge to move, even in my place, to sway, to undulate, to lose myself in the throbbing heat and thunder of the dance. *Restrain yourself!* I thought. I dared not turn my head and meet Tarzan's eyes. I was fixed on the blistering performance before me. Altogether paralyzed.

And all at once it stopped.

The drumming and revelry. The men receded from the circle to stand behind the leaf table, the night silent but for the sharp crackle of the fire. But the silence was short-lived, for now the drumming recommenced and the women—young and old alike—stepped delicately into the circle . . . and they began to move.

So different from the men were they, with bent bodies, crooked knees, and small shuffling steps. Swiveling and snaking, the women rose and fell with mild expressions and utter reserve. Some bore small children on their backs, and the little Waziri moved their heads and limbs in perfect syncopation with the drums.

I felt my composure returning. I chanced a look at Tarzan and found him staring unabashedly at me, his eyes gleaming, his bold, handsome features set in shadowy relief by the firelight. I found I could not draw my gaze away from his, but then the drumming stopped again and the women joined the men outside the circular table. All were perfectly silent. Riveted with avid expectation.

I anticipated more drumming, but there was none. Just absolute stillness. Cessation of the revelry. Nothing but the night and the flames and the soft sounds of the forest beyond the village.

Now on cat's feet, a single young tribesman padded into the circle before Tarzan and me. He was painted with stripes of white and ocher on all his limbs. He wore thick golden anklets, a necklace of long white fangs, and a lion skin pelt at his loins. He was joined then by a nubile girl, perhaps sixteen. Her bare breasts were small and tilted upward, her waist slender, and long legs shapely. She was clothed in a lion skin skirt and her ornaments were simply a golden bracelet and a necklace of dark claws.

They took their places standing face-to-face and locked eyes for what seemed to me an eternity. Then, without cue or the sounding of the drums, they began to move. It was at once apparent that the rhythm of drums was deep inside the couple. The dance itself—its raw thrusts and grinds, its quivers and shakes—was utterly profane. Where I had felt heat and pounding at my center, now I believed I was drunk. *The palm wine—I had had too much.* My head swam as I feasted my eyes on the exuberant, blistering passion that spanned the space between them, an invisible current connecting the pair altogether abandoned to this voluptuous public coupling. Their shaking quickened, their bodies nearly touching, never touching. Thrusts insanely carnal.

And then the drums began! Pounding out a swell of sound to match the movement. Louder and louder! Faster and faster! Arms and legs a blur. Sweat glistening. Shouts and groans. The dancers' arms reached out, finally touching. A frenzied climax. Clutching rigid forearms, their eyes mad.

They stopped. Panting, their faces streaming, the couple broke out in smiles. The spell was broken.

I was unsure what next to do. I did become aware that the circle of Waziri behind the leaf table had strangely thinned. When I dared turn my head and look, I saw that pairs of men and women were quietly peeling away, disappearing into the dark of the village.

I felt a hand on my shoulder. Two women who had bathed and dressed me helped me stand. Inebriated still—with the wine or the shocking spectacle I had just witnessed—I allowed myself to be led from the fire to a hut bordering the main clearing. The light was dim inside, but there squatting on the earthen floor was Tarzan.

When he saw me, he stood. Even in the dim light I could see he was taut, straining, as a stallion set to be loosed upon a fertile mare. *I was dreaming. Intoxicated. Outside of myself.* He took a step closer and I felt the heat pulsing from his body in waves so strong I staggered backward. He caught hold of my shoulders, fixed me in his gaze.

There is no tenderness there, I thought with sudden clarity, *only savage, quenchless desire.* There in my thin native shift, holding in my power this magnificent primal man, I trembled with my own wanton appetites. I reached out slowly and laid my palm to his breast. It was warm stone against my skin, and all at once I knew the depth and breadth of Tarzan's staggering strength.

I took a single step forward. It was all he needed. His arms clamped around me and he pulled me in. I raised my lips to be kissed, but he buried his face in the soft of my neck. Spikes of fire weakened my knees and I faltered. He caught me, lifted me, and laid me down on a blanketed floor bed. Knees on either side of me, he pinioning my two hands behind my shoulders.

Here was a ravenous beast. Nothing left of my nurse or gentle protector. This greedy creature was set to devour me, and I wished with all my might that he should. He plunged, his mouth suckling my breasts through the cotton shift. I moaned and writhed, ecstatic with pleasure. My hips arched toward his and I struggled to free my hands, for I yearned to touch him, feel his burning skin, pull him down, down onto me, into me . . .

Then I heard it. Heard the earth roaring, like thunder coming closer, closer. Heard it before I felt the movement beneath my back. The ground was quaking! I quieted under him. Now the hut's mud walls and the central pole began to jerk and shudder. Small creatures fell from the thatch onto us. He leaped from the bed, lifted me in his arms, and hurtled out the door.

Villagers were pouring into the central clearing, now lit only by the dying embers of the bonfire. I clung to Tarzan, trembling. Small children wailed. We heard spoken around us a single word, again and again, whispered in tones of fear and reverence—"Sumbula . . ."

Chief Waziri appeared, surrounded by his several wives, and spoke in soothing tones to the rattled villagers. Then Ulu, bald without his feathered headdress, frowning and somber, strode out among them. All were silent as he raised a great rattle above his head and shaking it in an easterly direction began to sing in words that made the people tremble and huddle close to one another. He sang till the earth stopped its tremors. Sang till the last embers died and the clearing was pitched into utter blackness.

"Sumbula," intoned an old woman clutching her neck charm.

"Sumbula," I heard as the Waziri melted away into the night.

"Sumbula," I whispered.

Tarzan clutched me to him, but the fire had left my body, as it had his. Feeling his way in the dark, he led me to our hut, but we did not enter. We sat on the earth shoulder-to-shoulder, our backs against the mud wall. After a time I slept, my head upon Tarzan's shoulder, but he sat silent vigil till the sun showed its first faint light through the Waziri village trees.

The quake had brought me to my senses. I'd have had to have been drunk on palm oil wine or unnaturally aroused by the frenzied dancing to be so intoxicated as to lose all inhibitions as I had. Perhaps it had been the lewd details of Cecily Fournier's escapades in France that had ignited my passions. Yet this morning I felt no mortification in Tarzan's presence. I'd made my change of heart very clear once I had awoken sitting on the hard ground outside the hut. And his even-temperedness at the rejection after so tempestuous a seduction did nothing but improve my regard for his character.

I must stop at once any thought of a romance with Tarzan. It was simply absurd. He had taken me to the Waziri village with the intention of learning news of Father's whereabouts and the Porter Expedition. And what of Ral Conrath?

The village women had pressed ground banana meal cakes on us just after the sun rose. Chief Waziri and Ulu were overseeing the clearing of rubble from a collapsed portion of the men's house, and so Tarzan and I left quietly on foot. To my surprise, we continued to head east.

Not far out of the village I stopped him. Looking him straight in the eye this morning, I found, was more difficult than I had at first supposed it would be. His gaze was soft and affectionate and, I thought, a bit amused. But there was business to be accomplished, and I wasted no time.

"I must find my father," I reminded Tarzan and gestured back toward the village as if to ask what he had learned there.

He nodded, then looked at the ground. He walked away from me, still looking down. I followed, becoming annoyed. But then he squatted and beckoned for me to join him. He had found a patch of soft earth and was smoothing it with the palm of his hand. He was creating a clean slate for us to "talk," and began by signaling that the Waziri had indeed seen much. I knelt beside him.

He first drew the stick figure of a female, clearly myself. Next to this was a figure with male genitals that was connected by a single line at the chest to me. This Tarzan named "Jane fah-thah." A second male he drew he pronounced "sord." It meant "bad." This had to be Ral Conrath. *Fascinating how clearly his evil nature showed itself,* I thought. I could see Tarzan's mind working before he put his finger in the dirt again. The next figure lacked breasts, but neither did it have male genitals. Tarzan had begun to make small squares around the four figures—the Porter encampment, I surmised—when I realized the third male must be D'Arnot: a weak man with no testicles.

Concentrating deeply, Tarzan drew to one side of the camp four large triangles together. This had to be the range of mountains to the east at the base of which we now were located. Outside the camp he drew a fourth man. Yabi, I thought. Now using his drawings, hand signals, and the words we knew between us, Tarzan explained what the Waziri had seen happen in our camp.

After Yabi had left, Ral had climbed the largest of the mountains. "Sumbula," Tarzan declared, placing his finger on the peak.

"This is Sumbula?" I asked. It was the single Waziri word Ral had insisted D'Arnot should have knowledge of and was furious when the Frenchman declared his ignorance of it. In the Waziri mind it was also in some way yoked to last night's earthquake.

Pointing alternately to the figures of Ral and Sumbula Tarzan repeated "sord" several times. Ral and Sumbula were both somehow bad. Then indicating my father, Tarzan pantomimed what could only be illness. I felt my eyes beginning to sting, remembering that terrible moment when I realized his heart might be failing.

According to the Waziri telling, and true to the facts as I knew them, Archie had gone in the tent. The weak man, D'Arnot, had followed.

Tarzan gave me a look I could not wholly read. I wondered if this man experienced astonishment, for when he said, "Jane go Sumbula," I was sure his expression was one of amazement.

"Yes, I did go up Sumbula." My heart was beginning to pound, remembering the awfulness of that day. How my life had forever changed the morning I followed Ral Conrath up the mountain.

"Jane Sumbula *sord*," Tarzan said, looking grim.

I thought hard. This story was being told through Waziri eyes. They had known Ral to be a bad man. They saw Sumbula as somehow bad. And I, ascending Sumbula, was *sord* as well. I waited for the next piece of the puzzle to be revealed.

But now Tarzan was showing Ral descending the mountain.

"Wait," I said, stilling his hand. "On Sumbula"—I touched my two eyes—"what did the Waziri see?"

Tarzan shook his head violently. "Waziri no go Sumbula. No Sumbula!"

Ah, I reasoned, *Sumbula must be taboo to the Waziri.* If they would not climb the mountain, they could not have seen what happened. But never mind. I knew very well what had occurred up there.

"Tarzan," I said, pointing to the story drawn on the ground, "where are *you?* Where is Tarzan?"

"Jane here," he answered unflinchingly and pointed to the peak of the mountain. "Tarzan here." He pounded the very same spot with his finger. Then he held my eyes and I felt warmth between my thighs. My face grew red remembering the previous night. Now I was sure—Tarzan had indeed been following me since the Mbele elephant hunt. He had followed me up Sumbula, despite the Waziri taboo. And now I understood by the passion with which he spoke the last simple phrase that he meant to be with me always. *Jane here. Tarzan here.*

"Good. Go on," I said, forcing myself to calm. "The *sord* man comes down Sumbula."

"Jane no come Sumbula."

I nodded. Here was the business I had been waiting to know. Had been terrified to learn.

"Jane fah-thah," Tarzan began and then with clenched fist screwed up his face in a fierce grimace, widening his eyes and clenching his jaws.

"Oh!" I cried. "He was angry. My father was angry with the *sord* man." I clutched Tarzan's arm with the greatest relief. *Archie was not dead!*

"*Sord* man, fah-thah . . ." He gave me a short shove with both hands.

"They scuffled. More, tell me more!"

"Jane fah-thah an-gree. Jane fah-thah go Sumbula."

"Oh, no! He climbed the mountain?" I clutched unconsciously at my own heart. "Where is my father?" I was shouting. "Where is my father?!"

Tarzan grew quiet. He looked pained and confused, frustrated without the words he needed. Finally, he wiped the dirt slate clean and drew two male figures standing a distance apart, a line connecting their shoulders, and a horizontal male figure floating above the ground between them. "Go," Tarzan said. "Jane fah-thah go."

I stared at the drawing. *They'd carried him away! In a hammock suspended on a pole! He must have collapsed. He must have been very ill.*

Then slowly, with a look of the greatest sadness, Tarzan traced with his finger an oblong box around the figure of Archie Porter.

"No! *No!* No, oh please no . . ." I folded over my knees and began to wail. The sound filled the trees and caused the creatures of Eden to answer with their own howls and lamentations. I felt the touch of Tarzan's gentle palm on my back, but there was nothing, nothing on the face of the earth, that could assuage the agony of this loss.

I sobbed and keened and whimpered like a little girl. I wept until I was empty, drained of all feeling, hard and hollow as a newly forged bell. When finally thoughts returned, sly creeping things, seeking the darkest corners of my mind, I knew at once that I had been wrong. Very wrong.

There *was* something that could be done to quench the fire that had gutted me. To temper the fury that racked my soul. There might be no civilized laws to bring suit against him. No prisons to hold him. No powers to seek redress of his unconscionable acts. But Ral Conrath was not invisible. And he believed me dead. When I returned to my world, I would find him. Find him and avenge the betrayal of my family. So I must be strong and I must be patient. I must bide my time in this forest. Cool my passions. Formulate my plans. My immediate future was more than uncertain. But the villain's greed would devour him in the end. Of this I was certain.

I lifted my head and saw Tarzan's steady gaze upon me, and I breathed the first painless breath in a long while. My beloved father was lost, but here before me was a true and trusted friend.

I reached out my hand and he lifted me up. I saw eagerness in his face. Some wordless purpose. And suddenly I found that I wished more than anything to know Tarzan's mind.

"Come," he said, and together we climbed Sumbula.

Mothers and Fathers

Now I followed Tarzan up the mountain path to the site of my near demise. With news of death below me, I had no desire to visit its memory above me, but Tarzan was oddly determined to ascend. I had asked him to explain his urgency, but he'd just gestured his frustration. Many times he had no words to make his thoughts clear.

Patience, I reminded myself. I thought that perhaps a lack of it might become my great nemesis here in the forest while, conversely, assimilation and education my greatest desire. Was this place not like Cambridge, a college of sorts? The University of Nature. And Tarzan my professor of all subjects.

Even in the depths of my mourning, I was forced to smile.

He had wanted to carry me on his back up the trail, but I had insisted upon walking, for some of the time at least, to trudge up the incline on my own steam. Tarzan was unnaturally strong, but he was, after all, human, and there were limits to his capabilities. The trees here were so enormous, the circumference of their limbs so large, and the distance between them so great, they made brachiation impossible. He signaled that if he took me high enough into the branches he could run along them with me on his back as we had done in Eden. But I wished to begin the recovery of my strength at once. I knew this would test me severely, and I wondered, as my thighs burned and my breath became short and labored, if I was up to the task.

Well, I *must* be up to it. That was all there was to it.

It had been a long and arduous climb, but finally we arrived at the site of the incident—the clearing Ral had hacked away to make room for his surveying equipment, all of it askew on the ground. But there—I could hardly bear to lay eyes on it—was evidence of the most terrifying violence imaginable. The picked-clean bones of the porter were already bleaching in the sun. The leopard's corpse, the great beast that had very nearly killed me, was sprawled not ten feet away. With its thick spotted hide, it had weathered the scavengers and the elements far better than its human counterpart had done. Only with the sight of it did the vision come clear to me what Tarzan must have risked to save my life—the Bowie sunk to its hilt in the man-eater's flesh, its snarling fury, writhing and clawing, its great jaws snapping at Tarzan's face. He would have seen the mad eyes, long bloodied fangs. Smelled the hot, rank breath. Felt its razor claws inflicting tears in his skin.

But what had driven him to risk life and limb for a stranger, an interloper in his world?

A thought came to me. I asked him in words and signs. *Did you see me and the bad white-skin here?* Tarzan nodded yes. So he had witnessed my angry confrontation with Ral Conrath. *Did the bad white-skin see you?* Tarzan shrugged at that.

"Sord tar-zan," he began. "*Goro hota bomba et-nala!*" I did not know the words, but by the ferocious look twisting his features and his harsh gesture down the path we had just come from, I knew he meant "he left you here to die!"

Tarzan picked up the tripod and gazed questioningly at it. "Why *sord tar-zan* come here?" he asked.

I was rendered silent. *How on earth could I explain the Belgians? Their greed and cruelty. A trade route through Eden?*

"Many *sord tar-zans* come here," was the best I could manage.

"Men-nee?"

I was lost for words, exhausted by the climb and agonized by the loss of my father. I conceded defeat. An explanation of Leopold's legions would have to wait.

Now Tarzan strode purposefully to the big cat's remains and knelt down beside it. He laid his hands upon the leopard's skull and was still for a long moment, softly muttering words I imagined were a prayer of sorts. Then he lifted the heavy back pelt—dark gold with round black rosettes—rotted through with numerous holes, and threw it aside. The belly skin had disappeared altogether, certainly consumed by armies of ants and microbes that lived in the rich soil.

The leopard's skeleton was now revealed, and I found myself

drawn to it, as I had been drawn to my first human cadaver. I knelt at Tarzan's side. He looked searchingly at me, but I was too curious at what lay below to attempt communication. I feasted my eyes on the long body and shortish legs, the massive skull with its pointed occiput and four great fangs. I touched one of the large flaring scapulas and moved a hind leg bone in its socket through its range of motion. The segmented tail, too, held me fascinated. But Tarzan had come with a purpose and, finally losing patience with my examination, grasped the spinal column and tossed the clattering skeleton away. Then he began raking through the dirt beneath the carcass. With a satisfied grunt he picked out of the soil an object that fit easily in the palm of his hand. He brushed it off and rubbed it on his loincloth. Then he held it up in front of me. The sight of so common an item in so uncommon a setting stunned me.

It was a large gold locket, a perfect oval, worked with fine filigree, hanging from a broken gold chain. This could belong only to Tarzan. He'd known exactly where to look. Clearly, the bauble meant much to him, and he had lost it as he'd been saving my life.

Now he was dangling it before me, insisting that I take it. This I did and examined the thing more closely. It was beautifully made, as was the thick chain, and by the weight of them felt like solid gold. It was an expensive piece. I continued cleaning the locket with the short skirt of my cotton garment. Soon it was gleaming in the sun.

"This is a locket," I said, pointing to it.

Tarzan parroted me. Once he had learned a word and spoken it one time, it never needed repeating.

"It is pretty." I had never attempted teaching him an adjective before. Making an expansive gesture with my hands, I said "vando," his word for "good." But this was an imperfect description. I saw a white flower entwined in a nearby bush and, pointing, said "pretty." A red-and-black insect fluttering past I called by the same word. But this, too, was confusing, for the word for "flower" was osha and the insect zut-tat. Tarzan, I could see, was listening intently, concentrating deeply.

"Pretty," I said again and ran my hand slowly across the least chewed portion of the discarded leopard skin. Then suddenly, as if one of Mr. Edison's electric lightbulbs had been switched on, understanding flared in Tarzan's eyes.

"Prit-tee," he said and touched the flower in the bush. "Prit-tee," he repeated, pointing to a red-and-yellow sunbird that had lit on a branch nearby.

I smiled broadly at the success.

Then he reached out impulsively and touched my cheek. "Prit-tee," he said.

I swallowed hard.

"Yes. Good." Happily taken aback and a bit flustered, I began fussing with the locket. Its clasp was sticky, and I was relieved to have something upon which to redirect my attention from Tarzan's unexpected praise. It took a good bit of fiddling with my fingernail to pop open the latch. But when I looked down at the tiny photographs in their oval frames, I felt my jaw drop.

On the right was the portrait of a lovely young woman stylishly coiffed and dressed in the fashion of twenty years previous. On the left was a fine gentleman in a starched collar and frock coat, his gleaming black hair short and parted in the middle.

Good Lord, I was staring at an image of Tarzan! I looked back and forth between the two, just to be certain.

There was no explanation save one. The man was his father and the woman his mother. I looked up and found Tarzan puzzling over the locket, but it was not the photographs that held him rapt. It was the latch. He took the necklace from me and, ignoring its contents, began opening and shutting it again and again. It occurred to me that the young man had no idea that the locket owned such capabilities, and that he had never before seen the inside of it.

Gently I took it back from him, spread the two halves wide, and held it before him. Finally he took notice of the pictures. He squinted at them with first a blank stare and then utter bewilderment.

I hesitated, unsure if I should speak the next words. *But how could I not?* I pointed to the man in the locket.

"This is Tarzan's father."

He shook his head. "No Tarzan fah-thah."

I must not be making myself clear, I thought. I touched the photograph now, then reached out and touched Tarzan's cheek. He looked perplexed.

"Tarzan prit-tee?"

"No, no," I said, frustrated that I could not express just now that, indeed, Tarzan was pretty—the handsomest man I had ever laid eyes on. I resorted to the method of communication with which we had had the greatest success. I cleared away some grasses and created a dirt slate. I drew stick figures of myself and my father, connected by a line through our chests.

"Jane. Jane's father," I said, pointing to the figures. Then, wiping them away, I drew another male figure and laid the locket next to it, connecting the two with a line. "Tarzan. Tarzan's father."

Still he resisted with a furious shake of the head. I must try another tack. I drew a female with breasts and a tiny male figure next to it. I named the *balu* Tarzan, then questioned what the female figure was called.

He answered quickly. "Kala."

Good, I thought. Kala *meant "mother."*

I pointed to the female figure in the dirt. "Tarzan's mother?" I questioned.

He nodded and uttered, "Tarzan muh-thah."

Now I set the locket over the top of the stick figure and, pointing to the woman in the golden oval, proclaimed, "Tarzan's mother."

He shook his head violently. "No! Kala Tarzan muh-thah."

Now it was I who was filled with confusion. *Why was he not understanding? Why did he not recognize the couple in the locket as his parents? And who was Kala?*

All at once he stood and, as was his way with coming and going, disappeared into the bush.

My mystification was growing. *Who was this man? What was his parentage, and how had he evolved into this brilliant and untamed adventurer of the forest?*

In the next moment Tarzan returned with a section of tough vine and from it peeled a single long fiber. He picked up the locket, snapped it closed, and ripped the broken chain from the necklace, tossing it away. Carefully he replaced the chain with the vegetal cord. Then he reached out and tied it around my neck atop the Waziri ornament.

"Jane prit-tee lok-it." He stared hard at me. I was, I supposed, as enigmatic a being to him as he was to me. And by the look in his steel-grey eyes, he was bound and determined to learn the deepest secrets of my heart.

To the West

It was less than a single day's travel, yet I felt it as a lifetime. Except for thoughts of my father and raw bolts of fury directed at Ral Conrath, I was feeling myself again. Tarzan had become a man possessed. He knew his direction and destination, and while he did not overwork me, mostly we traveled.

He called to a brown-furred monkey sitting in a tree fork feasting messily on juicy pawpaw, who called back in the same voice. He showed me a flower of insane beauty and appalling stench, and an insect that looked like a twig walking on legs. There was a puffing steam vent and the riot of colorful lichen that grew all around it. At first I hung on to Tarzan as though my life depended on it. I took my first independent steps among the webwork of trees high above the forest floor, but they were tentative. Tarzan, of course, could run fleet-footed along those limbs. I was reminded of my hunting dogs, a rich scent ahead of them, their legs seeming to move before their brains. They were always changing direction, backtracking, surging ahead, stopping occasionally to ponder an obstacle, but never for long.

Tarzan—a human animal—was a fine specimen of *Homo sapiens sapiens*.

Of course I had known, intellectually, that the human species was nothing more than the most highly evolved creature of the animal kingdom, remarkable for its self-awareness and imperative toward culture, language, and philosophy—none of which were to be found in other species. But the base animal quality of humans was almost always avoided in my world. Not a decade before, the merest glimpse of a woman's ankle, even one that was heavily stockinged, was thought altogether scandalous. Even piano and furniture legs were considered unseemly and swathed in brocaded draperies and fringe. Now here I was, moving barefooted, bare-ankled, and bare-legged along the limbs of an African forest canopy with a nearly naked man.

Indeed, following behind Tarzan I was acutely aware of how very little of him was covered by his loincloth. His genitalia were hidden by what was little more than a ragged flap of soft hide, a fact for which I was alternately grateful and mildly frustrated. I wondered why, when his buttocks were quite exposed, he chose to hide his male parts. I remembered the sorry, shriveled bits on my Cambridge cadaver and was certain that my admirer's would be a sight prettier than that. I had only once seen a naked boy—in the River Cam—or, to be more precise, when he'd been pulled out after a harrowing rescue. He'd fallen into the flood-swollen stream, and his clothes had been torn clean off him by the rushing water. I, watching as he'd been dragged onto shore barely alive, had not been able to take my eyes off those fascinating fleshy parts before a blanket had been thrown around him. As an only child—and a girl—I had never had the opportunity to observe young male bodies. Now I could feast my eyes on what I imagined was a perfect specimen of manhood.

Tarzan's back was a masterpiece of musculature. Under the slightly tanned skin rippled and bulged two mighty triangular trapezii, massive latissimi dorsi running from armpit to waist, a spinal column sunk within a deep canal and bordered on either side by a column of little erector spinae and intertransversarii muscles connecting one vertebra to another. The proud, well-formed head sat atop a powerful neck with its two brilliantly defined sternocliedomastoid muscles, providing maximum flexibility and strength.

I could not decide whether I was more fascinated by Tarzan's arms and hands or his buttocks. The forearms were nearly as large as the upper arms, with the most massive wrists I had ever seen on a human being—even the masons who worked on the manor's stonework. His hands themselves were living machines that allowed him feats of unbelievable strength yet were capable of the most extreme dexterity and tenderness. The thought of those hands moving over my body in the Waziri hut made me suddenly weak and giddy, and I admonished myself to concentrate lest I lose my footing and fall to my demise.

A moment later, however, I found myself contemplating Tarzan's thighs. They were meaty and well formed, with a quality that hardened them to steel when in use and softened them when at rest. The feet, and his toes in particular, could curl around a limb and grip with astonishing tensile power. But the man's arse, I thought, was one of the Seven Wonders of the Natural World . . .

Well, honestly, I must stop these licentious observations! I could tell myself all day long I was studying his magnificent physique "in the name of science," but that was blatant self-deception, and I was mortified by my prurient motivations.

For the next little while I lost myself in the challenge of this remarkable passage through the trees. But soon enough my concentration was broken by the sight of the astonishing body ahead of me. Tarzan brachiated through the tangle of vines and branches and liana with the ease of an ape, but more impressive still—and terrifying to watch—were his leaps across chasms with no hand- or footholds at all. He was flying though the canopy with the grace and confidence of a bird. I wondered if he knew how frightened I was every time he defied gravity that way. He would set his sight on a distant tree crotch or limb, leaping upon the vine that would begin the great arcing flight. Then his hands would release their hold, he surrendering himself to his confident calculations, *soaring free*, and always landing with graceful precision on his target.

I really must concentrate on my footing, I thought. *Really.*

Though I was aware we were traveling west, back the way we had come, it took me by surprise to recognize the fig tree that cradled Tarzan's nest among the other green behemoths of the forest, but we passed it from a distance, never bothering to stop there. I thought to ask Tarzan why we would not be pausing at his home before continuing west, but then it occurred to me that all of this forest was his home. His *kingdom*. How at ease he was in every way. It reminded me of watching my mother in the flower garden in front of the manor or moving through the house from room to room, making sure every painting, every chair, the fold of every upholstery skirt was in place, beds made precisely the way she expected them to be done.

My mother is a widow, I suddenly thought, *and believes she has lost her only child.* I did not like to think of Mother with pity, but she was most certainly in a piteous state. In another way, though, as I contemplated my own position now—engaged in the greatest adventure of my life—I realized the part that my mother had played in this strange and wonderful destiny. For so long she had represented all that was repressive about my existence. The strictures to which I was constantly forced to adhere. The social conventions that ordered so much of my world. I had come to believe my mother was my enemy— everything that the daughter wished desperately to avoid emulating in a woman. But now I could see I had been viewing her quite superficially. Every annoyance, every burst of rebellion had been a reflex on my part, like the knee jerk that happened when a nerve on the lower patella was knocked with a doctor's mallet. But suddenly I could see that Samantha Edlington had had to rebel against her own parents in order to marry an American commoner, even one with a medical degree and a good head on his shoulders. She had been destined for marriage with a peer of the English realm, one who would have enhanced the Edlington wealth and influence, and carried on the bloodlines of the British aristocracy. Instead she fell madly for Archie Porter, her own sort of "wild man," and married for love, an altogether untoward state of affairs for a girl of her station.

Without my mother's initial courage and rebellion against tradition, I realized, there would have been no progressive father to insist upon educating his daughter at Cambridge University, no assisting him in his home laboratory, no expedition to Africa for a twenty-year-old English girl who had been allowed to avoid any unwanted marriages till nearly the age of spinsterhood. I would not now be following on the heels of a large, handsome, feral creature who could swing through the vines and liana with the grace of an ape, who could speak in the voices of wild animals, and who knew of Bowie knives and the tender way a human mother checked her child's forehead for fever. Silently, I thanked my mother and blessed her. I promised myself that as soon as I was able, I would make my way back to England to inform Mother that she had not lost her daughter as well as her husband, and to properly mourn Father's death.

But just now Tarzan had paused in his forward motion through the canopy. He turned back to me with palm outward. Stop. Quiet. Look. Just below us was a family of lowland gorillas, peaceably feeding on vegetation. Some dozed in the branches. Tarzan and I, while I had been daydreaming of my mother and father, had been descending, so that the ground was within sight. Here I observed juvenile apes playing on the forest floor, smaller females lazily grooming a formidable silverback male.

With no warning to me, Tarzan hooted out a greeting to the little colony of gorillas. Nearly every one of them looked up into the branches above and Tarzan was spotted. I was farther back and hidden from their view. There was no alarm in the animals, though several hooted back. One youngster, half the size of the females, set up a screech and instantly began climbing through the branches in our direction. Though it was small for a gorilla, I felt a thrill of fear shudder through my body, for it was quite as large as I was. And who knew how strong? Tarzan's arms were outstretched when the beast leaped at him. He was nearly bowled over by the furred missile, but a moment later they were wrestling playfully as two friends might do. The play ceased abruptly when the young ape caught sight of the strange white-skinned female partially hidden in the foliage. With Tarzan leading along the thick limb, the pair of them came toward me. I hardly breathed.

Tarzan pulled me from my hiding place and quickly put both arms around me, a signal to the gorilla that this was no one to fear. Then he leaped to a nearby branch, allowing the gorilla to view me more, and I sensed above all a shy quality in the youngster. I had never seen a living ape in such close proximity. The London zoo had several sad specimens in cages, and I'd had occasion to view, in my father's collection of comparative anatomy, body parts of the species. But here was a living, breathing, and quite curious western lowland gorilla inching toward me and reaching out one of its long arms in my direction. I looked to Tarzan for guidance in behavior, but his face was passive, unalarmed. It reminded me very much of my father's expression when he had introduced me to a new wonder of nature from his pantry, one that would no doubt repulse or terrify most well-bred ladies. He had expected more from me than a turned-up nose or a shriek of disgust, as now Tarzan seemed to be expecting more from me than fright at this novel experience.

I inhaled deeply and reached out my hand to the creature who was reaching out to me. The instant our fingers touched, the young ape grabbed my wrist, causing me to cry out, despite the obvious lack of malevolent intent. The gorilla's hand was warm and strong and leathery. Feeling suddenly confident and wishing to prove my bravery to Tarzan, I moved toward the beast. But a tiny slip of the foot found me teetering dangerously and, with a shriek, losing the branch entirely. Now I hung terrified by one arm in midair, grasped by the ape with effortless strength. Aside from the hoots and grunts from the colony below, I heard, much to my indignant fury, Tarzan *laughing*. The gorilla hauled me up in an easy sweep and set me back on the limb. Tarzan swung down and, all smiles, embraced me. Then he gave the youngster a playful cuff on the head to thank it. Having had enough of the white-skins' company, it descended and rejoined its family members below.

There I was, in Tarzan's arms again. I had nearly plunged to my death and yet could not deny the ridiculous feeling of safety thus embraced and, more surprising, my utter contentment. Still, he had just put me in peril, allowing me to fall, only to be saved by a young gorilla.

And he had laughed about it!

I gave Tarzan a sharp poke in the chest and assumed the angriest expression I could muster. "You let me fall," I said and completed the spoken thoughts with gestures to the same effect.

"*Bolgani dan-do amba* Jane," Tarzan replied.

"*Bolgani* means 'gorilla'?" I asked.

"*Bolgani* gorilla," he said, pointing to the apes below and nodding. "*Dan-do amba,*" he added insistently.

I did not understand the meaning of the phrase.

Tarzan clasped both his hands together in a facsimile of the young beast's arm clutching my arm. He thought for another moment. "Stop," he said. It was an English word he had learned. Then he pantomimed falling.

"*Dan-do ambo* means 'stop fall'?" I guessed.

He nodded.

I found myself delighted at the communication. It was impossible to stay angry at Tarzan. This was how the two of us were proceeding with our joint education. A new word spoken would be quickly translated into the other's language. Our vocabularies for nouns were growing quickly. We had just learned another verb.

Then Tarzan was on the move again. I marveled at the dogged persistence with which my friend was heading toward his chosen destination. Wherever it was, it must mean a great deal to him.

Toward the end of the day when the forest undergrowth darkened and the patches of dappled light grew golden with the coming sunset, Tarzan's movements became slow and wary. He stopped often and lifted his head, sniffing the air. Now he kept me close behind him, many times reaching out his hand to help me, where before he had encouraged independent movement. Then he stopped altogether.

Before us was a massive tree, the species of which I could not determine, for it was dead, with no living leaves on its many crisscrossing limbs and branches. We approached from halfway up its trunk and now Tarzan tightly grasped my hand, leading me in the failing light up and up into those branches, and closer to its trunk.

It was clear that Tarzan had made this particular climb many times, and equally clear that this particular tree was the mysterious chosen destination. Having reached the trunk, Tarzan suddenly disappeared into a hole in its woody side. He turned and faced outward, very much the same as the grey parrot in the fig tree did from his nest hole. *Is this a nest in which the two of us are going to spend the night?* Tarzan reached out his hand and guided me up over the lip of the hole. Inside I was startled at the light that poured in from above, much more than illuminated the forest canopy. I gazed upward and saw that the trunk was entirely hollow, and it was sunlight that lit the great tubular giant, both above our heads and below our feet.

Tarzan began to descend, using sturdy foot- and handholds, encouraging me to follow him. I hesitated, for this was quite a daunting proposition. By now, I reckoned, we must be two hundred feet above the forest floor. One slip of my foot and—if not *dan-do amba* like I had been by the *bolgani*—I would tumble down the wooden well to my death. Tarzan was patiently awaiting my first step downward, his hand stretched up to assist the foothold. I should not delay. We were losing the light, and climbing down the hollow trunk in the dark would be suicidal. I steeled myself in the same way I did before taking a high jump on Leicester's back and lowered one-half of my body, seeking the foothold. The feeling of Tarzan's hand on my ankle caused an upwelling of relief substantial enough that I was able to release the grip of the opposite hand and find the lower handhold—a gnarled nub of air root.

Thus we descended slowly, but with ever more assurance. Once we had lowered ourselves three-quarters of the way down the trunk,

Tarzan stopped and, standing on what appeared as a broad ledge, helped me down to firm footing. I doubted I could have made that feeling of gratitude understood, but the rush of relieved tension in my muscles was so intense I nearly wept. I became quickly aware, however, that Tarzan was in a state of *increased* tension and awareness, and also that there was a foul odor wafting around our heads.

He was peering out a hole in the trunk. Coming to his side on the ledge I could see below me what appeared in the disappearing light to be a nesting ground for a huge family of *bolgani*, already tucked into the crooks of trees making ready for sleep. But here, at the view hole, the stink was nearly unbearable. When Tarzan gently pulled me back, I questioned him about the smell. He directed my sight in the final rays of sunlight to a dead, decaying monkey carcass hanging just under the opening.

When I signaled that the gruesome bit of carrion should be disposed of, Tarzan shook his head in a vigorous *no!* Well, I thought, a further explanation would have to wait till tomorrow. Just now Tarzan was guiding me to a place on the ledge and motioning that I stretch my whole body out. He lay next to me, his body facing out into the abyss. I knew that the closeness would, on this precipice, lead to nothing resembling the lustful gropings in the Waziri hut, and that the morning light would reveal not only the bizarre necessity for the dead monkey hanging a few feet away but also the great mystery that lay below in the gorillas' nesting grounds.

I wrapped my arm around Tarzan's waist, breathing in his rich musky scent, and closed my eyes.

As it had every night since I came into his company, sleep took me instantly.

Mangani

I woke as Tarzan pulled out of my grasp and in the weak dawn light filtering in from above made his way across the ledge to the view hole. He stood just above the rotting monkey carcass, clearly unperturbed by its foul odor, then turned and beckoned to me. I had not seen such a look in the man's eyes before, not when he was swimming in his favorite pool or communing with a beloved animal friend, or even gazing at me with obvious affection. The expression was at once hopeful and anticipatory, furious and fearful. He reached out his hand to help me negotiate the ledge with its dangerous drop and, thus assisted, I came to stand side by side with Tarzan at the blind.

The lowland gorillas in their nests below were beginning to stir. I counted more than five dozen hominids, adults and the young. Some began feeding immediately from piles of food they had placed in their nests the night before. Several *balu* descended to the ground and began frolicking and wrestling with one another on the thick bed of leaves and moss that covered the forest floor.

I had begun to wonder what significance this particular band of *bolgani* had for Tarzan when one of the females stood up in her nest. *Were my eyes deceiving me?* The furred, massive-bodied tree dweller had a backward-sloping skull and the face of an ape, but the creature was most definitely *not* an ape. She stood far too upright—like humans did. Others stood now. The largest of them were over six feet tall. The long bones of their arms and legs, like human limbs, were not bowed but *straight*. The creatures were not bent over, and their knuckles did not scrape the ground. Like human hands, theirs hung just at knee level. *Good grief, what was I seeing?!* Their fingers were excessively long. Their big toes—contrary to the rest of their very human legs—were not parallel with their other toes but set at right angles to their feet, a configuration that would allow them to grip all the way around a tree limb, like an ape's would do. On closer examination, their broad furred faces were more like a chimpanzee's than a gorilla's. The backward-sloping skulls could not leave much room for a large human-sized frontal lobe and cortex of the brain, yet the entire skull was much larger than a gorilla's, therefore allowing for a decent-sized brain. They were neither human nor Neanderthal, nor even what Java man must have looked like.

And what was this? The sounds coming from the creatures—it was a kind of *language*, guttural and very rudimentary. Some sounds were those Tarzan used as words. Were these beings using words, even small phrases, to communicate with each other? *But this would mean the species—and yes, it was most decidedly a new species—had the physical equipment for speech!*

I argued silently with myself. Surely this was impossible. Even if the creatures could manage a few word-sounds, could they possess the mental capacity to understand spoken language?

I watched as a mature female called in "words" to a small juvenile on the ground to join her on the tree limb where she squatted, and within moments he left his playmates and climbed to her side. She took him to her teat to feed. Now I observed two males who were attempting—with words I dared to believe were colored with *inflection*—to lure a young female down from a higher limb to join them in mutual grooming.

I felt my heart pounding hard in my chest. I was barely breathing. This could not be. *Could not be!* It contradicted everything I had been taught about evolution and the extinction of species. But seeing was believing. And right now, before my eyes, I was observing an entire colony of *living missing links!*

"Mangani," Tarzan said to me, not in his usual bold style of speaking but in a whisper. It was then I realized the import of the rotting monkey corpse hanging below the view hole. Tarzan did not want these creatures to know that they were being spied upon from the tree trunk. The carrion flesh would hide our human scent.

My mind was utterly shattered. Before me was the greatest

discovery in the history of biological science. My thoughts raced in several directions at once, and I strove to rein them in, to begin formulating questions, ones that Tarzan, even with his limited vocabulary, would be able to answer. First, I must know why he had come so far out of his way to make this tribe—the Mangani—known to me.

But now, standing so close to Tarzan, I became aware that my friend was more than excited. He was agitated. He, too, was attempting urgent communication with me about the creatures.

"Tell me about the Mangani," I said very quietly.

Tarzan nodded, then gestured to the female I had seen call to the small child who was still feeding at her breast.

"Muh-thah," Tarzan whispered.

"Yes, that is a mother."

"Tarzan muh-thah."

I shook my head. "No, not Tarzan's mother."

Tarzan grew visibly frustrated. "No Tarzan muh-thah," he agreed. "Mangani Kala Tarzan muh-thah."

I thought hard. Did Tarzan want me to understand that he knew this nursing female was not his mother, but that *another Mangani female called Kala* had given birth to him?

It was an outrageous idea, but it indeed appeared to be what he thought.

All at once Tarzan grew ecstatic. He was directing my sight to a well-formed adult female, gracefully brachiating her way through the treetops of the Mangani encampment.

"Jai!" he exclaimed, forgetting to keep his voice down.

"Who is Jai?" *Jane lul. No jai lul*, I remembered.

Tarzan's face twisted with the exertion of difficult thought. Finally he smiled. "Tarzan Kala *balu*. Jai Kala *balu*."

Mad as his logic was, I felt obliged to foster understanding and not split hairs. Tarzan was saying that he and Jai had the same mother.

"Jai is Tarzan's sister?" I said.

"Sis-ter," he repeated. He had never before heard the English word. But he pulled me to him and hugged me fiercely—in thanks for understanding, I presumed.

Tarzan's sister, and a beloved sister at that, I thought. I must formulate my ideas into words I could make Tarzan comprehend. In reality, his mother could not possibly be one of these Mangani females, and Jai was not his sister. How on earth had he come to believe such a preposterous delusion?

"Kala Tarzan muh-thah," he began. He balled his hand into a fist and, pounding the center of his chest, made the universal symbol of strong love. "Tarzan *eta balu*."

I remembered *eta* as the word for "small" or "weak." So Tarzan, improbable as it might seem, had been raised from a child by a female Mangani named Kala. I watched as Tarzan—unable to find the proper words—pantomimed loving care and tender affection for a little creature in a mother's lap. He held an imaginary infant at his left breast and smiled. "Tarzan," he said. Then he held another imaginary babe to his right breast. "Jai."

So Kala had suckled them both.

Lost in pleasant memory now, Tarzan's face grew animated. "Tarzan *ee* Jai *zu, zu-vo*." He signed that the two little ones had grown big and strong. Now he was smiling broadly. "Tarzan *ee* Jai *olo*."

I shook my head. "*Olo?*"

Tarzan grabbed me and made as if to wrestle. Clearly, he and his sister had play-wrestled with each other growing up, as many young animals were known to do in order to learn the art of fighting—as I had seen the juvenile Mangani do this morning.

"Where is Kala?" I asked Tarzan.

"Kala *bund*."

I had never learned Tarzan's word for "dead," but by the grim expression on my friend's face, the meaning of *bund* was all too apparent. And clearly, he did not wish to elucidate any further on that subject.

Regardless of Tarzan's odd misconceptions about his parentage, I found it impossible to tear my gaze from this stunning discovery. I was speechless. Paralyzed with wonder. If only I had pen and paper to begin recording my momentous findings and drawing the living missing link species in detail. But truly, I was satisfied for now just to stand and observe, to allow the enormity of it all to settle into my brain.

Pithecanthropus aporterensus erectus I would name the creatures, in memory of my father. Oh, how I grieved that he had left this world without seeing them. It was a universe of importance beyond the pile of petrified bones that we had come seeking in West Africa. What on earth would Eugène Dubois think when he saw *P.a.e.?* Imagine the furor this would create within the scientific community. Tarzan had not the slightest conception of what a crucial and magnificent gift he had given me.

Given the world.

Just then Tarzan, at my side, began to bristle. All the muscles in his body grew rigid, and with unconscious roughness he pushed me away from the view hole. A sound came rumbling from deep in his throat. A dangerous growl.

"Tarzan, what do you see?"

He seemed to me, at that moment, to be lacking all control of his senses. This frightened me. I knew his power. He had killed a giant cat single-handedly in my defense. But here in the hollow tree blind I was in no danger. What had so upset him? I placed a gentle hand on Tarzan's arm. When he did not respond, I took his face in both of my hands and forced him to look at me. What I saw in his eyes was murder.

"Kerchak," was all he said before stepping aside to let me back at the spy hole.

Standing tall and upright in a nest far above the others—one that I had not previously noticed—was the most fearsome creature upon which I had ever laid eyes. While he was surely Mangani, he far outstripped in size and proportion every other member of the tribe. If my eyes were not deceiving me, he stood at least six and one-half feet tall and weighed in excess of three hundred and fifty pounds, every ounce of it muscle, bone, and sinew. His chest and shoulders were massive. But his posture, and the cowering stance of the others below him who had, like myself, just become aware of his wakeful state, told a further story than simply one of a physically dominant male of the species.

Every single Mangani, despite its age or sex, lived in abject terror of the one Tarzan called Kerchak.

In ominous silence, he began making his way down to the lower nests, brachiating with arms the size of tree limbs. As he approached the blind, I caught a full view of him. It came as a shock to see that Kerchak was disfigured. One of his eyes was missing, the socket a sunken black mass. The other glimmered with silent threat. A huge diagonal scar across the whole of his face had healed, but it made the monster's countenance even more horrifying. There was quiet menace in every movement. If he approached a nest, mothers would pull their young closer. Males simply turned and disappeared into the greenery. As Kerchak went down, he picked morsels of food from the nighttime stores of the bowers, but no Mangani dared challenge the theft. When he reached the ground, a roundish clearing of beaten-down grasses, he settled himself into a seated position and began chewing on the berries and shoots he had taken from the others.

Now movement began in earnest all over the nesting place, which I had silently named the "Great Bower." Males came out of hiding, their arms filled with foodstuffs they had just gathered, and, climbing carefully to the ground, set it all at Kerchak's feet. Two females with groveling posture crept up behind the tyrant and began to groom his fur.

I could see the one Tarzan called his sister, Jai, just sitting on a bough, watching almost impassively the strange, animalistic drama playing out below. *But is it altogether of the animal world?* I wondered. The aging King Henry VIII was brought to mind by this spectacle of pathetic cringing and cowering of his courtiers.

I turned with a dozen questions to Tarzan but found that he had retreated to the ledge where we had slept, his back against the inner wall of the trunk, his knees pulled close to his chest. The morning light was filtering down from above, and I thought then that I had never seen a sight so heart-rending. Tarzan, bold and courageous in all things, was now much diminished. But when I went and sat beside him, I was at once disabused of any thought that my friend was abashed or humbled by the might of Kerchak. In fact, he was seething with so terrible a rage that his crouched, removed pose was an attempt to control an uncontrollable infuriation. I felt waves of violent heat pulsing from his skin. His face was hidden, but I was certain that if I could see them, his features would be disfigured with hatred. I therefore hesitated speaking and sat quietly beside him. Then I remembered to what great lengths Tarzan had gone to bring me here. He wanted me to see this. Wished me to understand.

"Tell me of Kerchak."

It took some time for Tarzan to compose himself.

"Tarzan *ee Boi-ee lu har* Kerchak." He whipped the Bowie knife from its sheath and sliced the air with it again and again, describing *lu har,* a fierce battle. "Tarzan *yuto yat* Kerchak."

I knew that *yat* meant "eye." So the young boy had been the one who had taken out Kerchak's eye.

"Kerchak *yuto-gash* Tarzan." He bit into his own arm. Raked his fingernails across his neck and chest. "Kerchak *aro* Tarzan Mangani." He pointed away to the east with a look of despondency. "Tarzan no here Mangani."

It was indeed a dreadful story. For daring to defy Kerchak, Tarzan had been badly mauled and sent away from his family and tribe with the memory of his abuse simmering like hot oil in his veins.

He stood and returned to the blind, both hands clutching the sides of the hole in a white-knuckled grasp. I became alarmed. I wondered if a brutal confrontation was inevitable. I had to prevent that. If something were to happen to my protector, I would surely die in the forest. My death would be tragic for my mother, but more important, news of the *P.a.e.* find would be lost to the world, perhaps forever.

These were selfish thoughts, I knew, but gazing at Tarzan—so heartsick and so murderously inclined—I realized how deeply I had come to feel for him. For his own good, I needed to put distance between him and the malevolent Kerchak. Was my influence strong enough to move him? I was not certain, but at the very least I must try.

Zu·dak·lul

All along our westward imperative, riding the Ogowe Mbele above- and belowground, I knew that our final destination must be the Atlantic. Yet my first sight of it as we emerged from the brackish mangrove swamp stunned my senses. In all the time I'd lived under the deep forest canopy I had felt no claustrophobia or even longing for the light that had largely gone from my existence. But here on the wide beach of fine-grained, blinding white sand lined with a pretty fringe of coconut palms (here was where Tarzan had harvested the coconut shells!), I felt a great rush of joy tinged with something akin to homesickness. There was a great dome of stark blue sky, gentle green waves rolling landward, and the equatorial sun that began in an instant to burn my skin (I heard Cecily admonishing me to put on a hat). Certainly the happiness was borne of the light and freedom, the diving seabirds, and the fresh breeze whipping my hair. It was, I decided, the sight of the sea that had made me nostalgic. *This is my ocean*, I mused. *The water here may once have touched the coast of England. It is the same in which I swam with my father as a little girl. This ocean bore his body home.*

I was all at once overcome with the urgent need to immerse myself. I strode—how odd it felt to be able to stride, unhindered by roots and matted vines of the forest and jungle floor!—across the sand and without hesitation waded into the shallows. I was grateful for the gradual slope and the calm, waist-high waves, and plowed through them, using my arms to push myself forward. The water was warmer than I had ever felt it, and utterly delightful. All the grime of the mosquito-infested jungle and the stinking mud of the mangrove swamp were washed away in moments. When I was chest-high, I pushed off the sandy bottom and began to swim. It was only then that I remembered Tarzan, assuming he would be right behind me in the water.

But when I turned, I saw him standing, unaccountably, on the shore, watching me. From this distance I could not see his features, but his posture was odd. As if he was straining forward and restraining himself all at once. In any case, he was immobile. I called to him and waved him in. He shook his head.

Well, the water was too glorious to abandon, so I had a good strong swim down the coast a piece. Finally, with no need for watchful stepping or hair-raising rides upon raging rapids, in and out of eerie underground rivers, and slogging through snake- and insect-ridden jungles, I was able to revisit my find of *P.a.e.* When this portion of the adventure, whatever it was, was done, I would insist on Tarzan taking me back to the nesting grounds so I could begin memorizing every detail for the time there would be pen and paper to record it.

I swam back up the coast to where Tarzan stood and saw that he had not moved from the place I'd left him. Reluctantly, I regained the shore and stood dripping and refreshed before him.

"Why did you not swim?" I asked him.

"Here Zu-dak-lul," he answered cryptically.

Large Water, I silently translated. I could see his expression, but I could not read it.

"Tarzan no swim Zu-dak-lul." This was spoken with such simple authority that, despite the mysteriousness of the pronouncement (he was a more than capable swimmer in Eden's pools), I refrained from further questioning. There was so much I wished to ask. But I forced myself to be patient. All would be revealed in time if I practiced patience.

"Come," he said and, turning north, began walking along the water's edge. It was strange seeing Tarzan on foot in so spare and open a landscape, without the wall of trees, the lush carpet and upholstery of greenery. And yet he walked the beach with assurance, as though he owned it, every bit as much as he did the forest.

What was this up ahead? Tucked into a monstrous baobab tree surrounded by a small forest of coconut palms was a man-made structure. As we approached, I could see it was jerry-built and weather-beaten, much of it the driftwood of some old shipwreck and the tattered remnants of a canvas sail. The thatch roofing had all but blown away, but there was a cleverness to its construction, a thoughtfulness and intention of purpose.

Now we stood below it and I could feel Tarzan immobile but agitated at my side, much as he had been standing at the Mangani blind. Here on this beach and above in the ramshackle hut must reside more puzzle pieces of my friend's origins and history, as surely as a limestone cave would give up the fossils of a man dead for a million years.

Suddenly Tarzan sprang to a horizontal palm trunk and up onto the lowest limb of the baobab. He climbed through the many branches, approaching a wooden platform near what appeared to be the hut's front door. A moment later, a frayed but still-sturdy rope ladder unfurled from above, and Tarzan jumped down to my side. I saw him hesitate before he put his foot on the first rung of the ladder. Hesitation was rare in this man, but here on the beach of Zu-dak-lul I had seen both refusal and hesitation in an otherwise fearless individual. Now he was climbing and turned to urge me to follow him. With the greatest eagerness, I did.

Tarzan gained the platform and held out his hand, pulling me up. What I saw then was a door made of several thicknesses of crate sides. Yet it was a proper door, with cleverly fashioned hinges and a latch. Tarzan opened the door and disappeared inside.

I followed.

What I saw then was so improbable, so mismatched a gathering of native and civilized cultures, that my mind fell briefly into confusion. Here were walls made of driftwood and crates, carefully sawed palm tree trunks, and a roof of the same. The palm leaf thatch had been an adjunct to the wooden construction, so that although the giant leaves had blown away from the roof, there was still a ceiling over our heads, and even though the boards beneath my feet squeaked, I felt the floor safe and sturdy. There was a porthole window to the side open to the sea, but I noticed the top half of a solid shutter, long ago broken off, that would have closed the window against the weather when necessary.

And what was this? Were those ragged remnants of lace curtains at the window? The single room was appointed with pieces of furniture, some of them rough-hewn, like the table—two broad planks of a ship's deck carefully nailed together—and benches on both sides, of the same construction. But near the window was a beautifully made rocking chair, looking very much like the one in the Edlington-Porter nursery. And there was a child's desk and chair. And a bookshelf . . . filled with books written in English!

Drawn to the most unlikely of objects in such a place, I took a step toward the bookshelf and felt something crunch underfoot. Shock at the sight of civilized trappings in that rude hut on a remote, palm-lined beach in Gabon was nothing compared to the horror of having crushed beneath me the bones of a human hand!

Recoiling, I saw that the hand was part of a complete skeleton, albeit in several large pieces scattered on the floorboards—an arm here, the rib cage, spine, pelvis, and one leg there. The skull sat a distance away from the rest. It had to have been, I thought, shuddering, the most violent of deaths.

I looked to Tarzan, who had, with quiet indifference, stepped around the bones on the floor and squeezed himself into the child's chair behind the little desk and had pulled a book from the shelf. He was turning the pages slowly, but too quickly to be reading.

As I walked farther into the hut, my eyes fell on a bed tucked into a corner. There, sprawled on the once-fine yellow silk coverlet, now in moldy shreds, was another bony corpse, this one smaller and, by the look of the wide pelvis, a female. Although it was intact, its posture— with limbs splayed and the mandible open in the shape of a scream— indicated that the woman's death had come at the end of an appalling struggle. Most gut-wrenching of all was the sight of a gold wedding band on the skeletal finger of her left hand.

Looking back at the door through which we'd entered, I saw quite clearly all the signs of a forced entry—three trunks that had been piled in front of it pushed aside, splintered boards nailed over the opening that now hung from a single nail.

Once more my gaze found Tarzan, but he was fully engrossed in his book, not in the least concerned with the carnage around him. *What on earth could be going on in his mind?*

Now my eyes fell on the floor beside the bed. There was a third skeleton, though this one was tiny—perhaps the size of a year-old child. I knelt beside the piteous remains of a short-lived life. But when I reached out to touch the bones, I was jolted with a further shock, something unexpected in this den of unnatural and macabre surprises.

The infant skeleton was not human. Most obvious was the shape of the skull—clearly apelike. The leg bones were straight and the fingers overlong. The big toe bone stood at right angles to the foot.

This was a Mangani child!

I glanced again at Tarzan, who was still entirely engrossed with his book, thus allowing me to continue this astonishing investigation.

Behind the open door I found a proper mahogany writing table, its elegant matching chair overturned. A dried-up inkpot, pen, and blotter were askew on its top. At my feet was a large journal of faded claret leather that had fallen to the floor, splayed open, facedown in an attitude that to my eye appeared obscene in its violence.

I hesitated before lifting it up from where it lay, as I foresaw the weight and profundity of its contents. I was certain that what was written within would change forever the life of the nearly naked savage squeezed now into the child's desk, paging placidly through a book he could not read.

I lifted the journal with reverence, keeping it spread to the page where it had fallen open, turned it, and placed it on the writing table. Even in the stuffy heat of the room, I shivered, knowing at once that the faded brown blotches that overlay the careful script were bloodstains, surely those of the man who lay in pieces on the hut's floor. With growing dread I righted the chair and placed it before the table, then sat myself down. I thought then how odd it felt to be sitting upright in a proper chair and not squatting in a moss nest or on the limb of a tree. To have in my sight the trappings, however few, of a familiar society. I closed the diary, squaring it before me. Then steeling myself for what was to come, I opened the front cover. On its title page in bold masculine lettering was centered:

The Journal of John Clayton

Below it had been added in a fine, spidery script:

and Alice Clayton

I found my eyes locked on those few words on the page, but my mind was racing. The family name was familiar to me, if only vaguely. Clayton. John Clayton. I turned the page to the first entry and stared at the date: 2 March 1885. Leaning my elbows on the table, I covered my face with my hands and went inward, searching my memory as I had taught myself to do when studying. I sifted and rummaged through the multitude of acquired facts and knowledge of my twenty years. It was far easier for me, I thought, to remember the names of the twenty-eight bones of the foot than it was recalling minutiae about a member of the English aristocracy for which I had so little patience . . . but that was what I must do, for I was quite certain that the name Clayton was of the peerage.

I had some faint memory of it. No more than gossip overheard at an afternoon tea. *Greystoke*. The title came suddenly and unaccountably to mind. Lord and Lady Greystoke. *A long and high lineage. A tragedy. Died prematurely.* Yes, dinner at the Blanchforts' London house was where I had heard it. A heated discussion of a vast fortune languishing in limbo with no heirs. John Clayton and his young wife, against the advice of his aging father, had taken a diplomatic post in some godforsaken outpost. The ship's wreckage swept up on remote shores. No survivors. The vulturelike families of England petitioning Queen Victoria to award the Greystoke title to one of them. A legal quagmire. What to do with the London mansion, the country great house, the many properties? Lost at sea. Lost at sea. Godforsaken outpost. John and Alice Clayton, Lord and Lady Greystoke. *The man and woman in Tarzan's locket. His parents!*

With trepidation and anticipation the likes of which I had never known, I began to read.

2 March 1885

I had not thought to begin writing in this journal until we had made landfall and set up our household in the port of Angra Pequena, but circumstance has a way of riding roughshod upon the best-laid plans, and the disquieting turn of events of the past several days has me concerned that my sweet bride and I shall never set foot on the coast of West Africa.

That we are here, hiding in our cabin of the Fuwalda—*a rough sailing ship with a crew of scoundrels and cutthroats—is a folly born of equal parts* ambition, loyalty to my Queen, and the influence of my wife. As a peer of the realm I had, as all men of honor do, served as a soldier when I came of age. But there had been no war worthy of making me a hero (and I sometimes wondered, had I seen battle, would I have even been one?). Instead I'd read the law and entered Victoria's service in the lower ranks of the diplomatic corps. There I would surely have languished had it not been for the family alliances of my lovely young wife, Alice Rutherford, an intimate of our queen's eldest daughter, the Princess Victoria, known to all as "Vicky."

Her marriage into the German royal family to the son of Kaiser Wilhelm—the Crown Prince Frederick—had taken Alice's friend away from her in all but letters. That passionate friendship (of a kind that only women seem able to continue from girlhood to old age) produced one missive that changed our lives forever . . . and if our luck runs out, may end it at the bottom of the sea.

Vicky and her royal husband were of a liberal bent. They sat in fierce opposition to that tyrant, Chancellor Otto von Bismarck, a man who held the German Kaiser in his thrall. One evening at a state dinner, she had chanced to overhear Bismarck's plan to begin the colonization of Africa, a policy he and the Germans had always eschewed as a serious fiscal blunder. The objects of Bismarck's colonial desires were territories along the west coast of Africa, including a puny port town (though any port is better than no port at all) called Angra Pequena. But the place was legally held by the English Crown and run by her consul of the Cape Colony at the southern tip of Africa.

It was well known that Bismarck had spies reading all of Vicky's letters to her mother, the English Queen, but no one bothered to read those sent to her girlhood friend Alice Rutherford-Clayton. In short, Vicky told Alice of the planned coup, Alice told me, and together in an audience with Queen Victoria, we passed along the secret intelligence. She, in return, rewarded me with a posting to Angra Pequena to keep a close but tactful eye on the German machinations.

I would have jumped at the chance had Alice not recently announced her first pregnancy, so instead I privately balked. But she would have no part of any refusal to help her Queen and Empire. She was young and strong, with several sisters who had had no trouble birthing babies. We were going to Africa together, and that was that.

With little fanfare, save the vigorous protestations from both our families— our true mission kept even from them—we set sail out of Portsmouth, with all believing me the purveyor of Victoria's new moneymaking enterprise . . . bat guano, which was found in abundant quantities on the islands off the coast of Angra Pequena.

Alice was a trooper from the moment we'd boarded that vessel and had suffered far less seasickness than I had. Indeed, her pregnancy nausea disappeared entirely, and she became a woman with a mission. My mild-mannered bride was suddenly bursting with confident purpose. Of course equatorial Africa was a foul posting and a dangerous place with its savages and malarial fevers, but she was certain that our destiny was calling us to this godforsaken outpost and that, of course, it would not last forever. Before we knew it we would be back in England with my diplomatic career assured.

Neither of us had expected the mutiny.

At the Gabonese port of Libreville, we had boarded a second ship, an aging barque, to take us the rest of the distance. If the crewmen aboard the Fuwalda are the minions of hell, its captain, one Marston James, is Satan himself, and his officers incubi. Vicious and ignorant, the captain takes daily pleasure in corporally abusing his men with a belaying pin and threatening them with his revolver. We, of course, loathed him utterly. We wondered between us why the men stayed under his captaincy and reasoned that their own histories must render them unfit for more convivial situations.

But two days south of the Gabonese port at Libreville, Captain James stepped beyond the pale.

While speaking on deck to Alice and myself, he stumbled over an old crewman scrubbing the deck, fell, and soaked himself in filthy water. Humiliated, he struck out at the poor man with the belaying pin, only to be confronted by another deckhand coming to his friend's defense. This crewman was a great hulking fellow aptly named Great Henry. He fearlessly put his body between the captain and the scrubber, who lay bleeding on the deck. Without hesitation, James withdrew his revolver and pointed it at Great Henry's head. A swift brush of my hand on the captain's firing arm caused the bullet to merely wound and not kill the sailor, who limped away. For this I was roundly chastised by Captain James and told to mind my business on his vessel.

Two days later, the crew was primed for mutiny. Great Henry gave us fair warning of the coming carnage and instructed us to stay below in our cabin.

Since then Alice and I have had the first serious argument of our marriage. I am a man of the law, and despite the appalling behavior of the ship's captain, I regard mutiny as a most heinous criminal offense. I felt it my duty to warn him. Alice would hear nothing of it. That Great Henry told us of the rebellion and cautioned us to stay below convinced me that he means us no harm, that he is grateful for my having saved his life and will return the favor by saving our lives. But I am morally torn and in fear of the outcome in either direction.

Good Christ! The first shots have been fired above deck! Alice, more stoic than I ever imagined her to be, is sitting upright on her bunk, knees pressed together, back straight as a rod. I must go to her now. Sit beside her and hold her hand. Await our fate. I pray that there will be another entry in this journal, and that a peaceful fate awaits us, one that will not have us fish food at the bottom of the Atlantic.

Written belowdecks in our cabin on the Fuwalda,
John Clayton

1 April 1885

There may be eloquent words to describe the predicament in which Alice and I now find ourselves, but I am no Daniel Defoe, and we, unlike his heroic creation, Robinson Crusoe, have not been battered, half drowned, or shipwrecked upon an island. We have instead been set down upon a wild, deserted shore by mutineers, some of whom wished, I believe, to throw us overboard with the abhorred captain and his officers, but one of which—Great Henry—was a man of honor and gave us our lives as well as our possessions, and even a promise that when they were next in a "safe port" he would convey our location to the authorities in order that we might be rescued.

Alice astonished me with her fortitude, never shedding a tear, even as the Fuwalda disappeared around the point, leaving us alone with piles of crates of our personal items, furniture, tools, rope, food provisions, two of the ship's old canvas sails, and, blessedly, my box of rifles and ammunition—far more than I might have expected from that scurrilous company of ruffians.

It is true that Alice had no earthly idea what we should do with ourselves as the sun set in a shocking blaze of crimson and gold. Nor did I. Thankfully she had bullied the sailors into piling our things as far back from the water's edge as possible, under the row of coconut palms, for we had no idea of the action of the waves, and sensible girl that she is, Alice did not wish for our belongings to be ruined in the first high tide. They grumbled but complied, and so placing the canvas over the great pile, and ourselves with them, we settled into the sand for our first night—with my Winchester loaded and close at hand.

I never slept, though she did. In the morning she said that she had had a prescience that we would be found in less than a week's time by a stroke of good fortune, having nothing to do with our mutinous benefactors. Choosing to trust her optimism, we spent the next day scanning the horizon for our saviors and I, therefore, failed to put forth any effort whatsoever in improving our circumstances.

That night, unfulfilled of our hopes, we huddled again under the canvas as a great tornado raged over the sea, whipping the waves so high on the beach that I blessed Alice's foresight a hundred times, as in the morning light we found all our possessions spared. But in the next two days, as we vainly awaited rescue, flotsam began washing up on our shore. Great chunks of a wrecked vessel, most certainly undone by the tornado. A good portion of the deck and timbers, and some of the aft with its brass porthole window still intact were gifts from the sea on successive mornings. When a jagged bit of the bow with the lettering "Fuw" washed ashore, I found it first and tried to hide it from Alice . . . most unsuccessfully.

Finally she wept, her premonition "a worthless scrap of wishful thinking," for now our location would never be passed along to the authorities, and if the wreckage were found, we, along with the unlucky crew, would be presumed lost. I began to berate myself for demanding we embark on this fool's errand. It was nothing of the sort, she insisted. We were doing our duty to God and country, and besides, she told me, we might still be found.

Nevertheless, sobered by this inconceivable reality, I began that day to build a shelter. The one large tree on the wide, sparkling beach would be perfect, I told her. I had never built so much as a wooden box, but there were tools and excellent pieces of timber at hand. Further, I had a brain in my head and a very serious purpose—to protect my wife and my unborn child from the elements until the time we were rescued . . . or died. I thought again of Robinson Crusoe, his courage and manly self-reliance, and silently vowed to emulate him. I counted myself infinitely more fortunate in having not a Negro servant as my companion but my young wife, who appeared to me more beautiful with every passing hour.

My marriage to Alice Rutherford was, as all marriages in our society are, an arranged one. We'd been pledged to one another from the time we were children by our fathers, who saw some great benefit to both our families. She *had always been a plucky girl, but I never knew her mettle till that day I spread my tools about me on the sand and took stock of the materials I might use for our new "home." I looked up and saw Alice, who, having crowbarred open a crate, was similarly taking stock of our food stores—salt meats and biscuit, even a small supply of potatoes and beans—with as much calm assurance as she might have overseeing a half dozen kitchen maids preparing for a dinner party at Greystoke Manor.*

God grant me the strength to keep her safe, she and our child who will, I fear, be born on this terrible shore. And let me build a strong fortress against the wild elements of nature that will surely test us in this great adventure, one that we neither asked for nor expected, but one, I pray, that will make better people of us.

Written apprehensively on a Gabonese beach,
John Clayton

I closed my eyes. I could not bear to read any more, nor did I wish to look at Tarzan, for my heart ached with grief for him. Yet I refused under any circumstances to regard him with pity. I must make him understand what the horrors within this room revealed of his past, unsure what result it might achieve. Here was a young man who had conquered unspeakable adversity and become extraordinary. He was not, for all I could tell, unhappy with his circumstances. Indeed, Tarzan had shown himself to be a man of courage, honor, and intelligence far surpassing any of my English suitors and equaled only by my father. Who was I to rip apart the finely woven fabric of his remarkable existence? What would be the consequences if I did?

I chanced a look at him and found that he was staring openly at me. There seemed to be hope in his gaze, anticipation. Tarzan had, I now reflected, quite deliberately and purposely taken me to see the Mangani tribe and brought me here to Zu-dak-lul. To this hut strewn with the remains of his early life. He *wished* me to unlock the mystery for him. He could not have been more clear about his intentions.

I must be brave. As brave as he had been to survive these many years, survive and not devolve into feral depravity. To retain deep in his mind snatches of humanity and language and civilized behavior.

I grasped the locket he had hung around my neck. *Open it, I thought, and you will be opening the door to his memory.*

"Tarzan," I said, "come here."

He padded over across the wooden boards to me. I knelt and, without being told, he did the same. I placed the open locket before Tarzan's face and pointed to John Clayton, Lord Greystoke.

"This is Tarzan's father," I said. Then with my heart pounding hard in my chest, I swiveled slightly and touched the rib cage of the skeleton on the floor. "*This* is Tarzan's father." I watched his eyes as comprehension began to manifest itself. He looked many times from the handsome image of John Clayton to his broken remains. Tarzan's breathing was even and his features stony.

"Do you understand?" I said, unsure he comprehended the question spoken in a language long forgotten.

Finally he whispered, "Tarzan fah-thah *bund*."

"Yes, your father is dead." I placed my hand over his, but he was still as a statue, and silent, trying to fathom the unfathomable.

I stood and walked with the greatest apprehension to the bed. I sat gingerly on the edge and called to Tarzan. He stood but refused to move from his place. My voice was gentle, but I felt like a trickster, for I knew that the invitation to my side was an ambush, anything but gentle or kind.

"Tarzan," I said, "please come." I held out my hand to him. *He knows*, I thought, *knows what is coming. Dreads it above all dreads.* But finally he came and sat by my side. He looked deep in my eyes and refused to look down. I held the locket before his face again and pointed to the woman's photograph. The words when they came were bitter as bile.

"This is Tarzan's mother." I felt hot tears burning my eyes. It was impossible. I could not say these words. I could not hurt the dear man beside me. But when I chanced a look at Tarzan fixed on Alice Clayton's image, I saw the faintest glimmer of recognition. His breathing came harder now as he beheld the portrait. *I must speak!* I reached out and put my hand on the dead woman's skull.

"*This* is Tarzan's mother."

He remained more calm than I had expected, but he slowly shook his head no.

"This is Tarzan's mother." I held out the locket, which he took and snapped shut in the palm of his hand.

"No Tarzan muh-thah." He shook his head from side to side,

again and again, squeezing his eyes tight to blot out either image. "Here no Tarzan muh-thah. Kala Tarzan muh-thah."

He wiped a hand across his face. His cheeks were wet.

I had begun this. I must finish it. I stood and walked to the tiny skeleton on the floor. Kneeling down, I touched the little bones. "This is a Mangani *balu*."

His expression was blank.

"Try to remember, Tarzan," I said, aware that I spoke in words of which he had no comprehension. "How did you go from being a *balu* of *tar-zans* to a *balu* of Mangani?"

Suddenly I saw him move, and his actions, macabre and repulsive in any other circumstance, choked a sob from me. He had pulled the skeleton of Alice Clayton into his lap. I did not dare move or speak, and I barely drew breath, for a great and terrible epiphany was unfolding before me. Tarzan tilted his head to one side to regard the remains in a different light. Carefully he closed the gaping jaw. But as he moved to pull the bony figure into a delicate embrace, the corpse, in the cruelest of all blows, crumbled suddenly into a pile of fragments and dust.

With a heartbreaking cry, Tarzan shrank back from the bed and bolted for the door.

"Wait!" I called after him, but he was gone.

I watched from the doorway as he leaped from the trees to the sand and, running pell-mell, dove headlong into the sea. He swam like a man possessed, slicing through the waves, farther and farther from shore.

My heart sank. I had done wrong in telling Tarzan the truth. My father always told me that while the truth might hurt, it would never harm. Now I saw that he was wrong. This truth had harmed Tarzan. He was a tiny speck in the ocean now, swimming farther from my sight.

All at once the air of the tree house felt filthy and choking. I escaped, climbing down the rope ladder to the beach. I walked slowly to the edge of the ocean. There was no sight of Tarzan. Shuddering with guilt and unutterable remorse, I sat down hard on the sand. If ever there had been a time to pray, certainly it was now. *But what savage god would have conceived of a punishment such as this for an innocent young family like the Claytons?* None that I would wish to worship, I thought angrily, nor one who would listen to my most fervent prayers. No, it was useless to pray.

The best I could do was wait.

I have no idea of how long I sat on the shore, knees pulled up to my chest, head sunk between them, mourning. All of my losses, mistakes, and this cruel fate. I had driven Tarzan into the sea with my well-intentioned ignorance. Why had I not left well enough alone? He'd been beautiful just as he was. Wild. Fierce. Untrammeled by his English lineage, a heredity no more valid than his Mangani roots. Now he was gone. Drowned in the sea. Drowned by his sorrows. The mutineers had been kinder to the Claytons, putting them ashore, than I had been to Tarzan, tossing him onto the shoals of unwanted memory. Shipwrecked. How could I have been so unfeeling?

"Jane."

I startled at the sound. My heart leaped at the single syllable of my name spoken by a someone I thought lost. I looked up. Tarzan towered above me, a mountain of a man. Then he fell to his knees before me, his expression suffused with equal measures of pain and joy. In the long silence that followed, his face twitched with fervid emotion. I was terrified to utter a word. To damage him further. And then he opened his mouth and spoke. Chillingly. In the voices of a woman. A man. A child.

"Give me my shawl, will you, dear?

"Are you ill, my darling?

"Look at him, Alice. He's so strong.

"A B C D E F G.

"Tickle me, Mummy!

"Let me help you, Papa."

He looked at me then, directly, piercingly, and in the voice of a four-year-old demanded, "Sing to me."

I was struck dumb, my limbs paralyzed. I could remember nothing of the songs my mother had sung me in the nursery. In the void of my silence, with only the waves as accompaniment, Tarzan obeyed his own command and began to sing in a sweet, wavering voice.

"Sleep, my baby on my bosom.
Warm and cozy will it prove.
Round thee mother's arms are folding,
In her heart a mother's love.

"There shall no one come to harm thee.
Naught shall ever break thy rest.
Sleep, my darling babe, in quiet.
Sleep on mother's gentle breast."

Now I remembered the lullaby. The words flowed back to me as though I myself were nestled in my mother's arms. My voice rose together with the little Clayton boy's.

"Do not fear the sound of a breeze
Brushing leaves against the door.
Do not dread the murmuring seas,
Lonely waves that wash the shore.

"Sleep serenely, baby, slumber.
Lovely baby, gently sleep;
Tell me wherefore art thou smiling,
Smiling sweetly in thy sleep?"

We buried the three skeletons with somber dignity far back from the highest level of the tide. There being no stones, we sank heavy pieces of driftwood deep in the sand over the graves. I had retrieved Alice Clayton's wedding band from her crumbled remains and, lost for words, placed the ring in Tarzan's hand. He stared uncomprehendingly at it.

"Here," I said, taking it and fitting it on the first joint of his little finger, the only digit on which it would fit. *She would want you to have it,* I thought but did not say. But I had no wish to dwell on remains and heartbreaking mementos. I had pried open the door to Tarzan's past, but the deep vault of his mind was yet untouched and needed the tenderest mining. He had begun parroting words and phrases he remembered, as he had recalled the lullaby, sung by rote. When we spoke now, English words were more liberally mixed with Mangani, and I encouraged him at every turn to use proper grammar, something he took to like a fish to water. I taught him the use of verbs and adjectives, as nouns were so easily learned.

Still, it was elemental communication.

There was in the tree hut on the handmade bookshelf of deck planking a fine and varied collection of titles, less blackened with mildew than I might have expected. It had, I thought, been planned by the Claytons to serve them during their years in the South African colony. Aside from the obvious—the classics from Pliny to Shakespeare—there were entertainments from the Brontë sisters, Austen, and Doyle. What looked to be a centuries-old family Bible had recorded on the pages of the front and back covers the marriages, births, and deaths of generations of Claytons, and the proud passage of the title of the lords of Greystoke. All twenty-four volumes of the 1880 edition of the *Encyclopædia Britannica* stood in neat alphabetical order on the top shelf. But it was the bottom shelf that most captured my attention. Here were books that had been brought along for the edification and enjoyment of the expected child (or children). Hans Christian Andersen's *Fairy Tales*, *Alice's Adventure in Wonderland*, *The Adventures of Pinocchio*, *Treasure Island*. There was a primer for spelling and grammar, worn and grimy from tiny hands fingering and turning the pages. It explained Tarzan's quickness of learning. And it was with this primer that I began his reeducation.

We would sit for hours in the shade of a palm with the primer between us, and I did my best to move him through the lessons. At first the letters were *eta go nene*, little black bugs to him. But Alice, I thought, must have been a gifted teacher, for her little Johnnie, by leaps and bounds, mastered and relearned his letters and numbers in days, even writing in a childish but steady penmanship. When I began to read the Andersen fairy tales, my friend grew dewy-eyed and enraptured, and though I could not be sure he understood every word (for as yet he could not speak in complex sentences), his responses to the stories were most appropriate. When the Ugly Duckling was bitten and pushed and made fun of, Tarzan grew sad. When in *The Snow Queen* the hobgoblin with his evil mirror froze people's hearts, he trembled. Clearly they had been read to him over and over again, and if the words themselves made no sense, then the memory of the stories came back to him by heart.

I thought it a leap but decided to graduate to the encyclopedia. Starting with A–B, we began. I had never been so appreciative of the many finely wrought illustrations in the volumes as I now was, for much of the text was in language far beyond the young man's comprehension. I was forced to translate into simpler concepts, for example, what a locomotive engine was. To Tarzan it was a huge creature the size of three elephants. I explained it was not a living creature at all, rather made of the same material as his blade. Though not alive, it was able to move along a "track," ate a hard black soil called "coal," and made a loud noise as it came, spouting from its top a thick cloud of "steam." It was, I discovered to my chagrin, impossible to explain the new technology of "moving pictures."

I had been suddenly thrown into the role of teacher, something quite unknown to me, and I did the best I could. But I soon discovered I was doing all the guiding and decided that Tarzan himself should choose the direction of his education, and to that end I taught him, along with the questions "why?" "where?" "how?" "when?" and "who?" the phrases "Do you remember?" "Now imagine," and "Tell me about." This served me in two ways. First, I was spared the constant responsibility of the fledgling tutor for choosing subject matter and, happily, it provided a window into the workings of Tarzan's mind—the ways he perceived his experiences and the world he knew. What fascinated him and the gaps in his understanding that wanted filling.

I spread out a map of the world on his father's writing table, and we stood over it together. I had enjoyed geography as a schoolgirl, but explaining the entirety of the planet was overwhelming. I began by pointing out the continents and seas, the great mountain ranges and rivers, countries, cities, and towns.

Almost at once he asked, "Where are we?" It was a simple enough question, but his comprehension thrilled me nevertheless. I pointed at Africa and more specifically to the coast of Gabon, explaining that Zu-dak-lul was known to me as the "Atlantic Ocean." I moved my finger slightly inland, eastward, and pointed to my best estimation of the Mangani encampment, his own nest in Eden, Waziriland, and the hills of Sumbula.

Once Tarzan understood what the map represented, it became his obsession and he reveled in pointing to a place and demanding that I describe it. Not simply the location but all the details I could manage.

There were huge mountain ranges that made Sumbula look like anthills. Peaks so high they were freezing cold and covered with "snow" and "ice." People crossed the Atlantic Ocean in great "ocean liners." Men like him, wearing "suits of clothes," drove "automobiles" in "New York City," a place that had as many "buildings, *wallas*, as the forest had trees," some of the *wallas* as tall as mountains.

One day he said, "Tell me about London." I found myself speechless. Here was a subject about which I was more than conversant but had never been called upon to describe. That answer took the better part of a day, my pupil absorbing hundreds of new words and ideas. The encyclopedia provided drawings of Parliament and London Bridge and Buckingham Palace. I was not much inclined to theatrics, but I managed with the help of pantomime and mimicry to impersonate a variety of characters one might meet in the city—from a merchant to a beggar to a bobby. I attempted a barrister, a washerwoman, and a lorry driver. For a few moments I was Queen Victoria. My performance delighted Tarzan utterly, especially when I collapsed into giggles at my own silliness.

When I'd pointed out the Sahara Desert, he'd insisted I tell him about the desert, somewhere I had never been. I picked up a handful of fine-grained sand between us. "This is called 'sand.'" He repeated the word and learned it instantly, as he always did. "Now imagine a world of nothing but sand"—I pointed to the western horizon—"to there and there"—I pointed north and south—"all the way back to your nest. Nothing but sand, some of it in huge piles called 'dunes.' There are hardly any trees and very little water."

"I will see the desert?" he said, as much a pronouncement as a question.

"Well, yes, if you like," I answered in as even a tone as possible, realizing the implications of that simple promise. Tarzan had taken me under his wing, nursed me, protected me, discovered the fate of my father, and led me on the strangest of odysseys, introducing me to *Pithecanthropus aporterensus erectus,* and here to this beach holding the mysteries of his past. I would certainly, at some point in the near future, be called upon to bring him out into the wider world. How far from his home should he be taken? Surely his help would be necessary to get me as far as Libreville, but was it my duty to bring him back to England, present him to society, assist him in retrieving his birthright and title? Was it my duty . . . or my desire?

I was forced to admit that when he'd uttered the words "I will see the desert?" I'd envisioned my new friend standing tall on a windswept dune . . . with me at his side. Visions of Jane Digby and her Bedouin husband assailed me.

Impossible!

Our chance meeting, this exceptional adventure, and Tarzan's unbreakable bond with the Mangani might suggest some ties between us in the coming years. But what of the nature of those ties? What were my responsibilities to him? What were my feelings?

I had less question of what his feelings were toward me. I would find him staring openly at me in any and every circumstance. Listening with a cocked head if I hummed a tune. He was protective to a fault.

He would endlessly demand to hear about my *walla* in England, and my "nest." I would describe as best I could the Edlington-Porter estate—the grounds and greenwood, the manor, the stables, my canopied bed. I told him of the long dining table made with wood from the mahogany trees of a forest like his, with their "legs"—so different from the Waziri banana leaf table. My explanation of glass windows left even me confused. I attempted to show him the way to drink from one of the Claytons' teacups, but all he could do was laugh at the ridiculousness of the too-tiny, too-delicate "coconut shells" in his muscular fingers. He did a sight better with forks and knives and spoons but refused to employ them outside our lessons.

He liked especially to hear about the animals in England. The horses—"Like a *pacco,* zebra, but all of one color" and many times larger in size, upon whose backs I would ride at great speeds and jump over "hedges" and "stiles," followed by a pack of yapping hounds.

He urged me to make the sounds of all the animals I described and added them to his already prodigious repertoire. His eyes would grow wide as he imagined my descriptions and was shocked to hear that sometimes a tiny *sheeta* I called "Tabby" would sleep in my bed and wake me licking my neck with its tiny pink tongue. He thought it very odd that we should be forced to feed our animals to keep them alive. Why did they not feed themselves?

The day we sat under the palms, me describing the roses in my mother's garden, I began with no warning to cry, surprising myself and alarming Tarzan.

"What hurts you?" he said.

It was so hard to explain that despite this magnificent adventure, I was homesick. "I want to see my mother," I finally told him, sniffing back the tears, which did nothing but cause a flood of them to follow.

I felt an arm pulling at my shoulder and suddenly found my head in Tarzan's lap, facing out to sea. The next thing I knew he was picking at my scalp with the gentlest fingers. He was "grooming" me, perhaps what his Mangani mother had done to soothe him when he was small. My heart broke, for his losses and my own, and there were no more lessons the rest of that somber afternoon.

It was time, I realized, to begin reading Tarzan his parents' journal. There had been moments I'd been tempted to read on by myself, for my curiosity was intense. But there was fairness to be considered. This was young John Clayton's life to be revealed. What gave me the right to gain knowledge of it before he did?

For the reading of the diary I chose the inside of the hut, in order to protect this precious and most irreplaceable document. Since the burial of the remains, Tarzan and I had tidied up the place as well as we were able, and after remaking the bed with the least frayed linens found in a wooden trunk, I had begun to sleep in it, very grateful for its comforts. He had chosen to sleep on the porch just outside the door, the closeness of the walls unbearable for him for more than an hour or two. Likewise, he was loath to sit on the bed, and this I put down to that tragic experience of his mother's bones crumbling in his hands on this very spot.

And so I began reading, slowly and deliberately, stopping here and there to explain, simplify, or translate a word or passage Tarzan could not yet comprehend.

8 May 1885

While we thank God Almighty for our kindly treatment by the mutineers setting us down with all of our belongings, Alice and I yet find ourselves trapped in a nightmare from which there is no waking. We do our best, I with the building of the shelter, which I suppose could be called a tree house, and she furnishing it with the contents of her dower chest—the finest French linens, which we view with some irony laid across the crude bed that I have fashioned from the straightest of the found boards—and trying to eke out our stores of food by fishing, collecting small mollusks and seaweed, and partaking of the coconuts that have already fallen to the ground. Alice will not allow me to try my hand at climbing the long-necked trees, for if I should fall and injure myself or worse, all will be lost. She is right, of course, so I do not fight her on this, though I must admit to wanting more of the hairy-shelled fruit, its delicious white meat and delicate milk, the most refreshing of beverages.

In the last few days Alice has taken to helping me with my carpentry, something I at first protested, citing her delicate condition. She appraised me with a quirk of a smile and said, "I am not ill, my darling. I'm pregnant and perfectly capable of hammering a nail. The more help you have, the sooner we will have a shelter." It surprised and delighted me more than I could have imagined that Alice is no wilting violet. That she is indeed a true helpmate and what Coleridge called a "soul mate." I am blessed, so blessed.

Written with great hopes of rescue from a beach in Gabon,
John Clayton

23 June 1885

How odd it feels to take up the pen, for while I have since girlhood been an inveterate writer of letters to my friends, aunts, and cousins who lived a distance from Rutherford House, it had never occurred to me that my thoughts were worthy enough to warrant diary keeping. But here I am gazing over the sea from the window of the hut my hero of a husband built with his two hands, sitting at my mother's antique writing table—a wedding gift—preparing to pour out the contents of my heart on these pages next to John's own.

How it has come to this is all but inconceivable. How strange are the Fates that placed me first in the marriage bed of Lord Greystoke, who strayed far from the path set down for him by his father, instead following the commands of our Queen, then boarded us on a certain ship and, by the whimsy of a mutinous sailor called Great Henry, finally set us down on so deserted a shore as this.

I cannot say the Fates have been unkind, for we are not at the bottom of the sea. We've not died of malarial fevers, nor even suffer in the brittle cold of an English winter. The sun shines every day, breezes soothe our heated brows. We eat fish of a freshness indescribable and drink sweet rainwater collected in halves of coconut shells lining our porch. Our skins have grown golden tan (how horrified Mother would be!). But my belly bulges high and round, and by the sharp kicks and the tiny footprints that, to our delight and laughter, there appear, our child grows strong and healthy within.

John will read this, I know, but Diary, here is the truth of it: My husband, while always kind and attentive in our brief married life in England, held me as all men do their wives—as a sweet appendage and companion in the times set aside for family pleasures. Men work, attend to matters of business and estate. Women tend to social chores and children. Had we safely arrived at his post in Africa, our lives would yet have been separated by roles and rules, masculine and feminine.

But here on this beach no such lines of distinction apply. Some days I fish for our supper. He washes our clothes. I will collect wood for the fire. He will cook a crab and coconut stew. Still, I'll sew on a button. He will lift a heavy load. But that such sweet equality should exist I never imagined in the world.

I would be lying if I said I do not long for a feather bed, Bessie's apricot scones slathered in sweet cream, a stroll in Hampstead Heath on a crisp autumn morning, and most of all my mother's hand to hold when this babe is born.

But I do not curse the Fates or God for this strange adventure, one that I believe in my heart will end with eventual rescue. But it will leave its indelible mark on my life with John. Of this I'm sure. Once so tightly cleaved together, we shall never be torn asunder. We are one creature now, and for *that I can only give thanks to God and the Fates and to Great Henry himself, who, by the look of the wreck of the* Fuwalda, *is already in the arms of Jesus.*

Written in gratitude from a beach in Gabon,
Alice Clayton

18 September 1885

I have in the many months of this sojourn thought myself a brave man. But I have in the last day been rudely disabused of that notion. For without benefit of physician or midwife I was called upon to bring my child into the world. Before Alice's true labor began, I had time to muse on the sheer unorthodoxy of a husband presiding over this most primal of occasions. I would in the society we once knew have paced impatiently, whiskey and cigar in hand, in the downstairs salon, far enough away from the birthing chamber to be spared the womanly shrieks of pain, and I, like all men, would wait for news of a joyous birth (or the tragic death of mother or child, or both).

Modesty prevents me from imparting the sometimes gruesome particulars, but finally the moment came and there I stood between Alice's thighs, she the picture of courage to my knee-clacking terror, pulling the slippery head and shoulders of our son from her heaving body, waiting breathless to hear the first squalling cry that would signal he lived.

But it did not come. An eternity passed in terrible silence broken only by Alice's exhausted panting and my own feeble gasps of defeat. My eyes met hers, her face wet with sweat and tears of pain, lips twitching, but no words came forth. She should have been shouting out to God her fury at this betrayal, but she was silent. "Alice," I thought but could not say aloud, "I love you more than words have meaning to express. I love you to distraction, whether this child lives or dies."

And then it came. From the bloody bundle I held in my two hands a sound more welcome than a chorus of angels. Not a whimper or choked spluttering but a demanding bawl, a raucous cry, a clamorous announcement of new life!

Alice collapsed into sobs of relief as I laid our son on her breast and cut the cord, tying it twice. Little John Clayton, having taken his place in the world, lost no time seeking his first meal. I helped Alice to sitting, and the boy sucked noisily. I left them, she staring down at the miracle in her arms, *and sought the narrow porch outside the door, gulping in fresh air and trying to still my knocking knees.*

The sun had commenced its setting behind a great wall of grey and gold and orange clouds, a storm far out to sea. Here the waves still lapped lazily on the shore as though unaware of what forces behind would whip them soon into frenzied foam, and before them a rude hut in which a storm of a different kind had already been weathered.

I laid my head on the rail and began to weep, relieved of unutterable terror and racked with unspeakable joy. We have borne a child, Alice and I. Little Lord Greystoke. John Clayton. Johnnie. Our son. Beloved. Beloved. Beloved.

Written with all the beauty and blessings of Heaven and Earth about me,
John Clayton

I looked up from the page blinded by tears to find Tarzan standing behind me.

"I was born here?" he said, as much a statement as a question.

I looked across the room. "You were. In that bed."

"My father was John Clayton?" Tarzan was thinking very hard. "*I am John Clayton? I am . . . Johnnie?*"

I nodded a vigorous affirmation.

"Who is Lord Greystoke?"

Ha! What a question. How on earth could I possibly explain the idiocy and ridiculous complexity of titles and noble lineage? That Tarzan, a naked jungle dweller, was a peer of England, heir to a vast fortune, owner of farms and greenwoods, houses in country and town, master of servants, tenants, gardeners, gamekeepers, client to groveling lawyers and accountants, each at his beck and call? A seat in Parliament awaited him! It was ludicrous and altogether indescribable.

"I will explain this at another time. Is that all right, Tarzan?"

He nodded, then said, "My mother is Alice."

"That's right."

"My mother is Alice Clayton."

My mother was Alice Clayton, I wanted to correct him. But I could not bring myself to make a grammatical point that might remind Tarzan of his loss.

"Why don't we read more some other day?" I suggested, and after a considerable moment of thought, he agreed.

I could see that Tarzan was mesmerized by the stories of his mother and father and the innermost workings of their hearts. He would sit alone staring out at the sea mouthing words or phrases he remembered from the journal. I tried to avoid disturbing his thoughts, for it seemed to me he was piecing together all that he knew of Zu-dak-lul with everything he had learned from the diary: *Fuwalda*, Great Henry, writing table, Heaven and Earth.

"Beloved," I heard him whisper as he sat below the hut cleaning a fish he had caught for our dinner, "I love her to distraction."

We were scouring the beach for small delectable crabs and the long strands of salty seaweed I had come to enjoy.

"Tell me about your mother," he said.

"My mother?" The question took me by storm. Where to begin? How could I make Tarzan understand the complexity of emotions I had for her? Here was a man who had known feelings for his two mothers, deep and purely loving, unsullied by resentment or contentious battles. Mothers who had urged him to his full potential, whether swimming or climbing or wrestling, whereas mine had straitjacketed me in innumerable ways. Her social etiquette was intolerable. She was stubborn to a fault. And yet I had, from the earliest days of my childhood, been altogether certain of her maternal affections. Too, she had in the end given her permission for me to come to Africa—a courageous act by any standards.

"My mother's name is Samantha," I finally said. "Like your mother Alice, she is very beautiful. Her eyes are green and her skin is very fair. Many people say my features 'resemble' hers"—I touched my eyes and nose and mouth—"meaning they are very much like hers. The same way your features resemble your father's."

"So you are beautiful, too. Like your mother."

I marveled at Tarzan's improving skills of logic, even as I acknowledged the compliment with a shy nod.

"She and my father were married for many years."

"What is 'married'?"

"Uh . . ." I stalled for time, scooping up a long strand of seaweed and winding it around my arm, but I could see that Tarzan was eager for an answer. How could I ever begin to explain the typical marriages of our society? Here was an institution that was in almost all instances abhorrent to me. There were exceptions, of course. My parents had wed for love's sake, and apparently John and Alice Clayton's arranged union had blossomed into deep affection.

I would, I decided, simply avoid any explanation of forced marriages whose sole purpose was the enrichment in fortune or status, or the continuity of a family's high and mighty bloodline. I would describe only the romantic ideal.

"When a *tar-zan* man and woman love each other," I began as though treading on a path of broken glass, "they give each other rings." I pointed to the gold band on Tarzan's little finger, "like your mother and father did. The man and woman promise to live together in the same *walla* all through their lives. They . . . mate . . . and have many children—*balu*."

I sighed, wondering how so simple a sentence could be fraught with such huge and labyrinthine ideas. Tarzan had grown silent, contemplating my explanation. I shuddered at the thought that he might ask me next what love was.

How on earth would I answer him? What did I know of love? I was probably the only person alive who found *Romeo and Juliet* preposterous—two children who, in the course of several days, conceive a passion so violent that they would rather die than live without each other. I'd always assumed their affair was simple lust, wallpapered over with flowery words and chivalric ideals. Suddenly I realized with horror that any explanation of married love would certainly entail some mention of the sex act, and I began to flush red remembering those wild gropings in the Waziri hut. Here before me was a man of primordial desires but possessing no more than a childish grasp of emotion.

And suddenly I was faced with the most embarrassing irony: When it came to the subjects of love and passion, I was no less naïve than Tarzan of the Jungle.

He helped me fill the skirt of my shift with the crabs, and we started up the beach for the hut. To my great relief, no further mention of marriage or love was made.

* * *

Tarzan had asked if I would read him more of the journal. This time he sat on the floor of the hut with his back up against the bed in which he had been born. When he closed his eyes I knew he was ready to begin. He was picturing it all as I read, I thought, teasing from his lost memories the faces of his parents, imagining his mother on the beach at Zu-dak-lul bending to gather sticks of driftwood, his father cooking a crab and coconut stew. How I blessed them, John and Alice Clayton, for leaving this warm and brilliant record, illuminating for their child that which would otherwise have left him blind and groping in the dark, bereft of his beginnings.

Further, I apprehended that this young man had been raised in his earliest days by parents who shared the exact sensibilities, society, and intelligence as my own. Had Tarzan been born John Clayton in England, I might have known him, sipped tea with him, perhaps even had him put forward as a suitor. The thought took my breath away.

"Read, Jane," he said.

"*Please* read, Jane," I corrected him, then caught myself. *By ingrained habit I am turning him into a gentleman of manners, the kind of person I most abhor in the world.* I smiled when he did not obey my correction. He might come to speak the King's English, one day come to be a man of the world, but he knew his own mind. He was still Tarzan. I would never, I realized with certainty, wish him otherwise.

18 September 1886

John has insisted on keeping a calendar, simple marks with his Bowie knife upon a wooden plank, and by his reckoning, Johnnie is one year old today. Not much in the way of celebration, just a "Happy Birthday" song. Our boy, having never heard both his parents singing at once to him (I croon him all his lullabies), began to giggle madly, putting his fingers to our mouths to quiet us. But we wouldn't quiet, and sang it again, even louder. He fell about laughing and rolling in the sand, parroting the words "Happy Birthday," which he repeated all day long. For a present, John carved him a boat with three sails, but the waves were too rough to set it in the water. Otherwise the day was like any other.

My favorite times are when John reads to me while I feed my child. I know full well that women of my station never dream of suckling their infants. That is the job of a wet nurse. Most would grant that a "Mrs. Robinson Crusoe" cast away on a desert shore, having none to serve for this task, must take it on herself and, while pitying me, would not chastise me, for the child needs feeding. What would scandalize the matrons and disgust brides-to-be is my passionate love of having my son drink from my milk-swollen breasts and the pleasure of his peaceful, contented gaze into my own. At first he was ravenous, fastening hard and biting my nipples till they grew red and sore. But I sang to him, rocked him in the chair by the window, and soon he softened, knowing his wants would always be met. It is a miracle to me, and one on which I had never spent a second thought, that a mother's milk is all a child needs to live. That my body provides rich sustenance, a fountain of life. Oh, they would be scandalized, my cousins and friends, even my mother, to hear such ruminations, but they are all far away. My child, however, is close as he can be, and my husband, too, head tilted down at the book as he reads me Romeo and Juliet, my favorite of the Bard's plays.

"My bounty is as boundless as the sea,
My love as deep; the more I give to thee
The more I have, for both are infinite."

It seems outrageous. Dare I say it? I am content.
Written on our son's happy birthday on the beach in Gabon,
Alice Clayton

17 January 1888

I have few complaints except, perhaps, the monotony of food. Our stores from the ship are long gone and now we eat only what is at hand. I have fashioned a long pole allowing me, from the roof of our hut and various branches of the baobab, to knock coconuts down that would have taken longer to fall, so we have all the milk and meat of that fruit that we desire. I'm frankly sick of fish and would give my eyeteeth for a slab of rare beef and a pile of roasted potatoes. Bread pudding with hard sauce, a glass of aged port.

Enough of that. Johnnie is doing marvelously well, sharp as a whip. Alice and I split his day, me with my "manly chores," she with lessons. He loves his books. At three he's learned to read and knows his numbers. The child is a chatterbox and can barely be silenced. If he is not reading aloud, he is singing. If not singing, then spouting off the thoughts in his head— what he sees, what he hears, what he imagines, what he wonders. He is a gushing fount of questions. Why does the fish stop moving when you knock it on the head? Why is the sun yellow in the day and orange as it sets? How many crabs are in the sea? Why do birds fly? When they dive into the water, how do they always come up with a fish in their beaks? Why does Mummy have breasts, and not me? And on and on . . .

The only way I can silence him is by working him, and even at three, he is quite a good apprentice. He has learned to hammer a nail, however crooked. He is a patient fisherman and has caught a great many of our dinners. He is a prodigious collector of crabs and turtle eggs and does not mind handling the slimy seaweed, which Alice prefers not to do. To her horror, I have allowed Johnnie to place his little hand around the grip of my Bowie knife, for one day he must learn to wield the blade, though I draw the line with my machete. This I wield with some violence in order to chop coconuts in half. Alice holds him in her lap as I swing downward, hoping to split it cleanly, catching the milk in a bowl below, and as many times, like a circus clown, I miss it altogether (on purpose, to give them a show and a giggle).

But our favorite times, Johnnie's and mine, are swimming in the sea. He is fearless of the water and shrieks with delight as I carry him through the breakers to the calm. I do admit a certain worry as I release him and push backward away from him, watching his doggy paddle, the excited grin, the shining eyes, he waiting for the moment I say, "Come on, Johnnie, swim to me. You can do it!" Then he comes, splashing arm over arm, legs kicking wildly. He's fast and strong, my boy, and when he reaches my arms he laughs triumphant, holding me tight and kissing my face.

Written with pride and happiness from a beach in Gabon,
John Clayton

30 March 1888

Our boy is very agile. Today John took him to the roof of the hut and, standing below the lowest overhanging limb of the baobab, allowed him to reach up and grab on, instructing him to throw a leg over and pull himself up and onto the bough. How pleased Johnnie was to be sitting there! His father followed, and together, very carefully, with John the safety net, me with my heart in my throat, they climbed their first tree.

John and I did not hear the end of it all day, how high he had gone, the bird nests into which he peeked, the lizards he saw that changed colors from red to green to brown. And the question: What would happen if he fell from such a height? Johnnie babbled all through supper and was only quieted as a storm came thundering upon us from the sea.

There were great explosions of lightning and waves crashing far up on the beach below. We three pushed back in the corner of our bed, John holding an arm around each of us, pulling us tight and weaving stories of flying horses and brave guardian angels so that, as the tornado roared overhead, there never was a moment that we were gripped by fear, but rather swam in our private sea of happiness, contentment, and love.

Written on a peaceful morning after the storm,
Alice Clayton

It was not all about lessons or reading from the journal, our time at the edge of the world. Tarzan and I swam every day in the sea, and I grew stronger. We played in the waves when they were gentle, one morning diving below to follow after an ancient turtle studded with barnacles, its paddle-shaped feet speeding it out from the dappled sunlit shallows into the depths of a blue-black abyss.

Tarzan would race the length of the beach, glorying in the space and freedom unknown in the forest or jungle. I found I could not tear my eyes from the sight of his magnificence. He was more beautiful and more dear to me with every passing day.

"You run, Jane," he commanded me one afternoon. "You run."

I hesitated. Had I ever run before? A little girl was taught to walk with proper composure. A young lady might leap about in short bursts after a tennis ball. But to run unhindered with the wind in her hair? It was unheard of.

He was standing there waiting for my answer. "We'll run together, side by side," I said.

Tarzan's smile was mischievous. He sat himself down in the sand. "I will watch you run."

"No!" I cried, suddenly shy at the thought of this handsome voyeur appraising my nearly naked body in motion. I pulled him to his feet. "You will run with me."

And so, with this mighty athlete at my side, I ran for the pure joy of it, racing the length of the Gabonese beach till my thighs ached and my lungs burned. Ran until we fell laughing onto the sand.

That night the air was thick with salted wind, and I fell into a restless sleep, dreaming of my father. We were in the sea together, he a distance away calling, "Come on, swim to me, sweetheart!" His wide-open face beamed, and the spray glinted like chipped diamonds around his long, curly hair. I stroked toward him with smooth grace, relishing the moment he would catch me up and praise my efforts. Then in the sweetest collision I was in his arms, face-to-face. But when I looked up, it wasn't Father. It was Tarzan, his grey eyes sparkling, his black mane curled and dripping around his broad shoulders. "Beloved," he murmured, "I love you to distraction," then he kissed me deeply, hungrily. In the cold water, flesh seared against naked flesh causing steam to rise all around us. My head swam and I drowned happily in his embrace . . . till I woke with a start, momentarily disoriented at my whereabouts.

The dream had rattled me. What could I be thinking! What was I feeling? I forced myself fully awake. I needed to keep my wits about me. I really did.

I felt a sudden urgency to continue reading the Claytons' journal, and now my listener sat rapt at his place on the floor beside the bed.

<u>2 December 1888</u>

An unsettling occurrence has got me on edge. Worse still, dear Alice is quite unconcerned. I think she has been lulled by our strangely idyllic existence and her perception of me (a quite incorrect one) as a hero. I feel anything but heroic after this morning's sighting of a most frightening creature.

I have for all of these nearly four years been able to keep at bay any wild animals that happen onto the beach and threaten us in the least. On several occasions, a large crocodile has wandered from the brackish outlet of the mangrove swamp and onto the sand. The first time a blast from my rifle gave the animal a fright and it turned tail, returning whence it had come. The second time it emerged in the night, and in the morning it was Alice who received the fright when she opened our door and found the armored reptile, twelve feet long, sunning itself just below the porch. I dispatched the thing with a single shot. It proved my first experience with skinning and butchering an animal. We tried to cook and eat its meat, but we all found it distasteful. Its pieces (quickly putrefying in the sun) had to be hauled down to the shore and set out to sea.

The spotted leopard that came padding up the beach from the south was scared away by warning shots from the Winchester and never returned. These incidents, I presumed, imbued Alice with a false sense of security of which I (quite wrongly) failed to disabuse her. For it was from these incidents I came to believe that I, with my weaponry, could repel any and all threats to our well-being.

But this morning there emerged from the mangroves perhaps 300 long paces from the hut, a "thing" that struck such unreasoning fear into my heart that these many hours later I am still unnerved and trembling. How shall I describe it? It was an ape . . . but not an ape.

T he whole of my body tingled with gooseflesh. I looked down and the hair on my forearms stood erect. All at once Tarzan swept past me, a blur, and out the hut door. By the time I had laid down the journal and followed him, I found that he had attained the highest branch of the baobab above the tree house. He squatted there on a limb staring out to sea.

"Tarzan, come down!"

He disregarded my call as though he had not heard me. The problem, I knew, was that he *had* heard me. Heard the words I had read from the journal. The frightening "ape-man" that had emerged from the swamp was Mangani. I was dangerously close to opening the door behind which lay the darkest and most terrible secrets of young John Clayton's past. It must be true, I thought, gazing up at perhaps the strongest human being on earth, he crouched in a pathetic posture avoiding my call, refusing to hear more of the story that had, until now, so delighted him.

I considered climbing the baobab. It would be unwise, I decided. I was yet unskilled for such a feat without Tarzan's close assistance. And besides, he had fled from the story in the journal for a reason. Though it pained and frightened me to see Tarzan in so weakened a state, I must give him all the time he needed. He would come down when he was ready to go on.

Just after the sun set in a blaze of outrageous crimson and serpentine green, he descended and came to sit with me on the porch outside the hut door, the place from which John Clayton had first spied the ape that was not an ape.

"I must tell you," he said, his voice choked with misery.

"What? Tell me what?"

He raked his fingers across his forehead.

"Is it a story?"

"A story, yes."

"What is it about?"

"About *Boi-ee* . . . Bowie," he corrected himself. "And Kerchak. And Kala." His voice quavered at this last.

"I was a . . . boy." Tarzan raised his hand five and a half feet above the floor. Perhaps he'd been thirteen or fourteen. "I stand in the mangroves, there." He pointed inland. "I have come from Zu-dak-lul. The blade"—he balled up his fist as if gripping the hilt—"it is in my hand."

As he began to weave the tale in words he had recently learned, I saw it clearly in my mind's eye—like a moving picture. Heard the words as if in a play. Felt the depth of feeling he so simply and perfectly conveyed . . .

Blade

The cool, salted air of Zu-dak-lul had disappeared quickly as the boy plunged inland through the mangrove swamp. He thought about the blade hanging at his waist from a hide thong and sheath, the way the knife felt as if it belonged there. It was his. It had always been his.

As he pulled the blade from its sheath, he wondered at the perfection with which the handle of the blade fit the palm of his hand. But then he had never once left Zu-dak-lul without the sensation of wonder, confusion, or elation. Sometimes an unnameable fear. This was, however, the first in all of his solitary visits to the bower by the great water that he had taken something away with him.

It was not as though before this he had found the blade of little interest. He had handled it on innumerable occasions since its discovery. The first time he'd slid his fingers across the sharpened edge he'd sliced the flesh. Surprised, he'd cried out, but as he sucked the blood away, his surprise was mild, perhaps tempered with the same wonder he now felt at the grip of the knife's hilt. Somewhere within him was the sure knowledge that the artifact could cause harm. It was meant to cut and stab, and that with it held in his hand he could become a brave hunter, like ko-sabor, the mighty lioness.

As he moved from mangrove swamp to jungle, he felt a gnawing in his belly. He knew his hunger would be sated by a handful of nuts or pawpaw, or the white worms he could pick from the wood of a rotting log. The watering holes with snails and crabs were still far ahead of him. But he longed to employ the blade. So he stopped, ceased all forward movement. He lifted his eyes and attuned his ears to the canopy above. He drew breath equally between his mouth and nose, tasting the air in a long slow pull.

Oh, the kambo was rich with life! The sweetly rotting stew of the jungle floor, the animals in all their abundance. The perfumed flowers in profusion.

He should hunt before the rain began again, he knew, for the scent of his prey would weaken in the downpour. There! He inhaled the faintest whiff of manu just above his head, but he hesitated. Monkey meat was hearty and delicious, he knew from the bits of it left on the bone after a kill and before it had been picked clean by vultures or ants, but the furred creature with long agile limbs had a form and a face close in shape and features to the Mangani—his clan—and eating its flesh always left him uneasy. He found a fat dan-sopo tree, its trunk encircled with roots, and began to climb, the footing so easy he ascended quickly. There were myriad meals along the way. The nuts that grew on the tree. A fat lizard. Curled green fern fronds tempted him, for they were tender and luscious and required only that he pluck them and put them in his mouth. But Tarzan longed for something more. Something upon which he might use the blade to subdue.

The barest movement and swish along a burly limb below him was loud to his ear, and before he saw histah the skin beneath his forearms shuddered, the hair rose, and his loathing for the creature was felt as a fleeting jab in the pit of his belly. He saw the snake then, almost as long as the boy was tall, just now finishing a curl into itself, yellowish with its black bars hidden within the coil, and its head drawn down to settle at its apex. It was a night hunter, he knew, but even as it had found shelter from the heat of the day under a broad leaf, histah would not hesitate to strike if provoked.

Tarzan nearly ceased his breathing and drew the blade from its sheath with slow and infinite care, for even if histah could not hear well, its incessantly flicking tongue could taste the most delicate scents—the faint wafting of musk from the pit of his arm. His breath. His fear.

He remembered the Mangani balu who had fallen victim to the yellow snake. She lay on the ground spasming violently. When blood began to seep from her eyes and out from under the fur of her arms and chest, all life left the child's body, and a great wailing went up from the clan.

The boy's mother, Kala, had pulled him and his sister, Jai Kala, close, clutching them to her with such ferocity that her long fingers dug into his flesh. "Histah uglu utor," she whispered. Hate and fear the snake. From that moment, all and every histah, small or harmless though it might be, was avoided by the boy. Now as he watched the creature sleeping below him, he saw that he could kill it with the blade. If he ate its flesh, he would not simply quell his gnawing hunger but also gain the strength of histah, if only for a while.

I must be quick and clever, he thought, or I will die like the Mangani balu. *Then he saw, not a hand's breadth from his face, his salvation—a bright blue* rok *staring placidly down from the white-petaled flower in which it was cradled. The boy well knew this frog, its habits, the distance of its leap. He also knew the creature's language, its sounding. Never taking his eye from* histah, *the boy croaked hoarsely.* Rok *echoed the sound precisely. It was a greeting, given and returned.* I am a friend, *it said, sharing the same branch.*

Histah *remained immobile, unmoved by the conversation above it. With another call, Tarzan moved carefully and took up the* rok *in his hand. His fingers curled like a small prison around the frog. Then before* rok *could begin to struggle, the boy threw it down to the branch upon which* histah *rested. But not for long. The movement, the scent, and the sight of perfect prey caused an uncoiling, jaw-expanding assault that, in its speed, rivaled a lightning strike.*

Once the snake was stretched to its full length, devouring Tarzan's sacrifice, he dropped with perhaps less grace than purpose and began his assault. The long, muscular body twisted around the boy's body, causing great terror in him. The dangerous head whipped from side to side, poisonous fangs snapping at him, keeping all of the attacker's limbs employed in a frenzied defense. But something burned in the boy, even it the midst of his struggle.

With a burst of strength that he never knew he possessed, he grasped the snake's neck with one hand and with the other slashed the head from it. While the long body still writhed, curling around the boy's leg, there was, he realized with some shock, nothing left to fear. He had killed histah *with this blade! He shouted with joy.*

The body of the beast had finally stilled and now Tarzan slit the skin of the belly from end to end, taking great and slow pleasure in the precision of his task. He stopped then. Snakes were strange creatures. Did they have entrails like monkeys and birds, that might be removed and eaten separately from the flesh? With the knife's tip he made a deeper cut and pulled it the length of the flaccid body. Yes. There were entrails, but Tarzan had no stomach for them. Pulling them out, he threw them to the ground—a good meal for the jungle pigs.

He wrapped his fingers tightly around the top of histah's *headless, gutless body and pulled the skin from the flesh, cleaning from it the remaining blood and membrane. Then filled with satisfaction, Tarzan sank his teeth into the flesh of his once-feared and hated enemy.*

It was surprisingly sweet.

The triumph over histah *brought added strength to the boy's body and a new clarity to his senses. Wrapping the snakeskin around his forehead and tying it in the back, he continued his journey.*

When the first of the monstrous tall and thick-trunked trees came into sight, his heart grew calm. Soon he would be among his tribe and the warm embrace of his mother, receive the playful jabs and jostles of his sister.

Tarzan began to climb the first of the trees that divided the jungle from the forest. He stood in the crook of the tree and leaped into what, for anyone but him, would have seemed an endless void. Tarzan lived for this feeling of flight, of soaring. Through these branches he swung his lithe body hand over hand above the forest floor. To home he flew. To Kala, his mother, her warmth and indulgence. He knew that in Mangani eyes other than hers he was dwarfish: "The Scrawny One." "The Weakling." "The strange white-skin . . . tar-zan."

He'd long suspected it was his stunted proportions and pale hairlessness that had forced Kala's nest and that of her two children to be built at the farthest edge of the clearing. That he was a shame to his race. To Kerchak, their leader, the boy was an affront, an abomination.

Nevertheless, Kala loved him. He had never known a time when her strong, brown-furred arms had not tended his many scrapes and bruises. He could not remember when her deft fingers had not tenderly groomed him. When she had not uttered soothing words of mother love and kissed his one puny patch of fur on the top of his head.

Kerchak plagued Kala with threatening displays, pounding his massive chest, baring his teeth, sometimes lashing out, even striking her. But where other females cowered, Kala stood tall. The boy would watch amazed as she held Kerchak's eyes, mad and flashing with unreasonable fury—amazed that his menacing did not frighten her. Finally he growled, and with one last pounding of his chest turned away and climbed to his nest, twice as high as all the others.

There were words to describe the rages into which Kerchak would sometimes fly. He was "gumado b'nala," Kala told her son, "sick in head."

Tarzan could hear, before he could see, the circular grove of giant trees that was the Mangani bower. He knew by the commotion of sound, excited hoots and howls, the calling of names and instructions that something was afoot. All of the bower's members were on the ground and gathered tightly around something Tarzan could not yet see. They did not know of his arrival.

He thought to surprise them. Enter the clearing with no warning calls that the Mangani used to announce their coming. But just as this thought crossed his mind, the head of a female snapped back, her flared nostrils twitching.

It was Kala, his mother. She had smelled him, perhaps sensed him in that strange way all mothers felt their children's presence. How simple of him to think he could take her by surprise.

"Tarzan!" Kala cried, her rich, throaty call resonating beyond the bower clearing.

His heart bursting with joy, he darted from the bush toward the gathering of Mangani. Some looked up at his approach, others fixed too intently at their feet to care. He sprinted in Kala's direction, saw her smiling eyes and teeth bared in a happy grin. He was proud of his mother—the strongest and most beautiful of the Mangani females. But before he reached her long outstretched arms, the boy was knocked off his feet by the furred projectile that was Jai, his sister. They rolled and tumbled together, wrestling and pummeling as they had since their earliest youth. She was as strong as he and enjoyed biting his hairless neck with a soft, playful mouth. He liked to tickle her to hear the grunting laugh, so different from his own. Suddenly he felt a strong hand on the scruff of his neck. Kala pushed her children apart and Jai tumbled away to let their mother embrace him.

Ah, those arms, the clasp of affection that had, from earliest childhood, been the soul of his world, the web of safety, warmth, and the purest love. He sank his face onto her shoulder and inhaled the rich scent of female musk, her fur suffused with fragrances of all the leaves and mosses through which she had moved.

She pushed him to arm's length to observe his face, learn by his expression how he had fared on his solitary adventure. It was then she noticed the skin of histah tied around his forehead. She recoiled in a moment of unguarded reflex.

"Bundolo histah," he said. I kill snake.

Her look demanded to know how this had been accomplished, and with care, so as not to further alarm her, Tarzan withdrew the blade from its sheath. Jai came close and stared openly at the terrifying adornment on her brother's head and the strange stick he held in his hand.

"Boi-ee," he said, naming it. The word came to him unbidden in that moment, surprising him. It was the merest fragment of a memory, and he was unsure from where it had come.

"Boi-ee," Kala repeated and moved to touch it. He stayed her hand.

"Uta," he said. Danger. Now he had attracted the attention of several of the huddled group. They stared at the shining object of a shape and material they had never before encountered. Now, too, the boy could see the locus of the crowd's interest.

On the ground lay the body of a pacco. It was quite dead, a fresh kill, yet there were but two puncture holes in its neck. No mangling or mauling had been visited upon the animal.

"Pacco," Jai said.

"Numa Bundolo. Ho tantor b'zeebo numa." A lion had attacked the zebra, but before it could be eaten, a family of elephants had come stampeding and the cat had been trampled to death.

"Dako-za rut," said Kala. The flesh is tough. Tarzan could see there was no way to extract the meat. The many sticks the Mangani had been using to tear at the hide had broken, the puncture wounds too small to allow even the sharpest stones to rip them open.

Tarzan felt an upwelling of assurance. He stepped to the center of the gathering, well aware that all eyes, suspicious and contemptuous, were on the puny Mangani. Without a word, he knelt beside the pacco and raised the blade high over his head. There was awed silence at the sight of its point, dangerous as the fang of histah and so much larger. But as a ray of sunlight struck the metal shaft, its glinting fire wrenched from every Mangani's throat a cry of terror.

Then with all force he could gather into both hands, shoulders, and arms, Tarzan brought the blade down into the haunch of the zebra. Now the boy, using the sharp edge, cut the hide from the leg, exposing the dark pink flesh and white sinew. Working with precision, he removed the muscle and cut it into pieces, handed one first to Kala, one to Jai, and then to the other suddenly admiring Mangani.

Without looking up from his work, the boy could feel the warm pride of his mother, the delight of his sister, and the begrudging and bewildered murmurings of respect for Kala's hairless runt . . . or at least the dreaded weapon he now possessed.

Then, without warning, a seething storm of rage roared down upon them, fists and feet flying, great fanged mouth snapping, eyes fixing with murderous intention on all and any that did not flee the might of Kerchak.

Most did run, mothers snatching up their little ones, all making for their nests, cowering in twos and threes, teeth chattering.

Jai, too, had fled for the trees. Tarzan and Kala alone stood their ground, she with eyes blazing, and he, back straight, clutching the blade with white-knuckled terror. The rank smell of fear hung above the neatly butchered carcass.

The tar-zan had received more blows from Kerchak than he could remember. Even at the distance Kala's nest was set away from the clan's and from their leader's nest high above, any and all chance encounters between the two would end with a clout of a fist to the head, a blow to an arm or leg or torso with the shaft of Kerchak's favorite weapon—a stout branch—or a tear to the flesh with its ragged end.

These attacks, much as Kala raged against them, could not be avoided. They had begun before the boy could remember and continued till the day he had left on his most recent journey to Zu-dak-lul.

"Kagado balu-den Kerchak." The great beast, three times the boy's size, weight, and strength, was demanding the blade, what he called a stick, to be surrendered to him.

"Tand," Tarzan said. It was the word for refusal, never ever spoken to Kerchak.

"Tand kagado?" A sound came from deep in the creature's throat. It was a rumbling growl and, as it grew, the expression on Kerchak's face became more frightening than anything the boy had ever seen.

"Kagado balu-den!" Kerchak roared in Tarzan's face, the stench of his breath fouling the air around him.

The boy raised his arm and put the knife in Kerchak's palm. The moment the beast's face settled into satisfaction and his long furred fingers closed around the blade, Tarzan, his own fist tight on the grip, drew it backward with swift force.

Kerchak howled with surprise and pain, as the razor edge sliced through the thick pad of his hand.

The boy could see the pupils growing black, the whites red veined, and the face beginning to twitch with fury. Kerchak raised the bloody hand, but before he could strike, the boy, with a defiance he never knew he possessed, sent the blade flying end over end through the still, silent air. It sailed for so great a distance that it disappeared into the thicket of the far boundary of the bower's clearing.

He could see, however, that Kerchak had raised his uninjured hand into a fist nearly the size of the boy's head. In a moment it would come down into the center of his face. The blow would certainly kill him.

But suddenly, there at Kerchak's back was Kala with a rock held in both her hands. No, Mother! Tarzan thought. The rock is too small. Its blow will only anger him further! But in the next moment the rock found its mark—the side of Kerchak's skull above his ear. This deception by the runt and now this adding of insult to injury was more than Kerchak could bear. The eyes, already black with rage, transformed into that madness that all Mangani most feared.

The blow to the boy's head came rapidly and with such force that he was suddenly sprawled supine across the pacco, his ears ringing and his body paralyzed.

But Kala had, as Tarzan vaguely realized, accomplished her intended purpose. Diversion.

Cut and tricked by the tar-zan runt, then battered by the most unmanageable of females before every member of his tribe, a humiliated Kerchak now watched Kala race across the clearing. Deranged by frenzy and forgetting the boy, he took chase.

Kala began to climb the tree farthest from where Tarzan lay, still struggling to rise. She was strong and nimble, but massive as Kerchak was, the power in his limbs made him fast. Once high above, her foe in close pursuit, Kala shouted down to her son.

"Boi-ee!" she cried. "Boi-ee!"

He understood at once. She had drawn Kerchak away so he could retrieve the blade. Now, fighting pain and dizziness, he rose to his knees and finally his feet. He scrambled best as he could and, blotting out the sound of Mangani screeching above him, crossed the clearing and dove into the thicket into which he had thrown his knife.

He pushed aside branches and leaves, scouring the ground with his eyes. Where was it? With the knife in hand he could face Kerchak. Save his mother. There! The handle was barely visible among the woody stalks, but the moment it was in his hand he felt power returning to his body, clarity to his mind.

He ascended the closest tree and emerged on high with a view of the bower—the screeching, cowering Mangani, and the only movement to be seen in the whole canopy: Far across the central clearing his mother evaded her enemy. She was running on her long straight legs along thick boughs, arms outstretched for balance. She leaped over voids where thin branches would not hold her, knowing all the time that Kerchak was gaining, knocking terrified Mangani from the forks and nests in which they cowered, unable or unwilling to come to the aid of the female of renown. Now, for Kala, there was no way out.

Tarzan, too, was gaining on Kerchak. He had learned well from his mother the art of upright limb running and was as fleet on his feet as she.

Kala had stopped and stood in a nest of fresh cuttings. Here she turned to face her pursuer. The end had come for her. Running was futile.

Kerchak came slowly now, his eyes altogether mad, every muscle straining and pulsing. Keeping sight of his prey, he reached out and snapped off a thick branch. Weapon in hand, he advanced. There was terror in Kala's eyes as she backed away, back from the nest. He followed her into the matting of woven leaves and branches.

He felt his mistake at once.

The nest was newly built, a first attempt of a young male recently gone from his mother's bower. It had easily held Kala's weight, but it was far too flimsy for Kerchak's.

The nest collapsed and Kerchak fell straight down, the leaves and twigs falling after him, raining on his head and shoulders.

There were hoots of Mangani laughter, but not for long. For the final trickery, the unconscionable humiliation of the leader by a female, was nothing short of a death sentence.

Kala began swinging arm over arm amid the branches that hung over the clearing. It was then she saw, to her horror, that the boy she had risked her life to save had not retrieved his Boi-ee and fled from the fury of the insane beast she'd drawn away from him.

No, Tarzan was running along a branch high above Kerchak—Kerchak, who had found footing on limbs below ones through which Kala now swung. He was thrashing upward with his club, trying to break her legs. She did not stop. Just moved, finding handhold after handhold and pulling up her feet to avoid his blows.

Yet her eyes searched for her son. She wanted to cry out that he should save himself. Now she lost sight of the boy and slowed to find him, stopped for the briefest moment and hung by both arms far above the forest floor.

She was not, therefore, aware that Kerchak had found an angled limb and deftly climbed it. At the moment she found sight of her child, she sensed Kerchak suddenly above her and knew without seeing that the club was rising above his head. Tarzan's expression told her as much.

She loved the boy so. Knew him to be fine and strong and clever. She had meant to save him today, he, never knowing himself to be the child who had once saved her.

"Busso, Kala, busso!" the boy cried out to her. Flee, Mother, flee! But she did not flee. He watched in helpless horror as Kala reached out one furred arm in his direction. Her warm brown eyes found his and held them steady . . . steady . . . steady as the stout club arched above her head, swinging down with a force and fury that crushed her beautiful face to bloody pulp.

The long fingers that had once guided his mouth to the sweetness of her milk loosened, and she fell arm over leg with the gracelessness of violent death, meeting the ground with a dry thud.

In that moment, Tarzan lost all reason. Became, in fact, as mad a creature as the one he now pursued. With a flight across an impossible void and with a mangled cry of agony, he leaped full upon Kerchak and sliced with the blade a great gash across the monster's face.

Kerchak roared with pain, dropping the death-dealing club. It mattered not. He wanted nothing but the blade. Kerchak grasped for the knife as the boy pummeled with his feet, seizing every moment to sink the sharp tip into flesh. Once he managed a hard blow to the heart, but the armor of Kerchak's chest hide was impenetrable.

It was then that Kerchak grasped the small white wrist with his massive hand, and with a menacing snarl moved with his other to relieve the tar-zan of his weapon.

The boy stared into the eyes of obscene wickedness and with a more easy movement than any he had in his young life made simply opened his fingers and let the blade fall, end over end to the forest floor.

Roaring with rage at this final bit of trickery, and caring less for the runt's death than possession of the weapon, Kerchak began a swift descent, arm over arm, limb running, nest crashing, his eyes always fixed on the glinting prize below.

The attack from above, therefore, was quite unexpected. The puny one had jumped on his back and was tearing at his face. Fingers found the knife's gash and pulled it painfully apart. Kerchak inflicted punishment with teeth on the boy's arms and legs, scratching and tearing flesh and pulling muscle from bone.

Then came a searing pain the likes of which Kerchak had never before felt. A bony finger was pushing and gouging at his eyeball. So great was the agony that momentarily his arms could do nothing but flail helplessly. By the time he'd regained his faculties and before he could reach the small hand, he heard a great sucking noise and felt the eye plucked from its socket. The viscous globe now hung by sinew down upon Kerchak's bloody cheek. Engorged with a fury so consuming it could raze the forest itself, with both hands he reached above him and found the slender white torso of the tarzan. He raised the boy high overhead and, turning on his feet, set his one remaining eye on the boundary of the bower. He wished the son of Kala to be gone forever from the Mangani, the Clan of Kerchak. He knew that alone and without the protection of his band the boy was as good as dead. He would be torn limb from limb by lions or leopards or trampled underfoot by elephants. And so, with all the force that his massive arms could muster, and with knowledge that he had been dealt a disgrace that even the tarzan's death would never mend, he threw the puny one far out into the forest.

Tarzan's fall was broken by many limbs, but those limbs broke him as well. He crashed finally to the ground, more dead than alive, blood flowing from a dozen gashes, and an arm that felt no longer attached to his shoulder. He was beyond pain, but he retained sense enough to know that on the floor of the forest he was easy prey. So gathering all the strength of his spirit and remembering the sacrifice of Kala, he crawled, battered and broken, his dimmed eyes searching for a tree, any tree with hand- and footholds that he could somehow climb

And then he remembered nothing.

When the boy awoke, his eyes swollen shut, the pain that he had evaded in his flight from the Mangani bower had found him and was tearing and burning every fiber of his body. Yet there was some comfort here. His head and shoulders rested not upon the hard bark of the tree. There was softness beneath him. He struggled to open his eyes, and in the slitted view above him, he saw his sister, Jai.

She was stuffing m'wah wa-usha into her mouth and dutifully chewing the bitter blue leaves. From her mouth she took the paste, and as she applied it to a gash on his shoulder, she saw that he was back in the world with her.

Her expression was unreadable to the boy. She did not speak. There was not, he realized, a single thing that could be said. As she worked the wa-usha paste into his wounds, he tried not to cry out or wince. He wished above all to be brave before his sister, Jai Kala—daughter of Kala—in their mother's honor.

Then he saw a twinkle in her eye, the same as he had seen in the moments before she had tricked him onto his back while wrestling.

*"Jai," he managed to whisper and questioned her with what expression
was left in his battered face.*

She reached behind her and held something in her fist above his head.

It was the blade.

The boy smiled and closed his eyes.

I was speechless, shaken to the core. Tarzan stood then.

"Come inside," he said and gave me his hand to help me up. In
the dark he led me to the bed and drew me down with him, curling
around my body as he had done so many nights in his nest. Now I
felt that the protective and comforting gesture was as much for his
own benefit as for mine. I did not hear Tarzan's breathing slow or feel
his muscles twitch as they always did as he was falling to sleep. He
was wide awake, remembering, reliving the terrors and the pain of
his darkest memories.

How had he managed to grow into such a fine, remarkable man?
To escape profound damage to his innermost being? By what subconscious means had he melded the noblest of human qualities with the
strongest primal instincts of the Mangani?

I pondered these questions for hours, occasionally recalling the
horrors that had taken place in this room, unaware that I had finally
fallen asleep. When I opened my eyes at dawn's light, I found Tarzan
sitting in Alice Clayton's too-small writing chair gazing down at the
open journal on the table. I could see he was not reading the hand-
written script, just staring blindly at the hateful words. He looked up
at me finally with an expression both resigned and confused.

Gathering my courage, I picked up where I had left off in John
Clayton's journal.

*It was an ape . . . but not an ape, covered head to foot in fur and as large as
a gorilla. But this was the strange thing: It was too upright and humanlike
to be one. Humanlike? What am I saying! At first I thought my eyes were
playing tricks on me, for the creature disappeared from where it had been
standing on the boundary of the beach and the mangroves behind. Perhaps,
I thought, I had been a castaway too long and my contented life was naught
but the delusions of insanity.*

Then Johnnie came out from the hut and wrapped himself around my leg asking for a swim in the sea, and I knew that this life was all too real. My son and wife were real, and as if to prove this reality, the beast emerged once again from the mangroves, this time farther away yet altogether recognizable. It stood very still, staring at the baobab.

"Go inside," I told Johnnie, unsure if he had seen it. "We will swim later." I reached around and took up my rifle, closing the door after him. I aimed, knowing very well the thing was too distant for a kill shot. I was not, however, sure I would have wanted to kill it, for it did have the aspect of a man . . . and would that have been murder?

I fired, and the gunshot's effect was gratifyingly instantaneous. Unhurt, the creature bolted into the mangrove swamp and did not reappear. Alice was by my side a moment later. What had I shot at? she inquired. She well knew my reluctance to waste even a single bullet, for when our stores of ammunition were gone we would be quite helpless against wild animals, however infrequently they might visit our home.

I thought to spare Alice news of the ape-man (which is how I had come to think of it) but thought better of keeping it to myself. I needed every iota of tact and diplomacy I had learned in my service to the Crown to describe the brute so that I would not frighten her unduly, yet frighten her enough so that she would be wary herself and take special care of our son. So I told her, but I fear I succeeded too well in comforting her, or perhaps it is merely my unfounded belief that I am capable of protecting them from all eventualities. That I can scare it away with the Winchester if it returns or dispatch it if it comes too close.

She has, however, promised me that she and Johnnie will stay close to the hut unless I am there with them armed with my rifle.

Written with trepidation from a beach in Gabon,

John Clayton

1 March 1889

I have seen it, seen the creature! Some months have passed since John's first sighting of it, and I (ashamedly) had grown complacent. I think that part of me had chosen to believe that the story of the "ape-man" was a misperception or a wild fantasm brought on by my husband's compulsion to keep Johnnie and me from all harm. But my eyes were not deceiving me when I walked out my door in the morning and saw the enormous furred monster standing in plain sight on the beach not two hundred feet away, its eyes fixed on the hut.

I quelled the instinct to shriek but quietly called for John to come with the rifle and shut Johnnie in. He was there at my side in a trice, but his appearance caused the agile creature to bolt for the swamp, and John's shot missed it. Our boy pounded excitedly from the door calling, "What did you shoot, Papa?" John pushed me inside, requesting that I ready all the Winchester shells that we owned and load the pistol as well.

It is dark now and I write by the light of a candle, one of the last left in our stores. We spotted the creature twice more this day, farther down the beach, peeking out from the mangroves. John shot both times and it disappeared at last just after sunset. He stands sentry now outside the door, unsure if the thing will return again. Tomorrow he will fashion a lock, a luxury he deemed unnecessary before, from the hardware of the Fuwalda's wreckage. Tomorrow as well, he will teach me the use of a pistol, for there will come a time when he must sleep, and someone must hold back the night.

Johnnie, the ever-cheerful child, now whimpers in his sleep. We have not told him there is a monster outside the door. Yet he knows his world has changed. His lighthearted mother and hale, undaunted father are strained and speak in terse, worried phrases.

How foolish was my optimism! This is no sweet dream of paradise. There is no rescue. No vaunted homecoming with stories of adventure to tell. No royal garter from the Queen for John's unswerving service. There is only this dark beach and stinking mangrove swamp out of which come nightmare creatures to stalk us. The idyllic years are shattered like Venetian glass, never to be whole or beautiful again.

I am so afraid.

Written tremblingly in the black of a moonless night,
Alice Clayton

<u>7 July 1889</u>

I can barely keep my hand from shaking or my wits intact for in the hut in the dead of night I hear the weeping of my wife and child huddled ball-like in bed, outside the palm leaves swishing and flapping in the tropic winds, a sound until this day I found a comfort. Now it is a sinister noise, a frond falling on the roof enough to make Alice cry out as though struck.

The events of the week past have been worse than the mutiny and our abandonment on this shore. Worse by far. The creature returned and with him brought a tribe of his hideous brethren. They ARE ape-men! They stand upright and yet bear the face of a monkey. Having come in numbers, they grew bold, day by day drawing closer to our shelter. I had always thought it strong, and in truth, it weathers the fiercest of storms. But will it withstand the attack of an army of monsters? Few of them walk in plain sight on the sand, but from our porch where I've stood every nightmarish day, I can see dozens in the mangroves, swinging by sinuous arms and calling not in hoots and howls but in WORDS AND PHRASES OF WORDS, incomprehensible to me but a language known to them!

I have fired and fired my weapons. Shot and killed them, but still more come, besieging us, urged on by the giant who first came here last year in July. This abomination leads them as surely as a general leads his troops. Admittedly I find it as horrible as I do touching that they drag their dead away as humans on a battlefield do. My skin crawls at the memory.

I am so tired. I have not slept for days. How could I? For a time my brave Alice stood beside me on the porch firing the pistol as I did my Winchester. Then all at once the giant emerged from the swamp just before the door and I, forced to reload, watched as he fixed her with his terrible black eyes and, pounding his massive chest and clutching his erect masculinity, roared his animal lust to possess her. I froze in horror, unable to pull the trigger. By the time I took aim, he had fled again to the swamp, and Alice collapsed weeping into my arms.

We are all but spent of our ammunition. I have locked us in, barricaded the door with our trunks and extra wood hammered across the entry. Alice begs me to keep a candle lit for she so dreads the darkness, and so by our last candle I write. She is wild with fear, clutching our child, and I am altogether helpless, have no words of comfort. I am sorry, Alice, I wish to say. Sorry, John, my son, for I have failed you.

What is that! A sound on the roof? A falling frond? Dear God, dear God, they are footfalls

A groan escaped my throat and a violent shuddering shook my whole frame. The expanse of blank white pages splattered brown with blood told more a story of horror than any words could do. I could not bear to look at Tarzan but recalled the trembling rage at his sight in the Mangani bower of the one called Kerchak, and of his murder of Kala. Now this. The hellish tale of his father, mother, and his tiny, tender self finally cruelly besieged on a dark, windy night by the very same loathsome beast.

I must force myself, I thought, *and gather my courage as Alice Clayton had for four years on this beach.* With hands shaking, I closed the journal and looked up. Tarzan sat on the bed, frighteningly still, his back to the wall, eyes open, staring sightlessly, no doubt gazing with clear vision into the past. The air was warm, but I shivered uncontrollably. I crossed the room and sat on the edge of the bed. I wished to embrace him, but some restraining force kept me seated, still. Not my corporeal body but my love must flow across the space between us to enfold and comfort him, for I knew it was Tarzan's own ordeal to suffer, one without which he owned no future. He began to speak in the voice of a small child, words flowing one into the other, a rush of terror and grief.

"mummy screaming . . . crashing door . . . papa where is papa? cannot see mummy holds me tight too tight too tight . . . cannot breathe cannot see . . . john! she cries . . . screams . . . the door at the door oooh . . . HAIRY MONSTER BITING PAPA! . . . blood blood . . . papa screaming, screaming wet and red . . . mummy crying no no god no jesus help us . . . it is coming red with papa's blood coming it is COMING! monster monster monster . . . falls on mummy I will hurt him cannot hurt him CANNOT hurt him! mummy screams and screams and screams . . . strong arms around me lift and carry . . . out in dark and mummy's screams and waves and wind . . . warm fur chest . . . mummy screams no more . . . beating heart thub thub thub . . . splashing croaking clicking . . . soft arms strong fur arms and chuffs . . . *balu balu* kala *balu* . . . eyes close . . . sweet milk in mouth so sweet . . . all I know all I know all I know . . ."

It was more than a minute before Tarzan came back to himself, as if from a daze, and stared hard at me. "Jane, we are going," he said, rising and rushing out the hut door. I followed to see him jump to the ground. Then he was moving quickly across the sand, south, in the direction of the mangrove swamp's inlet.

"Wait for me, Tarzan," I cried several times as I struggled down the rope ladder and ran, trying to catch him. "Stop! What are you doing?!"

"Kerchak will die!" he called without turning.

I sought some logic, any logic that might stop him. "Kerchak is an animal, a wild animal!" I shouted after him. "You are a man, a human being! *Histah* coils and strikes—that is what snakes are born to do. *Sheeta* kills prey—that is what leopards are born to do!"

"Mangani are not born to kill!" he shouted back at me, never slowing. "Only Kerchak kills! He is sick in the head!"

"You can control yourself!"

"I can put *Boi-ee* in Kerchak's heart!"

"I don't want to lose you!" I blurted suddenly, the words surprising me, painful and joyful and true. Tarzan slowed perceptibly at this but kept striding forward, nearing the brackish outlet.

"Wait, please wait!" I was crying now, tears washing my cheeks, desperate to stop him. "If you fight Kerchak . . . and if you are hurt, if you are killed, what will happen to *me*? Think, Tarzan, think! What would Kerchak do to me?!"

The image those words evoked was like a dart to Tarzan's brain. He stopped in midstride and turned, saw me running toward him. I flew the remaining distance between us, but he caught me by the shoulders and held me at arm's length, holding me in a piercing gaze. Then he crushed me to him. I lifted my mouth to be kissed, but the lips that met mine were less tender than ferocious, for murderous rage had, with but a moment's grace, transfigured into passion. Bloodlust to wanton lust. Now his hands were on my breasts, and though I'd expected this, wanted it, still the extravagance of his touch was shocking. The hands lingered but a moment, then followed with voluptuous restraint down the curves of my waist and belly. All at once I came fully alive, in places he caressed and those I wished him to caress. He buried his face in the soft of my neck, biting me gently, then fiercely, then gently again. He pulled down my shift and was on me everywhere, licking my breasts, licking with a long, catlike tongue that jellied my knees. He laid me down in the sand and straddled my hips, hanging above me with a look that spoke of hard animal craving. Yet poised as he was to strike, he waited. A sign was needed.

The smallest sign would unleash him.

I raised both my hands to his waist. Flat palms snaked around him, my fingers playing on the taut ripples of his back. Then all restraint abandoned me. Hungrily I surrendered, and as I pulled him down, a primal growl sounded deep in Tarzan's throat. I lost myself then. Lost time and the world around me, hearing only the ecstatic cries of seabirds.

Cries that I finally, wondrously, recognized as my own.

It was an idyll like no other, two of Nature's innocent creatures at one with the sky, the sea, and the land. We worshipped together at the altar of pleasure, learning the secrets of our bodies—the rush of exquisite sensation, the languorous exploration of willing flesh. For days on end I thought little . . . and felt much, though I did consider Cecily Fournier and how thrilled she would have been to see me here—naked in Paradise with this astonishing, virile man.

Whether it was love I was feeling, or merely lust, I did not dare to think. But while Tarzan—who had grown as quiet as he had tender—spoke of neither, I sensed that in his heart and mind I had, irrevocably, become his "mate."

We slept close every night, a tangle of limbs. Many times I'd awake to feel his warm breath on my neck. Often he cried out in his sleep. Once when his moans were piteous and protracted, I gently shook him awake.

"What is it, love? What were you dreaming?"

It took awhile for the answer to come, as though he were replaying the night visions over in his head.

"Kerchak . . ." he finally murmured, "trying to come in."

I kissed his face and smoothed his hair, whispering, "Sleep, sleep, but only sweet dreams."

He took my hand and draped it around him, holding it to his breast. He twitched, then fell into a slow rhythm of breathing that told me he slept.

I would have followed him, but my own night demon had awakened. As Kerchak menaced Tarzan's thoughts and dreams, Ral Conrath menaced mine. In both instances, a single monstrous individual had wrought devastation on an innocent family. Certainly the Claytons had suffered a more gruesome end, but Conrath's intent was no less vile than the crazed Mangani's.

I was no Dr. Freud, but I nevertheless attempted to analyze the psyche of the man. With icy precision he had chosen his victims. He had set the trap, baiting it with irresistible promises, then orchestrated our meeting. It haunted me that Ral, like myself, might have witnessed Father's brief chest clutching at the Zoological Congress and held knowledge of that weakness to later exploit. In the end, with that jaunty two-fingered salute, he had left me to be eaten alive on a lonely mountaintop.

Kerchak's actions were overtly violent, clearly fueled by insanity. Unforgivable, yet somehow understandable. My tormentor's mayhem was more subtle and devious, but was his premeditated crime any less horrible than Kerchak's? Was Ral Conrath any less mad than his bestial counterpart?

I found myself trembling at the thought and pulled my hand from Tarzan's lest I wake him with my black thoughts. I imagined Conrath even now in fine evening wear at some European gaming table gambling with his ill-gotten fortune from King Leopold, his paid-for women every night, perhaps scheming his next adventure, keeping a keen eye out for his next "mark."

I loathed the man. Desperately wished to avenge my father's death. Of course it would have to wait till my return from Africa. It would not be an easy thing, but I would find a way. Then I shuddered, remembering the words of a wise old friend of Father's, Dr. West. "If you go looking for revenge," he'd said, "you had best dig a grave for your victim and another next to it for yourself."

I didn't care. I would see to Ral Conrath's demise whatever the cost.

I no longer stopped to reflect upon how strange my life had become, for every moment was needed to live it. Every afternoon without fail, I laid Tarzan down with his head in my lap and bit by bit picked at his dark matted locks with one of the Claytons' dinner forks. The hair, once untangled, was thick and beautiful. As I picked, I could see in my mind's eyes my father's long hair blown backward as the Packard sped home from Cambridge on a Friday afternoon, and my mother pulling him into the house with mock horror that he looked like the "Wild Man of Borneo." What, I thought, would she think of *my* wild man?

We sat every evening to watch the setting sun, and on this night a great tornado of purple clouds began to form on the horizon.

"The rains will come soon," Tarzan said.

"Soon? When?" His words shook me, waking me from a beautiful dream. "How long before the rains come?"

He thought for a very long moment, considering the shape and movement of the clouds and sniffing the air. "Less than two moons."

All at once the passion that had ruled my life before coming to Africa came surging up, like a plugged well unbound. How could thoughts of such a wondrous thing as *Pithecanthropus aporterensus erectus* have slipped my mind? Maybe I had *lost* my mind. First I had become Tarzan's analyst, then I had become his concubine, mistress, mate. He had, likewise, shown the profoundest affection for me by stifling his natural instincts to do away with the mad Mangani. Concern for my welfare had trumped his primordial urge to destroy his enemy.

"Tarzan," I began, feeling horribly uneasy and praying for clarity, "I am a 'scientist.'"

He regarded me with curiosity. "What is that?"

"A scientist is someone who studies, as you've studied from books and learned to read and write. Scientists study *things*—like animals or the stars or earth or trees. We learn all about them so we can write books and teach others about animals and stars and earth and trees."

"What do you study?"

Here is the deepest part of the quagmire, I thought. Tarzan had learned to think and reason more quickly than any human being could be expected to do, but there was no way in the world to explain to him the theory of evolution or fossils or the science of paleoanthropology. I would have to lie, or at least modify the truth.

"I study apes," I finally said. "*Bolgani* and *manu.*"

He narrowed his eyes, sensing the dishonesty of my explanation. "You study apes, yet you were . . . *afraid* when the *bolgani balu* touched you."

"Where I am from, a scientist might study a gorilla but never be touched by it, and never do the studying standing high in the limbs of a tree."

"Trees are where *bolgani* live," he reasoned.

I expelled a discouraged breath and began again. "I am most interested in studying the Mangani," I said, relieved to be speaking the whole truth once more. "When you took me to the hollow tree and we saw the Great Bower through the hole in the trunk, I grew very excited."

He regarded me with a bewildered tilt of the head.

"The Mangani are a rare tribe. 'Rare' means that there are very few." I made the sign of "few" with my two hands close together. "There may be no other tribes of Mangani in all the world."

"No other Mangani?"

"That is correct. So every single one that lives is precious." *Even Kerchak*, I thought but did not say.

"Precious," he repeated.

Did he know the meaning of that word? I wondered.

"Tarzan, you are precious to me, and I am precious to you."

"Because you are the only Jane and I am the only Tarzan?"

"Yes!" I cried with a relieved laugh. *But for so many more reasons*, I thought. He was silent, waiting to hear what it was that I clearly desired. "Will you take me back to the hollow tree so I can study the Mangani?"

"No."

"No?"

"Kerchak is there. Danger is there."

Even in the warmth, I shivered. I knew the violence and depravity of which the monster was capable. What savagery he had inflicted upon the Claytons. But I could not allow fear to rule over reason.

"We can be hidden—*mel-cot*. You can protect me."

"No."

I cursed myself for having convinced Tarzan too well about his need to protect me.

"How can I make you understand? It is very, very important that I go to the Mangani bower. I *must* study them." It was as much in Father's memory, his legacy, I realized, as it was in my own self-interest.

"I cannot take you. You are weak and slow."

And if you see Kerchak again you will want to tear him apart, I thought. Instead I said, "I *am* weak and slow. But I can become strong and fast. You can teach me. I beg you. But I must do this before the rains come. Before you take me out of the forest. Before I take you to England."

I held his eyes, now reflecting the last rays of *kudu*, and saw his resolve wavering. I knew how deeply the man wished to please me. I saw his desire to see the places on his father's map of the world.

"I will teach you. Then I will . . ." He was seeking the word.

"Decide?"

"Yes. Then I will decide."

"Will we leave tomorrow?"

He lay back in the sand and pulled me onto him. His face was a welter of conflicting emotions. These weeks at the great water had transformed him, pained him, but most important pleasured him beyond his wildest dreams. Searching my eyes, he must have seen much of the same in me. Why would we ever wish to leave this place? For a moment, even I wavered. Perhaps we could stay just a bit longer . . .

"We will go tomorrow," he said.

Then he drew me to him, and in that moment all but his sweet lips and fervent embrace was well and truly forgotten.

Student and Teacher

The journey back to Eden was longer and more difficult than the one we had made to the coast, as so much of the previous trip had been achieved by downriver rafting on the Ogowe tributary.

The shallow water and tangle of slippery roots in the mangrove swamp behind Zu-dak-lul made footing difficult and dangerous, and here mosquitoes in profusion swarmed us. I constantly feared losing the Claytons' journal that I'd packed into a crude satchel of sailcloth I had stitched to the best of my abilities. Tarzan was least at ease in the swamp of all terrains, and once having crossed into the jungle he seemed to find relief in the overgrown paths and impenetrable canopy of foliage. He was comfortable and familiar with the dim light of the jungle floor, the thick, sodden carpet of decaying vegetation between his toes. I was less than comfortable with palm fronds slapping my face and thornbushes scratching my legs. And the snakes—they were everywhere slithering and hanging in the branches of trees. We stayed well clear of the army of red ants that moved in a long roiling column devouring and denuding everything unable to move from its path.

We stopped at night, resting in whatever crude nest Tarzan could quickly fashion of banana leaves, eating a simple meal of fruit and nuts before laying ourselves down on our bed to sleep. He lost no time teaching me the simplest skills of survival. How to see and how to listen and detect the scent of any creature that might do us harm or become a meal. I learned to use every sense to its finest degree. How to become invisible in the forest.

I had never realized how hard and ragged my breath was after exertion, or how difficult it was to stand so perfectly still that an ani-mal thirty feet away was unaware of me.

A split bamboo cane could be used to collect water to drink. Beans were to be found in the most unlikely-looking pods. And raw bananas, though bitter, could always be found and would stave off hunger if nothing else was edible. Feeling my teeth gritty, I crafted a toothbrush of sorts from the fibers of a palm tree, an invention that Tarzan found very clever and began to employ himself.

Though my training excited me, I was increasingly eager to begin my study of the Mangani. I had with me the Claytons' journal with only eighty empty pages, and all the fountain pens and nubs of pen-cils I'd found in the hut. I fretted about the limited space for so pro-digious a documentation as well as running out of writing materials, but there was nothing to be done about it. I had better be careful with my words and keep the illustrations small. When ink ran out, perhaps a substitute could be made from blood or berrry juice. The notes could always be enlarged upon when I returned home. It con-cerned me that living things were not at all my area of expertise. I was neither a biologist nor an anthropologist. I studied *fossils*, for pity's sake, at the very most the tissue of cadavers.

On our fourth day out, the raucous sound of an elephant's trum-peting up ahead stopped us in our tracks. Visions of Ral Con-rath's butchery and my own guilty part in it made looking Tarzan in the eye all but impossible. I saw by his grim expression he'd been witness to the Mbele slaughter.

"Have you been angry with me about the elephants?" I said, com-ing around to face him.

He bore deeply into my eyes. "I know . . . why you shot the bull. He would have hurt your father and . . . the black-white tribe." We had spoken very little of the Porter Expedition, but this was his name for the strange conglomerate of native people and *tar-zans*. "Why shoot the female?" he said. "She was down. There was no danger."

"She was suffering, Tarzan."

He cocked his head to indicate his ignorance of the word.

"The female had already been shot many times with a terrible weapon."

"The one that made a great thunder in the jungle?"

"Yes."

"I saw many . . . wounds in her side. There was much blood."

"That is right. The wounds were causing her awful pain. When I went to her in the clearing, I saw the hurt in her eyes. Where I come from, if an animal is suffering and cannot be healed, we take its life quickly. We end its suffering." I paused to compose myself. "I did not *wish* to kill the elephants, the male or the female. I'm very, very sorry."

"Your father is dead, like mine?" he said a moment later.

The question took me by surprise. I felt my throat tighten with the answer. "Yes," I whispered.

"Why did he die?"

A *bum ticker*, I thought ruefully, though the news of my death on the mountain would certainly have been the shock needed to kill him. I placed a hand over my breast and patted it.

"His heart was sick."

"Why did the bad man leave you to die on Sumbula?"

How could I possibly answer so complex a question? Would Tarzan understand how Ral had tricked Father and me into believing his promises and lies? I could hardly admit my earliest feelings for the man. And how to begin explaining the Belgian incursion into Africa? The genocide of ten million tribespeople, and King Leopold's desire to cut a road through Paradise.

"The bad man's name is Conrath," I finally said.

"Conrath." Tarzan spoke this with the same repugnance he reserved for the name Kerchak.

"Tonight when we lie down to sleep, I'll tell you the story of how I came to your forest."

His eyes softened and his mouth curled into a slow, lascivious smile. "And I will tell of the first time I saw you bathing in my pool."

The first time he saw me naked, I thought. I hadn't been mistaken about a near presence that day in Eden. He had watched me. Perhaps grown aroused.

"Is that why you followed me up the mountain?"

He nodded, not at all ashamed of his decidedly lewd motives. I wondered at the outcome of our fates had Ral Conrath not left me to die on Sumbula's peak. If Tarzan's primal urges had not, of necessity, been supplanted by his softer, more protective instincts.

"Take me to see the elephants," I begged.

"*Tantor*," he said. "They are *tantor*."

We lay stretched across a broad limb above a clearing where they drank and bathed in a muddy pool. There was an old bull, monstrous in size, seven females, four of whom were mothers of *balu*. We watched them frolic, showering each other and twining their trunks together affectionately. But it was the *balu* sliding and flopping gracelessly in the slippery mud that held us rapt, and the sweet attention of the mothers who used their strong, sinuous trunks to help the young ones stand, only to watch indulgently as they fell again.

They craved bathing—splashing and swimming in clear deep pools and lolling about for whole afternoons in muddy ones, endlessly flapping their great ears to beat the mosquitoes from their eyes.

The largest of the females had recently birthed the youngest and smallest of the *balu*. This baby was the clumsiest, forever slipping with splayed legs in the mudholes. Once we watched as the tiny creature sank in a deep hole, its slopes so steep and slippery that none of the females could extract him from it. They had begun trumpeting in panic. With a deafening bellow, the trees parted and the bull came charging out of the bush. In a graceful sweep of his immense trunk, he encircled the body of the youngster and lifted him up, depositing him gently onto the muddy shore.

We slept that night and rose early. Tarzan led me to a deep, sandy-bottomed pool, and we slipped into it moments before we heard the low rumbling of *tantor*'s soundings, the snapping of twigs and branches that heralded their arrival.

Following Tarzan's lead, I dove deep and swam underwater in the direction from which the elephants were coming. I felt the water disturbed as the huge beasts entered the pool. Now as we drew closer with our eyes open, we could see the great hulks of their bodies and the tangle of their paddling legs.

Taking my hand, Tarzan silently urged me to follow him closer to them, but I couldn't. I was terrified at their immensity and their wildness, and I begged Tarzan not to go. I begged in vain. He took a long breath and submerged, breaking the surface surrounded by four of the females.

They stared with little fright but some curiosity at his head—all that protruded from the water, bobbing on the surface. I could see him smiling as the trunk of one touched him delicately on the back of his head. They were curious. Carefully, he brought his hands above the surface and reached out to the female before him with fingers spread. Eyes fixed on him, she wrapped her massive trunk around his arm.

They all took turns touching him, finally realizing there was more to him below the water's surface. I heard him laugh as they explored his body. But when the giant bull began paddling his way, a bolt of real fear tore through me. Would the male be as curious as the females, or would he regard this stranger as an intruder, and with a glancing blow to Tarzan's head with his trunk, or an upward thrust of a sharp tusk, kill him?

It seemed to my untrained eye that the bull was indeed wary. He swam close, then the long, thick trunk snaked below the surface. I had rarely seen alarm in Tarzan's expression, but it was now apparent that the male had wrapped his trunk clear around Tarzan's torso. In the next instant the elephant dragged Tarzan beneath the surface.

I fought panic as more than a minute ticked by with my lover fully submerged. He had barely had time to suck in a full breath. Two minutes, and more . . . I was poised to create a disturbance, shouting and flailing about, when suddenly the bull's grasp loosened and Tarzan exploded out of the water astride the back of a baby! He gasped a breath and one of the females trumpeted loudly. With this, the bull turned and paddled away, as though to leave this strange white, fuzzy-headed *balu* to the females.

Soon after, I, too, was welcomed into the company of the herd. Once my fear had sufficiently subsided, we spent the morning in joyful communion with the elephants, bathing and playing. We'd dive deep and encircle their thick legs with our arms. Once I slid beneath a female and caressed her leather belly, examining the two teats between her forelegs. We bobbed near their heads and splashed water on their ears, closely observing these magnificent appendages.

The air grew ever thicker and hotter, the swarms of insects unbearable. Late in the afternoon the herd took refuge in a shallow watering hole and found relief from the flying pests in the cool brown-black mud at its edges. Hand in hand, we followed them gingerly in. Standing waist-deep in the pool, I understood why *tantor* sought these baths. No mosquitoes swarmed us. No sand flies bit us. Mud cooled the skin. We went back to the shore and rolled in it, covering ourselves—hair, face, limbs, and torso—in the stuff, and laid ourselves out in the sun, baking. Tarzan dove into the pool and wallowed amid the herd, cooling himself. One by one, the females and *balu* allowed him to mount their slippery backs. Tarzan's laughter echoed across the water as he slid and splashed down, and climbed up again, only to careen back into the mud for the sheer joy of it.

"Jane!" he cried, beckoning to me broadly. I was all at once observing myself, sitting mud covered on that slippery shore, invited by a near-naked English lord into a pool of elephants. I shook my head in disbelieving wonder . . . and joined him.

Return to Eden

The homecoming to Tarzan's fig tree was sweeter than I ever had imagined it would be. There was a great and raucous welcome from Mr. Grey, who, upon our arrival, flew rather than walked down to the nest and began shouting out the whole of his vocabulary as he paced back and forth on a branch above our heads. "Tarzan!" the crimson-tailed parrot cried. "Tarzan! Tarzan, piggy, piggy, Jane."

The bird was, in fact, so happy to see his old friend that he jumped down on Tarzan's head. His needlelike claws became stuck in the long hair and were soon tangled. We both laughed at his clumsy extraction from this "bird's nest."

When the commotion of our arrival had quieted somewhat, another grey parrot flew to the fig and perched quietly just inches away from Mr. Grey. On first observation the two looked identical, but the closer I looked, the more differences I saw—a slightly smaller, sleeker head, the coloring of the plumage lighter.

"Have you gotten yourself a wife?" I said to our friend. "Is this Mrs. Grey?"

He answered, uncannily, by reaching over and gently grooming his companion's head feathers, a gesture she accepted by moving a bit closer to him and closing her eyes.

I saw Tarzan smiling. "They are mates," he told me. "Now they will never part."

I had come to expect Tarzan's absence from the nest when I awoke in the morning. It had always been his habit to climb the fig before sunrise, and I had never questioned the ritual or begged to join him. But in the hour before dawn on the day after we had arrived home, Tarzan shook me awake. I was instantly alert, needing no time to rouse myself or rub the sleep from my eyes.

"Follow me," Tarzan said. "Very careful where you step. Where you hold."

It was strange climbing in the dark, though I saw at once that it was not pure dark. Here and there leaves glittered with moonlight like tiny lampposts showing us the way. Tarzan, who knew the route perfectly well in pitch-black, was most certainly moving upward through the branches with unaccustomed slowness and deliberation so I could safely follow.

The limbs and branches thinned out as we neared the top, and he demonstrated how to lay a foot upon a slender bough so as not to bend or break it with my weight. Finally he reached down and lifted me handily to the crown of the fig. I found to my delight that Tarzan had fashioned a second nest here which, though smaller than the one below, was adequate to bear the burden of two bodies sitting side by side. We sat facing east—a direction he called "Sumbula"—where the merest glow of light could be seen behind the mountain range. I saw a few stars still shining brilliantly in the dome of the sky. Few, as the moon was full and bright in the West, low on the horizon.

"It's so beautiful," I said.

His reply was a long silence during which he lay back, resting his head on his hands.

"*Kudu* will come soon," he finally said. "The sun will rise," he corrected himself. "When it comes, the black will turn to . . . purple. Then"—he was searching for the word—"the color of the hornbill's cheeks."

"Orange," I said, and he nodded.

"From the mountains smoke will rise. Like smoke from Waziri fires, though *many* times greater. I think there is a tribe that lives in Sumbula that makes these fires."

I was quiet, for he had never spoken so long or so eloquently.

"When the sun rises, the moon . . . it will still be in the sky."

"Is that why you brought me here today?"

He affirmed that it was.

I was humbled by Tarzan's broad knowledge of his surroundings.

I knew little of astronomy but was aware that it was a rare occurrence in a year when a full moon and rising sun shared the same sky.

"You are a naturalist, Tarzan," I said.

"What is that?"

"A kind of scientist who studies plants and animals, the earth and the sky."

I saw him nodding in agreement to the title I had bestowed upon him, visibly pleased.

"Today I will begin the teaching, so you can grow strong and fast," he said.

I resisted the urge to hug him, but thought, *You were my student, now I will become yours.*

"You will follow me. Do as I do. Go when I say go. Stop when I say stop. You will be silent. You will see and hear and smell *everything.* Or you will die."

Suddenly despair overtook me. *How on earth could I learn everything expected of me in time to study the Mangani before the rains began?*

Tarzan's eyes were fixed on me. "You will learn quickly," he said. "There will be time."

Then the sun rose in all its violet-and-orange glory. Tarzan stood and gave me his hand, helping me up. Assuming a pose of reverence, he stretched his arms out before him, chin lifted. I did the same, feeling the first warm rays on my chest, envisioning the full moon at our backs. We inhaled the fragrance of the fig leaf bower, and I knew without words that here, standing at the top of the world, we were giving thanks that *kudu* had risen again to begin its travels through the arc of blue sky and another day had come. With the years of our diverse lives behind us, I could feel that something great lay ahead. Adventure. Discovery. Danger. We were joined together in a strange destiny . . . my wild man and me.

And I was ready. Ready as I would ever be.

So it began. We climbed trees endlessly, he instructing me in the art of finding hand- and footholds—some obvious, some mere toe- and fingerholds. I had to learn to trust that these would support me, and my courage grew as the size of the nubs by which I perilously hung over the forest floor diminished. I became adept at gathering fruits and nuts and ferns, and more than once caught myself literally "going out on a limb" to secure the ripest cluster of berries or the pinkest figs, a feat I would have blanched at watching Tarzan do just months before.

The mature liana of the great forest afforded us our "campus." On the broad branches I felt confident almost at once, using my outstretched arms as a circus tightrope walker would do. But I was leery of narrower limbs, and Tarzan patiently educated me in which of them were sturdy enough to hold my weight, which looked large enough but were made of brittle wood and might crack beneath my feet. And soon I knew the crisscrossing of pathways in the canopy as a network of roads—one that led to the warm pool or the pawpaw tree with the ripest fruit, or to the Enduro Escarpment and the Waziri village.

Above our heads, a tangle of branches, air roots, and vines provided a perfect environment for brachiation. I admit I found it daunting at first. I was not a petite girl, nor was I small boned, and though years of riding had strengthened my legs, I regarded the musculature in my hands, wrists, arms, and shoulders as inadequate for the task of swinging from one branch to another.

But Tarzan was a clever and patient teacher. At first he guided me to webworks close to the ground so that fear of falling was all but eliminated, and my feet touched the forest floor as much as they dangled above it. To begin, he chose a liana of small hardwood branches around which my fingers could curl completely. His body behind, his hands over mine, he placed them for me (in the same ways I had "danced" with Father as a little girl, standing with my feet on his shoes). This allowed my grip to be firm and complete before Tarzan released his. Thus we worked, arm over arm, he instructing which branches or vines might be crawling with biting red ants and those that were slippery or poisonous and to be avoided at all costs.

My strength and dexterity increased daily. I grew calluses on my soles and palms. I knew my progress to be good, for Tarzan acted the proud parent when I leaped across the ever-widening gaps between branches. Soon I was surprising myself with prodigious feats of brachiation, exploding with most unladylike whoops of triumph.

Tarzan insisted I learn the use of the Bowie to kill prey. I could not yet hunt, but he would subdue an animal with his sheer strength or dexterity and insist I deal the deathblow. I was of course horrified to be taking the lives of animals, even for food, but learning even the most gruesome of the forest arts was the price I was forced to pay if there was to be any chance of my returning to the Mangani bower.

I enthusiastically applied myself to the tasks of daily living and so determined to broaden our diet, in particular to encourage Tarzan to eat cooked meat. I was still very thin and my limbs wiry. I wondered if it was the loss of weight that had caused the cessation of my menses—a circumstance that although worrisome made matters in the wild far less complicated. I recalled the frenzy when my female hounds came into their season. The last thing I wished to be out here in the forest was a "bitch in heat." And of course without ovulation there was no chance of pregnancy. But whether for health, appetite, or vanity's sake, I contrived to put some meat not only in my stomach but on my bones as well.

To this end I had Tarzan take me back to the Waziri village, where we were given a warm welcome and, and at my request, lessons in the art of fire making. We were shown how to hammer one piece of split bamboo into the ground and use another, held horizontally and stroked up and down, to produce a spark. It was hard work to raise the wood's temperature high enough to ignite, and we learned to take turns rubbing and blowing on the coal. Too, the tribeswomen seemed delighted to teach the "ape-man's mate" how to prepare certain of their delicacies. Grubs raw disgusted me. Grubs roasted were quite delicious. And the once-shocking lizard on a stick touted by the women as one of their favorite hors d'oeuvres became eatable.

Tarzan, who had relied solely on the Bowie knife for his infrequent meals of flesh, was given the gift of a spear and then taught by the men how to use it. In no time we were enjoying meals that satisfied my palate, though Tarzan was slow to appreciate cooked flesh. One afternoon he speared a fish in the nearby watering hole. The taste of it when it was baked in banana leaves in our fire was a cause of delirious lip-smacking celebration for me, and finally Tarzan admitted to enjoying it, in particular the oily-crisp skin.

It was a small triumph, but one by which I was entirely delighted.

* * *

Some small creature had taken up housekeeping in the nest under my head, and after several nights of disturbed sleep I decided to evict it. Tarzan had gone to spear us a fish. It had amused me to see shining in his eyes the memory of and craving for a particular food, this craving that—for probably the first time in his life—moved him to secure for himself that same meal.

I had set about on my hands and knees picking apart the thick mattress of twigs, leaves, feathers, and moss and the soft fibrous tufts from the silk-cotton tree in the places I remembered hearing the scuffling about and chewing which, in the deep quiet of forest night so close to my head, had sounded like the downstairs maid cleaning out the hall closet.

Less than a foot down I came upon an object foreign in size and shape to the nesting material. With a bit more digging I uncovered an artifact that, once uncovered, literally set me back on my heels.

When Tarzan came swinging acrobatically through the curtain of vines near the fig—a sight that never failed to thrill me—I was sitting waiting for him. He dropped down feetfirst with immense grace just in front of me and his eyes fell immediately on my find. The expression I saw flitting across his face surprised me, for embarrassment was one emotion he had never once demonstrated.

"Why was a Waziri bow and arrow buried in our nest?" I inquired mildly.

He produced a blunt-nosed fish, holding it out for me to see. He was clearly unready to confront the issue of the hidden weapon, so I exclaimed brightly at his catch and climbed down the fig tree to the clearing to where we had taken to building our cook fire.

He followed shortly, having wrapped the now-gutted fish in a neat package of banana leaves tied with a length of fiber. I was nursing the first tiny flame with bits of dried twigs. Now he knelt down beside me and began feeding larger sticks into the crackling fire.

"Bow and arrow?" he asked, as though no time had elapsed since my question in the nest.

"Yes," I said, "that is what the weapon is called. Did your mother never tell you the story of Robin Hood?"

Tarzan shook his head.

"Well, many, many years ago in England a man, not so different from you, lived in a forest much like this."

"There are forests in England?"

"Not anymore, I'm afraid, but back then there were, and the man called Robin Hood was a good person who wanted to protect the forest and his friends from a very bad person called the Sheriff of Nottingham who was making trouble for everyone. So Robin gathered a small tribe around him—'the Merry Men'—to fight the sheriff. And the weapon they used for hunting and fighting was the bow and arrow."

Tarzan was wide-eyed. "In England they had Waziri weapons?"

"Something very similar and, strange as it may seem, these weapons are still used, though not for hunting meat to eat."

"For what, then?"

"Sport."

Tarzan shook his head uncomprehendingly.

"Sport is something people do for the pleasure of it, not of necessity." I thought for a moment. "The way you dive from the cliff into the deep pool, that is sport."

Now he was quiet.

"Why did you hide the bow and arrow, Tarzan? Why did you not use them to hunt?"

He lifted his hands in a helpless gesture. "I cannot."

This was an odd statement. There was nothing physical that my friend was unable to do. Or so I had thought.

"Robin Hood loved a woman," I said, surprised at how shy the statement made me. I saw Tarzan's eyes brighten at the words, but he remained silent. "Her name was Maid Marian, and this woman was very good with a bow and arrow. As am I."

"You?"

"Would you like me to teach you?"

"Yes!"

I smiled at his uninhibited enthusiasm. What "civilized" man would welcome instruction in so manly an art from a woman?

"Shall we begin today?"

"Yes," he answered. "After the fish."

Tarzan and I journeyed to the Waziri village for a second bow and quiver of arrows that would be needed for our endeavor. On the

234 ■ Robin Maxwell

way he described how he had first come across the tribe and their weapons.

Once his injuries at Kerchak's hands had healed, Tarzan had begun to climb the fig and greet the dawn. He'd felt strong again and swung through the branches with ease, moving in the direction of *kudu*'s rising and the mysterious smoky mountains. It was here he first became aware of creatures so far below the crush of leaves that he could hear but not see them. Their words and voices were somehow Mangani and somehow not. Then he recognized that the sounds and tones were more the kind that he—an inferior Mangani—made. This surprised him.

Carefully descending, he had seen a group of the creatures moving with swift grace on two legs along a forest path. He thought his eyes had deceived him. These were *not* Mangani, though their bodies were the same dark brown. But the brown was not fur. It was skin, and except for color, the skin was smooth, the same as his own.

Too, they were not as broad and powerful as Mangani, nor their arms and digits as long. Their faces and the shape of their heads were—as he remembered seeing the reflection of himself in an undisturbed pool—much as his own.

They carried long sticks with sharp points and used them to throw and bring down several *wappi*—these were a small species of antelope—at one time. And they slung on their shoulders another odd pair of sticks, one of them curved and tied on two ends with the thinnest of twisted vines. From this shot a sharper pointed branch, shorter and thinner than the other, that flew into treetops with a speed that Tarzan had never imagined possible, bringing down *manu* and *neeta*, the thin sticks having pierced through the bodies of their prey.

All the while they moved through the forest they spoke in a language that sounded strangely familiar and soothing to his ear. With great stealth, Tarzan, keeping to the treetops, followed them on the whole day's hunt till they reached a place at the foot of the four mountains. Here he had come upon a great pile of stone, very narrow but very tall. Taller than the top of the trees. He'd climbed to its highest point, a long rocky ridge, and looked down upon a puzzling sight.

It was—it had to be—the black-skins' Great Bower. But this bower was set upon the forest floor and not above in the crooks of trees.

Their nests were as high as the creatures stood and had holes through which they passed to go inside, much as the grey hookbills had a nest hole. There were many of the brown, two-legged, short-armed creatures, as many as the digits of his hands and feet, and that many times over. He saw males and females and young ones of every size. Short animal skins covered the males' dangling parts. The females' hips and upper legs were wrapped as well, though their rounded breasts hung as female Mangani's did, and infants fed from them as he had done from Kala's more pendulous ones.

The word he heard most was "Waziri," and so the creatures came in his mind to be known by that word. Their chief—Tarzan knew him as chief by the heads that dipped as he passed, so like the cowering postures of Mangani as Kerchak came into their midst—was named "Waziri" as well.

The tribe became for Tarzan an endless source of wonder. He did not show himself to them, and he, deft in the treetops and silent as a cat, was not known to them for many long cycles of rain and drought. Once, while he was tracking their hunt to watch and learn of their weapons, the small party was set upon by *sheeta*. One Waziri was mauled, and in the sadness and confusion of carrying his mangled body back to the bower, one of the hunters left behind his curved weapon and pouch of pointed sticks.

Now they were Tarzan's, and he determined to learn their use. So many times he had spied upon the hunters to copy their stance, their positioning of the bowed branch and the pointed stick. So many times the stick sprang prematurely and uselessly to the ground at his feet. Nothing he had yet attempted, save trying to kill Kerchak, was less successful than this. In the end the weapon defeated him. He finally set it aside in his bower, covering it with leaves and moss so he should not be reminded of the cursed object.

He did persist in observing the Waziri in the village, and Chief Waziri, who was much loved by all. Tarzan learned the name of the four sloped mountains to the east of their village, that which they called Sumbula. Though they spoke the word often and with a reverence greater even than the name of their chief, the Waziri did not go to the mountains. If a small child strayed too far in that direction, he was swept up into his mother's or father's arms and beaten. From this, Tarzan learned that Sumbula was feared above all else. And when smoke rose from the tree-covered mountains and the earth shook beneath them, the Waziri fell to their knees, trembling, and chanted the word again and again until the shaking stopped. We had seen as much during our first visit to the village.

As theirs was a great and proud tribe, if they feared the mountain, Tarzan believed he should fear it as well. He never, therefore, strayed any farther to the east than where the Sumbula foothills began.

It was here above the village that Tarzan saw a girl of his age, her taut brown flesh moist and shining in the day's heat, pounding the *gomi* root into paste, saw her high round breasts . . . and felt something stir between his legs. He remembered with fear and loathing how Kerchak wielded the flesh stick against the female Mangani with as much violence and pain as he did a wooden branch. Tarzan slunk away flushed with shame, wishing never to inflict such anguish as his hated enemy had. After that day he began to wear, as the Waziri males did, a skin that hung from his waist to cover his loins. He continued to visit Waziriland often in secret, but never again did he feast his eyes on any young female.

Instead he'd fashioned for himself a long pointed stick weapon and learned to throw it with deadly force. He took Waziri words back to his own nest and laughed to hear the grey *neeta*, Lu-lu, speaking in that tongue. Too, Tarzan marveled at the fires, the "captured lightning" that danced all yellow and orange in pits in many places in the village, fires over which the Waziri placed their kills. It had been the sight of the strange flickering flames that had caused the undoing of Tarzan's secret presence.

As he was drawn from the rocky ridge and treetops, his descent had taken him lower and lower. Then suddenly his sure footing failed him, and with a resounding crack, he crashed through boughs and liana, catching himself finally just above the heads of the Waziri females at the fire. They shrieked at the shock of a white-skinned, four-limbed, long-haired creature dangling by one arm with an expression they perhaps perceived as fierce but was to Tarzan more akin to shame. He must escape from this humiliating confrontation!

With the sound of Kerchak's most bloodcurdling roar, Tarzan had risen in a wide arc and, gaining a barely existent foothold, catapulted himself—flying—through an immense void. Then catching hold of a gnarled vine and soaring up and away with the effortless grace of a *manu*, he vanished in the deep folds of the canopy.

The fearsome "Wild Ape-Man of the Forest" became Waziri legend that day.

The first time he'd swung down from the trees with the purpose of "making talk" with the Waziri, he had caused a great sensation among the tribe, with females shrieking and little *balu* crying. The males had drawn their spears and bowed weapons, but Tarzan had quickly begun to speak in their language, all the words he had learned by secretly observing them from above. He repeated "*Waziri*" many times, "*bongullo*" for food, and "*mpinga*" for village. He pointed to a young one, saying "*lunimi*," and to the growing delight of the tribe cried "*tinkalo*" and began kicking a large nut pod with his feet as they did while playing their favorite game. But when he uttered "*Sumbula*," the spears were raised again, if only briefly, for Tarzan quickly assumed a pose of submission as a Mangani would do when an angered Kerchak approached. He later learned that "Sumbula" was a sacred word, not spoken lightly, and he silently vowed never to say it again. He stayed only a short time to assure the tribe he meant them no harm and only wished to make talk with them.

On the second visit, they'd complied, even inviting Tarzan to eat with them, and bringing him into *zozo-thango*, the "men's house," in which all the Waziri males involved themselves with palaver of great and minor import—the need to hunt and kill a man-eating leopard that had struck for the third time in one cycle of the moon, negotiations for a marriage, the punishment for a stolen pig, even jokes and pranks they played on one another. So besides talk, there was laughter, and this was pleasing to Tarzan, as the laughter sounded not like the shrill Mangani squeals but like his own.

Here he had met a man, the only one of his tribe to ever have left Waziriland and gone *seta*, in the direction north, and come back alive. His name was Ecko, and he stood examining Tarzan very closely for a long while, pointing north and bobbing his head up and down in a signal that he had learned meant "yes." Then Ecko said quite loudly to all the males at the palaver, "*Techa mpinga* Tarzan, Tarzan, Tarzan." He had on his journey seen a village of Tarzans.

But what did *techa* mean? Tarzan had asked.

"Large. Very large," Chief Waziri answered.

Ecko. This, then, was the man whom Ral Conrath and Paul D'Arnot had met at the dock in Port-Gentil, the one whose golden pendant had led the Porter Expedition to Eden. It was all very strange indeed.

Once back in the clearing beneath our fig, I fashioned a crude target of banana leaves tied to a tree, the concentric circles drawn on with charcoal from our cook fire. I stuffed it with soft nesting material so that the arrows' carved wooden tips with grooved teeth would not be damaged by repeated practice.

The bow, a simple affair with both ends of its stave wrapped with narrow leather strips and the string of twisted leather, was, not surprisingly, shaped and weighted differently from its European counterpart. It took some practice of my own before I could hit the bull's-eye. I could see Tarzan watching me with slack-jawed admiration (or was it amazement?). For in all the physical disciplines that had preceded this moment, he had been the teacher and I the student.

When I was confident myself, I stood Tarzan before the target. By my observations of him I guessed he was ambidextrous, and I could not determine which was his dominant eye. I was right-eye dominant and wished to make it easy all around, so I placed the bow in Tarzan's left hand, as I would do myself.

"This is your bow hand or bow arm," I said of his left, "and this is your drawing hand or string hand." I stopped then, annoyed at the outset with the plethora of useless terminology. I would just *teach him*, simply, not talk him to death.

Picking up my own bow and arrow, I stood before Tarzan and assumed the correct posture, my body sideways to the target and shooting line, feet shoulder-width apart.

He copied me, striking a perfect stance almost instantly. I went to him then and had him watch as I loaded an arrow into my bow, careful to point it toward the ground and placing my fingers close to his eyes so he could see their positioning—the index finger above the arrow, two below, with the string held in the second and third, as I had been taught.

I lowered my weapon then to watch Tarzan's loading of the arrow and adjusted his fingers accordingly. He was altogether silent, concentrating deeply.

When I was satisfied of his finger placement, I again took up my equipment and demonstrated the raising and drawing of the bow in one fluid movement, the string hard drawn to my face, resting lightly at the corner of my mouth, while the bow arm rose toward the target.

Again I went to Tarzan and, assured that he was ready, had him pull back the arrow to the anchor point. I stood close behind him, enjoying the feeling of him near me. My new physical obsession—becoming "strong and fast"—had for the time being superseded the more sensual pleasures we had enjoyed so frequently at Zu-dak-lul.

"Aim for center," I said, "and when you are ready, let go of these three fingers on the bow."

I watched Tarzan's teeth clench and his eyes narrow as he homed in on the center of the target, the picture of single-minded absorption.

He let fly, and the arrow missed the banana leaf target by a fraction of an inch. I expected an angry oath, the usual reaction of a frustrated beginner. But Tarzan simply reached back to the quiver slung around his shoulder and withdrew another arrow. With intense deliberation, he reloaded and aimed. Then with perfect form took his shot.

When the arrow thwacked into the outer ring of the target, Tarzan turned and smiled fully at me. I was beaming with pride and admiration. Of course I had expected no less from the man, but that I had succeeded in my instruction of the art of archery gave me inordinate pleasure.

For the next several days Tarzan did next to nothing but practice, and in no time the pupil's adroitness with his new weapon exceeded the teacher's. But hunting with the bow and arrow was, after all, the point of the exercise, and he soon moved out into the forest and taught himself that skill. After delivering his first kill—a wild pig—and partaking of its succulent cooked flesh, he decided to take me with him on the hunt.

It proved an electrifying experience, first learning the skill from my student, then attempting, with little success, to bring down my prey. With a bow and arrow I had never practiced on a moving target, and with a rifle on the skeet range the target moved at a uniform rate. Even the bull elephant I had brought down had been coming straight at me and was therefore a reasonably fixed target, but here the prey was small and flitted about, or jumped sideways in short, jerky bursts of movement. But it was not so much my aim as the nearness to the prey that proved my problem.

Rare delicacy was required, as well as a quietness of being, to narrow the distance between me and my intended mark. I used what I had learned about quieting my breath and becoming still as stone. Yet I lost count of how many targets I missed.

I had become less squeamish about killing living things, for this was the wild, after all, and for better or worse I had become the wild man's mate. Taking example from Tarzan's dignified response to his early failures, I refrained from angry expletives when, time after time, my target evaded me.

But in this exercise Tarzan was stern. He meant for me to bring down our dinner, so I shot and missed, shot and missed, till my right arm burned with pain. When the blue-green *neeta* sitting above on a branch and twenty feet away was in my sights, Tarzan came to my side. He said nothing, merely breathed in a slow, steady rhythm near my ear. He wished for me to take up the same rhythm. And so I did.

This calmed me, and almost by magic the pain in my shoulder vanished. I felt steady on my feet, and the target came clear in my sight.

I released my fingers from the string and loosed the arrow. The bird was falling, lifeless, before I knew I had hit the mark. I turned and clasped Tarzan in a rough, triumphant embrace, then ran to retrieve my kill.

When I'd taken down my first antelope, Tarzan had run his hand over the animal's flank, his fingers coming up deep ocher. He had painted my face with the pigment, and I'd worn the markings with quiet pride for days after. The Bowie had been put to a further use—to prepare a garment from that kill to replace my now-shredding native cloth. Tarzan showed me how to skin it and finally soften it using the edge of the blade, along with repeated drubbing on a stone set beside the warm pool.

When the hide was ready, he watched as I clothed myself in it. I moved to hang it around one shoulder like I had the Waziri cotton, but he reached out and pulled it down to my hips. I watched as he draped the thing this way and that, like some wild couturier pinning together his latest French creation. Finally he was satisfied with his placement, which closely approximated the tribal women's "skirt." I was speechless. My bosom was entirely uncovered. What shocked me especially in wearing this revealing garment was how unperturbed I was with my nakedness. I quite liked the feel of my breasts preceding me as I moved through the world. There was a bounce and shimmy as I walked, and when I brachiated through the canopy, they stretched and elongated. The sensation when I swam in the warm pool was one of unimaginable sensuality, the finest silk dragged slowly across that delicate skin.

Never had I thought of breasts as anything more than fleshy protuberances to be carefully covered, imprisoned in the hated whalebone corsetry. I could not deny the growing pride in my figure, lithe and strong and quick. I liked it when Tarzan gazed openly at me, whether I lay in repose in the nest or was in motion, running along the jungle floor, chasing through the liana.

I had become shameless. Utterly shameless. And it was, I decided, an excellent state of affairs indeed.

It was Tarzan's way to swim almost daily. It was the moment in the day that he relished above all. He would stand high on the cliff above the pool nearest the nest. Its edges had sandy shores, but below the falls it seemed to have a bottomless depth. I loved to watch him straighten his back and square his toes on the black rock beneath his feet. There was no hesitation as he raised his arms high above his head, palms touching, and sprang, first rising and then streaking downward, breaking the water with hardly a splash.

This day we descended to the forest floor from the upper nest after our dawn greeting of *kudu*. The anticipation of the crashing falls never failed to excite me, but when we breached the curtain of water and beheld the sight of the loveliest of pools, I stood stunned and horrified.

Floating on the surface and strewn along the black sand beach were hundreds of fish. All dead. Upon examination, their delicate flesh disintegrated under my fingers—as though they'd been boiled alive.

Tarzan stared in dismay.

I remembered the warm tendrils of water the first time I'd bathed here. But this was something more. Volcanism, perhaps. But it was far beyond my capacity to explain.

242 🍲 Robin Maxwell

He snapped off a banana leaf and wrapped a dead fish in it. "We will go to the Waziri."

Tarzan and I squatted across from Chief Waziri and Ulu in the dirt of the charm doctor's hut, as women were forbidden in the men's house. Tarzan had asked the question about the cold pool turning hot, and there had been a very long silence that followed it. I could see Tarzan's concerned expression. He would be wondering if he had spoken foolishly or somehow offended our hosts. Yet he remained calm, and I watched as he began breathing in rhythm with the chief, keeping his eyes respectfully on the dirt floor in front of him.

"*Jaljuma*," Ulu finally said.

Tarzan touched his hands to the sides of his head, a gesture that said he did not know the meaning of the word. In answer, the charm doctor stood and took hold of the central pole of his hut with both hands, pushing and pulling it with all his strength so that the house shook and small creatures living in the thatched roof fell down to the floor and scurried away.

"*Jaljuma*," Tarzan repeated with certainty. Clearly the word meant the shaking of the ground—an earthquake.

Tarzan had described to me these tremors that he had experienced all of his life. Some had been so small they could be felt only if he was walking on the ground, but some were so mighty they shook the trees, causing the birds to take flight from the canopy, and set the *manu* howling.

"*Koho dak-lul ee jaljuma?*" Tarzan asked the headmen. Hot water and ground moving? Chief Waziri and Ulu had honored the ape-man by learning several Mangani words. *Dak-lul*, they knew, meant "pool of water."

Ulu nodded.

But Tarzan's expression was mystified. He turned to me. "How does the ground shaking make the cold water of the deep pool hot?" he said to me in English. Then he looked questioningly at Chief Waziri.

The man shook his head and touched his mouth to gesture, *I cannot say*. However, the worried expression on the headman's face was clear to both of us.

"*Ekumbu lata gomali Sumbula*," the chief said to the charm doctor.

"They speak of Sumbula, but they know nothing," Tarzan said to me.

Then the two Waziri stood. The meeting had come to an end. Tarzan rose and I did as well.

Ulu said to him, "*Lata ntembe bongullo.*"

Tarzan politely refused the offer of food, and we returned home no wiser than before.

Tarzan had come to trust my skill and wits enough to allow me freedom to move in a narrow circuit around the fig. But he always armed me with the Bowie, and his instinct to protect me assured that my solitary travels did not exceed a quarter of an hour without his gaining sight or sound of me. Unspoken as it was, I knew that Tarzan was bound and determined to make me his equal in self-sufficiency and competent to defend myself.

Despite the growing mastery of his native tongue, he chose oftentimes to be silent. Yet we were constantly "speaking," employing a subtle language of bodily gestures and the eyes. Using both Mangani and English words. It was rich with nuance and proved altogether satisfying. I had never before conceived of how very verbal was my home society. How little anyone touched each other. These were human behaviors that, before now, I had never considered. *How cold and rigid was the civilized world!* Many times I simply thought a thing—*Where is my quiver? I would love a handful of ripe figs*—and there Tarzan would be, holding out the arrows or the fruit. In short order I came to view it as the normal state of affairs.

I had, I realized with astonishment, become a familiar forest dweller, and I found this deeply satisfying.

Our late meal done, we had climbed to the nest and stood together in a happily exhausted embrace. It was Tarzan's way to fold his arms around me and simply hold me in perfect silence, my head on his chest, his hand over my breast, waiting for our hearts to begin beating in the same rhythm before we kissed and laid ourselves down to sleep.

I saw the foot-long brown viper as I lifted my head, dangling an arm's length over Tarzan's right shoulder. Its target was the back of his neck. *No time!* I thought. *No time!*

"Down!" I cried, and in the instant he obeyed my command, I snatched his Bowie from its sheath and sliced in a broad, furious arc through the air where a moment before Tarzan had stood. The snake dropped in two pieces onto the nest floor, and both continued to curl and wriggle for a time, I watching in horrified fascination, Tarzan gaping at me with astonishment and gratitude.

The next morning, with little fanfare, we left for the Mangani bower. It occurred to me that while I was forbidden to graduate from Cambridge University, I had passed my courses at Tarzan, Lord Greystoke's College of Eden.

I could not have been more proud.

The Great Bower

We arrived at the hollowed tree with little time to spare before losing the light. The climb down that had been so perilous for me the first time was now easily accomplished. On the narrow ledge, the monkey's carcass was nothing but desiccated skin, fur, and bone, a circumstance that I appreciated and one that Tarzan found alarming.

"Tomorrow," he whispered, "I must find another. They will smell our . . . presence."

Just then the last rays of sun blinked out, leaving us in shadows that soon turned to pitch-black. Using my sack holding the journal as our pillow, we lay down and he pulled me into the crescent of his body. The excitement of the next days' undertaking set my mind afire, but as was the case every night under Tarzan's stewardship, I slipped effortlessly into slumber.

By the time I awoke, Tarzan had returned with the putrefying corpse of a small anteater. I stifled my repugnance, setting my mind firmly to ignore it, for I would be forced to work directly above the rotting flesh. But the moment I peered out at the scene of the waking Mangani village, all else fell away. I feasted my eyes on the matrons, their infants and the older *balu*, the young females in their own nests, and the males of indeterminate age. I asked Tarzan to enlarge the blind's hole so that he might stand by my side and answer innumerable questions.

"What is that female's name? And why does she have two *balu* of nearly the same age?" It was Gamla. Her sister had given birth just after Gamla had, then died. Gamla had taken her sister's *balu* to raise. *Like Kala had done with Tarzan and Jai,* I thought.

"Who are the two youngsters wrestling on the ground? Are they brothers? Cousins? Unrelated? What do they eat? How far will they travel to forage?"

With the sun pouring down through the trunk, I had picked up the Claytons' journal, written on the first blank page, "A Study of *Pithecanthropus aporterensus erectus*, the 'Mangani' of Gabon," and was about to begin writing the first of my observations when the trees across the clearing high above us began to shake. I felt a sudden sinking in the pit of my belly, and Tarzan stiffened at my side.

I turned to him and saw the effort of unfathomable restraint harden his features and knots of tension in his neck and shoulders. His fists clenched into solid rock.

I spoke in the gentlest voice. "Tarzan, come away from here."

I led him like a blind child, for he was blinded by the fury of Kerchak's presence. He had not even laid eyes on the brute and was yet coiled tight as an overwound spring ready to snap. Strangely, the stories of Kerchak's three murders left me more curious than terrified. Here, above the bower hidden behind the view hole, I felt safe, immune from his hideous brutality.

"Why don't you go get us something to eat?" I said. "I'll be all right here."

He was too overwrought to speak, but he nodded and climbed dutifully away up the hollow trunk and disappeared.

The moment he was gone, I took my place at the blind. Kerchak had appeared and made his descent to the ground, thieving his breakfast along the way, terrorizing males, females, and *balu* alike.

The morning grooming of and groveling before the brutish tribal chief had begun. How to write about this creature in a scientific manner? Had my objective eye already been sullied by knowledge of Kerchak's previous actions and character? Or must these be considered no more than hearsay? Did I dare write in this scientific documentation any more than the most dispassionate observation?

What a glorious dilemma to have—a provocative and unstudied species literally at my feet and a singular partner in the endeavor to boot. I believed myself, at that moment, the luckiest woman in all the world.

Tarzan returned with enough fruit and nuts and sweet baby ferns to last us the day. He had, in his own way—I refrained from asking how—managed to calm himself so substantially that he was a great help with my study, despite Kerchak's belligerent and overwhelming presence at the bower. It quickly became apparent that the Mangani were a naturally peaceful species. The mothers doted on their young with more physical affection than I had ever witnessed "civilized" women bestowing upon their children. If a Mangani mother moved from one place to another, the little one would ride on her back or chest. Constant grooming of her child's fur was the most intimate of activities. The teat was at all times available, and as much a source of comfort as nourishment.

Of course my fondest observations were of those qualities that set the Mangani apart from other prehuman primates—their upright posture and their ability to speak. It thrilled me beyond measure that there were words of the language that I recognized when spoken by a member of the tribe, and I rather quickly learned the names of individuals, as the Mangani had the habit of preceding much of their communication with the name of the one to whom they were speaking, and identifying oneself with not a pronoun but a name. "Gamla, yud b'zan Kerchak" was clearly "Gamla, come groom me"; "Eta, yud so kal," "Come, little one, drink my milk"; "Kai, dan-do kob abulu" was "Kai, stop hitting your brother." It was all so human, I thought, and yet to see the creatures swinging so effortlessly through the trees with their overlong fingers or clutching a branch with that strange perpendicular toe left no question in my mind that Tarzan's adoptive tribe was as far from human as it was similar.

A strange and intoxicating paradox.

Adolescents too young to breed, males and females alike, were devoted to playful activities, their favorites of which were wrestling and chasing one another through the canopy. Of course there was foraging for food, but I (in my stationary blind) was prohibited from observing it. Mangani left the immediate bower for hours at a time. I resigned myself to Tarzan's descriptions and the obvious results of the food search—a diet quite similar to the meals he had returned with for the two of us, though the P.a.e. ate leaves in quantities and fat white grubs as a kind of delicacy. There were pools in the vicinity, but the Mangani did not eat fish. Tarzan reported that their refusal to swim was the cause but that the species was not adverse to eating snails and tiny crabs they found at the water's edge.

Tarzan's spirits lifted considerably with any sight of his "half sister," Jai. He told me that after Kala's death and his banishment from the Great Bower, Jai had been the only Mangani who'd not abandoned him. Even after he'd moved his nesting place far enough from the bower to guarantee his safety, Jai had found him and visited him there. Lately, though, her disappearances from the bower had begun to provoke Kerchak.

All of his attempts at *kin-ga* (mating) with her had as yet come to nothing. She had no desire to mate with her mother's murderer, and while Kerchak wished to show his dominance over every female in his tribe, he was leery of Jai, perhaps remembering the consequences of killing her mother and Kala's *tar-zan* son (he did indeed believe Tarzan had perished after his beating and expulsion from the bower).

Late afternoons were a time for rest. Matrons called their young back to the nest for feeding and a nap. As everyone dozed, the buzzing of ten thousand insects rose and melded into a single solid sound.

Tarzan had gone scouting for our evening meal, and I sat contentedly writing up the morning's observations. Aside from the quickly dwindling time for study before we would have to leave the forest (fewer than three weeks now), the Claytons' journal was filling at an alarming rate with my smallest handwriting and dozens of illustrations, and endless data was still to be recorded. It had been the only blank paper I'd found at Zu-dak-lul, Alice's precious box of stationery scattered about and destroyed by the elements of the previous sixteen years. When the awful day came, when the last blank page of the journal was full, I would have to resort to my memory of a thousand tiny details—a very daunting prospect.

I heard a gravelly voice from the forest floor and, knowing at once it was Kerchak, went quickly to the view hole to peer down. As yet there was no movement in the bower, but the Mangani chief repeated his call, this time louder and more demandingly.

"Gamla, *yud* Kerchak!" Gamla, come to Kerchak!

My eyes sought the female in her nest nursing her two infants. I had looked up but had yet to move from my place.

"Gamla!" Kerchak roared and pounded the ground with both of his clenched fists. "*Yud!*"

I scanned as many nests as I was able, attempting to observe the Mangani response to Kerchak's unwelcome summons. Many of them had already shrunk away into the shadows. Others leaned over the lips of their nests and watched, for Gamla had laid down her *balu* and begun her reluctant descent to the forest floor.

It was with a sick feeling that I watched the handsome furred female walk on her straight legs to the center of the clearing—what I had come to call the "throne room"—where Kerchak still sat, idly chewing on a pile of that day's offerings. I was grateful Tarzan was not present to witness what I guessed was about to happen. From this height there were no facial expressions visible, but I could clearly see the posture of defeat as Gamla turned her back to Kerchak and dropped to her hands and knees. Then Kerchak, as if possessed by sudden rage, swept away the food with a swipe of an arm and rose to his full height, pounding his chest with balled fists, exactly as John Clayton had described the beast's display before his terrified wife.

Do not watch, I commanded myself. *Turn away from this spectacle of violence.* But I could not. I was a scientist. The Mangani were my subjects. It was my privilege and duty to observe every aspect of behavior, no matter how repugnant.

Kerchak, larger by half than all the adult Mangani females, mounted Gamla from behind, roughly grabbing the fur at his partner's neck. Yet she bore the frenzied copulation quietly. Mercifully, it was short-lived.

Once Gamla had regained her upright stance and began climbing back to her nest, I pulled back from the view hole, slumping down with relief. My heart was thudding. Bitter bile rose in my throat and I thought I might vomit. But I calmed myself, aware of Tarzan's imminent return. I would not allow him to see me upset, and under no circumstance would I write of Kerchak's rape of Gamla in John and Alice Clayton's journal. It would be sacrilege, I thought, an insult added to injury. No, I had committed every moment of the scene to memory, and once returned to England I would record it in detail.

A sudden jolting of the earth caused some screeching and scrambling in the Mangani bower. Even Kerchak, busy stuffing his mouth with grubs, jumped to his feet in fear. Though the earth tremor was brief, in the hollow tree its consequence nearly proved fatal, for the journal in my lap as I sat on the ledge flipped up and out of my grasp and, to my horror, tumbled down through the trunk, clattering and echoing loudly as it fell. I looked at Tarzan, who had returned. He was standing at the blind and had braced himself for the shock. But now that it had passed, his body was stiff with attention. His eyes were fixed out the view hole, and he clutched the interior vines and ridges for another quake. When all was still, I joined him and looked down on the clearing.

Kerchak was now on his feet and moving slowly toward the base of the hollow tree.

I cringed as the journal, momentarily resting on a rotted lattice-work twenty feet below us, slipped off and fell an additional distance, coming to rest with a thud near the bottom.

When Kerchak started to climb, Tarzan and I pulled back quickly. I saw him look up and determine that a hasty escape out the top would be impossible. Climbing down would trap us in the well of the trunk.

Now we could hear Kerchak's progress up the outside of the tree. I fought panic and wished desperately to speak to Tarzan, to make a plan. But we must remain silent and at all costs stay out of Kerchak's sight.

I could see Tarzan's mind at work, his eyes flicking in every direction. Reverting to sign language, he gestured me to follow him. Squatting backward at the lip of the ledge, he lowered himself down till he was hanging by his fingers, his body suspended perilously over the well of the hollow tree. Swinging his legs forward and back, on the next forward movement he released his grip and disappeared.

I stifled the urge to shout, "What do you want me to do?" for clearly Tarzan meant for me to do exactly as he had done . . . and even with my rigorous training, it appeared impossible to me. The sound of Kerchak nearly at the blind hole forced me to act and to trust implicitly that Tarzan's plan was viable. I leaped to the ledge, turned my back to the abyss, squatted, and placed my fingers around the lip. Praying that my balance and newly strengthened body parts would not fail me, I carefully lowered myself down. I dangled only by my fingertips for a moment that felt an eternity. Pain shot down my arms. They would not hold! I felt my fingers slipping, and the very moment they lost the lip, Tarzan's arm shot out, clutching my waist. He pulled me to him where he clung by the other arm to a mass of tangled roots and ropy bark.

Not a moment too soon.

By the sounds above us, Kerchak's grunts into the blind hole were echoing up and down the tree well. Shortly he was done entertaining himself with the strange racket, and a brief silence ensued. A moment later we saw the anteater's carcass tumbling down the trunk. The thought that Kerchak's hand was feeling around inside our blind struck such fear into my heart that, but for Tarzan's strong arm supporting me, I would have lost all control of my muscles and followed the anteater's stinking corpse to the bottom of the well.

Kerchak was ripping the bark and the brittle wood from the dead tree's blind hole. How long it would take him to enlarge it enough to enter, I thought, was the remaining length of my life.

There was little light beneath the shelf, and I could not see Tarzan's face. I buried my own in the musk of his smooth corded neck and thought there was nowhere else on earth I would rather spend the moments before death than in this man's arms.

But Tarzan had pulled himself from my grip, giving me his handholds. I heard the sound of the Bowie knife being withdrawn from its sheath. Silent as a cat, he edged along the inner trunk and raised one arm, feeling for the lip of the ledge. He was going up to face the beast!

"Kerchak!"

Even from our hiding place below the ledge we could hear the name called and the widening of the blind hole cease.

"Jai! *Kin-ga!*"

Tarzan's sister was deliberately luring Kerchak away from us!

When Tarzan was certain the beast had abandoned the hole, he helped me regain the ledge while he quickly recovered the fallen journal in the tree well.

From the blind, I watched as Jai, in the center of the clearing, fell to her knees and presented her rump to Kerchak, who was quickly descending to claim his prize. But the moment his feet touched the ground, Jai stood and, baring her teeth at him, turned and raced for the nearest tree.

Tarzan pulled me to go, but I urged him to observe his sister. I felt his fingers digging into my flesh and saw that his face was twisted with hatred. It was not lost on him that Jai was luring Kerchak away from him as his mother had done all those years before . . . and she had died for that sacrifice.

In the canopy, Kerchak was gaining now, bellowing in anger (was he, too, remembering the trickery?). Jai leaped into a mango tree, clinging fast to its branches, and began a careful climb. A moment later Kerchak crossed the void and landed in the limbs under her.

But they were *not* limbs. They were feathery leaves on delicate woody stalks. They could barely hold Jai's weight. They could not hold his at all.

With a shocked and furious roar, Kerchak fell, crashing through the branches until his body hit the forest floor.

Now Tarzan was pulling me away from the blind, pushing me up the hollow trunk to make our escape.

I heard Kerchak's blustering oath. "Kerchak *bundolo* Jai!" I will kill you!

Yes, I thought. *He will kill her. But he will have to catch her first.*

Kala's Children

I learned more of the character of the Mangani from that day's observations than I had in all the previous days combined. Of course there was no question of returning to the Great Bower now that Kerchak's curiosity had been aroused. The danger was too great.

The loss of the observation blind was a massive blow for me. The few precious weeks left before our enforced departure were now useless. I was far from done studying the Mangani. I had, in fact, barely scratched the surface of their anatomy, physiology, and behavior.

Back in Tarzan's nest, I fought despair by counting my blessings. Simply to have discovered *Pithecanthropus aporterensus erectus* had been the greatest thrill of my life. I read my writings endlessly, adding to them, even beginning an analysis of them. But it was no good. How could I possibly analyze the data if it was incomplete? I found myself unable to sleep, obsessed with the idea that in a single moment of weakness—allowing the journal to fly from my hands—I had destroyed, once and forever, any chance of a worthy study of the living missing link species.

"I should not have taken you," Tarzan said, brooding and angry at himself for putting me in danger. I knew it was futile to ask to return. I grew short and snappish, but Tarzan bore my moods with quiet dignity and even tried to draw me into lovemaking, but in my obsession I had lost the desire for all but intimate friendship. In fact, his attempted embraces irritated me, and this reaction, in turn, disturbed me greatly. A constant war raged inside my head.

What have I gotten myself into? This outrageous adventure and the unearthing of Tarzan's harrowing secrets had drawn me, *seduced* me into a most bizarre affair of the heart. There was no doubt we cared deeply for one another and most certainly lusted after each other. I was nearly sure I loved him and was certain he believed me his fated companion for life.

But was he mine?

He said he longed to travel the world outside Eden, go to the places he'd seen in his mind's eye after poring over his father's map and hearing my descriptions of them. He was more than bright. Brilliant, I thought, and had powers to adapt that were stunning. But he had spent a whole lifetime believing himself to be an animal. He was a savage wild man who would chew the bloody flesh from the bone of a fresh kill with obvious relish. I could take Tarzan out of the jungle. *Could I take the jungle out of Tarzan?*

Or was this thinking an attempt to rationalize my selfish worries that he could never adjust to my life in England, my career as a scientist? I wondered if our unbridled abandon on the beach at Zu-dak-lul had made a sensualist of me. A muddled fool living a fantasy?

I knew I was driving myself insane with such thoughts. It was probably no more than the impossible frustration of knowing how near I was to *P.a.e.* with no way to observe them, and the time for my stay in Africa running out.

As Tarzan hunted one morning, I sat in the nest rereading my notes for the hundredth time, the Greys perched above me chattering to each other in a language that was a charming mixture of forest sounds, whistles, clicks, Mangani, and English, peppered with human laughter, both Tarzan's and mine. I was aware of just how much I conversed with the pair, and how we had become a strange family foursome. In fact, I was reading the passage aloud to them, glad for an audience (I dreaded the thought of becoming the proverbial addled professor), and was so engaged that I failed to hear the sound of something climbing up from below. When the long furred fingers gripped the edge of the nest and I saw the top of the Mangani skull, I screamed and leaped upward, clutching the branch overhead to make my escape. But the rest of the simian head, when it followed, was not Kerchak's. From where I hung, rather humorously by one arm and one leg, I saw that the Mangani was a female.

It was Jai, and on first sight of me, she also screamed in fright.

I quickly gathered my wits, realizing I held the advantage, having known of her existence while Jai had no knowledge of mine. Who, the Mangani must be wondering, or *what* was this creature in her brother's nest?

"Jai." I spoke the name gently, but the female's teeth were still bared and her eyes were bulging. "Jai *zabalu* Tarzan." Jai, sister of Tarzan, I'd said. "Tarzan *unk pacco*," I added. Tarzan go zebra. There was no word in the Mangani language for "hunt," but the words, no matter how imperfect, had the desired effect. The expression of fear on Jai's face transmuted into bewilderment.

I tried again. "Tarzan *popo pacco*." Tarzan eat zebra.

With this, Jai climbed into the nest and squatted there. I untangled myself from the upper limb and came carefully down, sitting on the edge farthest from the Mangani. I patted my own chest.

"Jane," I said.

"Jay-en." Jai's voice was rough and throaty, but she had gotten the word right. This thrilled me to my core. It was the first time I had conversed with *P.a.e.*, and the creature had spoken my name!

A savage cry echoed in the canopy, and Tarzan came crashing through the foliage onto the scene, his blade unsheathed, his features set in a fierce grimace. It took but a moment to realize that all the female shrieking had been harmless vocalization. Here sat his sister and his mate in amiable conversation.

It was a strange tableau, I thought, stifling the impulse to say, "Tarzan, won't you sit and join us for tea?"

He didn't sit. Indeed, with a happy cry, he threw himself bodily upon Jai and they began to wrestle. Once again I sought safety on an upper branch, giving them all the room needed for the playful melee. Mr. Grey, also attracted to the ruckus, beak-over-toed his way down and perched on a limb above my shoulder and began shouting out, "Jai! Jai! Piggy piggy Tarzan!"

The parrot and I watched the roughhousing until the siblings sat back on their haunches panting and exhausted and altogether pleased with themselves.

Thus ensued the most exquisite experiences of my research. For daring to challenge and humiliate Kerchak, Jai had lost her position in the Mangani bower. She would certainly be killed if she returned, and so she built a small nest of her own near Tarzan's. Here, with him translating the Mangani to English, Jai became my willing subject. Many times, I was aware that Tarzan's *zabalu* scrutinized me with equal fascination. It had proved difficult to explain where I—a *tar-zan* female—had come from (and fully grown!), but Jai could see the open affection between the white-skins, and she made her approval of me apparent almost immediately.

I hardly knew where to begin with my close study of "The Mangani Female, Jai." The pens and pencils were brought out, and the pages of the journal began to fill again. The new anatomical drawings became the most thrilling aspect of my study, for not only was I able to execute an artist's rendition of a body part, but the gentle Jai allowed me to examine, palpate, and move the part as well. Like a child in a sweetshop, my head spun with choices of what to study next.

Hands and feet with their specialized fingers and toes were of keen interest, as was the skull, though measuring cranial capacity was approximation and guesswork. The mouth, teeth, tongue, and throat took days of observation. It was not an easy thing explaining to the Mangani why another would wish to put fingers in her mouth, move her tongue around, and request that she open and close her jaw.

I could only guess what lay within the larynx—how it differed from an ape's and a human's. It amused Jai no end that I insisted that she make the same noise over and over again while I held my fingers over her neck.

The examination of the femur, hip joint, and pelvis to study the upright stance became a great source of merriment, for the palpations tickled Jai, and she—playful by nature—could not resist tickling me back. We rolled around the nest snorting and shouting with laughter, Mr. and Mrs. Grey happily chiming in with their own. But it was this wild grappling that put into Tarzan's head the idea that Jai should teach me to wrestle Mangani-style, much as she had taught him as a young boy.

I demurred at first, as this physical exercise was more foreign and exotic than anything that had come before.

"It will be useful to you," Tarzan suggested, though for the life of me, I could not see how.

In the end I acquiesced, and the three of us repaired to a clearing on the forest floor. With Tarzan standing guard against any ground predators, we two females fell together, arms and legs atangle, with Jai almost gingerly (for she knew her strength) and in silence (for she had no words for description) giving instruction in the fine art of Mangani wrestling—*another course in Lord Greystoke's Forest Curriculum,* I wryly thought.

When Jai thrust her head into my chest and pushed me to the ground, my lower limbs with next to no prompting wrapped around Jai's legs, and the grappling that commenced was far more instinctual than I could ever have imagined. Fingers clutched forearms. A leg was trapped between two knees. I saw how a head could be locked in the crook of an elbow. There was constant movement—rolling, flipping, tumbling, and escaping each other's grasp. Of course, Jai's advantages, besides the obvious, were fingers longer than mine, and the flexible perpendicular toe that was, by far, the strongest of all her digits.

Tarzan could not resist joining in, and while he never did wrestle me, brother and sister would sometimes demonstrate a particular maneuver, something that was quite new to them both. It was in this way that I first observed that a wrist grabbed by an opponent might be released by the rotation of the wrist in the direction of the tip of the thumb. I thought it a rather elegant escape and insisted upon practicing it with Jai until I had perfected it.

As exciting as the anatomy and language and the physical exercises were to me, most riveting of all were those times when, with Tarzan translating, Jai would allow me to peer into the interactions of Mangani society, a history of the tribe, and analysis of particular individuals.

Of the greatest interest to both Tarzan and Jai was their mother, Kala. She had clearly been a remarkable creature. Though Kerchak's dominance had been established before Tarzan's adoption and Jai's birth, there were *pan-tho* (a word I translated as "memories" or "tales" or "legends") that were told and retold down through generations. Tarzan had heard many of them, and now he was called upon to take the *pan-tho* in the uncomplicated Mangani language and interpret them into English, every word of which I recorded in the Claytons' journal, with some interpretation of my own.

"Kala and Her Family"

It became apparent to all, shortly after reaching her sexual maturity, that Kala was the most attractive of the Mangani females. Every male, young or old, desired to mate with her. Her coat was soft, more hairlike than furlike. She was larger and stronger than other females, and her scent was irresistible. Challenges were fought over Kala, but even when a challenge was won, she remained aloof and did not choose the winner for kin-ga. The first mating season after her maturity came and went without pregnancy, and it was during this time that Kerchak rose to dominance.

Of all the males, he had grown the largest by far, and all were aware—but did not speak—of his strange behavior. Where the Mangani were quiet and lived peaceably, Kerchak was loud and flew into violent rages, fighting when there was nothing to fight about.

When the females next came into season, Kerchak began challenging every male for every female, something unheard of in the tribe. There had always been sharing, and females might choose with which male they wished to mate. Some of the males were injured by Kerchak, and one died of his injuries, further shocking the tribe. But Kerchak had grown uncontrollable. There was no one strong enough or brave enough to stop him.

Then, in a moment that all living Mangani would never forget, Kala refused kin-ga with Kerchak, even after he had won a challenge for her. She disappeared from the Great Bower, never returning until her season had finished. Even Kerchak, with his furious moods, would not mate if a female was not in season.

In the seasons that followed, Kala grew wise and powerful among the females. Even Kerchak let her be. Her only sadness was her childlessness. She was good to all the tribe's balu and longed for one of her own. (Note: There seemed to be no understanding that mating was required for a female to give birth and, as partners were interchanged so frequently, no concept of "paternity.")

Kerchak began disappearing from the bower for long periods of time. The Mangani were so happy to have him gone they did not question where he had gone. They grew unhappy whenever he returned, for it was then he displayed the foulest of tempers and flew into the worst of rages.

After one of his absences, a strange thing occurred. When it was least expected, Kerchak ambushed Kala and forced kin-ga upon her. (Note: The estrus cycle had not begun in the females.) Even her size and strength were no match for him, and she succumbed.

After this, Kala's anger grew very large. She said to all that Kerchak was gumado b'nala (sick in the head). He was shunned by the tribe, which caused more violence. He did, however, retreat from the lower bower where the sleeping beds were and made his nest far above everyone else's.

Kala's belly began to swell at a time when no other females' bellies grew, and to her great joy, she gave birth to a healthy balu. She was the best of mothers, and the infant thrived on her copious milk.

Kerchak returned from his absence this time with madness in his eyes. He shouted and roared and flung himself around like a great wind in the trees. He broke the arm of another male and forcibly mated, out of season, with nearly every female. When he approached Kala, she withdrew, holding her balu to her tightly and baring her teeth at Kerchak, enraging him further. It was then he broke off the limb of a tree and began swinging it around him. No Mangani had ever seen anything like this. They had neither weapons nor tools.

Kala ran from him, but not fast enough. The branch upon which she had fled was shattered by Kerchak's club. She fell, and her infant tumbled from her arms to its death.

The uproar was great, but no one was strong enough to challenge Kerchak. The one Mangani who had always had the courage to do so was Kala, and her spirit had been broken by the death of her balu. She grieved so deeply that for a time she lost her senses. She would not let the body of her infant go. She clung to it and wept over it, or just sat staring sightlessly into the canopy. The sadder she became, the angrier Kerchak grew.

One day he came with the club that he now used as his weapon and forced all the Mangani to follow him out of the Great Bower. Even Kala was pushed along, carrying the decomposing body of her child with her. The tribe moved far beyond their foraging grounds, traveling for many days, lost in the forest that turned to jungle and finally to mangrove swamp. It was confusing and terrifying, and Kala, the true leader of the Mangani, was unable to lead, still so deep had she sunk into her grief.

The mangrove swamp scared the tribe with its razor-jawed croco-diles and stinking black water. What came next was sha-ka (beyond their comprehension). Kerchak led them to the edge of the swamp and out onto white, gritty ground, beyond which was Zu-dak-lul (the greatest water the tribe had ever seen). It was endless and moving in terrible swells that made a horrifying roar. Above them was not the protective green canopy of their home but a sharp blue dome with a burning yellow orb that blinded them to look at.

But there was no turning back. Without Kerchak, they were lost. They would never be able to find their way back to the bower, so they followed him up the white, gritty strip of earth, staying far from the dak-lul, and came upon a tree of the strangest form—a great trunk that, up at the level of a Mangani nest, grew very large. And on this nest were two creatures who appeared sick, for they had no fur except on the tops of their heads. Their skin was white! From inside the closed nest came the sound that they knew to be the voice of a balu. It was wailing in a thin, pitiful tone. None were moved by the sound . . . none but Kala, whose ears pricked up. For the first time in so long there was life in her eyes. The stinking corpse she had held close to her breast since its death now dragged along behind her by one arm.

The larger of the tar-zans (white-skins) raised a stick and pointed it at the Mangani, and suddenly came the sound of thunder, as if a terrible storm had descended upon them. There was no water com-ing down from above, or lightning either. But Baldor, who had come in curiosity to Kerchak's side, lay bleeding from a hole in his chest. Then he stopped moving and lay still. Dead.

All the Mangani ran back to the mangrove swamp. Kerchak as well. Night was falling. No one wanted to stay with the crocodiles, but no one wanted to be near the strange bower where tar-zans with their thunder sticks could make Mangani fall down dead where they stood.

All of a sudden Kerchak was moving, splashing through the black water, back in the direction of the strange bower. And Kala, still drag-ging the dead baby behind, followed.

The Mangani shook and shivered in terror without either of their leaders—one hated, one beloved. They were alone with the sounds and the stench in the mangroves on the darkest of nights.

Finally came splashing, and there was Kerchak, covered in blood *and crazed as they had never seen him before. But it was Kala who was most changed. She no longer carried the corpse of her Mangani infant. Now she held most protectively at her breast a small, hairless tar-zan balu. He was completely silent and clung to Kala with scrawny arms. Despite her strange acquisition, Kala was calm and happy. As the moon rose, they watched her offer the little one her teat. When he took it in his mouth, Kala closed her eyes and smiled.*

No one understood why Kala would want the strange hairless creature. But finally Kerchak was ready to take them home, and none questioned it.

In the Great Bower again, Kala, with her tar-zan balu, withdrew to her nest outside the clearing and kept even more to herself. This made Kerchak angrier than before, as did the puny white creature she had brought back with her from the Great Water. But Kerchak was powerless against Kala's will. She had become strong again, and even her distance from the clearing did nothing to diminish it. Females would come and visit with her and little "Tarzan," as she had named him. Even males would chance a visit with the beautiful Kala, and in time her belly again grew swollen. A female was born and was named "Jai," which meant "brave." Tarzan suckled on one teat and Jai on the other, and so the "Family of Kala" was complete.

So intent was I on transcribing every word into the journal that it was not until later that I had the time to pore over the legend. It was, I realized, a stunning bit of social and behavioral history told in the oldest spoken language on earth, and also the missing piece of the puzzle of Tarzan's life.

But another revelation buried in the tales truly set my mind afire. Kala was a far more extraordinary creature than I had previously realized, for she clearly possessed an intelligence that surpassed that of every other Mangani in her tribe. Perhaps every other Mangani who had lived before her. Could it be that this individual was "the next step" in human evolution? And if this was the case, did her offspring, Jai, possess what Brother Mendel called the "dominant gene" for the trait of increased intelligence? Too, Kala seemed to have conceived outside the females' seasonal "heat."

My study of Tarzan's "sister" took on an even greater intensity. I was frustrated by having no other *Pithecanthropi aporterensus erectus* to which I could compare her. Clearly Jai was intelligent and physically strong. But unlike her mother, she had fur, not the silky body hair that Kala had been described as having. That trait had not been passed down to Jai. Perhaps the gene for increased mental capacity had not either. Too, I spent endless hours pondering Kerchak. Was he the last vestige of an older *P.a.e.*, a species that was prone to brutishness and violence, or the first recorded hominid to display signs of madness?

As happily awash in mysteries as I was, two conundrums constantly haunted me. The first: Which aspect of Tarzan's nature was dominant—the feral animal or the civilized man? As I watched him with Jai, his persistent apelike traits were obvious. Lying comfortably with her in the nest, he would groom her, picking the nits from her fur and sometimes (to my horror) popping them in his mouth. I believed that sixteen of his formative years living as a Mangani had so deeply imprinted on his mind their habits and culture that no amount of memory retrieval or retraining in the world into which he was born would ever fully "civilize" him.

Frequently he would speak of his desire to sail on an ocean liner and ride in an automobile, but moments later he would forget them, fully immersed in the task at hand—hunting, eating, playing. All of my conversations about the "future," "present," and "past" had proved outside his comprehension. There was simply no way to explain the "finer" (and more stultifying) aspects of civilized life to him, circumstances that would no doubt chafe at his wild nature. If John Clayton returned to England, would he be lost to me, swallowed up by the uproar that would invariably ensue, transformed by the responsibilities of his title and fortune?

Yet another worry had begun to intrude upon my thoughts. In the excitement of my discovery and research, I had given little or no thought to what the news of a "living missing link species" would bring down upon the heads of these precious creatures. The academic, scientific, and religious establishments in all their ravening exploitation. Comparative anatomists. Vivisectionists. Taxidermists. Theologians. Zookeepers. Adventurers like Ral Conrath who would sell "specimens" for freak shows to the highest bidder.

How could the modern mind ever appreciate the gentle humanity of the Mangani? The American Indians and the Congo blacks who were themselves *Homo sapiens* had been slaughtered like animals. What chance would the Mangani have once the world discovered them?

Where did my responsibility lie?

As the days passed and the air grew thick with moisture, I stifled my misgivings and made plans for the inevitable homecoming with Tarzan. There was so much he needed to learn simply to get by. On the forest floor twenty paces apart I had him come through an imaginary door to where I was standing erect. He practiced saying "How do you do?" hundreds of times until he had mastered the correct inflection, learned just how far he should bend at the waist, the correct nod of the head, and the difference between the force of the grip on the hand of a lady and a gentleman. I explained that other than a handshake, there should be no physical contact with *tar-zans* unless he knew them to be "friends." Looking people in the eye when speaking to them was important. Otherwise they might consider him "devious" or "untrustworthy."

In our rush to leave Zu-dak-lul, it had not occurred to me to bring dinnerware from the beach hut, so I fashioned approximations of plates with rounds of bark, napkins with banana leaves, and silverware with slender sticks carved into forks, knives, and spoons. I had Tarzan build a simple table of appropriate height and, as we sat on stumps, I taught him how to properly eat a meal. For some reason, every time he uttered "Pass the salt, please," I fell into a fit of giggles.

I tried to explain the clothes he would be expected to wear, garments even more stiff and confining than the bush suits he'd seen Father and D'Arnot and Ral Conrath wearing. For his questions of why a collar should be so tight about the neck and why someone would wear shoes, I struggled with answers. I dreaded his one day asking why a woman would strap herself in a whalebone corset.

I considered making an attempt to explain to Tarzan his true station in English life, but as the thought made me gloomy, I decided to wait until it was altogether necessary.

K*alan galul?*" I said, pointing between Jai's legs. Females bleed? I had asked.

Jai nodded her head as Tarzan had taught her to do for the affirmative. A sideways shake meant "no."

I was unsure how to proceed with the questioning about the Mangani estrus cycle, for they had no discernible sense of time. From what I gathered, the females appeared to go into an annual or biannual "heat," as lower mammals did, but I needed to be sure. I scolded myself for failing to learn the correct wording for my query from Tarzan before he went off to hunt. Jai, bless her heart, was becoming fidgety and bored with the *tar-zan* female who, it must have seemed to the Mangani, talked incessantly.

Perhaps a simpler question.

"*Zu* Mangani *balu galul?*" I said and with my hand showed increasing height, hoping Jai would understand. How old when a young Mangani menstruates?

Jai thought very hard and, grabbing my hand, took it to a height of four feet, then pointed to her own vulva.

"Brilliant!" I cried, delighted Jai had made sense of the question and pleased she continued to show signs of real intelligence. When Tarzan returned, I must ask him how old a four-foot Mangani female would be. I began scribbling the questions and answers in the journal, all the while fretting about the wording of the next query.

I heard rustling in the fig boughs below me and looked up to find Jai gone from her spot. *Unsurprising,* I thought. *I'm taking forever with this interview.* And it was true that the Mangani shared Tarzan's propensity for coming and going with little or no fanfare. But by the time it registered that the fingers of the furred hand on the lip of the nest were too long and broad to be Jai's, I was staring into the hideous one-eyed face of Kerchak.

The speed and silence with which he rose like a mountain over the nest's edge and flew at me left no chance to cry out for help. I was vaguely aware of the panicked fluttering of grey feathers above me before the monster's blow landed on my chin. Then dark night descended on me suddenly and completely.

It was all the better that it had.

The Beast

I t was the stench of fetid breath on my face that woke me. I knew
before I opened my eyes some approximation of what was before
me and wondered, in growing panic, if my eyes remained closed
would I stave off the inevitable. I heard short sniffs as Kerchak ranged
over my body with his flattened nose, down into the pit of my arm
and lower to the V of my thighs. This was more than I could stand,
and through gritted teeth a moan escaped me. Steely fingers gripped
my belly and I screamed, eyes springing open against my will. The
face I dreaded to see—the appalling fanged visage—was leering down
at me. I refused to meet his gaze. His immense furred body throbbed
with a sickening heat that threatened to choke me.

Get hold of yourself, I thought. Do something, anything, but do not die
without a fight. I chanced a look at the Mangani, and with all thoughts
vanished, I moved. My foot smashed into the bull ape's testicles and,
massive as he was, his soft parts proved vulnerable as any man's. He
cried out in shocked agony, falling to one side. I twisted away only to
find myself a hundred feet off the forest floor in Kerchak's nest.

He leaped at me, but I found footing on the thick limbs he used
every day to descend. Now I could see the Great Bower and its Mangani in their nests peering up at the perplexing scene—a tar-zan female in Kerchak's nest. Now I was running away from him. Running
on light feet as he lumbered after me, clutching the fleshy sac between his legs, growling in fury.

"Hay-ee! Hay-ee!" I cried, begging for help. "Tarzan, Tarzan! Jai-
Kala, Jai-Kala!" The familiar names drew heads farther out of their
nests. "Gamla!" I shouted, "Gamla, hay-ee!"

I saw the female spring out onto a branch in front of her nest and begin climbing toward me. Then another female. And another. I was closing the distance between us, using the narrowing limbs, down to the gathering of maddened females. Having failed to come to Kala's aid years before, they were perhaps unwilling to allow their tormentor another murder right before their eyes. *Almost there, almost there . . .* I could see the warm brown eyes, the outstretched hands. And then he fell—the furred devil—as if out of the sky, heavily onto the branch between us. He stood with his back to me, a jagged club in his fingers, thrashing it in my rescuers' direction. He snorted his displeasure with the mutiny, but forward they came, through with his tyranny, ready to die. The club arced high and with a sickening thud of wood on flesh and bone, Gamla fell bloodied to a lower limb. The others pressed in. *No, no! I will not allow it! My precious Mangani females . . .*

"Kerchak," I shouted. "Kerchak, *kin-ga!*"

He turned slowly and faced me, a ghastly cyclops with flecks of foam around his snarling red mouth. I turned and made for the nest, luring him behind me, cursing my mad, irrational ploy. I would reach the nest, and when he came near I would jump to my death, die of my own will and not be murdered by a loathsome beast.

I could see the nest before me. Almost there. *Gather your resolve*, I thought, *death will come quickly*. But he leaped from behind, sweeping me under one arm, propelling us up and up to his nest. Trapped in his clutches I prayed for unconsciousness. It would not come. I felt the coarse fur against my skin, heard the lewd growling whisper, *"Kin-ga tar-zan."*

In the nest, he threw me down on my back and, reaching out a hairy hand, ripped the hide skirt from my body. Kerchak rose tall, showing me the vile weapon of his masculinity, that which would rend me and kill me as it had Alice Clayton. He threw back his head and roared his supremacy, a horror of a sound, I thought, that would surely be the last I would hear in my life.

The arrow that thwacked into Kerchak's side had barely time to register in either my vision or the monster's senses when out of the clearing swung Tarzan, a furious titan, a human projectile slamming with such velocity into his mortal enemy that the giant was knocked to his knees. I rolled away, crouching on the nest's lip as the combat began.

Kerchak snapped off the arrow shaft, and coming to his full height, he turned. Tarzan was ready with a downward thrust of his blade into Kerchak's upraised arm. But the cut barely fazed him. He merely stared with the outrage of recognition—Kala's puny *tar-zan balu* had returned to vex him. Never was the disparity of their sizes so clear. The sheer bulk of the monster was matched only by the madness that fueled his being. All Tarzan wielded against him were his wits and the Bowie, and the knife was of no use unless it pierced a vital organ.

"Go! Run!" Tarzan shouted at me. I hesitated, unwilling to abandon the sight of him. "Go!"

I leaped to a close branch, never taking my eyes from Tarzan, his fixed upon the dreadful Mangani. Kerchak's first blow—his great arm thrashing in a wide arc—knocked Tarzan clean out of the nest. I screamed, for the ground was a hundred feet down. I found him clinging to a branch. But only for a moment. He scrambled upward to a tangled liana, hanging like a monkey by feet and hands above the nest.

Now Kerchak broke off a limb the size of his arm and began savagely beating the thick mattress of twigs and leaves around him.

"Tar-zan!" he snarled. "Kerchak *korag* Tarzan!"

A promise to destroy him.

"Kerchak *kora*—"

Tarzan's feetfirst swing smashed Kerchak's face, cutting short the threat and knocking him backward. But he grabbed Tarzan's legs and held them fast. Clinging to a limb with one arm and his large-toed foot, the creature dangled his antagonist far out over the clearing.

Then in a feat of inconceivable prowess, Tarzan swung himself sharply upward, stabbing with his knife the arm that held him. The grip suddenly released, he *climbed* the beast's body! They fell back into the nest, a blurred tangle of furred and white-skinned limbs. Tarzan's fingers grappled over Kerchak's face, clawing at the one good eye. Kerchak knocked it away, scissoring Tarzan's torso with colossal legs. Tarzan landed punch after punch on unyielding flesh. Kerchak lunged at Tarzan's neck with his terrible fanged mouth, ripping the skin but failing, barely, to sink his teeth into the jugular, rip out the throat as he had John Clayton's. The beast's mighty fisted blow to Tarzan's belly knocked him back, but the punishing arm was laid bare as Tarzan's blade sliced the length of it. Blood spurted. Kerchak roared in fury and thrust upward with the other arm. The Bowie flew from Tarzan's grip only to be snatched in midflight by his adversary who now, gracelessly, punched the air with the blade, exultant in his victory.

Tarzan unarmed!

In that moment of Kerchak's self-delusion I saw Tarzan again retreat to the higher perch. What was he planning? What was he thinking?

Tarzan took flight, diving down on Kerchak's back. The unexpected assault from above took him by storm. Tarzan's powerful legs clamped viselike around Kerchak's middle, the muscular hands gripping his mammoth head. Kerchak thrashed with the knife to no avail, violently bucking his rider, bellowing his rage.

The twist and loud snapping of Kerchak's neck was sudden, choking the beast's roar in his throat. The look of stupefaction lasted but a moment, then the one eye rolled back in his head. Tarzan shoved the suddenly inert figure to the brink of the nest and tipped it off and over.

Kerchak was dead all the while he tumbled heavily down. Dead as the bulk of him snapped heavy branches like twigs. Dead when his behemoth's body crashed with a thud to the forest floor.

Tarzan flew to me, holding me to him, murmuring my name and wordless sounds of joy . . . I felt surging through every pore the furies that had driven him relentlessly to this moment in time. But he tarried only long enough to confirm I was whole and uninjured, for the Mangani—all of them—were streaming silently from their nests to the ground . . . and Tarzan was drawn to join them.

I followed after him slowly, savoring the sight of this gentle tribe longing for proof they'd been freed from its tyrant. A cry from above announced the arrival of Jai, her head bloodied, swinging to the Great Bower, and my heart soared with the sight of her.

And Gamla lived! Limping painfully and carrying the club that had wounded her, she was first to reach the reviled corpse. She swung the branch above her head and came down on Kerchak's face—once, twice, three times, till it was red mash. The others gathered around, jostling and murmuring quietly. *Balu* played with the flaccid hands and feet of their once-feared oppressor.

But when Tarzan came, they made way for him, he stained red and brown with blood. He'd regained the Bowie and, once at Kerchak's side, he fell to his knees. The blade arched high and drove violently downward into the leathery chest.

Hardly a sound was heard from the tribe as I made my way to the ground. They parted for the naked white-skin female. Tarzan was working with rough, jerking strokes at the body as I came to his side. I saw that in his hand he held the dripping, scarlet heart of the killer. I stared transfixed as he drew the glistening flesh to his mouth, ripped out a piece with his teeth, then thrust the heart high over his head, triumphant in his vengeance. The silent clearing erupted with ecstatic howls and cries of revelry. Mangani fell at Tarzan's feet in the worship of gratitude.

Something raw and primordial surged through me then. Something ancient and long unbroken. Knowledge that the creatures about me were sisters and brothers in blood. Tarzan I saw with perfect clarity—a mighty, gore-stained savage. A wild, ungovernable animal.

I had never desired him more.

We stood in the shallows of a nearby pool. Tarzan's eyes were closed as I washed him with cupped hands. His body was coming up in angry bruises. One shoulder was bitten, the skin of his neck torn in several places. He appeared to be still, but when I laid my flat palms on his chest I found him pulsing, tremulous beneath them, his heart pounding a strong, steady rhythm. His eyes still glittered with remnants of violence, and he clasped me fiercely to him, bruising me with a feverish kiss. He grasped my shoulders hard, pushing me to arm's length, desperately searching my face as though it were a map, something, *anything* to guide him back from the throes of insanity. Instead I lifted my face and licked the fresh wound. He shuddered under my lips.

In that moment all in me that was civilized fell away like a snake shedding its skin. I'd seen Tarzan for the brutal creature he was. An animal mad with the lust to kill. Here he stood, pulsing with heat and sweat and blood. His hands ranging over my breasts, thighs, belly were rough. And I wanted him rough. Craved him inside me. Moving hard.

I drew him onto the shore. He pulled me down, atop him. Pierced me. Sweet fire tore through my body. Snarling, he began to thrust. The world fell away and our coupling, our wild exultant cries, were lost amid the roars and calls and screeches of the great forest canopy.

We were one. The bond unbreakable. Forever.

We came to our senses slowly, never straying far from the Great Bower. I found myself shaken to the bone by my raw carnal raptures coming so soon after a brutal bloodletting. I had always believed Tarzan was in part a primal, feral animal. Never myself. In the sentimental shadow of genteel Lord and Lady Greystoke's beach hut, our lovemaking had been eager and ardent enough. And while I had reveled in the wantonness of our last joining, it had frightened me. *Had we been possessed by jungle demons? Intoxicated by violence?* The experience seemed to have electrified Tarzan, left him primed, cocksure, possessive. And for a time afterward, I basked in our glorious mating, certain that no other woman who'd ever lived had so sublime a lover.

But when the tumult of roiling black clouds signaled that the rains would soon be upon us, making the swamp to the north impassable, I again came to my senses. The pragmatism and science that had been temporarily usurped by libido once more prevailed.

Kerchak's carcass had been left where it fell and was, to the contentment of the Mangani, rotting away before their eyes.

Meanwhile, I had come to a momentous decision. I could do nothing that might harm the Mangani. If that meant never revealing the "living missing link species" to the world, so be it. In fact, I had barely scratched the surface of my study of *P.a.e.*, and subsequent expeditions would be carried out with secrecy and precaution. There was no telling how many years, or decades, it would take to complete the work. And perhaps by then a way might be found to protect their existence.

Yet Kerchak's corpse enticed and tempted the scientist that I was. Beneath the decomposing fur and leathery skin was a skeleton—some of its bones broken but otherwise complete. I could not be certain when—or if— I might acquire so perfect a specimen again.

I therefore asked Tarzan to strip as much flesh from the bones as possible, and with the Bowie I dissected out the larynx and voice box. These we packed in salt and minerals, hoping to preserve the soft tissue, though I was not at all optimistic. Of course the bones of the face had been crushed and it was hard to know what would be salvageable. We set the carcass down at the borderlands between the Mangani's forest and the jungle.

When we returned to the bower, we found the warmest of welcomes, with every member of the tribe gathering around us with grave solemnity.

"Tarzan *ben gund,*" Jai intoned, and the others responded with a guttural chant of the same words.

I understood none but his name, but Tarzan appeared surprised.

"They wish to make me their chief," he told me. "Great chief." It was, I thought, a proud announcement.

The males and females alike began touching him imploringly. To my dismay, he did nothing to correct them, just smiled sweetly and returned their caresses, even lifting a tiny *balu* into his arms. I was dumbstruck watching the scene, seeing him gaze around with such warm affection.

These are his people, his kin, I thought. *But could he actually consider such a thing?*

Our eyes met then, and I saw a moment of confusion there, as though he'd been caught in the act of a petty crime. He *had* been contemplating staying!

The breath went out of me and I looked quickly away. But my expression had betrayed me. A moment later I heard Tarzan say to the Mangani, "Jai *gund vando.*" Jai good chief.

There was concerned murmuring, but then Gamla spoke, "Jai *gund vando.*" She pulled Jai into a rough embrace. One by one the others grasped or nuzzled Jai, assenting to her leadership.

Tarzan caught my eye as if to assure me, *I've said no to them. I am yours,* and I nodded my affirmation.

But I'd seen that moment, brief as it was, when the man had in his heart accepted his title as chief of the Mangani.

We never spoke of it again, but it worried me. It raised doubts and uncertainties about the journey home. Even Tarzan's feasting upon Kerchak's still-warm heart had not given me so much pause as his fleeting moment of desire to stay among the Mangani.

When we returned to collect my specimens, we found that the army ants had done their job well—Kerchak's bones had been picked altogether clean. I found, as expected, that delicate folded muscles of the vocal cords had badly decomposed. But the larynx was made of sterner stuff—tough cartilage—and was largely intact.

The greatest part of our task became the fashioning of two carriers that would safely convey the top and bottom halves of the skeleton back to England. The sturdy bark of the mango was stuffed with tufts of fluff from the silk-cotton tree, rare in this season, harvested by Jai, Gamla, and the other female Mangani and delivered to us as grateful offerings. Many times I found them gazing at all that remained of their torturer. I had not observed the species long enough to recognize the varying emotions in those simian expressions, but I think in those days I learned the appearance of profound satisfaction by studying their sweet faces.

Tarzan hunted a *pacco* and with its supple hide fashioned sturdy straps to close and protect the cases and the pouch and the Claytons' journal, now filled with my scientific observations.

We'd been postponing the inevitable—our good-byes. Even now, memory of that parting brings me to tears. Jai was, of course, the most difficult to leave, as Tarzan was forced to make her understand that we would be gone for a protracted time and that we would be nowhere to be found. There were no words in the Mangani language for such a thing, and when she did finally understand, she wept, a sound that was as heartrendingly human as it was primal.

The Mangani in their farewells could not understand our need for a hasty departure. They were unsatisfied with warm and fulsome embraces and in the end compelled us to stay another day, insisting on languid sessions of delicate grooming and sharing of succulent foods. But when the first raindrops penetrated the canopy, we knew we had tarried too long. We slipped away the next morning before the bower had come fully awake.

I had long dreaded our leave-taking from the parrots with whom we shared our tree—the only of our friends that could not be made to understand our absence. Indeed, I owed Mr. Grey an enormous debt of gratitude, as it had been he who had sounded the alarm when Kerchak had abducted me. It was while Tarzan was feeding the birds some of their favorite pawpaw seeds that I understood his unspoken anxiety about leaving the only home he had ever known. To look at the man, such a strong and heroic figure, one would naturally assume the wider world to be his oyster, exploration and feats of daring the everyday occurrence. But I had sung a lullaby to the tender little boy who still lived within him. He might never again show fear to another human being, but beating inside that strapping chest was a bruised and wary heart.

Indeed, it was an overlong good-bye with our feathered friends, and I saw Tarzan's jaw clench as he climbed for the last time over the lip of his nest.

"You take good care of each other," I told the parrots, "hatch many *balu*," and followed Tarzan down.

We were climbing to the ridgetop of the Enduro Escarpment, as I'd wished to view the whole of Eden one last time. Each of us carried one of the bags holding Kerchak's bones, so the upward passage was slow. We'd nearly reached the summit when the forest air erupted into sound.

Distinctive and unwelcome sound.

I have been such a fool, I thought in sudden panic. *Such a bloody fool.*

Conrath

There was no need to explain the calamity to Tarzan. He'd already set down his bag and was scrambling to the highest vantage point. I did the same.

The scene below us was hard to make out from so great a height. Only a fraction of the village was visible and a mere slice of the central clearing. But it looked as if the tribe's population was gathered in a tight group at one side of it. No Waziri weapons were in evidence. Their postures suggested cowering.

We would have to move closer.

It was a silent scramble down the rock into the canopy and from there to the outskirts of the village. Tarzan leaped down to the thatched rooftops first and I followed. In this way we moved undetected toward the central clearing.

Without warning, the racket of rapid-fire explosions rent the air again. When it was silenced, I could make out the sounds of screaming. Children wailing in terror. Tarzan grasped my arm and pointed below. Hiding behind the men's house was a pair of tribesmen armed with spears who had somehow evaded capture. Tarzan made the call of a bird, and they looked up at us at once. He signaled that they should continue stealthily forward along with us.

We arrived at the hut closest to the clearing and, dropping to our bellies, peered down. Now we could see the whole central square, the place where we had feasted with the Waziri and watched them dance around the fire. All of their spears, bows, and arrows had been tossed in a pile. Two dozen white men, some tough and wiry, others large and brawny, were spread about the clearing. They were European mercenaries, two who manned the still-smoking Gatling gun and the others, skittish, standing at rigid attention with their rifles aimed at the villagers. Before them were the bullet-ridden bodies of fifteen tribesmen. One of the soldiers lay dead with an arrow stuck in his eye. It appeared an attempt had been made to charge the invaders.

"Ulu is there," Tarzan whispered. "I cannot see Chief Waziri."

The charm doctor stood in the center of his people, giving no indication of his status to the captors. But the grey-haired leader was not to be found in the congregations of the living or the dead. Nor could I see Ral Conrath. I could hear his voice, though. He was right below us, under the thatch overhang.

"Damn savages," he snarled.

Now striding across the clearing came Paul D'Arnot, red faced and raging. "What in God's name do you think you're doing?" he shouted.

Conrath finally appeared below the lip of the hut. The sight of him made my stomach churn.

"Defending your pathetic ass from unprovoked attacks like that." He jutted his chin at the dead mercenary.

"I was making progress with the chief . . . till this," D'Arnot said.

"What do you call progress?"

"There is enough Bantu in their language so he understands you wished to go to the source of the necklaces—Sumbula. Of course he resisted at first, but with time . . ."

"Who said we had time?"

"Well, now you have nothing."

"McKenzie!" Ral called out. "Bring him over here!"

On the far side of the clearing, a red-haired giant with his rifle dug into Chief Waziri's back pushed the old man toward Ral Conrath. The headman's face was expressionless, but his eyes fixed on the corpses bleeding out into the sacred ground.

"I have had enough," D'Arnot spat. "I will not be a party to killing these people."

"What's this bleeding heart act all of a sudden?" Ral went toe to toe with the Frenchman. "I saw the look on your face when I told you what your cut would be. You would have slit your own mother's throat for it. Don't tell me now you didn't know what you were getting into."

D'Arnot glared at him. "How many more are you willing to kill to bring out this treasure?"

Ral smiled jauntily. "All of 'em eventually." He appeared pleased by the horrified look that twisted D'Arnot's face. "You know something, Paul? You haven't been thinking straight. Did you really imagine the Waziri were going to let us waltz into their gold mine anytime we wanted?" He put a threatening hand around his interpreter's throat. "But in the meantime, you're going to tell the chief here I need a little guided tour—him and me and ten of his strongest men. And you're going to make him understand that if we don't all come out alive, everybody else dies—men, women, children."

"I will not."

"*You will not?*" Conrath looked genuinely shocked. "Well, I guess that's that, then." Ral released D'Arnot, who turned away.

I felt my heart leap to see the Frenchman, finally, after all this carnage, do an honorable thing.

"D'Arnot," Ral called to him.

Paul turned back with a hopeful look. Perhaps Ral had come to his senses. But in the next instant Conrath drew a pistol from his belt and with the most placid look fired into D'Arnot's gut. Paul staggered backward, as surprised as he was agonized. He stood staring at his employer, covering the gushing wound with both hands, then collapsed faceup into the dirt.

That was all I could stand. I took aim at the subhuman beast with my arrow.

Tarzan stayed my hand. "Wait," he whispered.

Chief Waziri was in the line of fire. Ral Conrath was gesturing for several of his men to separate out the required tribesmen and bring them to him.

I could see Ral fingering the gold ornament around the old man's neck. "Take me there, where these come from," he said, his voice icy. "I know you know the way. You'll be my guide. You understand me, don't you, you dumb jigboo." He pointed to the Gatling gun, then pantomimed bullets taking down the Waziri tribesmen.

"I love this weapon," Ral muttered and with his pistol dug into Chief Waziri's back, led him, ten mercenaries, and an equal number of Waziri out of the village in the direction of the Sumbula peaks.

"We've got to do something," I said.

"Wait until they are gone." Tarzan's eyes were following the party out of the village. "Till they cannot hear." Then he peered down at the two tribesmen below us. "Stay here." He leaped to the ground with the grace and silence of a cat, and gathered the men with an arm around each of them. He spoke quietly, making a plan.

O ur arrows were loosed simultaneously and found their marks at the same instant. The mercenaries manning the Gatling gun were stunned by the projectiles that pierced their necks from behind and came protruding with a gush of blood from their throats. A pair of spears came hurtling from *walla* rooftops, impaling two men, and an instant later the Waziri fell down onto two others and dragged them silently from the clearing. Those who were as yet unmolested turned and began shooting with their rifles at the roofline from where they perceived the attack had come. But no enemy was to be seen. Tarzan and I had run stealthily to another rooftop position and let fly with our arrows. Another pair of men fell dead in their tracks.

The Waziri's confusion had held them in their places at first. But when Tarzan and I raced into the clearing, Ulu found his voice.

"*Jacuma tek gomadi!*" he cried, and all at once the women and children fell back and the tribesmen, unarmed, crossed the clearing and charged the remaining guards, now firing in panic at the approaching mob. The Waziri fell on them in a frenzy.

Their screams as they were beaten and torn were less disturbing than how strangely pleasing the sound was to my ear. Only then had I time to reflect that I'd taken the lives of two human beings. That such an act felt natural and right did alarm me. *Was savagery endemic to my constitution? To anyone's, given the proper circumstance?*

All of Ral Conrath's men had been violently dispatched. Waziri women were tending to the wounded and wailing over their dead. Though dazed by the carnage, I found myself drawn to the figure of Paul D'Arnot. Mortally wounded as he appeared, he was alive, squirming in pain, his head tossing from side to side.

I knelt beside him and saw his bloodied chest rising and falling. His eyelids were shut, flickering with pain.

"Paul," I said quietly.

He did not immediately answer, startled by the sound of the

familiar and altogether unexpected voice. His eyes fluttered open with difficulty and focused slowly.

"Jane? . . . Jane?"

"Yes, I'm alive."

"Auugh . . . dear God . . ."

"He couldn't stay away, could he?"

D'Arnot was silent and still for so long that I feared it was too late. Then forcing a painful inhalation, he began to speak.

"I should never have returned . . . should have resisted him. But he threatened me with my past deeds and the law . . . and he lured me with promises . . . I would have all the money I would need to begin a new life . . . He had found the Waziri village and the gold mine he sought . . ."

I cursed my gullibility. Why had I believed Ral when he said he'd not found any gold?

"When?" I demanded. "When did he find the mine?"

D'Arnot's eyes closed and a thin stream of blood and saliva leaked from the corner of his mouth.

"One day before he went up the mountain . . . to survey for those Belgians. You and your father were exploring . . . your 'Eden.' He found the Waziri mine . . . before . . . augh . . . before he found this Waziri village . . . He never came here until today. Belgians' cash . . . paid for mercenaries . . . for bringing out the gold . . . Waziri . . . 'easy to subdue.'" D'Arnot managed a chuckle but choked on his own blood.

"The Belgians," I whispered urgently, "are they coming?"

"Yes . . . just south of here. Far enough away from his find."

But not far enough away from the Waziri, I thought . . . *or the Mangani. Leopold's ravening colonists, American gold miners, European scientists— all of them would lay waste to Eden.* I turned away, unable to look at Ral Conrath's accomplice. He grabbed my arm with clawlike fingers.

"You don't understand. There is more."

"More? More than this . . . abomination?"

"He found a doorway . . . a symbol."

D'Arnot's voice was growing very weak. *What symbol could he mean?* I bent over him, placing my ear to his lips.

"More famous than Petrie . . ." D'Arnot whispered.

"Flinders Petrie?"

"New Eeg . . ." A long sigh escaped D'Arnot and he lay motion-less. I shook him less than gently. His color had gone grey, but there was the merest rise and fall in his chest.

Tarzan came and knelt at my side. "Conrath has taken Chief Waziri to lead him into Sumbula. We must follow quickly. Ulu will take us."

A sound of pain and surrender issued from Paul D'Arnot's lips, and I felt desperation overtake me. I needed to hear about the last moments of my father's life. A word, a gesture. Something. *Anything.*

But when I turned back to the Frenchman, he was dead, his glassy eyes reflecting the shimmering green of the canopy. I gazed around once more at Ral Conrath's butchery. There were no words vile enough for what I felt for him. I imagined it was something akin to that which had driven Tarzan to carve the heart from Kerchak's chest, and wondered what I might indeed be capable of when the man was again fixed in my sights.

I stared down at Paul D'Arnot. What a wasted life. How honor-ably he had begun in Libreville. Standing firm against the Belgians. Giving all he had for love. But time and circumstance and human cruelty had devoured that which was good in him.

I stood. "We should hurry," I said.

Following Ulu, we moved swift and silent along the forest floor. The path was narrow and overgrown above, but the earth beneath our feet had been tamped down to the hardness of stone. I followed the charm doctor, Tarzan following me. I felt a fierceness in me, a forward straining in my limbs. I was a hungry hunter, sights set on my prey.

I could only imagine Tarzan's fury at Ral Conrath, for he'd slaugh-tered many good people. He had stolen the chief and forced Waziri men—mightily fearful of Sumbula—to journey there.

The four peaks of the range and the small valleys between them were blanketed with trees of a size I had seen only on my climb up the slopes of Sumbula's tallest mountain. Entering this forest was made all the more strange by the thick mist that rose about us and obscured even the sight of Ulu, if I did not follow closely enough behind him. It muted all sound, even the shrill cries of the birds that I could hear, but not see, flitting in the branches high above us. Dan-ger might be lurking very near—*sheeta, histah*—but without sight or clear sound of them, there would be no warning.

Suddenly, Ulu called back for us to stop. He had led us off the main trail to the base of a monstrous tree, even its lowest branches too high to see, but by its bark it appeared to be a baobab. Its many thick roots seemed to grow as much out of the ground as within and formed a wildly braided wall before which Ulu now squatted.

The charm doctor uncovered from beneath a mattress of moss a pile of sturdy clubs and a pot of what looked like pitch. Without speaking, he went to work making a fire with the dry stick and leaves that had also been hidden below the moss. He took three clubs from the pile and dipped their ends into the pot, then held them to the fire.

They burst into flame. Ulu stood, his expression grave.

"*Umla hugar* Sumbula," he said.

"Ulu says he fears taking us . . ." Tarzan translated, careful to re-frain from uttering that sacred word, I thought.

"*M'boa kai* Waziri *ta* Ulu *don.*"

"Only the chief and he are permitted," Tarzan said.

Then suddenly the earth—as if giving the charm doctor a sterner warning still—began to shake violently underfoot. All three of us were thrown forcibly to the ground. My imperative to follow Ral Conrath into the mine was forgotten in the upheaval. While the tree beside us was too mammoth to shake, the canopy overhead grew noisy with panicked animals. A vent nearby—one of those cracks in the ground I'd seen emitting the dense mist of the Sumbula foothills—tore open to discharge a massive plume of steam. Our torches aban-doned, we scrambled away on hands and knees lest we be scalded to death. From below us in the earth I could hear the sound of great crashing and destruction.

Ulu had heard it as well, and even when the shaking stopped and we three regained our footing, he seemed poised with his ear angled to the ground, listening to the subterranean. His features took on a brutal cast.

"*M'tolo!*" he cried.

"We must hurry," Tarzan said. Ulu had returned to the base of the baobab and was kneeling at the tar pot, again coating the torch tips with pitch and lighting them.

Without another word, Ulu lifted a section of roots—a beautifully hidden doorway—and ushered us into Sumbula.

Underworld

I t did give me pause when we began our descent—a steep one—
into a steam-filled passage hewn from stone. We were belowground, ground that had been regularly shaking since my arrival
in Eden. Boiling mud pots. A pool whose cool water had turned hot
enough to cook fish. And what we saw up ahead did nothing to assuage my unease. The passage opened out into a vast cave. Even by
the light of torches and in the misty air I could see that the rough-
walled chamber was a mine. Ral Conrath's damned gold mine. That
for which he had lied, stolen, bribed, and murdered.

Ulu was staring at a giant wooden waterwheel that had toppled
over and broken into jagged pieces, blocking the way. This, I surmised, had been the crashing sound we'd heard from above, the one
that had troubled our guide. The channel that had moved the waterwheel, I now saw, was a noisy rushing river—the Mbele Ogowe tributary, gone underground. But the water was boiling hot, steaming.
Father's observation about the area's volcanism had never seemed so
obvious.

*Are we mad to be heading into an underground cavern that could col-
lapse and bury us alive?*

I willed myself to rein in my fears, and it was easier than I expected, for the sights around me were strange and extraordinary. I
was no expert, but even a child could see that the veins, the wavy
ribbons of gold in the mine, were plentiful and thick. It was ingenious how the engineers had used the wooden waterwheel built into
the underground river to power a kind of "conveyor belt" that
brought from two wide shafts—like arms that disappeared into the
black depths of the cave—tons of ore. Ore, I could see, that was so

rich with the yellow metal that the raw quartzite rocks shimmered in our lamplight. At the back of the main chamber was what must have been a stone smelter. It was cold now, but I could see it must have produced prodigious heat.

We were forced to scramble over the fractured waterwheel to move ahead. Under my bare feet, the broken wood skeleton was no more difficult to traverse than the twisted branches of a tree.

Ulu was urging us on. As we left the gold mine behind, we entered a room housing what I vaguely recognized in the flickering torchlight as presses . . . coin presses. This was a mint—a find beyond all expectation! Here were sophisticated dies and screw presses that had clearly stamped the Waziri necklaces. The whole thing was mysterious, miraculous—a mining and coin-making operation in the depths of the Gabonese jungle so far from everything. And abandoned, as though all in a rush. *But abandoned by whom?*

There was no time for pondering, as Ulu had not paused for even a moment. He was leading us through an archway into a further passage. Its walls, I could see, were constructed of stone blocks, more finely made than the rough-hewn ones in the mine and mint. But what we found at the end of the passage stopped me in my tracks and caused the hair on my arms to prickle.

It was a doorway, massive, with two polished marble columns on either side of it. The columns were deeply carved with hieroglyphs.

Egyptian hieroglyphs.

I stood unmoving. "Wait," I said. I lifted my torch high and stared in astonishment at what I saw carved into the marble lintel. The flickering light left it in long shadows, distorting the image. But I could see enough of it to know that the symbol above the doorway depicted a square maze, the same design the Waziri used over and over in their village.

This was the symbol D'Arnot had spoken of before he died. The one that would make Ral Conrath "more famous than Petrie."

I studied it, recalling the story of the pile of rubble Flinders Petrie had discovered near Fayum Oasis, all that was left, he believed, of the fabulous three-thousand-room ancient Egyptian labyrinth the historian Herodotus had visited and written about.

But this was anything but a pile of stone chips. It was all intact. And the hieroglyphs . . . I had nothing but the most rudimentary knowledge of Egyptology. But if what lay beyond these doors was what I suspected—what Ral Conrath believed he had found—we had just stumbled onto the greatest archaeological find in centuries.

A "New Egypt" near Africa's west coast!

I was snatched from my musings by a deep sonorous droning and turned to find its source, the Waziri charm doctor. Ulu was stock-still in a seeming trance, eyes wide and staring at the closed door. Now the droning intensified, causing his lightly closed lips to vibrate, the sound reverberating eerily in the empty hall. Tarzan's eyes were fixed on the man—confusedly, expectantly. I, too, found myself expectant. But of what?

In the next moment we understood.

As if a mechanism had been triggered by the vibrations emanating from Ulu's body, the great doors swung silently open. I was dumbfounded and could only imagine the chaos in Tarzan's mind. He had ventured into the taboo world of Sumbula and seen man-made wonders—wonders that were near to his home yet hidden all these years from his sight and knowledge. I wished I could speak to him, though I had no good explanation for any of it. But there was no time for talk. Ulu had moved through the doors and side by side Tarzan and I followed. Nothing that had come before prepared me for the staggering sight before us—a long, stately corridor lined with tall pillars of fine white marble.

Ulu stopped long enough only to extinguish his torch, gesturing for us to do the same, for the entire passageway was perfectly lit with sconces of filigreed glass, the flames behind them throwing off a soft, filtered light. *Light from what source? What was this place?!*

But the dazzlement was just beginning.

The walls on both sides of the hallway had been covered, every inch, with brightly colored frescoes. Though we were moving quickly at Ulu's urgings, I could see that the artistry was magnificent, but even more amazing was the content of the murals. Scenes of celestial bodies. The moon in its phases. The constellations of the zodiac. Strange, colorful billowing clouds set against the blackness of space. The rings and moons of Saturn! I lagged behind to gape at scenes of an erupting volcano, great waves towering over a coastal landscape, terrible winds flattening a forest. I was reminded again of Petrie's description of his labyrinth—"paintings that showed the whole history of the world." There were scenes familiar to Africa—mountain ranges, waterfalls, snaking rivers—but others that had no business existing in a place such as this—vast expanses of icy wasteland, a glacier cutting down through snow-covered peaks.

As we reached the end of the hallway, Ulu turned the sharp corner and disappeared. But Tarzan and I had stopped dead in our tracks. For here before us was a magnificent map that covered an entire wall. It vaguely resembled our world, though continents were somewhat shifted about, Antarctica was nowhere to be seen, and a great island was outlined between the coasts of West Africa and South America. But Ulu soon returned, shouting at us to follow. We ran down another corridor, this one lower ceilinged, though the walls here were similarly painted with frescoes.

These were neither celestial nor planetary features. What we were seeing was a spectacular *bestiary*. As I hurried past, I caught glimpses of gorgeously rendered paintings of every animal of the jungle—big cats, hyenas, crocodiles, elephants. There were herds of zebras, elephants, antelopes. Birds, snakes, the long-tusked boar. Families of great apes. Insects. Tarzan had run ahead of me, following Ulu, but now I could see he was standing still, staring hard at the wall. When I reached him he was slack-jawed.

"Look," he said, reaching out and placing his palm on the painted surface.

Staring back at us was a perfect rendering of a Mangani female, male, and *balu*. The implications were stupefying. Whoever were the occupants of this complex, they had had knowledge of the missing link tribe!

"*M'tolo!*" Ulu cried.

We dared not tarry, though the mysteries of this place were piling one atop another. I determined that when we had stopped Ral Conrath and rescued the captive Waziri, Tarzan and I would find a way to investigate it further.

But now we were moving through a dizzying maze of interlocking chambers, crypts, and corridors, some that followed one after another, others that dead-ended, then turned back in the opposite direction. It struck me then with the force of an Atlantic wave—*It is indeed a labyrinth*—here, a continent away from Egypt. This, then, was Sumbula! The secret that Waziri headmen kept from their people, the sacred and taboo, bringing out gold medallions and snatches of culture to be woven into the fabric of the tribe. *For how long, how many thousands of years, I wondered, had their ancestors been visitors to this inexplicable destination?*

Ral Conrath, looking for a fortune in gold, had stumbled upon a far greater treasure: a "lost civilization." It would have been the impossible dream of a boy's lifetime—one he'd dared not imagine—vast riches outshone by the unimaginable promise of worldwide fame and prestige. Scholars, scientists, noblemen, even kings groveling before him.

Sure-footed and confident, Ulu led us deeper and deeper into the tangled stone edifice. Some rooms were no bigger than a closet; others, soaring temples. We passed through a chamber that with its scroll-stuffed shelves could only have been a library. Its sole living occupants, I found to my disgust, were large shaggy rats gnawing unmolested on the ancient codices. I wanted to scream, shoo the horrible beasts away, and salvage all the precious documents I could lay my hands on.

But there was no time!

I was still reeling from the thought that the library was perhaps as old as the one destroyed in Alexandria when I found myself alone—for Tarzan and Ulu had already run ahead—in a room at the center of which was a long wooden table. There were no seats around it, and I was certain it was not meant for dining. Along one wall were shelves stacked neatly with metal knives and probes and wooden-handled saws. On another wall I saw painted an image that took my breath away.

It was a human figure lying supine on the table in the center of the room—a Caucasian male, the skin of his limbs flayed and the muscles perfectly depicted, the torso laid open and the organs exposed.

This was a dissection laboratory! I swiveled and faced the opposite wall, awash in wonder, hoping perhaps to see the dissection of the human back, but there, lying cut open on the same table, was a Mangani female, a full-term fetus still curled up in her womb.

"Jane! Come!" Tarzan had returned for his laggard partner. "You must come now!"

Loath to expose him to this gruesome image, I dutifully followed him out into a stone corridor. One of its walls had collapsed inward.

Ulu now stood staring down at the pile of rubble. I could see that at least two of Ral's soldiers had been crushed beneath the mammoth stones. There was a bare black foot poking out of the crumbling rock and a crushed Waziri skull oozing blood and brain. It reminded me again of the danger we were in. But there was nothing to be done about it now.

Ulu turned on his heels and rushed down a short hall, disappearing through a doorway. Tarzan and I followed and found ourselves in an altogether empty chamber. It was small, but the ceiling was very high. The only features were built into each of the four walls—what could only be called an "instrument" the size of the body of a cello. It was nautilus shaped, and the accordion-folded membrane covering it resembled the gill of a fish.

Grim and determined, Ulu strode to the wall facing the door we had entered (I had long ago lost my bearings and had no idea of its compass direction). With the back of his fingers, he lightly strummed the curved instrument. It produced a resonant, nearly inaudible tone that was rather more *felt* than heard around us. A moment later, the loud and distant roar of rushing water filled the chamber. It was the underground river in the mine!

I saw Tarzan's eyes widen with wonder, and I, too, marveled at the technology mastered by the ancients who had inhabited these halls. Ulu, who'd been listening closely, was clearly dissatisfied with what he'd heard. When the sounds of the Ogowe tributary subsided, he moved to the next wall and strummed the "listening instrument" as he had done before. At first there was complete silence. We all strained, trying to hear something. Anything. Then it came—faint rustling and scurrying and the distant sound of the library rats chewing the parchment scrolls.

The listening device was most certainly directed at each of the four quadrants of the labyrinth. Tarzan, as excited as he had been when rediscovering the English language at Zu-dak-lul, silently gestured to Ulu, asking if he might strum the instrument on the third wall. Ulu nodded his consent.

Tarzan ran his fingers over the membrane. Instantly, the sound of voices could be clearly heard in the chamber.

"Get me outta this dump, Conrath. It ain't what I signed on for." It was one of the mercenaries. "It's a goddamn tomb," another man muttered, though it was as loud and clear as if he had been standing in the sounding room with us.

"And I didn't sign on a pack of whining lily-livered chumps," Ral Conrath snapped.

"My brother's dead back there. What's my mother gonna say when I can't even bring home his body?"

"She's going to say, 'Thank you, Son, for bringing me back this lovely pile of gold,'" Ral replied in an old woman's voice. "And then she'll bake you a cherry pie. Hey, McKenzie!" he called.

"Yeah, boss."

"Fall back. I want a word with you."

I remembered that McKenzie was the tall red-haired soldier.

"You think we've got a mutiny on our hands?" Ral said.

"I dunno. Depends on how happy they are with what we find. And how soon we find it."

"*M'tolo!*" we heard Chief Waziri call.

Conrath's voice was decidedly shaky. "I don't like that guy," he said.

"Yeah, well, he's all we've got," McKenzie said.

Conrath lowered his voice. "Maybe there is no treasure room at the center of the maze. Maybe it's a dungeon or a well he and his buddies will try to throw us into."

"Hell of a time to think of that, boss."

"I don't like the way this place is starting to look. Look at those things."

"Yeah, it's giving me the creeps."

"You back there," Conrath called. "Keep a close eye on those black fellows!"

The voices faded out.

We looked to Ulu, who—though he could not have understood the overheard conversation—seemed more alarmed than ever. Tarzan spoke to him quietly in Waziri, then turned to me.

"He knows where they are. They are very close, he says. We must run."

"Close to what?"

Tarzan shrugged. "Words I do not understand."

I wondered how much of Ral's conversation with his men Tarzan had comprehended. The different dialects. So many colloquialisms.

But there was no doubt what must now be done.

Followed closely by Tarzan, whose head swiveled from side to side devouring the unfathomable sights, Ulu raced ahead, navigating brilliantly through the jigsaw of chambers, his urgency to rescue the chief and their men from the white devil his only driving force.

I had a purpose as well. Much as these surroundings astonished and confounded me, I knew with all certainty that there was nothing on earth more imperative than the ending of Ral Conrath's miserable existence.

As we continued inward, I saw that the man-made splendor of the labyrinth had been corrupted by the hand of nature. Roots of the gigantean trees above had invaded the rooms. With the slow, steady power of growth alone, they'd broken through solid rock as if it were custard, spiraling down around marble columns, snaking across floors, tangling around altars to obscure the faces of their deities. The next few chambers were small and claustrophobic, the roots almost entirely engulfing the walls. This, then, must have been what had spooked Conrath and given McKenzie the creeps. It did, in fact, have a sinister look, a reminder that the most magnificent of man's achievements were so easily crushed by the relentless hand of Nature.

We turned a final corner and found ourselves in a broad pillared court with a soaring ceiling, its marble walls glowing with soft white light. Here the roots had found purchase underfoot, and we were forced to pick our way carefully across the thick woven mat of wood. Before us was a set of stupendous double doors, larger by half than the ones that had led us into the maze.

They were covered in gold.

We fell silent at the sight. But as we approached the astonishing doors, our attention was drawn to the two walls that flanked them. On our left was a fabulously painted fresco—a vast square building of two stories—the labyrinth as it must have looked in the past, its top floor aboveground. Behind it rose the volcanic peak—the largest mountain of the Sumbula Range. But below it, where the three smaller Sumbula hills should be, were three pyramids of various sizes. The largest of the structures resembled that most famous of all Egyptian megaliths, the one on the Giza Plateau. I stared for a long moment at its bright white surface, what Egyptologists reckoned the

Great Pyramid had looked like before its limestone casing had been looted to build the nearby city of Cairo.

But where, then, were the Sumbula Hills? It took a moment to adjust my thinking. The smaller cones weren't hills at all. *They were tree-covered pyramids!*

Now I saw that Tarzan and Ulu were across the way, riveted to the opposite wall—this an even more complex mural. On the left end had been painted the labyrinth complex, its volcano and pyramids. On the far right was a huge walled city, nothing less than a metropolis, and built in concentric circles—the second of the Waziri's oft-repeated motifs.

All of it was gilded in gold leaf.

I made my way across to it and saw the city, its enormous circular grid of turreted palaces, broad avenues, towers, and stadiums. I now realized that the labyrinth and the city were two ends of a pictorial map. A caravan of figures—humans and elephants—appeared to be traveling from the Sumbula site to the metropolis. There were finely painted renderings of mountains, low hills, jungle, forest, rivers, rock escarpments, swamps, and desolate deserts between the two.

I had Tarzan ask Ulu about the painted city.

"Opar," he uttered, then fell silent.

An undiscovered city hidden deep in the wilds of Gabon. The maze in which we were standing—fabulous as it might be—appeared humble compared to what might in fact be "Opar, the Lost City of Gold." *What would Ral Conrath make of that?*

The Great Chamber

I will kill him," Tarzan whispered.

I held his eyes. "Let me."

We were standing outside the golden doors left carelessly open, a testament to Ral Conrath's belief that he would be unmolested during his endeavors.

I looked behind me. Ulu was still studying the extraordinary fresco of a people's journey to a golden city. Tarzan quietly called to the charm doctor and he joined us at the doorway. We stared in at a sight beyond all comprehension.

It was a great chamber, one of massive proportions. Four rows of columns of a size that rivaled Luxor soared to the ceiling, the true height of which was completely obscured by a thick forest of tree roots and vines. Some of the pillars, all of them entangled by the thick vegetation, leaned precariously at odd angles, displaced, I surmised, by the millennia of slow incursion by the roots or, more alarmingly, by the recent tremor that had toppled the waterwheel in the mine. One at the far end had fallen altogether and now cut the front of the chamber into two uneven sections.

From this vantage point we could see that the walls of the oblong chamber were shimmering with yellow fire, for they were entirely covered in the Waziri's medallions—the coin of this mysterious realm. In neatly spaced rows amid the gilded armoring were thousands of small alcoves, and in each of them were piled more coins. Millions of them.

This was clearly a vault. The very heart of Sumbula.

At the far end of the chamber, perhaps a hundred feet from where we stood, were two immense statues standing side by side—a male and a female, rulers of this culture, or perhaps deities.

I could clearly hear the voices of Ral Conrath to the left of center and his armed henchmen to the right who, by the sound of them, were forcing the Waziri to pull coins from the alcoves and toss them in piles. Chief Waziri was presumably among them.

Tarzan signaled to Ulu that they would attack the right flank, and the charm doctor began his stealthy move toward the front, using the thick columns to hide his approach.

Tarzan pulled me close and buried his face in my hair. Though no words passed between us, I clung to him, my fears for his life and my own overcome by the pride I felt for his confidence in me. He pushed me to arm's length. "In there, find me," he said, "and I will find you."

Then he was gone, scrambling up the nearest column using the circling vines for foot- and handholds. Halfway up the pillar, he leaped into the thicket of hanging roots and began swinging silently to the front of the great chamber. I followed his lead, grateful that my limbs and fingers were able to easily lift me into the bare "branches" of the strange inverted jungle canopy and to the far end of the massive columned room.

From my high perch, I looked down upon a scene of unspeakable greed. Just below was Ral Conrath inspecting a treasure trove of small statues, his features disfigured with his lust for gold.

"Holy Christ! Wait till you see this, McKenzie!" he called to his man in the opposite corner of the vault.

McKenzie and the other guards had their rifles pointed at all the native men and their chief, forced to work removing coins from the alcoves, throwing them into wooden crates.

Coffin-shaped crates, I thought bitterly, remembering my father, and found that my hand had quite unconsciously tightened around the Bowie's hilt.

Above the Waziri, well hidden in the tangled roots, Tarzan crouched, taking his bow from his shoulder. Slowly he turned his head and found me with his eyes, held my stare.

In the next moment, he loosed his first arrow and the melee began.

That shaft struck a guard in the chest. He shrieked as he dropped to his knees, alerting the others, who swiveled and fired wildly, trying

292   ▣   Robin Maxwell

to locate the archer. Another guard clutched at his neck where one of Ulu's darts now protruded. The man began convulsing violently, his back arching so extremely that a moment later a loud crack reverberated through the chamber as his spine fractured and he fell screaming to the floor. Another henchman watching his cohort in horror was next to receive one of Ulu's poison darts. This man's shrieking began almost at once, as though fire was coursing through his veins. Then he started to bleed. First from his nose and ears, mouth and eyes. A red stain spread across his groin. And soon he was bleeding through the pores of his skin. Face and hands. His clothing was suddenly drenched in blood. Moaning pitifully, he dropped to the floor and lay still.

Gunfire ricocheted off the metal walls. Stone shard projectiles went flying from the columns. Chief Waziri called out a single word to his men, who instantly scattered.

Ral Conrath stood gaping at this sudden chaos. His pistol was poised for a shot, but all the targets were moving. *Where were those damn arrows and darts coming from?*

The instant McKenzie took aim at his fleeing native captives, Tarzan, with a lion's bloodthirsty roar, took flight and leaped down upon the man's back. Conrath stared open-mouthed as a naked wild man fell out of the knotted roots onto his top soldier.

The rifle flew from McKenzie's hands. They punched and kicked and gouged till McKenzie reached down, retrieved his gun, and began crazily swinging the rifle butt at Tarzan's head. Tarzan—nimble on his feet—evaded it, looking for a way to bring the man down again and disarm him once and for all. But he couldn't see what I could from my vantage point: Ral Conrath waiting for a clear shot of this brute. The target . . . that broad muscular back.

"Tarzan!" I shouted in alarm. His head snapped up, but his turn to find me left him open to a perfect shot to his chest. *I have to do something!* I leaped onto a thick root and, with a savage cry, swooped down. Conrath never saw me coming, only felt a bare foot kick the gun from his hand and the force of the body that followed, knocking him to the ground. He rolled deftly and came to his feet to confront his attacker.

There I stood, bare breasted and back from the dead! My knees were bent, arms held wide like a wrestler's.

"Surprise," I said, brandishing a blade as long as my forearm.

He was gaping at me. "Son of a bitch . . ."

I lunged at him with the Bowie and opened the skin of his hand. He yelped.

"That's for my mother. Think twice about speaking rudely of her again."

He couldn't help leering at my nakedness but was clearly enraged to be trapped like this by a female. And of course he was shocked. I could see him struggling for his usual witty nonchalance.

"Aw, baby," he finally said, "you gonna make me have to kill you?"

"Again? You'd best do a better job of it this time, Mr. Conrath."

His eyes darted behind me. From the grunts and shrieks I heard, Tarzan was brawling with several more mercenaries.

"Who's the Romeo?" Conrath sniped. "That the 'ape-man' D'Arnot thought he saw in the trees?" My expression told him he'd hit his mark, so he added, "The one I'm taking back to the Ringling Brothers' freak show?"

Conrath darted quick as a viper and caught me off guard. The knife flew from my hand.

My weapon is gone, I thought. *But so is his.* With that I sprang at him. We fell, grappling, to the floor. *He is strong, but not so strong as my wrestling teacher,* I thought. My muscles, from the hours of playful combat with Jai, felt powerful and sinuous, even against this hard, dexterous male body. I was edging our scuffle closer and closer to the Bowie. I could hear Conrath's ugly grunts and profanity, furious to find a woman his worthy opponent.

The knife was in reach if I could just free my hand. I darted for it, but he used the moment to flip me onto my back. One of my legs twisted around one of his, and with that we began to roll, over and over on the stone floor.

I caught desperate glimpses of Tarzan—three more attackers had joined McKenzie. He'd struck them repeatedly with hard bare-handed blows. They'd fall but get up and charge him again and again.

For a brief moment I was on my hands and knees, steady, while Ral was searching for my dropped blade. I chanced a glimpse at the altar and saw one of Tarzan's attackers suddenly drop, his skull spurting blood. There was Chief Waziri standing with a rifle barrel in his hand, swinging the heavy wooden handle like a club at the head of a second brawler. This man ducked and the blow missed. He charged at Tarzan's middle. Lifting him bodily by the waist, Tarzan sent him crashing to the floor.

Tarzan had lost sight of me and was scanning the chamber with frantic eyes. He found me. Then leaving the others to battle Chief Waziri, Tarzan leaped upon the downed pillar and began to climb its diagonal length in my direction.

All at once a sudden and thunderous convulsion rocked the chamber. Sumbula had awakened!

The shaking earth split Conrath and me apart—he on a ledge below, me scrambling for his pistol on a new-made "rock cliff" above him. I watched in horror as the massive column Tarzan was climbing snapped in two, throwing him down on his back. The stone behemoth was inches from crushing his head! He rolled sideways, saving himself, but the rumbling went on. This quake was far stronger and harder than any we'd felt before.

With an ear-splitting *crack!* and a blast of searing heat, the floor opened up beneath Tarzan. He was now balanced over a widening rift in the ground, and it was upwelling with molten lava. I saw his hair beginning to burn! Springing swiftly to his hands and knees, he vaulted over the crack in the earth.

He was trying to reach me!

Keeping one eye on him, I raced for the skittering knife, all the while knocked about by the unending tremors that seemed to be growing more violent.

I watched Tarzan dart for the nearest intact pillar and begin scaling its height toward the shaking tangle of brown roots above. It was moving under him. *Everything* was moving, and the bubbling red gash was widening with every passing moment. *Were the sharp splintering cracks I was hearing the stone walls and columns beginning to crumble?*

I crawled to the lip of the new-made "cliff" and looked down. A mistake. Ral Conrath stood wobbling on two feet, the pistol gripped in the hand of his outstretched arm, waiting for me. He fired point-blank! But the stone floor jerked under him and the shot missed. I was knocked back hard against the wall.

"Jane!" Tarzan shouted above the calamitous roar.

I caught sight of him in the trembling roots above, clinging to a thick vine. "Jane! Bowie!"

Bowie? What did he want me to do with it?

It was then I saw that the chamber itself was splitting in two, a glowing orange river of lava rising over its banks and covering the floor. With a piercing metallic shriek, one of the immense gold deities toppled slowly forward, crashing into the viscous red river, and began melting at once.

"Bowie!" Tarzan barked in a commanding voice, and suddenly I knew his mind. I struggled to my feet and raised the knife high over my head. He leaped from his foothold in the roots, swung toward me in a wide arc, and snatched the blade from my upthrust hand. Then he disappeared onto the ledge below. Thrown to my belly, I watched as the falling blow of Tarzan's body knocked the pistol from Ral Conrath's hand. I thrilled as the Bowie sliced into the back of his knee, instantly severing muscles and tendons that held the leg together. Conrath's strangled cry was cut short when Tarzan lifted him overhead and heaved him like a rag toy far out into the middle of the chamber's floor, now a dozen feet below us.

Tarzan battled the ever-moving ledges that could, in an instant, have ground him to gory pulp, and climbed up to my side.

"We must go," he said, urging me to follow.

But if we'd thought that all hell had already broken loose, we had sorely underestimated the fury of Sumbula.

One by one, the giant pillars began to fall, dragging down from above the gargantuan trees whose roots twisted and entrapped them.

"Climb!" Tarzan shouted.

Climb we did, up and over a roiling mass of rocks and earth, roots and treetops. Ulu and the tribesmen were nowhere to be seen, but now I could see Chief Waziri bravely meeting his fate, back against the wall, a shower of coins falling down around his head.

Below us, Ral Conrath, hamstrung by Tarzan's blade, dragged himself toward the great double doors. He caught sight of us, struggling upward amid the torrent of stones, then looked behind him at the wide river of lava now streaming together with the fallen deity's melted gold and gaining on him fast.

I had to marvel, for even at the last, Conrath's arrogance prevailed.

"You're comin' with me, Janie!" he blustered. "You and your god-damn ape-man! To hell!"

"You're on your own!" I shouted down at him. "I don't believe in hell!"

Then the molten soup enveloped his legs and he shrieked, mouth open wide. But the sound was lost in the din of collapse. As daylight shone above us, I turned for one final glimpse of our enemy . . . now a hideous writhing statue of gold amid a forest of toppling root-bound columns.

Tarzan was pulling me up and away through the mountainous avalanche. The ground had never stopped shaking, and as we reached the surface I was stunned by the sight of the nearest Sumbula foot-hill crumbling before my eyes—not as a mound of tree-covered earth and rock but in blocks of cut stone.

A pyramid.

"Hurry!" Tarzan called, but as I made to haul myself out into the dust-and-orange-smoke-clogged air, I felt my ankle catch in a mass of tangled roots. They were dragging me down as they fell into the sink of the great chamber.

"Help me!"

Tarzan was there in an instant, hanging down from above into the pit, slashing with the Bowie at the tough, fibrous roots that trapped my leg.

"Please," I whispered, watching in horror as a massive slide of pyr-amid blocks came crashing toward us, tumbling heavily end over end.

Suddenly I was free, aboveground, and we were running for our lives, running amid a course of ghastly obstacles.

"On!" Tarzan shouted and gave me his back.

With me clinging like a barnacle, he hurtled across the deadly gauntlet, the ground alive with convulsions. Myriad vents erupted with scalding steam. Trees toppled, their crowns afire. Jagged crevices ripped apart, glowing red from the center of the earth. And heated stones, great and small, rained down around our heads.

The shaking ceased abruptly. The sound of all living things, nor-mally loud to my ears, had fallen into shocked silence. All that could be heard was the hissing of steam and the crackling of treetops burn-ing. Lava that moved on the surface in sluggish streams shared the scorched earth with pots of boiling mud.

Tarzan set me on the ground, and we surveyed what remained of the range. Rivers of molten rock flowed down the slopes of the high peak, its "trees that touch the sky" afire. The three foothills—all exposed as pyramids—lay in collapsed heaps.

Looking west, we surveyed what was left of Eden. The mountain had given us so many clues and warnings—the steam vents and the basalt makeup of the Enduro Escarpment. The many earthquakes. But never could I have dreamed of what catastrophe Sumbula might unleash.

A great swath of the majestic forest at the foot of the range had been inundated by the river of molten lava. It took only a few days for it to cool substantially and a thick crust to form—it was a brittle black mass of volcanic rock, a mile wide and in places twenty feet deep. Our paradise was a wasteland. There was nothing left of "the trees that touched the sky" on the mountain itself, and all that protruded from the hideous layer of black rock was a graveyard of charred, leafless skeletons.

The Enduro Escarpment—that bogus gold mine of paleoanthropology—proved valuable after all. Its great height had deflected the flow of lava and spared the Waziri village. It was intact, though many huts had crumbled in the shaking, and the forest to the south was largely untouched.

In strained silence, Tarzan and I hurriedly traveled west. Everywhere we went we found terrible devastation. Countless birds lying dead on the ground with their plumage brilliantly intact. Within a circle of fire-ravaged trees were the charred remains of an entire herd of elephants.

The Great Bower had been obliterated by the eruption. A few of the Mangani—the very old and the very young—had perished in the fiery inundation. We searched the forest and located the survivors. It was a strange and joyful reunion. When the shaking had started and the forest to the east had begun to burn, Jai had instinctively and courageously led the tribe south. While shocked by the unnameable catastrophe, they were now calmly grieving their dead and busily rebuilding their new home bower.

When we returned to the Waziri, we found them also mourning

their dead and rebuilding their village. For the help we had given them (though I was racked by guilt that all I had done was bring them ravagement in the form of Ral Conrath), they gifted us with as many gold pendants as we could carry and a length of the pretty woven cloth that the women wore. We retrieved Kerchak's bones and the journal from the top of the escarpment and, with heavy hearts at the loss of so much of our paradise, began the journey home.

To the North

It began to rain. Nothing had prepared me for the incessant deluge. The roaring *rat-tat-tat* on thousands of broad leaves was enough to drive a person mad. By and large we traveled in silence, deeply sobered by the inconsequential nature of man and beast in the face of unimaginable forces of the earth. I met all obstacles with the stoicism I had learned from Tarzan. Thoughts of the mysterious labyrinth, "New Egypt," and the lost city of Opar lying somewhere in the wilds of Africa consumed me nearly as completely as did the Mangani. Their mysterious existence. Their evolution and survival against all odds. The complicated ethics of revealing them to or concealing them from the world.

Tarzan and I did speak at night, curled up together in the dark in whatever hollow tree or jerry-rigged nest we could quickly fashion. He had endless questions about the maze and everything we'd seen within it, though I was at a loss to explain any of it. That it existed at all was a wonder to me. Its technology—"high antchquity," I called it—was as enigmatic to me as it was to him.

So perplexed was I that I instead urged Tarzan to imagine the places on his father's map where we would one day travel. Borneo, Stockholm, Mongolia, California. He told me he wished to know more of his mother's and father's life than had been written in their journal. That he hoped to ride on a train and in an automobile. To hear music and to see how *tar-zans* danced.

Yet I was plagued by doubts. I anguished compulsively over the question of whether I was in love with this man or simply consumed by lust. Whether our unique adventure and great passion were enough to move a couple through an entire lifetime. Did he love me, or see me simply as his "mate," his "woman"? I had come to him in Eden almost magically, and I was, after all, the only non-Waziri female he had ever known, save his mother. Would he cleave so tightly to me when there were other young, pretty girls (and surely there would be) fawning and truckling at handsome Lord Greystoke's feet?

I did some unselfish worrying as well. No amount of explanation, I argued with myself, could ever convey the claustrophobia of living the better part of life indoors—the loss of the freedoms Tarzan took for granted in a thousand different ways.

Oh, how I wished for some guidance in this endeavor! But there was none to be had. I could only hope for the best.

We nearly lost the journal in the mangrove swamp below Mbele territory, so treacherous was the rain-flooded tangle of roots. I hadn't counted on being welcomed into the Mbele village after our tragic visit, but Chief Motobe had successfully sold the ivories that Father had given him and, at least for the moment, the people were prospering. I sat with the women stitching from the Waziri textile a simple garment for me, one that would cover me sufficiently for polite company.

Tarzan was taken into Motobe's hut and emerged wearing the breeches and ragged linen shirt of the colonial officer whose jacket was the centerpiece of the chief's holiday garb. Thus outfitted, we were taxied in a dugout canoe up the tributary to the main branch of the Ogowe.

I had done my best to prepare Tarzan for the first shock of modern technology, but sight of the stern-wheeler chugging downriver like a great white monster set him back on his heels. It was hard to read his expression, for there was some fright and horror admixed with admiration and excitement. And I knew that he wished above all, in the face of extreme circumstances, to appear brave and manly in my eyes.

We were taken aboard the *Dangereuse*, a craft less well captained and maintained than *La Belle Fille*, and the offer to pay our fare with a Waziri necklace was eagerly accepted. My appearance caused considerable commotion, as the "death of the white Englishwoman" had occasioned gossip all up and down the watercourse for many weeks after the Porter Expedition had come out of the jungle.

The captain plied me with countless questions, few of which I was willing to answer. He looked askance at the peculiarly clad "John Clayton" and tried to keep him up late at night drinking sherry and learn what he was sure were the sordid details of my rescue. Tarzan refused to drink, but he did use the French-accented captain to practice at English conversation, and insisted that the man show him every detail of the vessel, from the steam-run engine to the maps in the wheelhouse.

But the closer we came to civilization, the more apprehensive I became. Nothing I could ever describe would have prepared my lover for the shock of Libreville—the noise and the stench and frantic activity at every turn.

The moment we disembarked, I learned that a freighter would be sailing for England the next morning at dawn, and I quickly made arrangements for our passage home. As I negotiated for a tiny cabin with the captain—sadly, not my Captain Kelly—I saw a wide-eyed Tarzan standing alone on the dock, watching the rush and clatter of human commerce all around him. Again I observed his embrace of new experience, yet many times I saw him recoil at a harsh sound or the mindless jostling he received by the dockhands, blacks who must have looked unfathomable to him—Waziri tribesmen dressed in white men's clothes, speaking the white man's language.

With so little time till our departure, I became an army sergeant, ticking off all that we must accomplish before the morning. I hastily wrote a message to my mother telling her that I was alive and coming home, and sent it off as a telegram. Tarzan dutifully followed me everywhere, and I was forever extricating myself from his clutching embrace, as men unknown to him—black and white both, but all of them loud and aggressive—came unreasonably close to my person. How to explain that the crush of humanity was to be expected in city life, and that I was in no imminent danger? And how odd that he had trusted me to fight hand to hand with a grown man in the great chamber of Sumbula yet worried for my safety on the dock at Libreville.

Tarzan survived his first rickshaw ride with more equanimity than I could imagine—the sight of four native men propelling us in a box down crunching gravel avenues with strange wallas looming on both sides. His eyes grew wide as we trotted through the marketplace, where he gawked at the gaily dressed seesters and mammies, their piles of ripe fruit and vegetables. He grabbed my hand when we passed small wooden cages in which colorful *neetas* sat passively on perches, and grew visibly alarmed to see a row of monkeys likewise imprisoned. "I will explain later," I told him, wondering how I would excuse this "civilized" practice of animal abduction and keeping. Only when we started out the coast road and passed beneath the scarlet bower of the flamboyant trees did he seem to soften and grow easy.

My disappointment was impossible to disguise when we arrived at Cecily's house to find it altogether empty and boarded up with no one to tell me what had become of her.

Thus with nowhere to stay and no source of clothing to put on our backs, we made a forced return to the center of Libreville. I deposited Tarzan at the town's only haberdasher, paying for a suit of clothes to be hastily assembled while I visited the dressmaker.

I felt my own clothes to be confining after the loose shift (and less) that I had become accustomed to. As Tarzan and I walked into the Libreville Hotel lobby, I could see he was chafing against his suit. It must have felt miserably tight around his limbs and neck . . . and the shoes had to have been unbearable.

He was staring openly at the trophy head of a lion mounted on the wall above the counter, and I cursed myself for failing to warn him of such monstrosities. As I traded gold for a room for "my husband and myself," I was grateful for the moral leniency of the French in general and their downright laxity in this colonial backwater, for we had no luggage, I wore no wedding ring, and in a questionable and most unladylike manner I was negotiating for accommodations with a strange gold artifact.

I determined we should attempt eating a meal in a civilized setting and so we were seated in the nearly empty hotel dining room.

Tarzan sat rod straight in his chair and I whispered that he could lean against the back cushion if he liked. So much minutiae we took for granted in everyday life! Would I become nothing more than a full-time tutor?

He did quite well with his plates and glass and utensils, but we both found the food atrocious. Cecily had been right about that. I managed to get Tarzan to spit the poisonous stuff into his napkin and not onto the plate. I admit I did the same.

I was determined, though, to have him practice the manners he would be called upon to use in short order, so I began some quiet dinner conversation.

"You asked me once about Lord Greystoke. Do you remember?"

He nodded once.

"It might be better if you answered, 'Yes, I remember.'"

"Yes, I remember," he dutifully parroted.

"In England there are many, many people."

"That live in *wallas*," he added.

"Houses."

"They live in *houses*, as many as there are trees in the forest."

"That's right. But some of the people live in small houses and others in very large ones. That's because the ones who live in large houses have more money than the ones in small houses."

"Money?"

"You know the Waziri necklaces I used to trade for our rooms on the ship and the room here?"

"Yes."

"Those necklaces are made of gold, and gold is a kind of money. The men in England who have the most money . . ." I stopped then, because what I was about to say was absurd and profoundly upsetting to me.

"Tell me about the men in England who have the most money."

"They get to be the headmen."

"There is more than one headman?"

"Many more. One for every tribe. Tribes are called 'families.' Your father was from the Clayton family, and they had a great deal of money."

"Do they live in a large house?"

"When they were alive they did. In a very large house."

"But who is Lord Greystoke?"

"Lord Greystoke is a title, like 'chief'—another name for a person. When your father's father was alive, he was Lord Greystoke. When he died, his son, your father, became Lord Greystoke."

Tarzan looked utterly perplexed.

"And now that your father is dead, his son, *you*, are Lord Greystoke. It means that you are an important man in England."

"A chief?"

"In a way you're a chief. You meet with other lords in an even bigger house in London—the House of Lords—and together you make the laws. Rules everyone else has to follow. You own a great deal of land, and horses and dogs, and you have many . . . oh, God . . ."

"I have many . . . ? What do I have many of?"

"Servants. Yes, I know. 'What are servants?' " I was finding it difficult to hide my agitation. "Servants are men and women who have very little money. So they work in the houses of men with lots of money and do the things that the rich men don't want to do for themselves."

"I don't understand."

"Neither do I!"

He looked at me quizzically. "Have I made you angry?"

"No. And I've done a pathetic job explaining the English aristocracy to you." I sighed. "You are John Clayton *and* Lord Greystoke. You are a wealthy and important man. And when you get to England and have a houseful of servants waiting on you hand and foot and everyone trying to push you this way and that and fit you into their stinking little boxes, you're going to be a very unhappy man indeed!"

With that I stood from the table, wiping hot tears from my face. "Can we go to our room, please?"

Tarzan leaped from his chair so quickly it toppled over behind him. I took his arm, and leaving a Waziri coin behind, we hurried out of the dining room.

Once in our room I tried to settle myself down, but Tarzan, obviously suffering from claustrophobia in the small hot space, said almost immediately, "There is something dead nearby."

It was the *air* that was dead, I thought, though I had no way to express such a thing. When I showed him the toilet and the bathtub rooms down the hall and explained their functions, he grew visibly confused. I thought then that if the word "ridiculous" had been part of his vocabulary, he would have employed it.

All of this worried me, for if today's sights and sounds and smells grated on Tarzan's being, what a horror he would find Liverpool or London. It might be necessary to keep him in the countryside for a good long while. He might never acclimate, I thought miserably. But I was too exhausted to make small talk or any more convoluted explanations of this strange world into which I was taking him.

I suggested we get some sleep, and we undressed. But when I went to turn down the gaslights, I found that Tarzan had climbed out of bed and was curling up on the floor under the open window.

From the dark I heard him say, "This is how people live in England?"

I wished desperately to reassure him that it wasn't, but that would have been a lie. "I'm afraid so," I said, and with a heavy heart, I lay myself down. I was gone as soon as my head touched the pillow.

My dreams were scattered and disturbing, the worst of them the sight of Tarzan strapped into an easy chair, struggling against the bindings in a drawing room barely as wide as his shoulders and as high as his head.

I awoke as I always did, long before sunup. When I reached for Tarzan he was not beside me, and I remembered he had chosen to sleep on the floor. It was then I felt something different about my hand. With my thumb I felt the top of my third finger and discovered I was wearing a ring.

Alice Clayton's wedding band.

Its meaning struck me with as much worry as it did joy, but the sentiment was so dear, so loving, that I leaped from bed and went in the dark to the window, dropping to my knees.

Tarzan wasn't there.

I felt my way to the gaslamp and lit it. I could see his new suit of clothes draped neatly over the back of the chair where he had put them the night before. The cases of Kerchak's bones and the journal were where I had left them. Out in the hall he was nowhere to be seen. I looked in the bath and toilet rooms.

I began frantic reasoning and rationalization. Perhaps he had wished to spend his last hours on the African continent out-of-doors rather than enclosed in a malodorous hotel room. Maybe he had found his way back to the scarlet bower of the flamboyant trees and was even now waiting to greet *kudu*.

But now the sun's first rays were lighting the hotel room. Panic rising in my head and heart, I hurriedly dressed. I tucked the journal under my arm and gripped a bone case in either hand. I descended to the deserted lobby and was relived to see a rickshaw with its four-man crew waiting at the door. I had them take me through the whole of Libreville, down the still-deserted avenues and out the coast road

306 🐾 Robin Maxwell

where the vermillion trees showed no inhabitants other than the still-slumbering birds.

When we reached the marketplace, it was strangely chaotic in the thin predawn light. Vendors were shouting angrily, and as we passed the wooden cages where the day before we had seen imprisoned animals, I could see now that they were empty. All of them. My heart pounded and my stomach turned, certain that I knew their liberator. What I did not know was the meaning of the gesture. Had it been Tarzan's final act—a universal declaration of independence—before vanishing into the green world he'd realized he did not wish to leave?

It was with the greatest trepidation that I allowed myself to be conveyed to the dock, continuing to peer down every street and alley searching for any sight of Tarzan.

There was frantic activity at the ship with the last of the coffee bean cargo being carried aboard. I accosted every man I saw, trying to ask if they had seen my companion, but I spoke neither French nor Bantu and could not make myself understood. Finally I spied the captain and pressed him for news of John Clayton, but he had not seen my "husband," a word he uttered with a dubious smirk. He told me that I should board quickly, as departure was imminent. Perhaps I might check our cabin. Mr. Clayton might have slipped aboard without having been noticed.

At this I felt tears burning my eyes, for I could not imagine him boarding without me. But the captain had become impatient and was calling, "Vite! Vite!" to the dockhands, hurrying on the last of the coffee sacks. I boarded reluctantly and rushed below to our tiny quarters.

There was no sign of Tarzan. I grew bereft. After all we had endured together, he had deserted me. No promises of adventure, title, fortune, or a life lived with me could replace the man's imperative for freedom. The wedding ring had been not his pledge of undying love but the only good-bye of which he was capable.

Oh, what a fool I'd been!

I felt suddenly ill, queasy and unable to catch my breath. I stumbled through the narrow passageway halls upstairs to the deck where I saw the crew pulling aboard the gangplank and felt the rumbling of the engine under my feet. The last vestige of hope dissolved then along with my composure, and I wept the bitter tears of the abandoned.

The ship lurched as it began to move and I was knocked off balance, dropping the bone bags. But in fact as my hands clutched the rail, I felt emerging within me a state of absolute equilibrium. My mind cleared and I saw the rest of my life spreading out before me. A grim life of work and loneliness without the man I desired above all other men. *The man I have fallen desperately in love with!* And he loved me—I knew he did—in whatever mad configuration of animal lust, possession, guardianship, and romantic rapture his singular mind could conceive. Yes, he had deserted me, but had I—since the moment he'd for an instant considered the Mangani's offer of leadership—been faithful in all *my* thoughts of our future together? Perhaps he'd fallen victim to his fears about surviving in the stultifying prison of society. Who could blame him? But here was the thing: I had learned to survive in *his* world. What I now saw with perfect clarity was that I could not live without him. I *would* not live without him! The dock was receding and I knew I must act.

"Captain!" I shouted. "Captain, stop the ship!" I was beating the rails with my fists, shrieking like a fishwife. "I have to get off! Now! Now!"

Chicago, April 1912

Miss Porter I . . . I . . ." Edgar was slack-jawed and mortified at his stuttering, as though his organs of speech had been impaired. He briefly wondered if a person could die of astonishment.

"I . . . I am beyond words."

"Oh, I think you will find all the words you need, Mr. Burroughs."

He noticed for the first time that morning sun was streaming in through the windows.

"Forgive me, but I'm confused . . . about so many things. If you're so worried about the Mangani being found, then why have you been presenting the *Pithecanthropus aporterensus erectus* skeleton to the academic world? And why have you told me this story today?"

The flush of her cheeks that had risen with the emotional climax of her story had now receded. She looked him squarely in the eye. "It took eighteen months to mount a second expedition—a hand-picked team, very secretive. Yabi leading. Timed to the dry season, we journeyed up the Ogowe and down its tributary. We found the Waziri intact. Ulu now led the tribe with the deceased chief's eldest son, also known as Chief Waziri. It had occurred to me that after the destruction of Sumbula they might have picked themselves up and followed the ancient map outside the Great Chamber doors to the lost city of Opar. But they were content to live their lives in the forest south of the Enduro Escarpment. They spoke with no great emotion about more white-skins who had come up from the south into their territory. When I asked what had become of them, Ulu and the young chief led me into a hut off the central clearing to view the tribe's proudest acquisitions. In the dim light of a *walla* made all of volcanic stone, I was startled to see a Gatling gun mounted on its tripod. And there behind it"—Jane Porter smiled remembering— "was one of King Leopold's Belgian engineers from Libreville—a grinning smoked mummy wreathed in gold medallions. Their rail-road must have made it as far west as Waziriland. Had a bit of bad luck with the 'cannibals.'"

"Just brilliant!" Edgar's imagination was running rampant with wild, colorful images. "But what happened to the Mangani?"

"Yes, well . . ." She grew very stiff, and for the first time since they had met seemed lost for words. She sighed not once but three times before speaking again. "We found the new Great Bower with no difficulty. But all of them—every male, female, and young one— were dead. Nothing but fur and bones was left. I could only surmise that disease had taken them—some organism wafting up from the bowels of the earth to the surface after the great quake. Or perhaps they, too, had made contact with the Belgians and contracted a deadly microbe. What kept me awake at nights, though, was the pos-sibility that, with all my good intentions, *I* had been their Grim Reaper." She looked at Edgar with the most forlorn expression.

"For all intents and purposes, the Mangani are an extinct species. Nothing can harm them now. There's not a single respected paleoan-thropologist who believes *P.a.e.*'s bones are authentic. And as I said, today's was my last presentation. I may be stubborn, but I'm not a martyr." Then she added, "The good news, I suppose, is that Leo-pold's road through Gabon was never completed, and then of course the murderous old thug died."

With that, Jane Porter closed and snapped shut the two cases of Kerchak's bones.

Edgar felt a kind of desperation considering her departure. "Do you have to go?"

"I'm afraid so. I'm going to visit my parents before I go home."

"Parents? I thought your father was . . ."

"So did I." She smiled happily then. "Yabi was suspicious the day Ral Conrath came marching down the mountain with his story of my bloody demise. Father was in a very bad way, and Yabi insisted that the bearers carry him out of the jungle in a padded wooden crate. There was no arguing with him. Once in Libreville, the 'newly-weds,' Mr. and Mrs. Batty"—Jane looked decidedly pleased—"took up the shift and accompanied him to England. Archie Porter was more than half dead when he got home, but my mother nursed him herself. She simply refused to allow that 'damn ticker of his' to have the final say."

"Where is home for you now?" Edgar asked, trying anything to keep the woman talking.

Jane Porter smiled up at him as she pulled on her suit jacket. "Africa, of course. Kenya. Though it's really more of a home base. I travel quite extensively."

There was a sharp rapping at the apartment door. Edgar cursed silently. It was probably the landlord coming by for the rent.

"Excuse me," he said and went to open it.

Standing there was a man, decidedly not his landlord. It was, he was quite sure, the episcope operator from the Chicago Public Library. He was tall and broad shouldered, and even in his expensively tailored suit looked more vital and alive than any other human being Edgar had ever laid eyes on. His grey eyes flashed with good humor and his long, wild black hair was thick and wavy.

"John Clayton," the man said genially and stuck out his hand. "I think you have my wife in here."

Edgar shook it, then looked quizzically at Jane Porter. *Good Lord, this is Tarzan . . . in the flesh!* But the woman who had been so animated in her storytelling the whole night before was now utterly silent and still.

"Will you come in?" Edgar said to the man.

"I'm afraid we can't stay. We have to catch the four-forty train to New York. We've booked a cabin on a ship taking us back to England on Wednesday."

Edgar stared with what he was sure was rudeness into the man's strikingly handsome face, imagining the taut, muscular body beneath the fine wool jacket and trousers and starched white shirt. What he might have looked like with that hair a mass of matted locks.

Jane Porter had come to stand beside John Clayton and looked up at him with a decidedly conspiratorial grin. He picked up the two bone cases and went to the door.

"Change, enlarge, and embellish upon what I've told you as you see fit," the woman said to Edgar. We haven't known each other long, but I somehow have great faith in your abilities."

"But what *happened?*" Edgar said quietly, suddenly uncomfortable in front of the man about whose life he knew such intimate details. "Did you find Tarzan in Libreville, or did you have to go all the way back to Eden?" Edgar's imagination took flight. "Or was he waiting for you there on the dock in his new suit of clothes?"

"You're quite greedy, aren't you?" The woman's smile was an infuriating tease.

"You're not really going to leave me hanging?" Edgar said. "What happened once he got back to England? He *must* have gone back to England eventually." He stared down at Jane's wedding ring. "Did you marry? In a church?"

"You're talking to two avowed pagans, Mr. Burroughs." She was moving to the door now.

"Wait, wait! Did Tarzan take up the Greystoke title? Did you ever . . ."

She moved to John Clayton's side, and he smiled down at her with a look that bespoke unutterable adoration.

"That, my friend, is a long story for another day."

Edgar's mind was exploding with dozens of scenarios to keep the pair from going. But here was the blasted landlord coming down the hall for his rent! The Porters, or Claytons, or Greystokes, or whoever the hell they were, nodded a reserved good-bye and turned to go. Edgar kept them in his sight until they disappeared down the stairwell.

"Well, have you got it?" the landlord said, holding out his pale, sweating palm.

Edgar closed his eyes then and saw before him the lush canopy of Eden, the four hills of Sumbula, the Great Bower of the Mangani, and vast shining waters of Zu-dak-lul. His mind drifted and he wondered if his *All-Story* readers would cotton to an overeducated—and shameless—tomboy like Jane Porter. Wouldn't they like somebody a bit more sweet and submissive? And what was the African jungle without a tribe of bloodthirsty cannibals? The ape-people were a touch of genius. And Tarzan himself—now, there was a hero everybody could love.

"Burroughs!" he heard the landlord bark at him. "I said, have you got it?"

Edgar's face twisted into a slow smile. "I do," he said. "I have it. All of it."

Then without another word, he slowly shut the door.

Mangani-English Glossary

abulu brother
amba fall
ang allow
aro forced to leave
balu child/children
ben great
ben gund great chief
b'nala head
Boi-ee Bowie knife
bolgani gorilla
bund dead
bundolo kill
busso flee
b'zan hair/fur
b'zeebo attack
dak-lul pool of water
dako-za meat, flesh
dan-do stop
dan-do amba stop fall
dan-sopo nut
ee and
el one
eta small, weak
galul blood/bleed
gash tooth/tusk
go black
gomi root
gumado sick
gumado b'nala sick in the head
gund vando good chief

har battle
hay-ee help
histah snake
ho many
jai brave/Tarzan's half-sister
jar magic
kagada surrender/I do surrender
kagado surrender/do you surrender?
kak or
kal milk
kalan female
kambo jungle
kin-ga mating
ko mighty
kob hit
koho hot
korag destroy
ko-sabor mighty lioness
kudu sun
lu fierce
lu har fierce battle
lul water
manu monkey
mat of
mel-cot hide/hidden
m'wah blue
m'wah wa-usha blue-green leaf
neeta bird

nene beetle/bug
numa lion
olo wrestle
osha flower
pacco zebra
palu son
pan-tho memories, tales, legends
popo eat
rok frog
rut tough
sha-ka beyond comprehension
sheeta leopard
sord bad
talu daughter
tand no
tandanda forget
tantor elephant
tar white
tar-zan white-skin person
tat insect
tat wing
tug want
uglu hate

unk go
usha leaf
uta danger
utor fear
vando good
wa green
walla house
wappi antelope
yad ear
yat eye
yati sight
yud come
yud b'zan come groom fur
yuto cut
yuto-gash cut with teeth
yuto yat cut eye
zabalu sister
zan skin
zu big
zu-tat insect
Zu-dak-lul big water/Atlantic Ocean
zu-vo tand defy
zu-zu-vo strong

This glossary is an abridged version of *The Tarzan Encyclopedia*, a complete Mangani-English dictionary, its language created by Edgar Rice Burroughs and compiled by John Harwood and Allan Howard. The full encyclopedia can be found online at www.robinmaxwell.com or www.tarzan.com.

Author's Note

Tarzan was my first heartthrob. After all, what girl wouldn't crave the undying affection of a gorgeously muscled, scantily clad he-man (and an English lord, at that) living free from the confines of civilization in a lush paradise? Though an avid reader of Tarzan comic books, I'd never read a single Edgar Rice Burroughs novel. Yet Tarzan and Jane were as hardwired into my fantasy life and consciousness as any other characters in popular culture.

As an eight-year-old girl, I watched with slack-jawed wonder as a blond Amazon—Irish McCalla—in her tiny leopard skin dress and thick gold upper-arm bracelets swung through the vines in the thrilling TV series *Sheena Queen of the Jungle*. And who didn't love the Johnny Weissmuller Tarzan films with the peppery sophisticate Maureen O'Sullivan as his "mate," Jane? I waited breathlessly for *Greystoke* but was sorely disappointed by the filmmaker's decision to keep their Jane (Andie MacDowell) from setting foot in Africa till the last frame of the movie.

I'd just completed my manuscript of *O, Juliet* when the question arose via agents and publishers as to the subject of my next novel. I'd had a ball with my take on Shakespeare's *Romeo and Juliet*, fleshing out the characters, their world and families, and expanding the time line from three days to three months. As I was riding down the road one day with my husband, Max, he wondered if I might want to choose another pair of literary lovers rather than a historical character. When I told him I liked the idea, he asked who they would be. Not three seconds passed before I blurted out, "Tarzan and Jane!"

"Where did that come from?" Max wanted to know. At the time I had no memory of Sheena or the old Weissmuller/O'Sullivan movies, but the images must have been bubbling in the depths of my subconscious just waiting to erupt like magma from a dormant volcano.

The new idea took me by surprise and started keeping me up at night. I was fortunate that two of my dearest friends—the writing/producing team of Alan J. Adler and Susan Jeter—had been dealing with the Edgar

Rice Burroughs Estate on a screen adaptation of ERB's novel *The Out-law of Torn*, and I knew from their experience that one trod on the copy-right or trademark of any Burroughs creation at his or her own peril. Of course I desperately wanted the blessings and authorization for my idea from the heirs and estate of this iconic and massively prolific author.

To that end I had my trusted entertainment attorney, Phillip Rosen, contact ERB, Inc., on my behalf. Before I knew it, the two of us were on a conference call with the company's president, Jim Sullos. "What's this great new idea you've got?" he demanded. It was the easiest, shortest, one-sentence pitch of my entire writing career. "The Tarzan story from Jane's point of view," I replied. And with the same lightning speed as I had plucked the idea from my brain, Jim exclaimed, "I love it! It's original. It's never been done like this before." I sagged with relief. The first and most important hurdle had been cleared.

I also learned in that phone call that the one hundredth anniversary of the first episode of *Tarzan of the Apes*—a serial in the pulp fiction magazine *All-Story* (October 1912), later published as the first Tarzan novel—was just three years away. Considering how long it would take me to write *Jane*, and how long it would take to see publication, we were on schedule for its fortuitous release in the "Tarzan Centennial Year."

This was getting exciting.

After a marathon five-hour pitch session at the ERB office and archive in Tarzana, California (where else?), the estate approved my story line, and Jim Sullos became *Jane*'s first and most ardent champion.

A bona fide Tarzan fanboy with a near-encyclopedic knowledge of the vast collection of the "Tarzan Universe"—books, comics, artwork, memorabilia, dictionaries, and bestiaries—Jim provided me with every resource I could possibly need to write my novel, a book he began refer-ring to as "the next Tarzan classic." He was as tickled as I was that this would be the first Tarzan title ever written by a woman.

We spent many long hours discussing the ERB novels (many of which I had, by now, read), comparing the original characters and sto-ries with my own take, on such topics as the age at which Tarzan was ab-ducted by the Mangani (not a year old but four years old); the reason Jane and her father go to Africa in the first place (treasure hunting versus pa-leoanthropological exploration); and how to handle the couple's physical relationship ("tastefully").

Jim always kept in mind the Burroughs Bibliophiles, a worldwide or-ganization of aficionados who share a love for the works and characters of

ERB—who would surely scour my manuscript with a fine-tooth comb looking for discrepancies or any desecration of their favorite author's intent. I am eternally grateful for Jim's understanding that while an homage to *Tarzan of the Apes*, *Jane* was a stand-alone novel, and a too-strict adherence to the original work would put a stranglehold on my creativity.

John R. Burroughs, the only living grandson of ERB, was another champion of *Jane* from the beginning. Having his support meant the world to me.

The research phase was more fun than a barrel of Mangani. Aside from my exotic and erotic jungle and wild man fantasies, I was for the first time free to indulge in some of my greatest longtime passions— human evolution and the mysterious "missing link" fossils and creatures found all over the world. From a very young age I'd also been fascinated by and read voraciously about ancient and antediluvian civilizations, and accounts of the geological cataclysms that had ended them. Had I not become a writer, I feel sure I would have made my career as a paleoanthropologist or archaeologist.

As it always—happily—happens when I'm researching a novel, exactly the right books find their way into my hands. Perhaps the most important one this time was *The Man Who Found the Missing Link: Eugène Dubois and His Lifelong Quest to Prove Darwin Right* by Pat Shipman. The title tells it all. Dubois's discovery of Java man (*Pithecanthropus erectus*, later redesignated *Homo erectus*) in 1891 gave me a plausible missing link species upon which to base the Mangani. But learning in Shipman's book that Darwin's insistence that the *real* missing link would be found in Africa gave Jane and Archie (faithful Darwinists) the motivation to go to the "Dark Continent" on expedition. It was heartbreaking to hear of the lambasting Dubois took from the scientific community—it nearly broke him—but the support of his old professor, Ernst Haeckel, kept him sane. While my dates are off by seven years (I needed to take some artistic license to make my story line work), Dubois did actually present *Pithecanthropus erectus* during the Fourth International Zoological Congress at Cambridge (1898) and was hooted and howled at by the audience until Haeckel stepped forward to defend his student's thesis. Much of Haeckel's speech in *Jane* are his words, verbatim, from that spirited defense.

A more glaring discrepancy in dates concerns the Boy Scouts of America, an organization that was not yet in existence when Archie Porter was a boy. Again, I unapolgetically claim poetic license, remembering the rich tradition of ERB. If a man can go to sleep in an Arizona cave and wake up on Mars, I reckon my readers will indulge me on a wonky fact or two.

In July 2010, just as I was about to write of Jane being introduced to the Mangani at the Great Bower, *National Geographic* published a story about a team of paleoanthropologists, Tim White, Berhane Asfaw, and Giday WoldeGabriel, who, fifteen years before, had discovered in the Middle Awash area of Ethiopia a full skeleton of *Ardipithecus ramidus* ("Ardi"). The female, with its straight leg bones giving it a human, upright, bipedal stance, also had opposable big toes perfect for grasping branches and the face and skull of a chimp. It was to my eye the closest creature to a missing link that I had ever seen. To my pleasure (and Charles Darwin's, if he had been alive), it was found in Africa. While Ardi's discoverers knew the species was too primitive to have the power of speech, I borrowed one of ERB's most important conceits about the Mangani—that not only could they make meaningful sounds but they also had language. Asserting this kind of artistic freedom is one of the greatest joys of being an author of fiction. I cut out the artist's rendering of what "Ardi" would have looked like and taped it over my desk. I dubbed her "Kala of the Mangani."

Finding Mary Kingsley's *Travels in West Africa*—in particular her exploration of the Ogowe River—was like striking gold. There was a reason I had Jane read directly from her well-worn volume. As she opined to Captain Kelly, she was unable to top Kingsley's extraordinary descriptions. Neither could I.

I wanted the Waziri to have a basis in reality, so I followed to its end point one of the lines of the Bantu diaspora out of Cameroon (some four thousand years ago). There I placed the tribe's village, a few days' journey inland from the Gabon beach where ERB's *Fuwalda* mutineers had set the Claytons with all their belongings.

Minnesota governor Ignatius Donnelly's *Atlantis: The Antediluvian World* was a big bestseller of the nineteenth century that sparked huge controversy about the lost continent. William Flinders Petrie—the premier Egyptologist of his time—did stumble on what he believed was the rubble of the ancient Egyptian labyrinth at the Fayum Oasis. He also famously bragged that when he died he wanted his head cut off and his brain studied for science. His wish was, in fact, granted, though the famous noggin was lost during the years of the Second World War . . . then later recovered.

I had also made contact with Helen J. Blackman, a scholar who had written extensively on the history of Cambridge University. She led me to several important books for my research about what life was like for an intelligent, progressive young woman during the Victorian and Edwardian years. *Period Piece: A Cambridge Childhood* was insanely relevant, as it was an autobiography of Gwen Raverat—Charles Darwin's granddaughter—who grew up in Cambridge society and was precisely Jane Porter's age.

As I strove to finish the manuscript, I developed a temporary problem with my vision that made reading and writing nearly impossible. I was saved from disaster by my own hero—Max—who became not only my eyes but also my story partner and first editor. Himself an athlete (a yoga master), he helped me work out in the middle of our living room floor the feasibility of many of the physical stunts that Jane and Tarzan executed in the book. When the first draft was completed Max performed a wonderful reading of the entire novel for me.

My literary agents at InkWell Management, David Forrer and Kimberly Witherspoon, were incredibly supportive. David in particular became instantly excited about *Jane* and encouraged—without hesitation—my decision to jump genres from historical fiction to commercial fiction. Also at InkWell, Lyndsey Blessing, Alexis Hurley, Patricia Burke, Charlie Olsen, and Nathaniel Jacks kept my project at the top of their pile and briskly moving in the right direction. At ERB, Inc., the staff was top-notch. Cathy Wilbanks and her mother, Janet Mann, saw me through a tough, complicated Tarzan and Jane proposal with amazing grace. Willie Jones and Tyler Wilbanks kept all communication running smoothly.

I cannot say enough about Katharine Critchlow, *Jane*'s editor at Tor Books. Right from the beginning she loved the project. More important, she got it, and her editorial notes were spot-on. When Katharine left Tor, I was blessed with an equally smart and enthusiastic editor, Steph Flanders, who seamlessly took up the ball and ran with it. Together with art director Irene Gallo and cover artist Mark Summers, everyone at Tor worked tirelessly to ensure that each detail of *Jane*'s publication was top of the line and worthy of Edgar Rice Burroughs's legacy. Cynthia Merman did a heroic job copyediting a manuscript jammed with Mangani language (created by ERB) and Waziri dialogue (a pastiche of Bantu and fantasy words that I dreamed up). Bethany Reis lent much-needed support on the electronic copyedit, a technology that we old-school authors are still learning.

When Joe McNeely of Brilliance Audiobook acquired the audio rights to *Jane*, our tribe gained a stupendous cheerleader. Not only did his enthusiasm know no bounds, but he rounded out the effort by engaging yet another Tarzan fanatic and recording engineer, Bob Deyan, to record it, and the wonderful British actress (and my dear friend) Suzan Crowley to perform it.

Illustrator extraordinaire, friend of the ERB estate, and Tarzan expert Thomas Yeates indulged me during the writing process with hourslong raves about our hero and inspired me with dozens of his brilliant illustrations of Tarzan and Jane. Bill Hillman, editor and webmaster of the extraordinary ten-thousand page ERBzine.com website, supplied me with fabulous images and information on every aspect of the Tarzan universe. Filmmakers Dave Miller and James A. Sullos were late but great additions to what was clearly becoming a labor of love.

My trusted first readers, Max, Billie Morton, Iris Zweben, Ginny Higgins, Gregory Michaels, Cat Kovach, and Thomas Ellis (who did the first proofreading of the book) gave me much-needed encouragement and amazing insights.

My West Coast team—Web designer Linda LaZar, publicist Tasya Herskovits, and *The Sun Runner* magazine publisher Steve Brown—were simply the best.

When all is said and done, however, my greatest debt of gratitude is owed to the incomparable Edgar Rice Burroughs. His iconic characterization of Tarzan and the story of the young English lord's feral upbringing at the hands of a loving "anthropoid ape" named Kala is one I never, in all my wildest fantasies, could have conceived.

In October 1912, *All Story* magazine printed Burroughs's *Tarzan of the Apes* in its entirety. The next year it was published in book form, and twenty-four novels followed. They have been translated into more than thirty-five languages, including Braille and Esperanto, and adapted into movies, musicals, comic books, comic strips, and video games. It is believed that two million people have read and watched the adventures of Tarzan, perhaps the most recognizable character in the history of literature.

Being granted permission to write my version of this classic love story was one of the greatest honors of my life. I can only hope that Mr. Burroughs would have approved.

Robin Maxwell
March 2012